Copyright © 2016 by Jay M. Bylsma
All rights reserved.

Green Ivy Publishing
1 Lincoln Centre
18W140 Butterfield Road
Suite 1500
Oakbrook Terrace IL 60181-4843
www.greenivybooks.com

ISBN: 978-1-945058-73-8

## ALSO BY JAY M. BYLSMA

FICTION

*Pitcher's Hands Is Out* (with Dan Bylsma)

*Slam Dunks Not Allowed* (with Dan Bylsma)

NON-FICTION

*So Your Son Wants to Play in the NHL* (with Dan Bylsma)

*So You Want to Play in the NHL* (with Dan Bylsma)

# The Reprobate

*by Jay M. Bylsma*

# Foreword

Although a garden-variety preacher in a small village church, I thought it my responsibility to attempt to bring the best of contemporary theological thought to my people. I did this through regular Sunday morning preaching and midweek study using biblical scholars old and new. The spectacular growth of this church to one of the largest in its denomination confirmed my belief that in order to be relevant to the culture, the Church should always be working at a fresh translation of the faith in order that theological expression and ongoing human experience stay connected.

These fresh translations, although always in serious and responsible wrestling with Scripture, pushed my theological expression past some of the traditional dogmas formulated in the sixteenth century held by the more conservative regional governing body of my particular denomination. This painfully led to an inquiry as to the appropriateness of my remaining a minister of the gospel in this branch of orthodox Protestantism, although the national leadership of the denomination regretted the action of the regional body that created the conflict.

Much was written and discussed in both the national press and various religious publications about this inquiry, which ultimately led to my separation from this denomination. Unfortunately, it became a reporting of only snippets and soundbites of the body of work that was this "fresh translation"—usually used as either to condemn or affirm, depending on the publication's agenda.

It has been said that only under the mask of fiction can one tell the truth. In this work of fiction, a long-time parishioner and fellow student has captured the core of the struggle that led to my being mislabeled a reprobate. *The Reprobate* is a captivating attempt to synthesize our work together over many years of struggle to find this fresh translation of the faith. It is my prayer that in reading it, the reader may come to understand, if not appreciate, the basis of the theological expression that attempted to connect with the contemporary human experience in order that the Church may remain faithful to its calling to address the ongoing human drama with the Word of God in fresh translation.

Richard A. Rhem

August 17, 2015

Since retiring from the ministry, Rev. Rhem has continued to be in demand as a guest preacher. He was the first Sylvia Kaufman Interfaith Leadership Award Recipient. A repository of over 1,000 of his sermons is archived at the Kaufman Interfaith Institute at Grand Valley State University and can be accessed at www.richardrhem.org.

# INTRODUCTION

*"I believe the theological task belongs to every generation and a living Church will always be working at the fresh translation of the faith in order that theological expression and ongoing human experience stay connected."*

Richard A. Rhem, February 29, 1996.

For twenty-five years, I was a member of a dynamic faith community that met in a small village in Western Michigan. Throughout these years, I had been engaged not only in regular worship but in mid-week courses of study. These had at their core a personal attempt to reconcile myself with the ultimate realities of life and a corporate attempt as Christians to connect the life and ministry of Jesus Christ to the contemporary experience.

These studies, led by Reverend Richard A. Rhem, the senior pastor of this village church, challenged me to think beyond the boundaries of my tradition, which had its roots in the sixteenth century Protestant Reformation. There were honest and open inquiries using several of the most influential Christian theological scholars of the last half of the twentieth century, Catholic as well as Protestant. It was our corporate "working at the fresh translation of the faith in order that theological expression and ongoing human experience stay connected."

As one might imagine, I grew in my personal understanding of God and His interaction in the world and my understanding of the life and ministry of Jesus Christ. I remain grateful for the particular evangelical Christian tradition into which I was born and was nurtured. It gave me a marvelous framework on which I could hang an evolving and more palpable faith that has emerged as the result of my studies. This was not without personal struggle. It's not easy to give up the paradigm on which one has hung one's soul and fearfully embrace another. But such is the process of growth.

There came a time when the ministry of this church and some of the theological positions of its senior pastor came under questioning by its regional ecclesiastical governance body. Unfortunately, this questioning did not remain a private matter, and the news coverage carried the story around the world. While the news coverage contained some of the highlights of what the media called a controversy, it could not and did not get to the heart and soul of the story.

*The Reprobate* is my all-too-feeble attempt to tell the story of my personal faith journey as well as an apologia, in a fictionalized form, of the story of this wonderful Christian ministry known as Christ Community Church of Spring Lake, Michigan, and the theology of my beloved friend, pastor, and *Papa*, Dick Rhem.

I quickly and humbly acknowledge that if there is a single sentence in this work that the reader finds fresh or insightful, it is most likely not original with me. The theological and philosophical ideas have been imbibed from my readings of Hendrikus Berkhof, Douglas John Hall, Hans Kung, C.S. Lewis, Richard Tarnus, and others, and from conferences I have attended led by Martin Marty, Krister Stindahl, John Dominic Crossan, Huston Smith, Marcus Borg, Karen Armstrong, Paula Fredriksen, N.T. Wright, Rabbi David Hartman, and others, and from my faceless friends on the Internet known only to me by their screen names like "1st Horseman," and from sermons I have heard, many of them preached from a stool by a theologian disguised as a garden-variety preacher with half-frame glasses, remarkable blue eyes, and a face surrounded by an immaculate snow white beard.

Yes, Jason Richards is alive and well and living in Holland, Michigan, under an assumed name.

# Chapter One

It is a phenomenon of life that a path pursued for a significant purpose sometimes brings serendipitous events or human interactions that are more life changing than that toward which we purposed. It was just such a significant purpose that brought a master's degree candidate in Hospital and Institutional Management to be summoned to the office of the Dean of the School of Business Administration of the University of Michigan at the beginning of the fall term.

Dean Donald A. Nixon's office was large and comfortable, as one might expect for the head of a Department of a major university. The furniture, however, was spartan. It was like the furniture in all the other faculty offices: gray steel desks and tall files, functional, but not fancy or modern by anyone's standards. There were a large number of books, mostly textbooks, in apparent disarray. They were everywhere, including piled on the chairs. Today's visitor, Jason Richards, had to remove several to sit down. He decided Dean Nixon looked and talked very much like an English character actor.

"You have a nearly perfect academic record, Mr. Richards, and in my classes, at least, you have demonstrated an unusual grasp of the practical aspects of institutional administration. Your interview impressed the selection committee, especially Mr. Davidson's widow, who told me that she thought you had what she called a 'rare blend of intelligence and horse-sense.' It is for these reasons that the Department has selected you for the prestigious Davidson Fellowship in Advanced Management Methodology. Congratulations!"

Jason's stomach went into the gastronomic equivalent of cardiac arrest, his mouth went dry, and his tongue muscles eluded his control.

"You may be interested to know there were forty candidates from this institution and others. The selection was difficult because of the outstanding qualifications of nearly all of this year's applicants, many of whom were doctoral candidates. It was your master's thesis on the valuation of nursing homes that set you apart. Most of our brethren in the colleges of arts and sciences do not acknowledge business and scholarship in the same sentence. Your paper was a very scholarly work and deserved every bit of the attention it created. It helped you carry the day with the selection committee. You are to be commended."

"Thank you, Dean Nixon. I . . . ah . . . will do my best to live up to their . . . the committee's . . . expectations and prove the wisdom of their selection." He heard himself say the words but didn't recognize the voice.

"Yes, I'm sure you will. Do you have any questions as to what's expected?"

"No, sir, and I'm anxious to begin." Questions? Questions? He couldn't remember his last name at the moment.

"Very good. Dr. Playdon will be your mentor. There will be a number of self-study projects. You will have staff privileges and be expected to attend Department meetings. There will be an internship with the University Hospital's Controller's Office and a seventeen-week Interreactional Requirement leading to a paper."

"Interreactional Requirement?" What was that?

"It's long been the policy of this Department that one cannot become a good administrator unless you have experienced the institutional setting from the perspective of the service recipient. Therefore, the Davidson Fellows are required to spend a portion of the first year in interpersonal relationship with an institutionalized person. Because hospital patients are typically short-term, we have used supportive care nursing home patients with great success."

Jason felt his eyebrows involuntarily arch and decided he didn't have the judgment just then to force them down to normal.

"Not to worry, Mr. Richards. It has typically been a patient who has a physical infirmity but has retained his or her mental faculties. I know nursing homes can be unpleasant places to visit, but after all, institutional administration must have at its core an appreciation for the quality of the environment we provide. If that environment is less than pleasant, we haven't done our jobs as administrators then, have we? You will be able to select your host institution from a number with whom we have working relationships. If your experience is similar to that of those who have preceded you, this will be a most educational experience. Professor Playdon will be your contact for this.

"Now then, there's some paperwork required by the University to document your acceptance of the Fellowship and stipend payment procedures. Stop in at the Administration Building to complete the forms. Professor Miller will be contacting you about your graduate assistant recitation requirements for Intro Ad 301 this semester. If you have no further questions, congratulations, again. The Davidson Fellowship is a most prestigious award, and I shouldn't wonder it will look as good on your resume as it has on those Fellows who have preceded you."

"Thank you, Dean Nixon. I'm looking forward to working with you and Professor Playdon." He rose and extended his hand. Dean Nixon shook it vigorously, offered him luck, and invited him into his office anytime he wanted to talk. Jason left.

He was the Davidson Fellow! One selected every two years from the cream of the Hospital and Institutional Administration schools of the six graduate departments in the country that offered that degree program. Unless he fell on his face, he would have his choice of jobs at graduation.

Dean Nixon had mentioned his master's thesis as carrying the moment for him. He reflected on the events that led up to the paper. He had an uncle who was a business valuator, a person who advised others as to the value of private, usually family businesses.

At a family Christmas party, his uncle had been discussing Jason's academic track and had chanced to remark that there was a growing need to develop a methodology for determining the market value of nursing homes. There were rules of thumb for many kinds of business—simple formulas to follow. But nursing homes, to that point, had been a problem for his uncle and other evaluators.

Jason had needed to find a topic on which to write his master's thesis. In addition, he had been short several credit hours in his field of specialty toward his degree. A faculty committee had agreed to grant up to three credit hours toward his requirements if the master's thesis would be more substantial than the requirements for a regular thesis. Jason had found the subject of business valuation in general and nursing homes in particular very interesting, and he had tackled the assignment as if his degree depended upon it, which it did.

The final work product not only was rewarded with the three credit hours, but excerpts from the paper had been published in the quarterly magazine of the Association of Accredited Business Appraisers. He had heard from his now very proud uncle that his methodology was being used in the field and was being informally referred to as the Richard's Method. But now the extra effort put into the thesis had paid off handsomely—the Davidson Fellow!

It was the fulfillment of his dreams, the answer to prayer. Jason Richards, Davidson Fellow. Jason Richards, Graduate Assistant. Jason Richards, staff privileges—which meant the most treasured perk of all, a window decal allowing him entrance to the staff parking ramp. No more eleven-block walk to the Business Administration School in Ann Arbor, where it seemed to rain every day but on the days it snowed.

His mind raced through the possibilities as he made his way back to his apartment. It would mean one more year of school than he had planned on, but the extra cost would be covered by the stipend and then some. The last Davidson Fellow had taken a job with one of the largest private hospital conglomerates at an annual starting salary rumored to be seventy-five thousand dollars. Then there was the chance to work closely with respected minds in this field like Nixon, Playdon, and others.

Plus, there would be the chance to teach. Intro Ad 301 was *Introduction to Administration* and was taught by Professor Charlie Miller who lectured twice a week to a class of fifty. This class was divided into two recitation sections, and he would be the Graduate Assistant (thus the nickname, Grad Ass) who handled one of these sections. Miller's lectures were brilliant, but not orderly, and it was the Grad Ass's job to organize the brilliance into some semblance of order so the students could reduce it to notes. The trick to acing Miller was to sit back and listen, absorb. It was folly to try to take notes. Then, in the recitation, organize what was heard into notes. Then use the notes as the basis for going back to absorb more of Miller. Jason's job would be to assist the students with this organization. The Grad Ass that he'd had for the same class had only qualified for the last half of his abbreviated title. Jason had attended the other section regularly and had benefited from the other instructor, who was also a Davidson Fellow. He could and would improve on the instructor he'd had.

Jason thought about the other Fellowship candidates that he'd met on the day the Committee had interviewed the finalists. He had felt out of place and at the time wished he had more to offer the Committee—more credentials like the fellow from Harvard, more personality like the interesting candidate from the Northwestern, or more Joe-Camel-cool like the guy from UCLA. Even though he had won the fellowship, he found he still felt that way, out of place. If they knew he had won the Fellowship, he was sure they would shake their heads in wonderment. That is, if they remembered him at all.

He was reminded of the line in a popular song; this was "the chance of a lifetime in a lifetime of chance." And what a lifetime of chance it had been. His parents were divorced when he was two. Both his mother and father were from strong Christian fundamentalist backgrounds where divorce was unconscionable.

But there had been adultery while his father was serving in the military. His father's accusations had been substantiated by the discovery of hospital records that his mother had been treated for a uterine infection resulting from a back-alley abortion. There was other testimony of maternal neglect and custody was awarded to his father, with care to be provided by the paternal grandmother until his father's discharge. Custody to the father in a divorce settlement was unheard of at the time.

Jason's grandmother provided stability and love at a time when it was needed most, and he and his older brother had thrived under her grandmothering. His father remarried when he was five. The stepmother was also from a very strong fundamentalist background. They read from the Bible at every meal, prayed long and, Jason thought, repetitiously. They went to church twice on Sunday, and he attended parochial schools from kindergarten through his second year of college. There were religion classes in every grade as surely as there were math classes. They were also long and repetitious, but they had their desired effect. He had been molded into a born-again, Bible-believing Christian, whose faith was as sure and unshakable as anything built on faith could be.

In college, he had been an English major with dreams of becoming the next great American novelist. But a chance remark by his father had challenged him to transfer to the Business School of the University of Michigan. He began his studies there as an accounting major with an eye toward becoming a Certified Public Accountant, but Jason was steered into Hospital Administration by his pastor, who had pointed out that someone with his obvious talents could be used "mightily by the Lord in Kingdom work."

"Kingdom work" was any occupation that was long on service to fellow man and short on pay, like being a minister, a parochial school teacher, a missionary, a doctor (with extra bonus points for being a missionary doctor). Doing tax returns as a C.P.A. somehow didn't fit the pastor's category of "Kingdom work," but Hospital Administration, the administration of the healing arts, was a calling worthy of his talents. That is, if he wasn't going to be a missionary doctor.

Jason hadn't known what exactly the talents were for Kingdom work that were so obvious to his pastor. They weren't obvious to Jason. He didn't have a passion to save the world or teach the world or heal the world. He had a love for math and the workings of the economy and the business school suited him just fine, now that he had stumbled into it.

All through his life, there had been these small but noticeable nudges that had irrevocably changed the course of his life. Admittedly, he had never taken charge of his life or challenged its direction, choosing instead to make the best of the hand fate dealt him at that moment. That was probably the result of his non-confrontational approach to everything. The only plan he ever had was when he was eight or nine years old. He had wanted to be a fireman. In contrast, his older brother always wanted to be a banker and never took a college course that wasn't somehow geared to being a banker. Though Jason's track had not been as carefully charted, here he was at the academic pinnacle of his discipline. The orthodox tradition in which he stood would prompt his father to say he was pre-destined to become a hospital administrator. It was "God's Plan" for his life. One of his college roommates would have contended it was his "joss" or "karma." The Davidson Fellowship cemented both beliefs.

As he walked, he could hear the sounds of the renowned University of Michigan marching band practicing for the Saturday football game. The familiar strains of "Hail to the Victors" wafted through the leaves that were beginning to be tinged with bright yellow on the sugar maples that lined Hill Street. It was a warm day, and the air carried the smell of new mown grass. And he felt so good inside, his chest was tight. He clenched his eyes tight and breathed a small prayer of thanks, for surely this *was* God's will operating in his life, his pre-destination.

As he crossed State Street, he passed a very well-dressed elderly gentleman pushing a wheelchair in which was an equally elderly woman. The woman was bundled up against a cold that wasn't present, and she appeared inert behind a vacant stare. Probably Alzheimer's, Jason thought, and he wondered about the personal hell the man was going through as he apparently attempted to be her primary caregiver.

He was instantly reminded of his Interreactional Requirement. He had been completely surprised by it and wondered what it entailed. He was familiar with supportive care and nursing home facilities. He had bad memories of visiting his grandmother who in her later years had suffered from dementia and was a resident in a nursing home. He could remember the pervasive smell of urine and disinfectant and the oppressive, almost suffocating heat. But other Davidson Fellows had survived the Interreactional Requirement. Jason would make the best of it.

Remembering his recent prayer, he secretly hoped that nursing home administration was not God's will for his life. And then he remembered that a Christian does not believe you can secretly hope.

# Chapter Two

His schedule for the fall semester was full. He had two classes on Monday and Wednesday and one three-hour class on Tuesday. His Intro Ad. 301 recitation was on Thursday morning following the Intro Ad. 301 lectures on Monday and Wednesday, which he was expected to attend. Department meetings on Thursday afternoon. Fridays were available for the Interreactional Requirement for which the final report was due in February. In true scholarly fashion, Jason dubbed the project with its initials. He went to see Professor Playdon the first Friday of the semester to see what the I.R.R. was all about.

"Ah, Mr. Richards, our new Davidson Fellow. Nice of you to drop in." Professor Emeritus William A. Playdon was a legend in both academic and industry circles. He was sixty-eight, which roughly corresponded with the number of widely respected books and articles he had written in his field, which was accounting. He had not taught for some years now, preferring a semi-retirement status where he was free to lecture and write. His name still lent considerable prestige to the faculty. He had a shock of white hair that he wore straight back, which made the red bowtie he was wearing all the more striking.

"This Interreactional Requirement has proven to be one of the most valuable educational experiences in which our Davidson Fellows are involved during their tenure here." His bushy white eyebrows fairly danced over his eyes as he spoke. "It's long been my view that a good administrator has the ability to oversee the institution, but an excellent administrator has the ability to 'under see' the institution—that is, see it from the bottom up. Think of it as an exercise in market research where you view the institution from the eyes of the consumer.

"Most of the candidates get so excited about what they

learn, they want to go back and make changes in the institutions they visit. The problems that are all too visible to them are almost invisible when looking at the institution from the executive suite. Your job, however, is not to make or even suggest changes. Your purpose is to learn how to appraise an institution's needs from the executive suite, with the eyes of the care recipient."

Playdon's enthusiasm for the I.R.R. was contagious and Jason found himself warming to the project.

"I have here a list of institutions from which you may choose an affiliation. After you've decided, arrange to meet with that administrator and get an introduction to the facility, and select a care recipient with whom you will interact. Let me know when you've made your selection."

Jason found himself looking at a list of five supportive care facilities in the Ann Arbor area with description of each. The second one on the list caught his eye:

>  CHRISTIAN ARBOR HOME, INC.
>  *A 75 resident total care facility providing loving Christian care for the elderly. Our care ranges from supportive care and maintenance to round the clock nursing in an evangelical Christian atmosphere.* Dirk Van Dam, M.H.A., Administrator.

Professor Playdon was concluding, "You don't have to make a decision today. In fact, I encourage you to visit a few that strike your fancy. Talk to the administrators, tour their facilities, and then make up your mind. If you have any questions, I'm here trying to keep out of mischief most of the time."

"Thank you, Dr. Playdon. I like the idea of making some initial visits. I'll do just that and let you know my decision as soon as I make it."

"Good. And now that you're a colleague, Jason, I'd like you

to call me Bill. When I'm called Bill I don't feel quite so old and emeritus. And frankly, feeling emeritus is worse than feeling old. I've come to suspect that emeritus comes from a Scandinavian word meaning useless. It especially humors me when young folks like you call me Bill. So please, it's Bill. Well, good luck, Jason."

"Thank you, sir." Yeah, right, he thought. I'll be calling Professor Emeritus William A. Playdon, C.P.A., Ph.D. "Bill." Not in my lifetime.

And yet, the distinguished professor had an unmistakable genuine quality and his gentleness and sincerity leveled Jason's perceived notions about intellectual and academic distinctions. It was no wonder he was revered as much as he was respected.

It was now nearly noon. Jason decided on a Blimpy Burger on the walk back to the apartment and then a drive to Stadium Boulevard and the Christian Arbor Home. He called the Home and arranged for a 1:30 p.m. appointment with Mr. Dirk Van Dam.

☦

Christian Arbor Home was a three-story building in a largely upper middle class neighborhood with huge old homes. It occupied well-maintained grounds on a block with an elementary school, a fire station, and a small, new strip mall. It bespoke of an architectural style of an earlier time. It appeared to be a solid building, made largely of random-fitting Indiana limestone blocks. Large, expansive windows had been removed, and the space refitted with smaller ones, which had been surrounded with panels in what appeared to be an attempt to prevent heat loss.

Jason parked his 2008 Honda Civic in a spot marked "VISITORS." As he walked toward the entrance, he noticed that what had appeared to be a flower border from the street was a backdrop for a long, very well-maintained vegetable garden that wound its way along the sidewalk. There were several tomato plants loaded with large ripening tomatoes, beans, carrots, cantaloupe, and the inevitable zucchini plant. It was obviously someone's labor of love.

Jason entered the building and presented himself at a reception window that invited him to ring a small bell for service. He had called ahead, and the administrator would be expecting him. A matronly woman in street clothes appeared and asked if she could help him.

"Jason Richards to see Mr. Van Dam. I believe he's expecting me."

"One moment please, I'll see if Mr. Van Dam can see you. Please have a seat."

Jason thanked her and found a seat.

There were two elderly women in the lobby, each sporting a lot of accessories and dressed in a style older than he could recognize. One of them wore a hat with a mesh veil. The other had a very large purple purse and an equally purple hat that he guessed had not been purchased at the same time as the darker purple dress she was wearing. Jason was reminded of a poem entitled "And I Shall Wear Purple" he had seen done up in calligraphy in a gift shop. The ladies said nothing, but both of them watched Jason intently as if he were their best bet for entertainment for the afternoon. He supposed they were waiting for a ride to some place or other. He hoped the ride would arrive soon.

He noticed that the magazines were all at least six months old and, not finding any that struck his fancy, his eyes wandered around the reception room. The tile floors were polished to a very high gloss. There were sidelights made of stained glass on either side of the exterior door, neat parallelograms of light green and pink and light blue hammered glass, except for one pane that was clear window glass, apparently a replacement. A thick coat of fresh paint covered the walls, but the plaster alongside the sidelights appeared rough, and some of it bubbled indicating water was leaking in from around the windows.

The furniture was simple divans and chairs with heavy arms and imitation leather covers. The coffee table on which the magazines were placed had a blue Delft vase containing an arrangement of silk tulips. A large ceramic pot contained a fig tree. Jason was determining whether or not it was real when a larger-than-life voice announced, "Mr. Richards? I'm Dirk Van Dam."

Dirk Van Dam was a larger-than-life person. He had the largest hands Jason had ever shaken and a toothy smile that started under his nose and spread to his ears. It seemed to Jason that the man was everywhere in the room at once.

"Thank you for seeing me on such short notice. I appreciate that."

"You'll come to learn that almost everything in a supportive care facility is done on short notice, and we have to be ready for it. People's need for us often comes on short notice and most of our residents leave us on short notice. Sometimes with no notice at all."

Van Dam didn't wait to see if Jason caught on to his little joke but plunged right on. "So you're the new Davidson Fellow, eh. We had one other Davidson Fellow here in the past. Douglas, Douglas . . ." Van Dam struggled to recollect the name. "Douglas something or other. I believe he went on to San Francisco General. Didn't mind speaking his piece, that one. He was something else. Visser. Visser was his name. Douglas Visser. Enough of that, come with me, I'll give you the twenty-five-cent tour." With that, he turned on his heel and began.

They wound through the supportive care unit—dorm rooms for grandparents, Jason thought—the laundry, the kitchen, a large and well-appointed chapel, which was as large as some church sanctuaries Jason had been in, and the nursing floor. Van Dam stopped to say something to each person he passed, staff and resident alike. He had a sense of ownership in the facility, the staff, and each of the residents that was easy to sense. The tour ended up in his office.

"Can I assume, Mr. Richards, that you're a Christian?"

"Yes, I am."

"It's not a hard call. We attract Christian interns just like we attract Christian residents, which is as it should be. We're supported by area churches who see us as a benevolent work in caring for their elderly in a way in which they're not equipped for. The funds to build the building and furnish it came from a fund drive conducted within the local churches. And we think we have a Christian concern for the needs of the elderly. God loves them and we try to."

"So your population is drawn from the surrounding churches?"

"All of them have some connection. Mr. Runner is the man who tends the wonderful garden along the front sidewalk. We don't think he's a Christian, but his daughter is a member of the local Dutch Reformed Church congregation, and she placed him here. The rest of the residents are from the local congregations. Mr. Runner, incidentally, is the gentleman with whom I'd recommend you interact if you chose our facility to study. He's a very bright, well read, articulate man. He actually rents two rooms from us—one to live in and the other to house his very extensive book collection."

"What's his field of interest?"

"Electronics and religion."

"An unusual combination. A specific religion or religion in general?"

"Some of the staff think he's Jewish because he doesn't believe in Jesus, but he appears to embrace the Judeo-Christian God. Some think he's New Age. Mostly, we haven't the time to find out. He doesn't attend any church that I know of and won't attend our chapel services. He's something of a reprobate, but a delight to have around."

"What was his vocation?"

"I believe he has an undergraduate degree in philosophy and took post graduate work in business and electrical engineering. I think that makes him a philosophical engineer." Van Dam laughed at his own joke. "Seriously, he apparently made a lot of money inventing some type of chip or diode that's still used in small, hand-held electronic devices. Be forewarned that he's a bit of an enigma, but frankly, he's one of the few residents with whom I feel you can interact meaningfully."

"Why is he a resident here?"

"He's almost a paraplegic. Degenerative arthritis, and some bad luck with some unsuccessful total hip replacements. He's wheelchair-bound and diabetic, as well. He can't manage by himself. His only daughter has a job that requires extensive travel and he can't live with her. That's where we come in. I suggest you meet him before you leave."

"I think I'd like that."

Van Dam glanced at his watch and then craned his neck to look out of his office window. "As I suspected, he's tending his garden. Come on, I'll introduce you."

Van Dam led Jason into the lobby through a private door and outside. The two old women were still in the lobby, still waiting for their ride. Down the sidewalk, he could see a man in a wheelchair manipulating some sort of gardening tool amongst the plants. His back was to them, and he did not seem to notice them as they approached. Van Dam circled the chair and stood in front of the man before he spoke.

"Mr. Runner, how are you this afternoon?"

Only the man's head turned as he acknowledged Van Dam and he rested his tool. "Good afternoon, Van Dam. Are you here to plunder my garden again?"

"It does look like those green beans need picking. Actually, I have someone here I'd like you to meet," and he extended his hand toward Jason. "This is Jason Richards. Mr. Richards, this is Howard Runner."

Mr. Runner turned his chair, looked up, and extended his hand. "Pleased to meet you, Mr. Richards."

Jason was struck by the blue eyes. Blue eyes embedded in a craggy face surrounded by snow-white hair. Runner wore a navy wool cap such as the captain of a fishing boat might wear and what appeared to be an expensive navy wool sweater with his initials on the left breast. Jason could not remember seeing a more well-kept beard and mustache, every hair seeming to go in the right direction. But he came back to the eyes, clear and deep and measuring. "It's nice to meet a stranger who is not trying to save my soul."

"And how do you know I'm not trying to save your soul?"

"You don't have one of those two-pound Bibles under your arm."

"I don't own a two-pound Bible, Mr. Runner. Actually, I'm from the University on a study program. It requires me to get acquainted with a supportive care facility from the bottom up. One of the requirements is that I get to know a resident and find out how he or she sees the institution. Mr. Van Dam suggested you might be a good person to get acquainted with."

"He did, did he? Truth is, Van Dam's running out of residents who can pass the test of twos."

Puzzled, Jason looked to Van Dam for a clue. But Van Dam just shrugged. Jason turned back to the man in the wheelchair, "The test of twos?"

"That's being able to string two sentences together and remember them for more than two minutes. It's hell getting old, young man, and I'm not sure it's better than the alternative," Runner said with a grin that set his skin to crinkling around those remarkable eyes.

Jason chuckled at the old man's remark. "I'd pay you a visit for an hour or so every Friday until Christmas. We'd have a conversation about the facility and its programs and how they meet your needs. Perhaps have dinner together."

"I'm finished here, let's get out of the sun." It was spoken as a suggestion, but Runner punctuated it with an exclamation point by turning his chair and wheeling it down the sidewalk toward the entrance. Van Dam and Jason followed.

Van Dam caught hold of the handles of the chair and pushed Runner along, down the sidewalk, through the lobby, down a long corridor, and into Mr. Runner's room.

Runner's room was not what Jason's experience with his grandmother led him to expect. It was very tastefully decorated with a recliner, an expensive cherry entertainment center with a flat-screen TV and DVD/VCR and CD player, and its bookshelves were crammed with books. There was a leather wingbacked chair, a small sofa, and an Early American style cherry secretary with a writing top and pigeon holes. A slightly opened door led to another room that Jason could see was lined with bookshelves.

"I'll just leave you two to get acquainted. Stop in to say goodbye before you leave, Mr. Richards." Van Dam left and closed the door behind him.

"Tell me about your academic track, Mr. Richards, and please sit down."

Jason chose the sofa. "Please call me Jason, Mr. Runner."

"Only if you'll call me Howard, Mr. Richards."

"Okay . . . Howard. I started in business school in accounting, but now I'm in a master's degree program in Hospital and Institutional Administration. Recently I was awarded the Davidson Fellowship in Advanced Management Methodology. This Fellowship requires some study, some teaching and a work study program that attempts to have the candidate see an institution from the bottom up. I'm to visit a resident in a care facility and get into his shoes, so to speak. I'd think I'd like to visit you and do my project around you, if you wouldn't mind the intrusion."

"The intrusion? The intrusion!" He paused and leaned forward in his chair and the blue eyes squinted, boring right into Jason and held his gaze. "I'd be grateful for the chance to interact with someone who hasn't quit thinking. Most of the folks here, including the staff, haven't had a new thought since high school. And most of those thoughts were borrowed from the sixteenth century."

Jason's mind raced. What happened in the sixteenth century? That was before the Age of Reason, before the Enlightenment. "Why the sixteenth century?"

Howard sat back in the chair. "This is supposedly a Christian Home. This branch of Christianity draws its philosophical and doctrinal roots back to the sixteenth century when the Heidelberg Catechism was formulated. They believe that particular statement of faith said all there is to be said for all time. For the most part, their attitude is: don't confuse me with the modern world and the scientific method; my faith is sufficiently grounded in the sixteenth century. Are you familiar with the Heidelberg Catechism?"

"Very familiar." The Heidelberg Catechism was a one of the great documents of the Reformation. Written at the University of Heidelberg by two young scholars in 1563, it codified in simple language the doctrines of a branch of the Reformation led by John Calvin. Jason had been forced to memorize a lot of it at church school classes.

The Heidelberg was in question-and-answer format—one hundred twenty-nine questions and answers—divided into fifty-two sections, corresponding to the fifty-two Sundays in the year. Some Protestant churches required their ministers to preach from these questions and answers every Sunday. Knowing some of the questions and answers was a requirement for membership in some churches, including Jason's.

"Do you believe the Heidelberg Catechism?"

"Actually, I believe what I read in the Bible. The Heidelberg is a formulation of some of the doctrines that are based on the Bible. So indirectly, I suppose, I believe in the Heidelberg."

Runner had no noticeable reaction. The blue eyes were fixed on Jason's eyes, looking through them into his mind as if he were reading what was in there. This was getting afield of Jason's purpose for being here, but this old man was an interesting study. Howard Runner—he of the white-framed face and the steely blue eyes—Jason decided, would be his candidate for his Interreactional Requirement.

Runner brought his hand to his chin and stroked his beard as if to further train it. "You believe in the Bible? What do you believe about the Bible?"

"Well," Jason leaned forward as he spoke as if to add

certainty to his words, "I believe the Bible is the inspired Word of God."

"Inspired Word of God? How, do you suppose, the Bible, as you know it, came to be?"

"What do you mean?"

"Describe for me, if you will, how the words came into being and wound up in the book you now believe to be the inspired Word of God."

This was curious. The old man had started with innocuous questions but now was becoming more probing—like a professor in a college religion class. Well, Jason had taken and passed those courses, as well. Perhaps all those religion classes he had taken would hold him in good stead. "God inspired people to write books and letters and poems, and these were collected and became the Holy Bible."

"I've always been fascinated by the notion that God inspired people to write. How did he do that?"

"I believe he told them, or perhaps influenced what was written."

"How do you envision that happened? Did these people hear voices? Did they have visions? The reason I ask is because very few of the writers themselves ask us to believe what they wrote on that basis or that they were so inspired."

Jason was puzzled. "What to do you mean, on that basis? What basis?"

"Mohammed had the good sense to reveal that the Koran was received in a vision and was the actual Word of God, which is the source of many of Islam's problems at the moment; but that's a different story. Joseph Smith, the Mormon, said the golden plates were given to him by an angel."

Runner continued. "Only the Book of the Revelations,

which, perhaps you'll agree, is the most confusing of all the books, is admitted to be a vision. Very few of the other books begin with 'I had a vision, and in that vision God revealed himself to me and told me to write . . .' And if God had done that, wouldn't that have been a significant enough event in someone's life that it would be worth repeating?"

"Well . . ." Jason suddenly realized that his ideas regarding the inspiration of the Bible were something he had taken for granted. He had just ingested it as truth. It was an accepted phrase, "the inspired Word of God." Jason had taken it as truth on faith.

"The inspiration of the Bible is something I take on faith."

"Every word?"

"*Every* word!"

"In spite of the evidence to the contrary?"

"I don't believe there is evidence to the contrary."

"There is, and I'd like you to allow me to show you a proof text."

"You have a proof text from the Bible that the Bible is not the inspired Word of God?"

Runner wheeled over to the cherry secretary and pulled a yellow Post-It note from a pad. He wrote something on it, folded it and took an envelope from one of the pigeonholes, inserted the note, and sealed the envelope.

He turned to Jason and handed him the envelope. "This will raise a question in your mind. I know it will because you're an intelligent member of the post-modern era. Unless, that is, you're afraid of the truth."

"The Bible says '. . . *the truth shall make you free*'."

"On that point, the Bible is right."

"But on other points, you don't believe it's right?"

"What I believe shouldn't be important to you. It's important that *you* understand that you believe. A belief structure based on other people's misconceptions may not serve you well." Runner paused and glanced at his watch. "Jason, it's time for my occupational therapy appointment. I have no idea why they call it that. It has nothing whatever to do with my occupation or any other I can see. And its benefit as therapy is also questionable. If I'm late, they piss and moan for the whole hour about how important it is to develop good habits. Never mind that the physical terrorist, as I like to call him, isn't worth a tinker's dam and that if I'm never on time again in my life, it won't be a career-breaker. But I do hope you'll come again, Jason. Perhaps next time we can discuss what you think of the text in the envelope."

"When would be a good time next Friday?"

"Eleven. Perhaps a good discussion will improve my appetite for the culinary disasters they pass off as food here."

Jason said his farewells and expressed his thanks to Van Dam on the way out and indicated he had chosen Mr. Runner as the person with whom he would like to interact. "He's a fascinating man. He has a mind like a steel trap. I think I'm going to actually enjoy my visits with him."

"Anything we can do to assist you, let us know." Van Dam's reaction seemed a bit perfunctory to Jason. Perhaps Van Dam had more to think about than Jason's intrusion in his busy schedule.

"Thank you and have a nice day. I'll look forward to my visit next Friday," Jason responded and turned to leave.

The two old women were still in the lobby. Jason decided it wasn't a ride they were waiting for, and the thought caused him to shudder.

Jason opened the envelope Runner had given him as soon

as he was in his car. It read "I Corinthians 7:12 NEB."

Dirk Van Dam stood at the window of his office and watched the young student leave the building. This situation called for watchfulness. Perhaps it was fortuitous that Runner was the only resident who could, as Runner had said, "pass the test of twos." Van Dam would have preferred the student had chosen some other home. But perhaps, just perhaps, this young man's presence was providential. When the student reached the parking lot, Van Dam turned and picked up his phone. He pressed the intercom line labeled "Head Nurse." When the ring was answered, Van Dam said, "Mrs. Veeringa, could you come to my office, please."

When the head nurse entered, Van Dam said, "Do you remember Douglas Visser, the graduate student who did a research paper on us a few years ago?"

"How could I forget?"

"Yes, well, he's back, only his name this time is Jason Richards. This time, he doesn't appear to be so aggressive."

"Who are you going to pair him with"?

"Howard Runner."

"Howard Runner! That's the last person I'd . . ." She caught herself and took a deep breath. "Howard Runner? That old reprobate? Why Howard Runner?"

Van Dam's explanation of the choice made very good sense. He concluded, "Here's what I want you to do . . ."

Yes, the head nurse had to admit, the choice of Runner was a good one.

# Chapter Three

The meeting with Runner so preoccupied Jason's thoughts as he drove back to his apartment that the autumnal beauty of the maple trees that lined Stadium Drive might as well have been rendered in black and white. He had no idea what the twelfth verse of the seventh chapter of First Corinthians said and tried to convince himself that he didn't care. There were more important things to accomplish than straightening out the theology of an old electrical engineer, as engaging a fellow as he was.

Runner had intrigued Jason from the moment he had gazed into those mesmerizing blue eyes. Seemingly brilliant, he also had a quick and able wit. And it appeared his powers of observation had not been affected by his disability. He did not fit the image Jason had of the typical nursing home resident. Runner would not be out of place in a faculty meeting. He was not only widely read, but current. He knew of the Post-Modern Period, the phrase used by some current social scientists to refer to their understanding that a new age had dawned, something Jason had only vague notions of. He appeared to be a biblical scholar of sorts, but he apparently was not a believer. Strange he should know about the Heidelberg Catechism and its historical origins.

Reprobate. Jason remembered Van Dam's categorization of Runner. If he was a reprobate, Jason concluded Runner's *Weltanschauung,* his world and life view, had come about after considerable consideration.

Jason realized that he had begun to share Professor Playdon's enthusiasm for the I.R.R. This project might not be the unpleasant drudgery he had first envisioned.

Jason needed a birthday card for his mother, and he noticed a card store in a strip mall. He pulled into the mall's parking lot and went into the store. It was called "Under His Wing" and when he entered, found it was it was a little too religious for his liking, but he found a suitable birthday card and went to the cash register to pay for it. There was a display of Bibles near the checkout counter and his eye fell on a copy of the New English Version of the Bible. It was not a version he was familiar with and he paused to pick up a copy and turned to I Corinthians 7:12. He was not prepared for what he read. *"To the rest I say this, as my own word, not as the Lord's: if a Christian has a heathen wife . . ."* Fascinated, he read on and when he got to verse 25, the theme was repeated. *"On the question of celibacy, I have no instruction of the Lord, but I give you my judgment as one who by God's mercy is fit to be trusted. It is my opinion, then, that in a time of stress like the present . . ."* and all the way up to verse 40 where the writer, the Apostle Paul, concludes *"that is my opinion, and I believe that I too have the Spirit of the Lord."*

Twenty-eight verses of Paul's opinion, not the words of God.

"Maybe this is a peculiarity of this translation," Jason thought. He would check out this passage with his own Bible, a copy of the King James Version.

The notion that there could be even as few as twenty-eight verses of human opinion caused Jason enough consternation that when he got to his apartment, he went straight for his worn copy of the only true scriptures, the King James Version. He found the passage and read *"But to the rest speak I, not the Lord: If any brother hath a wife that believeth not . . ."* And verse 25, *"Now concerning virgins, I have no commandment of the Lord: yet I give you my judgment as one that hath obtained mercy of the Lord to be faithful. I suppose therefore that this is good for the present distress . . ."* and all the way up to verse 40 *". . . after my judgment: and I think also that I have the Spirit of God."*

The venerable King James version also contained twenty-eight verses of Paul's suppositions and judgments and a written admission from Paul that this was Paul speaking, not God's inspiration. He read it again, as if he expected the words to change on the page. They did not.

Slowly, ever so slowly, Jason felt his skin begin to crawl, and an unsettling feeling crept into his being. It was as if he were on the middle of a bridge over a cavernous void and having one of the bridge's supports knocked away. A main support.

He brushed the image away. This whole thing was getting out of hand. So a few verses of scripture were not inspired. So what. There was the rest of the book. And he had an education to see to, and this question Runner had raised was of no consequence. It was like a mosquito heard buzzing in a darkened bedroom. It could be ignored.

But it was the words "jot and tittle" kept buzzing to the surface of his consciousness. "Jot and tittle" were the words of his pastor, and the pastor before this pastor, and the pastor before him.

"Every jot and tittle of this Holy Book is the inspired Word of God. You can bank your soul on it," they said. Jason's soul was in that bank. But then there was the question Runner had posed, "If God spoke to these people and told them what to write, why didn't any of them mention it?" He had to agree that it certainly wouldn't have slipped their mind.

He ruled out the ever-increasing possibility that the writings were simply human endeavors. First of all, this was the Holy Scriptures. Didn't that say it all? Besides, it wasn't logical that so many people writing about so many events could have done so independently without contradictions and errors. And perhaps inspiration could be called into question, but certainly not inerrancy. There were no errors in the Bible. It was the ultimate source of truth. Actually, it was The Truth. His pastor had made a point of that only recently.

His pastor. It was four fifteen on a Friday. Pastor Lipscomb would be in his office working on the Sunday sermons. He would have a quick answer to this apparent heresy and Jason could then get on with his life. Jason looked up the church's number and dialed.

"Christ's Gospel Church. Pastor Lipscomb speaking. How may I be of service?"

"Jason Richards here. How are you?

"Fine, Jason, just fine. Congratulations on your fellowship. I just heard about it. We're very proud of you."

"Thank you, very much. Do you have a moment to explain a fine point of doctrine?"

"Certainly, I need a break. I'm trying to tie Sunday night's sermon together, and I need some inspiration. Perhaps you can give it to me."

"Well, inspiration is what I'm calling about. I'm involved with an elderly gentleman in connection with a work-study program that is a requirement of my fellowship. We got to talking about my beliefs regarding the inspiration of the Scriptures.

"Now, I've always believed in the inspiration of the Bible—the whole Bible—and he challenged me on that. He offered me a proof text that the Bible was not entirely inspired." He could hear Pastor Lipscomb chuckling softly on the other end of the line and Jason paused.

"And tell me what this proof text might be?"

"First Corinthians 7:12."

"Well, Jason, let me look that up a minute. If I'm not mistaken, that's the passage where Paul is admonishing the Corinthian Christians regarding an appropriate lifestyle. Yes, here it is . . ." and there was a long silence as Jason supposed the man of God read the passage, and then re-read it, as he had. Pastor Lipscomb was no longer chuckling.

Jason broke the silence. "Well Pastor, can you help me out here?"

"Jason, the Devil comes in many forms to test our faith. But the Bible says, *'My Word is sufficient'* and *'All scripture is given by inspiration of God'* and that *'prophesy came not by the will of men, but holy men of God spoke as they were moved by the Holy Spirit.'* It's been my experience that the Devil's work is most insidious and clever in academic circles where the ability of the mind and the power of reason is glorified. Faith, by definition, cannot be reasoned. We have to be always on our guard against those who would tear down what the Church has carefully built up over the centuries. And, as the Bible says, *'gird our loins with Truth.'*

"The Bible also says that *'the Word of God is quick and powerful and sharper than any two-edged sword and is a discerner of the thoughts and intents of the heart.'* Keeping the Word of God in your heart will help you discern the evil nature of those who would revile the name of God and His Word, and hopefully its powerful life-saving message will show them the error of their ways and win their souls for the Lord. In the face of the naysayers, we must keep the faith, because, Jason, if we don't do it, who will? There must be absolutes. Take away the absolutes and there's nothing left."

"Pastor, I couldn't agree with you more. But in the case of these verses, I was hoping you could provide me with a rebuttal."

"Well Jason, would it help to say that Paul was inspired by the Holy Spirit to include this passage in this letter?"

"On the face of it, the passage would seem to deny that. Perhaps you could recommend some serious study on the inspiration of the Scriptures that would give me some answers."

"I have several works on the inspiration of the Scriptures in my library. I'll look them over. Perhaps I'll be able to find something of some help. The problem is whatever answer we come up with wouldn't be accepted by an unbeliever. They're not motivated by a search for the Truth. If they were, they would see it in God's Word. Pray the Spirit works mightily in the heart of this person that his eyes might be opened. And be assured I'll be praying for you in this time of difficulty. How are your studies going?"

"Fine Pastor, just fine. Thanks for your time. I'll look forward to hearing from you. See you on Sunday."

"Very good, Jason. Good-bye."

In the Pastor's Study of the Christ's Gospel Church of Ann Arbor, Michigan, Senior Pastor Alan Lipscomb sat at his desk with five Bibles open. All were turned to I Corinthians 7:12-40. If he had other translations, they would have been open, also. One of the Bibles was the Nestle's Edition of the Greek Manuscripts. He couldn't speak Greek, but his seminary training had included enough Greek so he could read it, and it was not difficult for him to translate this passage. The New English Bible translation was as close to the original Greek as any of the other translations, closer than some.

His training had included the knowledge that translators from time to time had shaded the meaning of their translations to favor or espouse a generally accepted doctrinal position. One example that came to mind was the passage in Isaiah 7:14 foretelling of the birth of Christ in which Isaiah writes: *"Therefore the Lord himself will give you a sign; Behold a virgin shall conceive and bear a son, and shall call his name Emanuel."* The Hebrew word "almah" used here was translated as "virgin," but the word means "young girl of marriageable age who has not yet borne a child" with no implications as to her previous sexual conduct. She *could* be a virgin, but didn't have to be. But it suited the translators to flavor the translation to emphasize the doctrine of the miraculous conception and birth of Jesus and that this passage foretold that event.

Nothing wrong with that, the pastor thought. It's the way the Church protects the Truth.

The Corinthians passage was a little more troublesome to explain. He had long privately held to a position he came to in seminary that Paul's inspiration was, well, indirect. He speculated that Paul didn't realize the letters he wrote to the churches would eventually become a part of the Scriptures.

Much of what Paul wrote was very theological, the kind of exposition that was "biblical." Other of his writings are more the practical living, folksy kind of stuff that an uncle might write to his college-age nephew giving advice on how to keep his nose clean. Things like whether it was good judgment for Christians to eat meat that had been sacrificed to idols, whether women should wear hats in church, and the passage before him now regarding celibacy and interfaith marriages.

The apostle Paul had had an encounter with Christ. He was one of the earliest writers who tried to synthesize and make sense of the birth, life, message, death and resurrection of Jesus. His was a valuable source of education to the early Church. It was not necessary, to Lipscomb's way of thinking, to maintain that all of Paul's writings were the result of God's telling him what to write.

Obviously, that's not always how it happened, as Paul clearly indicated in this passage. More likely, Paul had heard of trouble in one of his churches and he was moved, or inspired—if that word suits better—to write them a letter. These letters contained very folksy and un-theological salutations and greetings and sign-offs. The body of the letter contained the ruminations, the thoughts, the systematic theology of a man who had an encounter with the living Christ and a man who knew Peter and John and Luke. The ideas and thoughts of a man with those credentials provided the Church with a valuable body of insights and knowledge.

It was the official position of his Church that the Bible, the whole Bible, including I Corinthians 7:12-40, contained the very words of God, miraculously passed to the writers and just as miraculously preserved inerrantly through the translation process up to the King James version. He wasn't the best biblical scholar, but he knew that the Church was now in possession of manuscripts that were at least one thousand years older than the texts from which the King James version was originally translated. He wondered if the official position of the Church had been revised to somehow include these older texts into the chain of miraculous preservation. The Bible was held to be a book of facts. To preach or entertain notions to the contrary would create unnecessary doubt and questions among most of the faithful. It would undermine the absolutes. It would also raise eyebrows among his peers.

He was preparing a sermon on the famous love passage in Corinthians, Chapter 13 ending with the lines, *"And now abideth faith, hope, and love, these three; but the greatest of these is love."* He had the John Calvin's commentary on Corinthians open on his desk. He had hoped the great scholar from the sixteenth century had something to say about the love passage that he could bring to his sermon. He picked up the volume and looked for the reference to the passage Jason had questioned and began to read:

> *But why is it that Paul speaks of himself as the author of these regulations, while they appear to be somewhat at variance with what he had, a little before, brought forward, as*

> *from the Lord? He does not mean that they are from himself in such a way as not to be derived from the Spirit of God; but, as there was nowhere in the law or in the Prophets any definite or explicit statement on this subject, he anticipates in this way the (slander) of the wicked, in claiming as his own what he was about to state. At the same time lest all this should be despised as the offspring of man's brain, we shall find him afterwards declaring, that his statements are not the contrivances of his own understanding.*

Interesting, Lipscomb thought. Calvin opines here that Paul does not mean what he says. Interesting because Paul continues to say that the advice he is giving *is* a matter of his judgment and opinion. In reading further, Lipscomb could not find where Paul refutes his statement that these statements are his understanding and holds they are not his contrivances. A conundrum for which the Pastor had no answer.

If Jason raised the question again, Lipscomb would invite him in and discuss it, even admit to sharing some of Jason's questions. But no more. The job market for heretical former pastors was very small, and Lipscomb's training for doing something besides pastoring was even smaller. And his already slim chances of advancing in the hierarchy of the Church or moving to a bigger congregation would dwindle to none.

He put the Bibles aside and returned to the preparation of the Sunday evening sermon. Speaking of questionable inspiration," he thought, "the sermon in front of me is replete with it."

# Chapter Four

After Jason had put the phone down from the conversation with Pastor Lipscomb, he felt better, but not good. He hoped it wasn't a dismissal. He told himself there would be an explanation. Surely, this question had come up somewhere sometime before this and had been answered to the satisfaction of the Church. There were good minds in the Church. In fact, for centuries, the best minds in Western civilization were in the Church. Not that he had any notion that he would be able to convince Runner; he didn't need to convince Runner. Jason was the one who needed convincing.

He went about the regimen of making supper. It would not be supper in the sense that his mother made supper and the family sat down together for a meal. Jason would throw something together and consume it on the run or in front of the TV. Tonight, he was not on the run, except perhaps from Runner.

He had bought the fixings for chicken salad stuffed into pita pockets. He drained two cans of processed chicken meat and a can of pineapple chunks, diced a stalk of celery, and put the chicken, pineapple and celery in a small plastic bowl and mixed in two tablespoons of mayonnaise and one tablespoon of the brine from a jar of kosher dill pickles, and mixed all the ingredients. He spooned the chicken salad into two pita pockets, poured himself a Diet Coke, and with that and the remains of a bag of corn chips, went to the couch and clicked on the television set.

It was not a big news day, and when a feature began on the political wrangling over the funding of a new bridge to be built to Canada, he began to channel surf. There was a *Bay Watch* rerun, then a western, a *Gunsmoke* rerun, another news channel, he saw Barney Fife swaggering over the set in an *Andy Griffith* rerun, a porcelain bird was being displayed on the shopping channel, an Australian football game, a huge man with a hawk nose and a shock of white hair, meticulously groomed was pointing his finger at the television camera crying out in a ringing voice, "The Holy, Inspired, Word of God came to us, as it were, from the very throne room of Heaven!" Jason stopped channel surfing.

The evangelist was grim-faced and perspiring. "And God's Word is all you need to be saved from the condemnation that is to come! 'My Word is sufficient' the Bible says. In a world of passing fancies, the Word of God is steadfast. Adolph Hitler tried to eradicate Jesus Christ and the Word of God and couldn't." The man paused as an audience microphone picked up a chorus of amens from the crowd. "Godless communism tried to stamp out the Word of God and couldn't, give the God the gah-LOW-reh!" Another pause and another chorus of amens. "The courts of the land have taken away Bible reading and prayer from the public schools." Another pause and yet another chorus of amens.

"The scientists have tried to throw out the Bible with their godless evolutionism." There was another pause and more amens.

Jason watched, fascinated. He had never paid much attention to television evangelists unless they got in some kind of trouble, like Jimmy Swaggert or Jim and Tammy Baker. He knew they were regular features on cable television, but had never actually watched one in action. This one reminded him of the blowhard preacher in the George Burns/John Denver movie *Oh God* who pronounced "God" as "GAWD-ah." The television camera was panning the audience in a huge arena or church building, Jason couldn't tell which. The audience was as grim-faced as the preacher. If they had any joy in their lives, they were hiding it well.

"And they're coming after your Bibles." The evangelist paused, but there was no applause. "I hear you say, 'Brother Hartger, no one's coming after my Bible.'" Another pause. "Oh no? You take a few of your friends and stand in front of an abortion clinic and read your Bible aloud and you . . . will go . . . to jail-ah!" he said with a rising crescendo. He paused and there was silence. "It's now the law of the land. You see, brothers and sisters, it's not politically correct to be opposed to the murder of innocent babies, but it is politically correct to be against the God-ordained death penalty for murders!" he thundered and the crowd broke into amens and applause.

"If there's one lesson of history, it's that the Bible and the absolute truths in it will come under attack from every angle. Satan and his legions will not rest until and unless he can destroy the Holy Scriptures." Another chorus of amens.

"The Devil doesn't want you to read your Bible. The Devil doesn't want anyone to read the Bible because the Bible shows the way to salvation through Jesus Christ. Give God the gah-LOW-reh." The amens came on cue.

"Satan has tried to work his purposes through Hitler, and that didn't work."

"Amen."

"Satan has worked through Godless communism, and that hasn't worked."

"Amen."

"He has his minions on the courts of the land, but that hasn't gotten rid of the Bible."

"Amen."

"You know where the Devil's working now?" The preacher paused. "You know where he's getting a foothold now?" He was pacing the stage. "I'm gonna tell where the Devil is working now. He's working in the Church-ah." He stopped pacing and raised an accusatory finger and pointed it right at the camera and thundered, "He's working through so-called biblical scholars who would tell you the Bible, this Bible . . ." he was holding a large rolled up, leather bound Bible aloft, "this Holy Word of God is not the Word of God at all. It's just a collection of STOW-rees-ah. Thet you cain't take it at face value. They are telling you that Jesus wasn't really the Son of

God-ah, but just some itinerant rabbi-ah."

The crowd was silent. Hartger was working himself into a frenzy. "I have but one thing to say to these so-called biblical scholars." He paused and paced. "I hope they're listening tonight and hear what I'm about to say. I say 'Get thee behind me, Satan!'" The crowd broke into a roar of applause.

"I say 'Get thee behind me, Satan,' because that's who they are."

"Amen."

"Satan cain't use Hitler anymore."

"Amen."

"Satan cain't use communism any more-ah."

"Amen."

"Satan doesn't need Hitler and Satan doesn't need communism. He's got enough henchmen in the ivory towers of the Church!"

"Amen."

"These self-styled, so-called biblical scholars are denying one of the fundamental truths of Christianity that the Bible is the inspired Holy Word of God-ah!" The huge man paused and raised himself onto his toes and leaned forward like a heavyweight prize fighter getting ready to attack. "Ah am here . . . to testify . . . that every word—Ah said every word-ah," he had the leather Bible rolled up in one hand and was raising his other hand and lowering his outstretched palm onto the Bible with each word or phrase, "from Genesis one, verse one to Revelation twenty-two, verse twenty-one is the message of salvation . . . unto eternal life . . . from God himself, for sinful man, give God the gah-LOW-reh!" The crowd took the cue and responded with amens and applause.

Except the part that Paul says is not inspired, thought Jason. He watched a while longer. The huge man continued to rail against

Hitler, communism, fascism, the courts, the public schools, gays, lesbians, biblical scholars, and other "profligate sinners." Jason noticed the preacher was long on condemnation and short on grace. But then, how could you be bombastic and preach grace? Jason wondered.

Enough already. Jason clicked the television set off and turned to his studies. He had set aside this Friday evening to formally outline his thoughts as to how he would handle the recitation sessions for Intro Ad 301. He got out the text and his own notes from the time he took the course, a yellow legal pad, and a felt tip pen. He rifled through the notes to see they were in order and began to read. His eyes went over the words, but his mind was still back on the portly television preacher and his shock of white hair, thumping his Bible and saying, "every word, from Genesis one, verse one, to Revelation twenty-two, verse twenty-one is the message of salvation unto eternal life from God himself . . . to sinful man, give God the gah-LOW-reh!"

Except for the political overtones and the show-biz production, the theology was not dissimilar to his own tradition. In Jason's home church, it was presented in a sobering and seemingly intellectual atmosphere. It was comfortable, and it was believable. When the same theology was presented by the fear monger on television, wrapped in the cloak of fear of Satan and communism and whatever else, it became suspect. As a scholar, Jason was uncomfortable with the television preacher's denunciation of scholarship.

What is inherently evil about scholarship? he wondered. Scholarship is a search for the truth, the conscious expansion of knowledge for the purpose of enlightenment. Why would the results of the legitimate exercise of this discipline be suspect on its face? It occurred to Jason that what the preacher came off saying was, don't seriously study the Word of God, don't be a serious scholar, believe it superficially. "Ah'll tell you whachew gotta know-ah."

Jason realized that was how he had built his faith structure, superficially. Other people had told him what they thought he ought to know and how he ought to think. And that's what he knew and that's how he thought.

He clicked on the television. He wanted to hear more. The huge man was no longer preaching but placing his hands on the heads of people who were filing past him. Some were crying, some looked as if they were in a trance. One man fell over backward when the preacher touched him, to which the preacher thundered, "Give God the gah-LOW-reh!" while the man twitched convulsively on the floor. In the background, a large choir was singing softly:

> *Just as I am without one plea*
>
> *But that thy blood was shed for me.*
>
> *And that thou bid'st me come to thee*
>
> *Oh, Lamb of God, I come, I come.*

The picture changed, and the preacher came onto the screen. He was sitting in an office and he began an earnest plea for money so that he "could continue this vital television ministry for the gah-LOW-reh of God-ah!" Jason clicked the set off and went back to his notes on Intro Ad 301.

He found he still couldn't concentrate. The happenings of the day kept crowding into his mind. The meeting with the man-devil Runner. Runner's questions. The verses from Corinthians. The phone conversation with Pastor Lipscomb. Absolutes that were not absolutely absolute.

He felt a growing angst that the discovery that, perhaps, just perhaps, not all of the Bible was the actual words of God. It all had more of an influence on his faith structure than it should have on a rational mind. And Jason had a rational mind. So a few verses weren't inspired. If he had accepted only superficially, what did it matter?

But what if the biblical scholars against whom the television preacher had railed were as credible as the courts of the land, which the preacher had also railed on? What did these scholars know that was so dangerous to this preacher? Jason thought that probably these biblical scholars remained biblical scholars in spite of the discoveries that the preacher so vehemently denounced. Or was it . . . *because* of their discoveries?

If they were scholars of any integrity and they had discovered something in the tradition was false, wouldn't they leave the tradition? Wouldn't they become agnostics, or atheists, or Muslims? Wasn't every biblical scholar dealing with personal belief structures that relate to the ultimate realities of life?

Jason remembered the TV preacher's reference to "godless evolutionism." He had come to believe that the world was not created according to the biblical explanation of the creation process. There were too many scientific facts, too much evidence to hold on to the belief that the world was only six thousand years old.

Jason was convinced the world as we know it evolved over millions of years. He was equally convinced that evolution was neither profane nor sacred, godless nor godly. It was a natural process, no doubt set in motion by and controlled by God, but it was not the process described in the first chapter of Genesis.

So did that acknowledgment put him in the camp of the television preacher's evil-doers? And was he now an ally of what the preacher had called the "self-styled, so-called biblical scholars who are denying one of the fundamental truths of Christianity"? Is the inspiration of the Scriptures, as the preacher believed in inspiration, one of the fundamental truths? Did the words of the Bible come from the throne room of God? If they did, what of the verses in Corinthians that Runner had directed him to? What was the view of the inspiration of the Scriptures that these biblical scholars held? Was there another view of inspiration that was plausible?

Jason mulled these and other questions over in his mind until he became numb. By then, it was past eleven o'clock and he gave up on thinking about theology and how it related to his personal faith structure. He had been blindly staring at his Intro Ad 301 notes. He decided to get some sleep. There was time enough in this life to solve the riddles of the universe. He was running out of time to solve the riddle of Intro Ad 301.

He usually fell asleep before or just as his head hit the pillow. This night he could not sleep. He had never noticed the stream of light from the streetlamp outside his bedroom window before. It crept around the edge of the window shade and illuminated the floor where he had left his loafers. It would have made a great advertisement for Bass Weegins.

His mind's eye could see the huge television preacher pointing right at him and the preacher's glaring eyes accusing him of being one of those godless scholars who was denying the fundamental truths of the Bible. Jason blinked him away and tried to have his mind channel surf to more pleasant thoughts. But this night his mind seemed to have only one channel. The LEDs on his alarm clock lit up 2:16 before sleep finally overtook him.

He dreamed he was trout fishing on the Pere Marquette River. It was an overcast and foreboding day, so the trout should have been feeding, but he was having no luck. He switched from wet to dry flies. No luck. He moved upstream to the next deep spot in the river. No strikes from that hole, either. He switched flies again, this time trying a large orange streamer. Still no luck. He moved upstream again, trying the shallower riffles as he went. For some reason he was under heavy pressure to catch fish and whatever he tried, he was having no luck. He strained some sand from the river bottom to see what larvae were present. None. He tried dry flies again. He didn't even see a follower. He tried an imitation crayfish. Not a tunk. He began looking for the next likely hole.

As he waded upstream, he saw another fisherman in the water fishing some distance ahead of him. Aha! This might be the reason he wasn't catching any fish. This guy was probably spooking the fish just ahead of him. Jason decided to get onto the bank and walk some distance ahead of the other fisherman and try his luck farther upstream. As he approached the place where the other man was fishing, he took some notice of him. The man was wearing shiny black waders and a white turtleneck top. On his head was a large brimmed straw hat like the Amish folks at the Ann Arbor farmers' market wore. A strange getup. Jason had never seen shiny black waders before.

There was something else that was strange about this fisherman. For a minute, Jason couldn't put his finger on it. Then as the man prepared to cast again, it came to him. The man was fishing with a spinning rod! This was the quality waters—the "Flies Only" section of the Pere Marquette—affectionately referred to as "the Holy Waters." Spinning rods are used to fish with nightcrawlers or artificial lures. This man was violating the law. In common terms, he was a poacher. Jason sensed trouble.

Just as this realization dawned on Jason, the man noticed him and Jason could see the man didn't appreciate sharing the river with another fisherman. He challenged Jason in an agitated voice, "What do you think you're doing here? This is my river. You're on my property, you're trespassing! Get the hell out of here!"

Jason was taken aback. The river was not private and the land on both banks was part of the Manistee National Forest. It was public land. He decided to avoid trouble and continue on his way without responding. The man's tone was growing hostile, "Who do you think you are?" he thundered. "Cain't you see you don't belong here?"

Jason was startled. That voice was familiar and so was the face. But Jason could not remember seeing this man with the shiny black waders in the river before. Who was he and why was he upset?

"You young bastards are all the same, think you can do anything you want! Well, trespassing's a crime. More than that, it's a sin! You're a criminal and a sinner."

Jason was confused. Was he mistaken about where he was? No, he knew exactly where he was, he had fished this stretch of river many times before. A sinner? What did sin have to do with this? He decided nothing would be lost if he defended his presence. "This is federal land," Jason rejoined. "This is a public river. Anyone can fish here. I'm not bothering you. I'm on my way upstream. I'll be out of your way in no time."

Jason's protest sent the man into a blind rage. He snarled back at Jason. "You don't know where you are. You think you do, but you don't. You're trespassing and you're a sinner. You've crossed over the line. You'll have to be punished. You're going to Hell and I'm going to see to it! You and all your kind!" As the man spoke, he began wading toward Jason in the lumbering waddle of a man in water up to his waist. He was taking large and determined steps and would soon be at the edge of the bank.

Jason tried to calm himself. Just avoid confrontation, he thought desperately, just get out of here before Mr. Shiny Pants makes it to the shore. Jason turned and tried to go on his way, but the undergrowth and a steep clay bank that rose along the trail blocked his path. The man was coming closer. Jason was trapped. His antagonist was a huge man and continued his ranting about Jason being a sinner and going to Hell as he came closer. The man was pointing a large accusatory finger at Jason and railing at him. Suddenly, Jason recognized the man coming toward him in the river. It was the television evangelist! Jason forced himself awake.

The room was still stained with the darkness of the night except for the shaft of light coming peering around the edge of the window shade from the street lamp illuminating his loafers. The house was quiet. The street was quiet. It was 4:15 in the morning. He was hot and sweating and he turned his pillow over to the cool side. Jason body tossed while his mind turned until the day broke. All because of a retirement home resident in a wheelchair with piercing blue eyes.

# Chapter Five

Davidson Fellows had a rigorous regimen. Jason found he had time for the program and little else. There were the preps for his Intro Ad 301 class, study for his own classes, which entailed a considerable amount of reading, and then faculty meetings, department meetings, six hours per week of work for the Controller at the U. of M. Hospital, and a periodic meeting with Professor Emeritus Playdon for his I.R.R. paper. The busyness of his schedule helped his mind push the unwanted spiritual conflict back until it fell off the edge of his consciousness. When it fell, however, it usually landed in the pit of his stomach.

During the first meeting with Playdon, after his encounter with Howard Runner, Jason had indicated his selection of Christian Arbor Home and that he had met a resident there that he felt would make a good person with whom to interact. Playdon showed his pleasure that the selection had been made so promptly and that he had chosen the Christian Arbor Home.

He gave Jason a stack of bound reports. "These are the work products of the preceding Davidson Fellows who have gone through the Interreactional Requirement Program. They'll give you an idea of what's been done in the past. I ask that you give particular attention to the paper written by Douglas Visser. Mr. Visser also used the Christian Arbor Home for as the basis for his work.

"I'm curious to see if there have been any changes at the Home. As you'll see, his paper is somewhat critical of the Home for being long on compassion and short on up-to-date methods and procedures. He also was a bit chagrined that the Home wouldn't provide any financial information for his research, something the other homes have typically been very cooperative in providing. His paper was unusual, I thought, because he was from the religious tradition that supports the Home financially. Yet, as you'll see, he put whatever bias he may have had aside and pulled no punches.

"The institutions in the program are under no obligation to use the student reports. Some of them are grateful for the unusual perspective and use them as the basis for improvement and change. You're only the second candidate to use this particular institution, so this'll be the first feedback we get as to what they did with Visser's report, if anything. Incidentally, can I assume your selection had something to do with the religious nature or denominational affiliation of this home?"

"It started out that way. But I must admit, I made my choice when I met the individual with whom I'd be interacting. His name is Howard Runner, and he's extremely well read. He rents two rooms at the Home, one for an extensive collection of books. I think he'll be a great resource person and I chose him—or perhaps he chose me—rather than my choosing the institution."

"Very good, Jason. Finding a good person with whom to discourse is key here. I'd like to continue these meetings on a weekly basis, if you don't mind. I'm working on an article for *Hospital Administration Monthly* about our Interreactional Requirement Program. I'd like to be free to ask you some questions from time to time. If your input is included, the publishers will be asking for a release." Playdon was smiling out of one side of his mouth and his bushy eyebrows were arched almost to his hairline.

"I'm flattered and honored, and I'd be pleased to lend whatever assistance I can." Co-authoring an article with William A. Playdon? Would one meeting a week be enough? He could make it two or three, whatever. Lord 'a mercy! Jason was floating on a cloud of euphoria as he left Playdon's office.

Friday morning found him in his Honda on the way to visit Howard Runner. Jason was prepared. He had a small tape recorder, a legal size notepad. He also had "... *gird(ed) his loins with the Truth.*"

He had spent more time than usual in personal reflection and had read passages of the Bible, partly out of a curiosity about inspiration and partly in an attempt to exorcise the memory of the television preacher. Intellectual integrity had forced him to acknowledge that Runner had a point about not every word being inspired. Jason also had to admit that this was counter to what his tradition had taught him. But as far as he could see, the fact that one or two or twenty verses were not God's words changed nothing. He still had The Book; it was still the way to salvation through Jesus Christ. Yes, he reflected, he was prepared to meet with Howard Runner.

He took note of the vegetable garden as he drove up. The tomato plants had been tilled and watered and looked like something out of a seed catalog advertisement. He made a mental note to compliment Runner on his green thumb.

He registered at the window in the lobby. The secretary informed him that wasn't necessary and he proceeded to Runner's room. The door was ajar and he knocked.

"Come in, Mr. Richards, come in."

"Good morning, Mr. Runner. How are you today?"

"I'm fine, thank you. Just fine." He was seated in his wheelchair with both hands resting on a cane that was propped in front of the chair. His chin was resting on his hands. Classical music was coming from the CD player, which Runner turned down to a level of background music with a remote control device he had beside him.

Jason was struck by how kindly Runner appeared—the pure white hair and beard ringing his face and his striking blue eyes. A pair of half-frame glasses were perched on his nose. He was looking at Jason over the top of the glasses.

"I'm happy you've come back. I was afraid I had frightened you off. I'm pleased that you have either the courage or the curiosity to return. Tell me, which is it . . . courage or curiosity?"

"Perhaps a little of both. I must admit your reference in Corinthians was a little unsettling for a bit. I had never experienced those verses before you pointed them out. But on reflection, I don't think the lack of inspiration for a few verses changes anything in terms of God's redemptive plan for the world."

"I think those verses *were* inspired."

Jason cocked his head and looked straight at Runner, as if he wasn't sure he had heard rightly. Runner said nothing. Jason was puzzled. "Did you say the verses *were* inspired?" adding the same emphasis Runner had added.

"Yes, just like all of the Bible is inspired."

"But the Corinthians reference . . . It says that Paul wasn't inspired."

"No, it says that God didn't tell him what to write. I think there's a difference between being inspired to write and inspired as to what to write. You told me you believed that inspiration means God somehow told people what to write. I said I didn't think so because few of them mentioned such a spiritual visitant. You are from a tradition of proof texts. Heidelbergers need proof texts. You don't want to hear about reason, or logic, or the biblical scholarship of the past two centuries—or, for that matter, experience. You need a proof text. I gave you one. That text in no way dispels the notion of the inspiration of the Scriptures. It dispels the notion that the inspiration was magical or mystical."

"So how do you believe the Scriptures were written?"

"By human beings—with all the limitations that unfortunate condition carries with it—who thought they had encountered the living God. They were moved to write about what they thought they heard and saw. No more, no less. The Bible is not a revelation from God. Rather, it's the witness of those to whom God revealed himself. God wasn't proactive in the writing process. But listen, you're not here to discuss theology. You have work to do. Let's talk about the

Christian Arbor Home, which, I might begin with, is none of the aforementioned."

Runner was right. Jason didn't come to talk about theology. Last week's conversation had been more unsettling than he had thought possible, and he didn't need the distraction. But perhaps one more discussion would put the matter to rest. "So in other words, you believe the Bible's collection of books that were inspired to be written, but were written without any divine interaction or intervention."

"That's the only explanation that doesn't defy reason. Why are there four Gospels? Wouldn't it make more sense for God to have told just one of the apostles what to write, like one Acts? And why are they so different? If God somehow told them what to write, did God's perception of what happened change? Why did God think Jesus cleansed the Temple during Holy Week when He told Matthew, Mark, and Luke what to write, but right after Jesus turned water into wine early in Jesus' ministry when He told John what to write? Why did the Holy Spirit remember only a few of Jesus' words on the cross in each Gospel? If they wrote with divine intervention, why did the writers think the world had corners, and that the sun went around the earth, and that the earth was the center of the universe? If God created the world, surely He must have known what we know now. Why do these discrepancies occur?

"If you can accept the notion that they were just human beings—conditioned by their environment and the accepted paradigms of their day—the church's acceptance of scientific information that we now know to be different than the ancient notions can be considered normal instead of heresy.

"Think of the agony the Church went through with Galileo. The biblical writers wrote in the paradigm of the day. That is, the earth was the center of the universe and the sun traveled around it. Galileo was nearly excommunicated for daring to suggest that Copernicus, who incidentally was a bishop of the Church, was right in that the earth traveled around the sun."

Jason saw a chance to jump in. "I think the Church has come a long way toward correcting the mistakes it made with Galileo."

"Which church? I read just the other day that a seminary kicked out several professors for their espousing the earth is more than six thousand years old. The curse of Bishop Ussher!" Runner was holding his beard. His eyes were soft and squinting and, Jason thought, almost twinkling. "What about your church, Jason. Where does it stand on the age of the earth?"

There were a number of pastors in Jason's denomination that still clung to the Bishop Ussher timetable. "I personally have no trouble believing the earth is millions of years old. But I want to get back to something you said earlier. You asked why there were discrepancies. What discrepancies are you referring to?"

Runner put his mouth into the top of his hands where his chin had been and looked at Jason over the top of his half frames as he contemplated the question and whether or not he should answer. The young man hadn't run off yet—why not? He lifted his mouth off his hands. "How many do you need to dispel the notion of inerrancy your Church so desperately and futility clings to?"

"How many are there?"

"Enough."

"Give me a few."

"How good is your biblical knowledge?"

"Pretty good."

"How did Judas die?"

"He hung himself."

Runner didn't move for a moment, then directed Jason's attention to his entertainment center with his cane. "Get that book with the dark blue dust jacket."

Jason rose to get the book Runner was pointing to and recognized it as a copy of the New English Bible.

"I see you're partial to the New English Bible," Jason ventured.

"I'm told by folks who should know about these things that this translation is closest to the oldest available manuscripts. When you get home, look these passages up in your King James Version. You can verify that I'm not using a particular translation to prove a point. Turn to Acts One, about verse seventeen or eighteen."

Jason found the passage and read aloud, "*This Judas, be it noted, after buying a plot of land with the price of his villainy, fell forward on the ground, and burst open, so that his entrails poured out.*"

Runner's steely blue eyes bore right into Jason. "Two points here. First, what did Judas do with his money, and second, how did he die?"

"I guess I was mistaken. I thought he hung himself, and I also thought he returned the thirty pieces of silver to the High Priest."

"You *are* a biblical scholar of sorts. Your information is from Matthew twenty-seven."

Jason turned to the passage and read aloud about the death of Judas as recorded by Matthew:

> *So he threw the money down in the temple and left them, and went out and hanged himself. Taking up the money, the chief priests argued: "This cannot be put into the temple fund; it is blood money." So after conferring they used it to buy the Potter's Field, as a burial field for foreigners. This explains the name 'Blood Acre', by which that field has been known ever since.*

"You'll have to agree, they're two entirely different accounts, both as to what Judas did with the money and how he died." Runner cocked his head and lowered his voice. "I put it to you, which one is right? Which begs the question, which one is in error?

"Another obvious error is made by Luke when he reports that Jesus, in his own words, assured the thief on the cross on Good Friday that, 'Today, you shall be with me in Paradise.' But John reports that Jesus was not yet in Paradise on Friday. On Sunday morning Jesus, when he appeared to Mary, said to her, 'Do not cling to me for I have not yet ascended to the Father.'"

Jason was on the bridge over the vast void again, and another support for the bridge had just been kicked away by a kindly old man in a wheelchair. No, it was worse than that. Acts 1:18 had kicked away Matthew 27:5-9, or vice versa, and the Jesus of John had disputed the veracity of the Jesus of Luke. The old man in the wheelchair had nothing to do with it and was speaking.

"Would you like to know what I think?" and he didn't wait for Jason to respond. "I think it doesn't matter. In the first instance, both of these writers are trying to tell you that Judas was remorseful and went out and killed himself, and that the thirty pieces of silver went to buy the Potter's field. In the second case, the thief on the cross was Paradise-bound.

"Four men, Matthew, Mark, Luke, and John, inspired by their encounter with the living God, writing down their recollections perhaps as much as some sixty-odd years later. They were recording to the best of their knowledge and belief. The wonder is not that there were differences, the wonder is that there aren't more differences. Heavens, if the two of us were to record our recollection of this meeting tomorrow, it wouldn't be the same for a number of reasons."

"Outside of the differences in ability to remember, why not?"

"Because I'll be remembering this meeting through my bias, you'll remember it through yours. We will have different reasons for remembering, which will color not only what we remember but what we choose to write about what we remember."

"Which suggests some writers in the Bible had a bias?"

"Some of them were honest enough to admit it. Turn to John's

Gospel, chapter twenty, the last verses in the chapter."

Jason turned to the passage and read aloud. *"There were indeed many other signs that Jesus performed in the presence of his disciples that are not recorded in this book. Those here written have been recorded in order that you may hold the faith that Jesus is the Christ, the Son of God, and that through this faith you may possess life by his name."*

"Here, the writers are acknowledging that this is not a complete history. They had to pick and choose what was in the Book and admit they did so to emphasize what they thought was important, so you'd come to the same understanding they had. Read that, b-i-a-s. Some might say it was an admission of propaganda."

"*They* picked and chose? Didn't John write the Gospel of John?"

"Read the verses at the end of the book."

"'*It is this same disciple who attests what has been written. It is in fact he who wrote it, and we know that his testimony is true.*'"

"Doesn't the second person plural suggest that the writing of this book was a corroboration? Recent scholarship suggests this book was written up to ninety years after the death of Christ by disciples of John." Runner paused a moment. He stroked his beard with his right hand, the left held the cane upright between his legs.

He continued, "While we are on the subject of bias, biblical scholars have long held that Matthew had a bias. He was writing to the Jews, trying to convince them that this Jesus fellow was in fact the Messiah they were looking for."

"I've heard that."

"Good, look up Matthew 1:22"

Jason found the passage and saw that it was the familiar passage where the angel was foretelling the birth of Christ to Joseph. "*All this happened in order to fulfill what the Lord declared through the prophet: 'The Virgin will conceive and bear a son, and he shall be called Emmanuel.'"*

Runner had put his mouth on his hands, which were clasped over the crook of the cane. When Jason stopped reading, he raised his head. "I think Matthew was so determined to show the Jews who he thought this Jesus fellow was, he became a bit over-zealous with his use of the Scripture. In fact, I think integrity will force us to say that his bias may have caused him to make a mistake."

"How's that?"

"Let's look up the original prophecy to which Matthew is referring. I believe it's in Isaiah 7. As I recall, Ahaz, the King of Judah, was being threatened by the King of Israel and some other enemy. Isaiah was instructed by God to tell Ahaz he had nothing to fear at verse 10."

Jason turned to Isaiah 7 and began reading verse 10:

> *Once again the Lord spoke to Ahaz and said, "Ask the Lord your God for a sign, from the lowest Sheol or from the highest heaven." But Ahaz said, "No, I will not put the Lord to the test by asking for a sign." Then the answer came: "Listen, house of David. Are you not content to wear out men's patience? Must you also wear out the patience of my God? Therefore, the Lord himself shall give you a sign: A young woman is with child, and she will bear a son, and will call him Immanuel. By the time that he has learned to reject evil and choose good, he will be eating curds and honey; before that child has learned to reject evil and choose good, desolation will come upon the land before whose kings you cower now. The Lord will bring on you, your people, and your house, a time the like of which has not been seen since Ephraim broke away from Judah."*

Jason looked up at Runner as if to ask if he had read far enough. He knew he had.

Runner had his mouth on his hands on the cane and was

looking at Jason over the half-frame glasses again. He lifted his head to speak. "If we take the words of Isaiah at face-value, the young boy that was already conceived will have plenty to eat, and the two kings hassling Ahaz will be in ruin by the time the child is old enough to tell right from wrong. Is this a prophecy of the birth of Jesus, who was born centuries later? Is Matthew's quotation appropriate?" He paused.

"You'll agree it's not." He paused again. Then, "Is the quotation lifted out of context and shaded to say something not obviously intended in the Isaiah passage? I think so. Should we be surprised that Jews did not, and are not now, flocking to your Jesus if this is the proof text that he is the Messiah? Not surprised at all."

Jason didn't think that a response was in order and didn't have one if it was. He now recognized the classical music that was coming from the CD player. It was Tchaikovsky's 1812 Overture. At that moment, the cymbals were clashing and the cannons were roaring. Or was it his mind and his intestines. He was sorry he had kicked the sleeping dog.

Runner had his elbows on the arms of the wheelchair and was pushing his body up to shift his weight in the chair. He settled back and began afresh. "The translators of the King James Version are even more biased. They want so badly to make this passage agree with Matthew's mistake, they have the young woman in Isaiah's time being a virgin also. That makes two virgin births in the Scriptures . . . unless one of them is a mistake. And that begs the question, which one is the real virgin birth or is any of them genuine? Inquiring minds want to know," Runner said with a chuckle, a reference to a popular television commercial for a tabloid newspaper.

His eyes bore in on Jason again. "So now, my Bible believing young friend. Are you as convinced of the inerrancy of the Scriptures as you were when you came in?"

Tchaikovsky's cymbals and the cannons were at triple forte.

"I don't know what to believe. All my life, I've had this belief structure and, intellectually, I'm forced to admit you may have a point. If I accept your argument, a large section of the foundation of my belief structure has been taken away. But I'm sure the Church has an answer that will refute you on this. I'm just not enough of a biblical scholar to argue the point with you." Actually, Jason Richards was not sure of anything, except for the cannon in his stomach that was drowning out the Tchaikovsky.

"I think on reflection, you will come to see that I haven't taken anything away that was really there. Is inspiration a claim of the Book or of those who make it their responsibility to defend the Book? Does the Book make a claim for inerrancy? I think not. Inspiration and inerrancy are claims made by the Church. Claims which, in my judgment, are both uninspired and in error." He grinned broadly, and his eyes twinkled at the play on words.

Runner paused and sized up his young pupil. He observed that Jason's face had the haunted look of someone who was looking at a ghost. Something or someone had scared this young man more than anything he had said. Perhaps he was seeing the ghost of religion past, the theological equivalent of Scrooge's ghost of Christmas Past. Perhaps Jason needed a look at the ghost of religion present.

"Tell me, Jason, would the Bible be less of a book of faith if we were to discover that the people who wrote it were real people like yourself, doing the best they could with their human-ness? People with imperfect knowledge, people with a normal bias toward their personal insights, people who changed their minds, people who had encountered the living God and were inspired to write what they remembered about that encounter without the aid of tape recorders or television cameras. These were people with historical perspective—these are the people who wrote the Book. And these people's human-ness, their imperfections, their bias—it's all in there, as we might expect with any human endeavor.

Runner paused and began stroking his beard. "Jason, do you

have difficulty believing in the Roman Catholic teaching of the infallibility of the Pope?"

"Yes, that's a problem for me."

"Why?"

"Only God is infallible, and it's an attribute he does not give to us humans, regardless of our piety and station within the Church."

"Interesting. You answer as I rather expected you would. It has always fascinated me how the Protestant Church will not give infallibility to the Pope but does give it to the writers of the Scriptures when the fallibility of both is so apparent. Actually, the Roman Church's understanding of revelation is that it's an ongoing process, beginning with the Scriptures and continuing with the scholars of the Church today. The Reformers of the sixteenth century threw out the infallibility of the wicked Church of their time and said they based their belief in the Scriptures. And the Protestant Church, in what was a logical over-reaction to the Roman teaching of the infallibility of the Church, came up with the idea of infallibility for the Scriptures."

Jason looked at the book on his lap. What was this book now? Was it just a book, like *War and Peace* or *The Cat in the Hat*? Was it a bible? *The* Bible? What was the Bible?

Jason closed the Bible on his lap and laid it on the end table next to him, and his eyes followed the book all the way back to the table. He realized he was watching himself discard it, and he didn't mean to get rid of it. He didn't want the act of laying the book down to be symbolic. He needed to pick it up again, and he did. He held it by the binding and pointed it at Runner. "If it's not perfect," he said quietly, "why should I or anyone else believe in it?"

The blue eyes grew even more soft and kindly. "Was you father perfect?"

"No."

"Do you remember the first time you realized he wasn't perfect?"

Jason did. His father had been involved in a rear-end collision. A motorist had not been paying attention and had plowed into the back end of the family's brand new Ford LTD. His father had gotten out of the car and exploded at the other driver, using language that he had probably learned in the Army and had suppressed until that moment. "Yes, I remember," Jason said.

"Did you throw out everything your father meant to you, everything he taught you because you discovered he had feet of clay?"

"Of course not."

"Can you use your belief in your father as a model with which to mold your belief in your Scriptures?"

But this was different. The Scriptures were the Scriptures. The Holy Scriptures. Still, Runner's point was well made. When he was a small boy, he had thought of his father as having god-like qualities. He was all-powerful, all-wise, all-knowing—only later to become human as Jason grew older. But Jason still respected him. He had not thrown out his father with the bath water so to speak.

Perhaps one could accept this notion that the Scriptures were of human construction without eliminating its power and its wisdom and its revelation of the Who of God and his interaction in history.

Runner was continuing, "And another point. There were believers before there were Scriptures. I get the feeling that some Christians believe leather-bound Bibles magically appeared the day after this Jesus fellow was supposed to have ascended into heaven. There were several generations of Christians who believed on the basis of oral tradition. Bits and pieces of the Jesus story passed along orally. The books that were to become the Old Testament Scriptures were not canonized until the year 98 AD by the Council of Jamnia and the New Testament in 390 or so at the Synod of Hippo.

"Then over a thousand years passed before the average person ever saw a Bible, let alone have the ability to read one. The tradition was passed along in the relief sculptures on the doors of cathedrals and in stained glass windows. Gutenberg's press didn't exist until 1454, and the first English translation didn't appear until 1536. So the tradition was passed along orally, without the fine nuances of doctrine for which this tradition is famous."

Runner glanced at his watch and straightened up. "Goodness, it's time for lunch. If I don't get there in time for their opening prayer ritual, I'll have to listen to all the old women cluck about how wicked I am. Would you mind wheeling me over to the dining room? If they see I have a visitor, they may not cluck out loud. They won't forgive me, but they might let me eat in peace."

Jason rose and opened the door, and after Runner had wheeled himself out, he closed the door to the room and took the handles of the chair. Following Runner's directions, they went toward the dining room.

Runner didn't stop talking. "Now the next time you come, we have to get at your work, Jason. Left down the next corridor. Enough prattle about inspiration and inerrancy. It's not what you're here for. The double doors on the right."

Jason didn't need instructions. His nose could follow the heavy smell of roast beef and gravy. "There you are, Mr. Runner. Until next week, then?" Jason turned and began to make his way out of the Home. As he approached the doors leading to the lobby, a tall blonde woman in white surgical pants and a flowered print over-blouse called to him.

"Excuse me, but are you the Michigan student who's interviewing Mr. Runner?"

Jason nodded and stuck out his hand to greet the woman as she approached. "I'm Jason Richards."

She was about thirty-five, he judged, and not unattractive, but she had a tired look.

"I'm Sharon Veeringa, I'm the head nurse for the Home. Congratulations on your fellowship. I worked with Mr. Visser when he evaluated the Home. If you don't mind, Mr. Richards, I like a word with you about Mr. Runner."

"Not at all. If you know something that will help me with my report, I'd welcome the information."

"Well, this isn't exactly about your report. Mr. Van Dam told me that you selected our nursing facility because you were a Christian as well, is that right?"

"Well yes, I am. There were a number of facilities from which to choose, but I admit I did lean toward this Home because it was a Christian Home."

"Mr. Richards, you should know that Mr. Runner has upset a lot of the residents here at the Home. This *is* a Christian Home, and there are a lot of fine Christian residents and workers here. They come from strongly evangelical backgrounds and the last thing some of these people need is for Mr. Runner to be filling their heads with his liberal, humanistic blather.

"I know this is none of my business, but I couldn't help but overhear your conversation as I was making rounds earlier this morning. A word of warning, Mr. Richards. That man is the Devil incarnate. I've never known anyone so adroit at twisting the Bible to suit his purpose. If you know what's good for your soul, you'll confine your conversations with him to your graduate paper. I . . . I ah . . . I'm sorry. It's probably wrong for me to interpose myself, but that man is dangerous. I only want to warn you before you get involved with him."

"Thank you, Miss Veeringa. I appreciate your concern, and I'll be careful," Jason said as he offered his hand in a parting handshake.

She took his hand and held it for a moment, and after looking about furtively, drew closer. "Furthermore, I don't buy this electrical engineering bit either. I don't know who he is, but he's not who he says he is. You be careful."

Unbelievers on the left, evangelicals on the right. As Jason took his leave he felt like he had been through a *blitzkrieg*, and worse than that, he didn't know whose side he was on.

When he got outside, he noticed the vegetable garden again and remembered that he had failed to compliment Runner. Jason unlocked the Honda and slid behind the seat. In fact, he realized he had forgotten everything he came to accomplish. The small tape recorder had remained in his sport coat pocket, the yellow legal pad was blank, and he felt he had left two of his possessions back in the nursing home: the inspiration and the inerrancy of his Bible.

Well, maybe they weren't gone entirely, but they were certainly not in the same unassailable condition as they had been in a few weeks ago. It was as if he were on a bridge over a cavernous void and the bridge was in poor shape. Worse than that, he had come to realize that it wasn't because Runner had kicked out some of his bridge's supports. His supports were rotten and in the press of getting an education, he had not paid any attention to its decaying condition.

Runner had held this support structure up to the light of critical examination and Jason did not like what was revealed. Perhaps it was more honest to say that when he looked closely, he didn't see what he thought was firmly ensconced there. Or was it there, but he was temporarily blinded by Runner? Was Runner the Devil incarnate as the nurse—what was her name—Veeringa—had said? And even if he was, why did the nurse think it important to warn him? Jason and his soul were no concern of hers.

And what was the melodrama about Runner not being who he said he was? Jason dismissed the notion as the product of the nurse's over active imagination. Runner had not claimed to be anyone or anything. The engineering and religion—or was it philosophy—was information from Van Dam. The administrator would have no reason to lie or make something up about one of his residents. Still, it was an unusual combination—religion and electronics.

Jason wondered if she had been eavesdropping on their conversation. That had other implications. Who sent her and what were her motives? Was she just concerned for Jason's soul or did she have a concern for what it was that Runner was telling him about the home? Jason decided she merely had a religious concern for his soul and was merely carrying out her missionary duty.

Jason needed some answers and needed them soon before this man-devil in a wheelchair flagged any more flaws in what he believed. He would go see his pastor. He turned right onto Stadium Boulevard, away from the campus and toward the Christ's Gospel Church.

Runner had asked him about the creation story. Jason remembered his troubled thoughts of a few nights past. He had long since abandoned the Church's teaching that it was a seven-day event about six thousand years ago. He had been able to do that by intellectualizing that the first chapters of Genesis were the *who* and *why* of Creation, not the *how*. What he had difficulty with, and had failed to realize until now, was that his Church's struggle with the Creation was a struggle over the inspiration and inerrancy of the Scriptures—not a struggle between theology and science. If he had to believe every word in the Book was written by God and was without error, how could he allow for the possibility of some other explanation of Creation without giving up on either God's inspiration, or the Book's inerrancy, or both?

And how about every other social or scientific issue the Church faced? Or rather, that society faced and the Church sought to address. He thought of Galileo threatened with excommunication if he didn't abandon what the Church of the time considered to be his heretical beliefs that the earth was not stationary and was not the center of the universe and therefore the centerpiece of

God's creative process. And the Church's stand on the legitimacy of slavery prior to the nineteenth century. And the professors who were under fire even now for allowing that the world was older than six thousand years.

He remembered his father saying that the editor of the weekly national publication of their church had editorialized that John F. Kennedy's call for putting a man on the moon would never happen because the Bible didn't allow for it, and God wouldn't tolerate such a bold move into the heavens by sinful Man. And even now, his Church was divided on the issue of whether homosexuality was a sin or a genetic condition and whether women could assume roles of leadership in the Church, including preaching. These were not problems of the legitimacy of the claims or causes. They were problems of the function of the Scriptures and whether or not they were the inerrant "Words of God" in a book of facts addressing all societal and theological issues once and for all time.

When he did take the book as inerrant—the "Words of God" for all time—then when the role of women was discussed in the Scripture and the word "woman" was used by the writer, he couldn't see the writer anticipate the twentieth century university-educated person with suffrage and the right to own property. But is this woman to be treated the same by the Church as her first century counterpart who was little more than chattel in a patriarchal society—as housekeepers and brood mares. Could it be?

Jason's head gave him an answer his gut could not abide, or his head gave him an answer his tradition could not tolerate. And there was Ms. Veeringa's warning. How strange. She was afraid of Runner, thought he was the Devil incarnate.

The admonition Pastor Lipscomb had given Jason the previous week came to mind. "The Devil comes in many forms to test our faith."

If Runner was the Devil, Jason had a whole new appreciation for how the Devil works. Here was one of the most intelligent, kindly, harmless . . . . Harmless? Did he dare to think harmless? Try insidious. Insidious, that was it. He had used the Bible to disprove the Bible. Well, not disprove the Bible, exactly, but disprove truths about the Bible. Truths that had been gleaned from the Bible over centuries of study by the best minds in the world.

There was something wrong with the logic here, a flaw, and although Jason's intellectual integrity forced him to acknowledge the flaw, he refused to let his mind go down that road to see what the flaw was. Not until he had a chance to talk to Pastor Lipscomb. If he hurried, he might catch him at the church before he went to lunch.

# Chapter Six

As he turned into the church parking lot, he saw Pastor Lipscomb's mini-van parked the usual spot marked by a neatly lettered sign, "RESERVED FOR PASTOR LIPSCOMB." Good, he was in. The lack of any other cars in the lot indicated the pastor was probably alone and could talk.

He wheeled into the lot and pulled alongside the minivan. Before he could shut off the engine, Pastor Lipscomb came out of the office door and immediately saw Jason and waved. Lipscomb was a large friendly man, always with a ready smile and appetite. He reminded Jason of what Friar Tuck of the Robin Hood stories must have been like.

"Jason, what a pleasant surprise. Have you had lunch?"

"No."

"I was on my way to Dominic's. I've a hankering for some of their steamed shrimp. Care to join me?"

"Actually, I came to chat, but Dominic's is as good a place to talk as any. Hop in, I'll drive."

Lipscomb nodded his assent and walked around to get in the car. "Well, this is a wonderful coincidence," said Lipscomb. "I was supposed to have lunch with Paul Yatzie, a classmate of mine from Wheaton. He's the visiting pastor over at the Presbyterian Church until they can find a new pulpit supply. But he got called home. Apparently his wife fell and broke her leg and he had to cancel. You came in time to save me from a fate worse than a bad sermon . . . the solitary power-lunch. What brings you here? Nothing serious, I hope?"

"Nothing real serious. Just some minor things like the inspiration and inerrancy of the Scriptures. Some light lunch conversation."

"Aaaugh! That's the kind of stuff of which serious indigestion is made. I never talk about that sort of stuff over lunch. But for you, Jason, I'll make an exception."

"Good, but if this stuff gives one indigestion, I've a good reason for the knot in my stomach. The resident over at Christian Arbor, with whom I have this study project, is, well, I'm embarrassed to say, theologically kickboxing the stuffing out of me." Jason merged into the right lane of traffic on Stadium Drive, heading toward the campus.

"I consider myself a reasonably intelligent guy, with a fairly good knowledge of the Bible and the doctrines of our Church. I can handle myself with most folks who are either unchurched or from a denomination with a different viewpoint than ours. But this guy's something else. I get with him and I'm brain-dead and tongue-tied."

Lipscomb interrupted him. "What is he, this man, an unbeliever?"

"A nurse at the Home went out of her way to tell me he was the Devil incarnate. I don't know what he is. He's a scholar. Van Dam says he may be a Jew. The nurse indicated he was a humanist."

"Van Dam? Pardon me for interrupting, but who is Van Dam?"

"He's the Administrator of Christian Arbor. He says Runner may be a Jew. Apparently he doesn't believe in Christ but is very knowledgeable about the Scriptures."

"How does he cause this angst that I'm sensing?" Lipscomb asked.

"He uses the Bible against me."

"He uses the Bible against you? Come on. How does he do that?"

Jason continued as he drove. "He asks me what I believe, and he has a proof text on his fingertips to show me I'm wrong. Like last week, he had the text from First Corinthians about inspiration. I make it sound like he's playing with me, and I don't think he is. But he sure has me going. And the worst part of it, I can't think of any comebacks to what he says."

"And if I am understanding you correctly," Lipscomb said, "last week it was the inspiration of the Scriptures, and this week it was inerrancy?"

"Yes, and he did the same thing with inerrancy as he did with inspiration. He asked me what I believed and then gave me the proof texts to show me I was wrong. He doesn't play fair. He's supposed to let me show him from my Bible that he's wrong and he's showing me that I'm wrong and using my Bible to prove it to me."

Lipscomb remained lighthearted. "That *certainly* isn't fair. I'm curious, who *is* this man?"

"His name is Howard Runner and I'm told he's a retired electrical engineer with an undergraduate degree in philosophy. His body is in a wheelchair, but there's nothing handicapped about his mind or his education." They were approaching Dominic's and Jason slowed to find a parking place on the street. There were none. He circled the block. Still no luck. And then it struck him that Dominic's was only a half-block from the Business School; he could park in the staff ramp, and they could walk over to Dominic's. The privileges of rank!

He found a spot in the Bus. Ad. School ramp quickly and they got out to walk the short distance to Dominic's. As they walked Lipscomb asked, "I'm interested in how you think he used the Scriptures to disprove inerrancy."

"Well, I'll ask you the same question he asked me. How did Judas Iscariot die?"

Lipscomb did not answer immediately, thinking over the answer carefully. He didn't see the trap and walked right into it as they walked into Dominic's. "I believe he hung himself. There's my favorite table right there, is that okay?"

"It's fine by me." They made their way through the crowded room and delicious smells to the table Lipscomb had pointed out. Jason continued as they sat down. "That's what I thought. That's what Matthew thought. That's what I remember from Sunday School. That's not what Luke thought."

Lipscomb pulled up his chair and looked at Jason and raised his eyebrows like the tops of question marks.

Jason noted the raised eyebrows and continued, "I feel better that I'm in good company. Luke has it that he fell headlong and his guts gushed out."

Lipscomb thought a moment and then rejoined, "I seem to remember that being explained as the rope breaking or something. On reflection, that's a lame explanation, but it's also a pretty small technicality on which to throw out inerrancy."

Jason just looked at Lipscomb. "What did Judas do with the money?"

"The thirty pieces of silver?"

Jason nodded as their waiter approached.

Lipscomb acknowledged his presence and turned back to Jason. "Steamed shrimp?"

Jason nodded.

"We'd like two pounds of steamed shrimp, a loaf of garlic bread and a pitcher of Diet Coke with some lime wedges, please.

"Wery goot, sir!" The Slavic-looking and sounding waiter disappeared toward the source of the good smells that were filling the restaurant.

Lipscomb took the bait, as Jason had done earlier. "What he did with the money is he threw it at the feet of the priest and they bought the Potter's field with it."

"That's what I thought, and Matthew concurs. In Acts, Luke

has Peter saying that *Judas* bought the Potter's field."

"Well, again, a small technicality. In either case, Judas's money went to buy the Potter's Field."

"I agree, but if God told people what to write, why is it different? And a bigger problem emerges. If people wrote the Book, human folks, we could write it off as a different interpretation of the same event. But if God told them what to write . . . ."

Lipscomb let out a big breath and sat back in his seat as Jason continued. He was not lighthearted anymore. This discussion was obviously going to lead to indigestion, at best.

"You can see what he's doing to me. First, I say the Bible's inspired. Every word. God told people what to write. He then points me to a passage that by its own admission is human opinion. I then conclude that not every word was inspired as I understand inspiration. Today when I saw him and acknowledged that apparently not every word is inspired, do you know what he said? That he believed it was. Every word."

The waiter arrived with the pitcher of Diet Coke, the lime wedges and a large loaf of warm garlic bread. Lipscomb poured a soda for each of them. Jason squeezed a lime wedged into his drink, took a draft of the soda and continued. "He said that the inspiration was not a spiritual visitation wherein God appeared and told the writer what to write or had some magical influence, but rather, people who encountered God, or, I suppose, witnessed His hand in history, were inspired to write what they saw. No supernatural intervention, just folks moved by what they experienced to communicate that experience in writing.

"Then he went on to drop the bombshell of the day. He said that this explanation of inspiration accounts for all the *discrepancies* in the Bible. If the Bible were strictly a human effort, we'd expect discrepancies and bias. But if there were supernatural intervention, why would there be discrepancies or bias, even on, as you say, 'technicalities'?"

"Essentially, what Runner inferred is that I could have a perfect God who was not proactive in the creation of an imperfect book, or I was stuck with an imperfect God because the book was imperfect."

Pastor Lipscomb had been sipping his soda when Jason stopped. He set his glass down slowly and reached for a piece of the garlic bread. "This technicality aside for the moment, is that the only error he perceived in the Bible?"

"No, there was the implication there were more examples than I cared to hear about. The one he did mention was more unsettling than who bought the Potter's field. This one goes to the question of bias of both the writers and the translators. Where is the prophecy found in the Old Testament that Matthew refers to in his first chapter foretelling the birth of Christ?"

Lipscomb felt himself being painted into a theological corner with rapid brush strokes. A corner he knew existed but had not allowed himself to explore because he had been afraid what he would find. In fact, it was more like a closet than a corner, a closet like Fibber McGee's closet. Better to leave the door closed because you don't know what kind of a mess you'll have if you open the door and let the contents spill out. And at that moment, the arrival of a huge bowl of spicy steamed shrimp saved him from having to open the closet door, at least temporarily.

"Boy, don't these look good. I've had my teeth set for these little babies since Monday. Hold up your plate and I'll dish out some of these little morsels."

Lipscomb dished out a portion of shrimp to Jason and another portion for himself and broke off another piece of garlic bread. "Tell me, how does an unbeliever like your Mr. Runner come to reside in the Christian Arbor Home? I was under the impression that they had admission requirements there."

Jason had begun shelling the spicy boiled shrimp on his plate and talked as he shelled and ate. "His daughter arranged for the placement. She's is a member of the local Dutch Reformed Church congregation, one of the supporting churches for the Home. From what the administrator told me, they see him as a harmless old man and have given up trying to convert him."

"Sounds like a project worthy of someone with your intellect and understanding of the faith, Jason."

"Frankly, I think I'm doing well to hang on to what I think I believe. I don't think the goal here is to save Howard Runner, I think the goal is to save what's left of Jason Richards."

"I'm not worried about Jason Richards. God's Word says that *'nothing can separate us from the love of God which is in Christ Jesus our Lord.'* And to paraphrase the passage, not angels or principalities or the Howard Runners or the world."

"I'm convinced he doesn't have a nefarious goal for my soul. He doesn't bring up religion unless I do, and then only challenges what I say. He said an interesting thing the first time I met him. He said, 'A belief structure based on other people's misconceptions may not serve you well.' I've had to admit that my belief structure is dependent on what other people have fed me. I've ingested their structure and assumed the veracity of their proofs. In that context, it's more than a little unsettling to have at least some of those proofs called into question in a way I'm unable to refute. Would you like some more shrimp?"

Jason divvied up the balance of the shrimp and broke off half the remaining garlic bread. He continued to eat as he talked. "These brief discussions with Runner have caused me to think I've discarded some of the teachings of the Church, to my amazement, without a second thought."

"What teachings have you discarded," Lipscomb interrupted.

"I was taught in the Christian day school and in Sunday School that God created the world in seven days. I haven't believed that since . . . since I don't know when. Not that I don't believe he couldn't have, I just don't believe the first chapters were intended to tell us the methodology of creation—just identify the Creator."

"And what caused you to accept a different view of the creation process?"

"The Bible."

"The Bible?"

Suddenly, Jason realized he was about to use the same methodology to convince Lipscomb as Runner had used on him. When you want to make a point with a Bible believing Christian, drag out a proof text. "In the creation story, the sun was created on the fourth day and so there couldn't be 'morning and evening' on the first day or the second or the third. I concluded that twenty-four hour days, the time periods defined by the revolution of the earth in relation to the sun, weren't possible until at least the fourth day when the sun was supposed to be created. In addition, we know that the earth is held in place by the gravitational pull of the sun. Which left me with the question, how was it held in place in the days before the creation of the sun?"

"And you don't think it's within the power of God to do that without the operation of the natural laws?"

"Sure, I also believe it's within God's power to *age* the universe."

"Age the universe? What do you mean?"

"There's overwhelming evidence that the world is millions of years old. Science can tell by the age marks, geological stratification evidence, Carbon dating, the speed of light, the movement of stars—all kinds of evidence. God could have created it and aged it in one or two days. But should Christians throw out the entire body of scientific knowledge regarding the age of the universe and the laws of physics to satisfy the Church's need to have the first chapter of Genesis be a science book?

"Anyway, in spite of my position on the creation, it didn't occur to me to make the logical extension that the chapter wasn't 'every word inspired and inerrant.' In other words, Runner focused my attention on the fact that while I mouthed words 'every word is inspired and inerrant,' I instinctively knew it wasn't, through my understanding of the creation story and other old testament stories."

"Stories such as?"

"The flood covering the whole earth when we know the amount of matter in the earth is constant. Where did the extra water come from to cover the earth and where did it go when the earth dried up? To cover the whole earth, it would have had to rain at the rate of 30 inches of rainfall per hour for forty days or 960 hours over the whole earth. That's more water than is in the whole solar system. But listen, I'd like to get back to my discussion with Runner today and the passage that foretells the birth of Christ . . ."

"I'd like to comment on the Creation issue, if I may." Lipscomb's interruption was said stiffly. He paused and wiped his mouth so forcefully with his napkin that he left paper traces on the stubble of his beard. "There are many in the mainstream Church who accept that the creation process may have lasted over a very long period of time. I personally like a literal translation of the seven-day creation. But intellectually, I'm forced to admit a literal translation requires one to suspend the natural laws and accept that God's creation process may be a mystery that we'll never unlock. I'm willing to accept the Church's explanation of God's creative action by faith and still allow you to buy in to a different creation explanation, as long as we can agree on the Creator. And I think we can, can't we?"

The shrimp and the garlic toast was gone, and the ice was melting in the Cokes they were sipping.

Jason nodded and said, "You're more generous than the larger Church. Runner pointed out that he had just read about a conservative branch of Lutherans who had expelled several professors for holding to a longer-than-seven-day creation process. The Church shoots itself in the foot in public. It's supporting evidence that God is supporting the Church."

"How do you conclude that?"

"We humans have done so much to sabotage it, it would have self-destructed long ago without Divine intervention." Jason could read some negative body language coming from the good Pastor Lipscomb. Better get off that topic, he thought. "I'd like to go back to the passage in Isaiah that Matthew quotes as prophesying the birth of Christ."

Lipscomb drank the last of his coke. "And what does your Mr. Runner say about that?" The body was stiff and the tone was cool, and Lipscomb's eyes were boring in on Jason.

This was going to go nowhere, Jason thought. He didn't want to argue, much less concede that Runner may be right. In fact, right at that moment he was hoping that Lipscomb would rescue him from his emotional and intellectual dilemma with a rational answer, perhaps a proof text or the ruminations of some saint who had confronted this devil and had conquered it. He continued. "As I read the passage in Isaiah, Isaiah prophesied that a child, who already had been conceived, would be born and before this child learned to distinguish good from evil, the kings that were hassling Ahaz would come to naught. Read in context, this passage is a story about Isaiah, Ahaz, and a sign that God gave a belligerent king who didn't want one."

"And you don't think Matthew had his scripture straight?"

"The point is, I don't know what to think. I was hoping you could help me."

Lipscomb seemed to soften somewhat. He folded his arms and put his elbows on the table, lowered his voice, and leaned in toward Jason. "I don't know that I can. If Matthew thought the birth of Christ was Isaiah's prophecy being fulfilled, I'm not sure I'm anyone to contradict him two thousand years later. The best minds of the Church have accepted Matthew's word for centuries. That's the best I can do for you. Let me add, it's been enough for a lot of Christians over the centuries." Lipscomb smiled and straightened up.

Jason got the implication. If it was good enough for them, it should be good enough for him. The words of the old gospel hymn came to mind:

> *"Give me that old time religion,*
>
> *Some of that old time religion,*
>
> *Give me that old time religion,*
>
> *It's good enough for me.*
>
> *It was good enough for my brother,*
>
> *It was good enough for my sister,*
>
> *It was good enough for my mother*
>
> *it's good enough for me."*

Perhaps it should have been good enough for Jason. But it wasn't. He didn't mind accepting something on faith if the proofs were unavailable, but he had difficulty *rejecting* evidence in the name of faith. His head told him to drop this discussion with Lipscomb, his stomach forced him to press on.

"Forgive what may seem like impertinence, but you live and work within the confines of the Church and your sphere of influence is with believers. I live and work in the world of academia, with people from all and no faith persuasions. If I can't address simple matters like the age of the earth with my peers with intellectual integrity, how can I expect them to give any weight to anything I might say on important current issues like abortion, or women's roles in the Church or, the place of gays?"

"I'm not sure it's possible to ask unbelievers to accept for themselves what we take on faith."

"But if the Church insists on asking us to accept on faith things that are known to be disproved by science, can it wonder at our skepticism at its pronouncements on matters that should be taken on faith?"

"Meaning?"

"The Church has been wrong on a number of important issues in the past . . ."

"Such as?" Lipscomb interrupted.

"For a long time the Church was *the* repository of knowledge for Western Civilization. But you have to admit, it stubbornly clung to erroneous teachings in areas that were none of its business. It was wrong about Copernicus. It was wrong about Galileo. It had to change its position on slavery. Our denomination will reverse itself on its seven-day creation stand, as much of the mainstream Church already has. Why should the modern world listen to the Church about current social issues, given the Church's history of holding on to misinterpretations and misapplications of the Scriptures long after they've been disproved? Why should my colleagues listen to a word I say from my Christian perspective?"

Jason was surprised how much he sounded like Runner. "Runner rightly points out I am trying to address the problems of the twenty-first century with a sixteenth-century perspective. The Church is still fighting the Enlightenment while the world has gone on to the Modern and now, some say, the Post-Modern Period. The Church is two or three paradigms behind the world and stubbornly waits for the world to catch up. How can it speak to a world with which it does not communicate? More to the point, how will the Church communicate with me, here and now, in my crisis of faith?"

Jason paused and took a deep breath. He caught himself bending over the table and stabbing his finger in the air. He sat back in his chair. He almost hoped that Lipscomb would not understand that "the Church here and now" had meant Lipscomb, in this restaurant, at this time. Jason didn't mean to put him on the spot. But then, Jason was on the spot emotionally, more so than he wanted to be and more than he wished he had admitted.

Lipscomb shifted in his seat and turned the base of his empty Coke glass with his thumb and forefinger, but did not look up or seize the moment.

Jason continued. "Case in point. Several weeks ago, *Time* and *Newsweek* and *U.S. News & World Report* ran cover stories on current studies of Jesus that have been undertaken. They reported that more books have been written on Jesus Christ in the past twenty years than in the previous two thousand. They report that these studies are serious and being undertaken by scholars within the Church, and that they challenge some of the Church's understanding of Christ. A classmate asked me what I thought of these reports and what my Church thought about them. Fact is, our national weekly church paper hasn't reported or commented on these studies, and, no offense, but neither has my pastor. Are these studies major news to everyone but the Church? Isn't this *our* Jesus Christ?"

Lipscomb put his forearms on the table and leaned in toward Jason like someone who was about to tell a secret. "For the most part, Jason, these studies are by academics *for* academics. I'm not sure they're intended for, or should be for, popular consumption. Many of these books are speculative. No sooner is one position staked out than some other, equally respected scholar stakes out another that is entirely different. And frankly, my understanding is that many of these theoretical positions call some of the core teachings that we believe about Jesus as the Son of God into question on the basis of conjecture.

"And when I visit the sick and seek to provide comfort to the dying, they don't ask me about the articles in *Time*, nor do they want to hear some speculative theory about Jesus, the Wandering Jew.

They don't care if we've moved out of the Enlightenment or not. They want to be reminded of what is their 'only comfort in life and death.'" Lipscomb paused, tilted his head to one side, and raised his eyebrows as if to ask if Jason understood and at the same time indicate it was all he had to say on the subject.

Lipscomb then inserted his fingers into his water glass to moisten them and laboriously wiped his hands with what was left of his napkin. He continued as he wiped. "Listen, I have to get back to the preparation of Sunday's sermon and you're my wheels. Let's get together again and talk about this. I'd like you to keep me posted on your progress with your Mr. Runner." And with that, he put the shredded napkin down, pushed back his chair and stood up and picked up the check.

"I'll get the table," Jason said as he reached into his pocket for tip money.

The ride back was cordial. They talked about Michigan's football team's chances to win the Big Ten this year and about the next day's game with Michigan State. But the discussion at Dominic's had put a rift in whatever bond there had been between them, and they both knew it. Neither one of them liked it. Neither knew what to do about it.

# Chapter Seven

Saturday dawned bright and clear and with it the promise of yet one more sellout at "The Big House," the University of Michigan Football Stadium. A hundred-and-ten thousand of the faithful would soon be pouring into Ann Arbor to tailgate and watch the perennial powerhouse Wolverines play inter-state rival Michigan State for bragging rights for its respective alumni for another year.

Jason had been raised in a decidedly Michigan State household. Neither his father nor mother went to college, but his father was an avid Michigan State fan. Jason's decision to attend Michigan was only accepted by the family on the basis that Michigan State did not have a Hospital and Institutional Administration program. He was still considered somewhat of a traitor by the rest of the Richards family.

Michigan football games had been sellouts for years and extra tickets were tough to come by, unless one was willing to pay scalpers' rates at the gate. But rank had privileges and Jason was able to get two extra tickets on the forty-yard line from an accounting professor who had to attend a conference in San Francisco.

Jason had invited his older brother, Willard, and Willard's five-year-old son up for the game. Willard was a blithering State fan in the best Richards' family tradition.

Jason and Willard had a good relationship. It had not been strained by the fact that they had seen very little of each other since Will left home to attend State and get his degree in Economics.

Will had married his high school sweetheart, Karen VanderMey, and had the one son. She was a registered nurse; he was a senior loan officer in Fifth/Third Bank in Grand Rapids and worked out of the branch banks in an oversight capacity. It was a responsible position, and Will was doing well. The little boy was the first grandchild on both sides and was named after both grandfathers, each of whom fought to see who could spoil the boy first and best. Will would have acknowledged the race was a dead heat.

Jason left the apartment early to buy goodies for a picnic lunch. He started with the delicious sticky buns from the bakery that Mrs. Lundsaford ran out of the back of her house. He bought three for the picnic basket and one for immediate consumption. He then went to Crazy Cal's Take Out BBQ and splurged on the long-bone beef ribs for which Cal was more famous than he was crazy. From there, Jason went to the Bun Basket for some hard rolls and the Hill Street Deli for some pasta salad and their homemade potato chips.

Jason and Willard could talk about anything and did. Sports, family, women, school, careers, politics, theology, and then, most likely, sports again. On most issues, mainly politics and religion, they were soul brothers as well as blood brothers. On other issues, they had honest differences of opinion, although Willard felt that Jason's new-found allegiance to the University of Michigan wasn't honest. In all issues, they respected the other's intelligence and wisdom. Jason intended to bring up his discussions with Howard Runner.

Willard and Deiter Richards arrived at the apartment at ten o'clock in the morning. Jason was struck once again how much of Willard's image had been transferred to Deiter. They were both dressed in variations of State's green and white colors.

Jason swooped the six-year-old up in his arms. "Deiter Man! How's my boy? Look at you all dressed up in green and white! Hope your dad didn't have to pay for any of those trash clothes. Does your mom know you're dressed like that? Huh?"

Deiter giggled and puffed up. "Yup! And Grandpa knowths, too! He liketh it. I got thith at the mall!" he said proudly through his toothless grin.

"Was the store all out of maize and blue stuff, or were they giving away the green and white things? How come you aren't wearing anything maize and blue? Didn't your daddy tell you we were going to Michigan Stadium?"

"He thaid I had to wear thith or Michigan Thate might lose."

Jason let out a fake sigh. "Looks like I have no choice but to report this to Child Protective Services. Child abuse in its most insidious form, I say. It's too late for today's game, but next time you're at the mall, Deiter Man, you tell your mom to get you some real clothes with maize and blue on it. Okay?"

After some more lighthearted banter, they left for the Farmer's Market. They strolled through the stalls for an hour, sampling the sights and smells. Willard picked up a fresh apple pie from an Amish woman's stall to take back to Grand Rapids for Sunday dinner dessert.

They then drove to Island Drive Park for lunch. Island Drive Park was an island in the Huron River that went unused in the daytime during the week but was a favorite place of young lovers after dark. On Saturdays in the fall, it came to life with football-going picnickers who came to avoid the stadium crowds, to feed the Mallards and Black ducks who would take food out of one's hand in flagrant defiance of signs that prohibited feeding the ducks, and to enjoy the beauty of the setting.

They found an empty table and began spreading out the lunch. The ducks approached noisily but cautiously. Deiter was fascinated by them. Willard cautioned him about watching where he stepped. "If you're not careful, you'll have duck poop all over your shoes and then they might not let us in the stadium."

Jason laughed, "Don't worry Deiter Man. They'll let you in the stadium with duck poop on your shoes. I suspect there will be more than a few dressed in green and white that'll have the same condition. You'll just be forced to sit with the Michigan State fans." It was a barb at Michigan State's beginnings as an agricultural college and Willard seemed to appreciate the humor.

As they sat down to eat, Jason spoke. "I have to talk to you about Howard Runner."

"Who's Howard Runner?"

Jason told Will about the I.R.R. requirement and his initial trips to the Christian Arbor Home as they tackled the beef ribs. Willard listened and ate and interrupted from time to time to clarify a point here and there, but for the most part, he let Jason get the story out, all the way through the meeting with Jason's pastor at Dominic's the day before.

When Jason finished, Willard and Deiter were done eating. Deiter had left the table and was parceling out the balance of his potato chips to about two dozen ducks, which had encircled him at arm's length and were clucking softly as if to beg for a morsel to be thrown in their direction. Willard had his elbows on the table, holding a napkin to his mouth with both hands. He removed the napkin to speak. "So where are you on this now, little brother?"

"Not as far as I'm going to be, but farther than I was before I met Runner?"

"Aren't you letting this stranger have a disproportionate effect on you? I mean, come on. We got the inspiration of the Scriptures and inerrancy before we got cold milk. You take that away and what have you got left? Nothing."

Jason handed what was left of his roll to Deiter, who continued to fuel the feeding frenzy. He looked away from the ducks back to Willard. "I'm not taking anything away. I'm asking if it's there in the first place. Does the Scripture say that God told the writers what to write, or do theologians tell us that?"

"Look, *I'm* no theologian, but I seem to recall a passage from the New Testament or somewhere that talks about all scripture being given by God . . ."

As Willard spoke, Jason, anticipating him, fished around in the bottom of the picnic basket and drew out a King James version of the Bible. He handed it to Will and said, "Second Timothy, three, sixteen."

"Are you serious? We're here for a picnic lunch before a football game and you got Bibles in your picnic basket and want to talk theology? What's got into you?" Willard paused and then saw by the look in Jason's eyes that this was not something he should be taking lightly. "You're really into this aren't you?" Will said lamely as he fumbled to find the Second Book of Timothy and then the sixteenth verse of the third chapter.

As he did so, Jason pulled a New English Bible from the basket and turned to the same passage, and nodded to Will to read from the KJV.

"*All scripture is given by inspiration of God, and is profitable for doctrine, for reproof, for correction, for instruction in righteousness.*" Will looked up and appeared puzzled as to why Jason would have any question. It appeared pretty clear to him.

Jason answered the look. "What Scripture was he talking about? The New Testament, as we know it, wasn't written yet. But further, listen to what this version says," and he read the same verses. "*Every inspired scripture has its use for teaching the truth and refuting error, or for reformation of manners and discipline in right living . . .*"

Will still had the same quizzical look. "So . . .?"

"So . . . the King James says that '*all scripture is given by inspiration of God . . .*' It doesn't say God told each writer the words to put down. The New English Bible says something quite different: '*Every inspired scripture has its use . . .*'"

"Well, that's not the only place it says the Bible is inspired." The Bible he had was a chain reference bible and Will looked in the index under "INSPIRATION – DIVINE." "Here, look up Second Peter 1:21."

They each looked up the passage in their respective versions.

Will found it first and began reading, "*For the prophesy came not in old time by the will of man; but holy men of God spake as they were moved by the Holy Spirit.*" He looked up smugly.

Jason did not read from his Bible. "Does that passage say that holy men of God were told what to say, or that they were moved to say what they said? And does that verse refer to prophets and prophecy or to the poetic and historical writings that make up the Scriptures as well?"

Will's look went away. "What does that version say?"

Jason read, "*No one can interpret any prophecy of Scripture by himself. For it was not through any human whim that men prophesied of old; men they were, but, impelled by the Holy Spirit, they spoke the words of God.*" Jason looked at Will. After a minute, he spoke. "It's a long step from saying that when the prophets prophesied they spoke the words of God, to saying the Scriptures are the words of God. In fact, the Timothy passage seems to separate inspired Scripture from another kind, and verse twenty of Peter separates prophecy from the rest of Scripture and puts prophecy in a separate category from the words of God. Look up First Corinthians Seven and start at verse twelve and look for the place where Paul says God told him what to write."

Will sat still for a second. He didn't like where this was going. There was a strange look in Jason's eyes. Will couldn't tell if Jason was troubled, scared, or both. He loved Jason like a brother should, so he would humor him for one more proof text.

He found and read the Corinthians passage, thought for a moment, and then said, "So you think because Paul says these are his words and not the Lord's words, and he has no word from the Lord, that God didn't tell him what to write, and therefore, these are not God's words?"

"That's what it says to you too, doesn't it?"

Will's jaw seemed to set. He checked on Deiter who had

wandered over to a swing set and was attempting to swing himself over the bars. He broke off a piece of his roll and threw it into the river. Several ducks rushed pell-mell into the river after the bread. Will concluded Jason needed a good dose of attitude adjustment.

Will turned away from the river and faced Jason again. He tried to sound more confident about what he said than he felt. "I don't necessarily see it that way. Besides, I don't think the likes of you and I ought to be questioning these matters. What do we know? I'm finding out that I don't know a tinker's dam about banking, and that's the field I'm supposed to be educated and trained in. With our limited training and pea-brains, we have no business trying to challenge these ageless truths about inspiration or inerrancy.

"I remember Doug DeBoer getting his butt kicked in High School Sunday School Class once because he challenged the preacher's interpretation of the Scriptures. Reverend LaGrande had just come to our church. He said in a sermon that the Roman Catholic confessional booth was not biblical because the forgiveness of sins was a power God reserved exclusively for Himself. He challenged anyone to show him where God delegated that power to anyone else. In the Sunday School class after church, Doug asked him about the Great Commission when Jesus told the disciples *'whosoever sins ye remit, they will be remitted in Heaven.'*

"LaGrande went ballistic. Told Doug he was going to Hell because he was changing the Bible. Threw some passage in Revelations at him about the plagues and Hell."

Jason let the comment set for a moment, then he parried. "Are you like LaGrande? You don't want anyone confusing you with the facts because your opinion is already formed?"

"You are the one confusing the facts. The Bible is facts, and facts don't change."

"The Bible isn't facts, it's someone's version of the facts. You know, as in the victor gets to write the history of the war."

Will countered, "Well, regardless, I like my belief structure. Systematic theology has a certainty and completeness and stability that's comforting. It has answered all the questions in a logical and thoughtful way."

"Questions from when?"

"What do you mean, questions from when?"

"How do you know it answered all the questions when it didn't know all the questions?"

"What are you saying? What questions?"

"How did the sixteenth-century theologians who wrote the systematic theology know what the questions of the twentieth century would be?"

"They are the same questions." A hint of exasperation crept into Willard's voice. "Facts don't change, evil doesn't change, sin doesn't change, God doesn't change."

"Evil does change. Slavery was not an evil in the sixteenth century. It is now. Treating debtors as chattel wasn't evil in the sixteenth century, it is now. Abortion wasn't known in the sixteenth century. Evil and sin have changed. And how about euthanasia, and the bomb, and righteous war, and the right of kings, and the societal role of women, and genetic engineering, and pollution. There are new questions the sixteenth-century theologians and the Bible, for that matter, didn't contemplate."

"And the implication is . . . ?"

"We think we know all the answers. Some of our answers are to questions that no longer exist. And we don't acknowledge or address many of the important new questions."

"I don't think you can honestly say that we don't acknowledge new questions."

"What did your pastor, Wayne what's-his-name, do with the

recent covers of *Time* and *Newsweek* on the new studies of Christ?"

"Wayne Wright. He hasn't mentioned it."

"That's how I can honestly say we don't acknowledge the new questions. This is *our* Jesus Christ, the author and finisher of *our* faith—to borrow one of LaGrande's well-worn phrases—that these studies are about!"

Jason paused to see if there was a reaction. There was none, and he continued. "What have you done with these articles? Did you read them?"

Will looked away again. Maybe if Jason's attitude couldn't be adjusted, perhaps it could be fine-tuned. He broke off another piece of his roll and threw it to the ducks. Then he slowly turned back. "Jason, I think we need the Book to be God's Words as we've always understood it. I believe the Book is inerrant. I take it on faith. I believe it has stood the test of time because it *is* God's Words. You start messing with that, and the whole thing may come down around your ears. The old Jesus suits me and my family perfectly well, thank you very much. We don't need someone else's idea for a new one. You can have your Jesus for your needs, my Jesus is mine for my needs. I'm going to stick to banking and leave the far-out speculation to these liberals who call themselves theologians. And my advice to you is to think less and believe more. You need to accept it with your heart, not your head."

"You sound like a television evangelist I heard the other night," Jason said. "His message clearly implied we shouldn't study the Bible too deeply, just superficially. On reflection, I got the impression he was afraid of what the current scholarship was espousing. But I'm asking myself, and I ask you, should we be afraid of the truth? "Shouldn't we be willing—better yet—shouldn't we insist that the theology be held up for scrutiny by the best minds of any generation? Does your bank do business by the most up-to-date methods? Do you insist on the most advanced medical care for Deiter? In every area of our lives, we seek the most advanced thought, whether it be in medicine or banking or football gear. But when it comes to our theology, we're suspicious of any thoughts or ideas less than two hundred years old."

Will was silent for a moment, as if he were allowing for the possibility that Jason had a point. He was looking out over the river and threw the last piece of his roll to the waiting ducks. His little brother was way too serious about this. Young Jason had a clear need to lighten up. When Willard turned back, he had an impish grin starting to form around the corners of his mouth, and he handed the Bible he was holding back to Jason. "I think you should put my Bible away, but you should keep yours handy because it's clear to me you're going to need it." And with that, Will held Jason's gaze to see if Jason understood the last comment.

Jason saw the grin and a twinkle in Will's eyes but didn't understand where Will was going with this.

"Little brother, you're going to need all the spiritual consolation you can get after we watch the Spartans whup your Wolverines' butts all over the AstroTurf in Michigan Stadium. Come on, let's get to the game. I want to watch the pre-game and see our band beat up on your band while our football team warms up to beat yours!"

They packed up the lunch and the Bibles, collected Deiter from the swings, and headed for the Michigan Stadium.

# Chapter Eight

Bragging rights for the season went to Michigan State after they eked out a victory by six points. The sights of the game and the sounds of the bands quickly faded into the hectic pace of the ensuing week. Jason's schedule was crammed well into the night. During a late night session on Thursday evening, he organized what he thought were the elements of good care in a long-term care facility into a plan for an in-depth evaluation of the Christian Arbor Home.

He would start with the food, its variety, nutritional value, presentation, and weigh that against any special dietary requirements known to exist for the elderly or any special needs of the residents. He then would review the physical plant and mechanical systems that provided for the comfort of the residents, then evaluate the programs provided. His schedule provided for twelve weekly visits of one- to two-hours each. That would bring him to the middle of December.

He figured he would have the three weeks of Christmas vacation to write the paper, a week for review and still allow for one or two weeks for revisions and perhaps a peer review before the paper was due on the fifteenth of January.

He read the report that Visser wrote and found it to be quite critical. Like other I.R.R. reports Jason had reviewed, Visser's report was organized into seven main sections. There was a section each on care, amenities, nutrition, plant, program, staff, and management. Visser reported deficiencies in each, although unlike most of the other reports Jason had read, Visser had indicated a level of what he had called "Christian concern for the person" at the Home that had not been mentioned in any of the reports he had read whose authors had interacted with "for profit" or secular homes. Visser had warned the management of the Home, however, about substituting platitudes for up-to-date care methods. He wrote, "Statements purporting to model care and concern demonstrated by the ministry of Jesus Christ when in fact the methods used were out-of-date were self-serving at best." Jason thought there was an unnecessary harshness in the tone of the report.

Jason arranged for his meeting on Friday to begin at noon and to include reservations for eating lunch with Howard Runner. He thought the best way to critique the food was to eat it. He wondered if it would be the same as the previous Friday's fare, remembering the pungent aroma of roast beef gravy.

On Friday morning, he equipped himself with his portable tape recorder, several pencils, and a black, three-ring binder in which he had begun to organize his notes and outline. It was a beautiful fall morning, and the drive to the Home was uneventful. Jason realized that he hadn't had a theological thought since his discussion with Willard the Saturday before. It was nice to be back in control, and he was determined to prevent Howard Runner from side-tracking him again.

Runner could be seen tending his garden as Jason drove up. He parked and walked over to where Runner seemed to be pruning the hedge that provided the backdrop for his plants. As he approached, he could see that what appeared to be a hedge from the street was actually a section where the hedge had been removed and in its place was a verdant grape vine. Runner was clipping large bunches of purple grapes from the vine and carefully placing them into a container that hung from the side of his wheelchair.

"Jason! Nice to see you. Do you like grapes? These are Van Burens, a variety similar to Concords, but they ripen about four weeks earlier, and they're larger and sweeter. Here," he held out the bunch he had just clipped, "try them."

Jason took the large bunch, removed one of the large purple grapes and squeezed the skin, forcing the contents into his mouth. "Mmmmm . . . they are good. Van Burens you call them?"

"Yes, there're a recent development of the New York Agricultural Extension Service located in the Canadice region of New York State. It's a large grape growing area. Table grapes mostly, although I understand some wines worth mentioning are being produced there. My produce is my small contribution to variety in our otherwise monotonous menu here. If you wouldn't mind carrying this container, I think it's time to eat."

The container contained a number of bunches of grapes. Jason put the bunch from which he had been sampling into the container and unclipped the container from the arm of the chair. Together they went into the Home, Runner propelling himself by spinning the large wheels of his chair. As they went, Runner spoke.

"I was a little surprised to hear you'd be eating here. I can't imagine anyone eating with us if they didn't have to. In fact, I thought about calling you to see if you'd be willing to bring something, and we could kill two birds with one stone, so to speak. Something good to eat and peace and quiet while we ate it. Now we'll have neither."

"I thought the best way to critique the food was to eat it. Will I be sorry?"

"That remains to be seen. One thing's certain, both you and I will be critiqued while you critique the food. These old crones, and the staff right in there with the old birds, can't seem to rest until they've secured my soul in their version of heaven. They'll be beside themselves with joy at the prospect of saving two souls. You, of course, will be assumed to be condemned to perdition by your association with me. Follow your nose. It's rainbow beef and gravy, so this must be Friday."

They entered the dining hall through double doors and Runner turned to and directed him to a table to the right. Almost immediately, Runner stopped his chair. There were seven people seated at the table toward which Runner was headed, a table with eight places. Runner got the eye of a woman of about thirty-five who wore what could have passed as a uniform. She had a clipboard in her hand and came over toward them. "How are you today, Mr. Runner? Is there a problem?"

"First, please pass out the grapes this young gentleman is carrying. Some of our residents may like some fresh fruit. Then it seems we have a problem. I've made a reservation for my guest to—what I have come to euphemistically call—dine with us. It appears the reservation has not been honored. The usual residents are at Table Two in their usual places. Have other accommodations been made?" His tone was polite with just a tinge of sarcasm. The rest of the diners sensed some trouble, and the room grew quiet except for a few whispers. All eyes were on the three of them.

"Well, let's see here, Mr. Runner. My list doesn't include a reservation for an additional guest, but I'm sure we can accommodate him. How would it be if I put the both of you at Table Eleven? It is empty and it will just take a minute to get it set up." And she turned toward some large doors to what appeared to lead to the kitchen.

"I'm afraid that won't be acceptable. The purpose of Mr. Richards' visit is to evaluate the Home for a research paper. It's important for him to get the pulse of our fine Home here and to do that, he should dine among us, immerse himself in the conversation and the cuisine. Don't you agree? I've made the proper arrangements. I insist we have a place at Table Two."

"Well, okay, we'll see what we can do." The woman gave a sigh and had the look of one whose life revolved around trying keep molehills, molehills, and one who was sure this molehill would become a mountain.

"Ladies, it seems Mr. Runner has a guest, so we're going to have to ask one of you to move. Let's see . . . there is an empty place at Table Six. Who would like to move to Table Six for this meal?"

No one at Table Two looked up. One lady moved her chair forward and hunched over her place setting. Another quickly reached for her water glass and took a drink as if to establish territory.

Another folded her arms across her chest.

"They ain't moving," Jason thought and was conscious that his presence had created this stir.

"Come now, ladies, we all have guests from time to time. Let's accommodate Mr. Runner. Who's going to move to Table Six?"

A lady in what looked like an expensive blouse and skirt and looked up said, "I'm not moving. Mrs. Douma's eating habits are not very appetizing. I don't pay four thousand, four hundred dollars a month to experience that. Let *him* sit a Table Six." Several heads nodded in agreement.

The lady with the clipboard set her jaw and moved over to the other table with a vacancy. She approached a lady in a wheelchair and said, "Mrs. Overbeek, today you'll be privileged to dine at Table Two," whereupon she unlocked the wheels of the chair and pulled the lady away from the table and began negotiating between the tables toward Table Two. There was no reaction from the lady in the wheelchair, only a vacant stare.

The lady with the clipboard caught Jason's eye and she jerked her head toward Table Six and said, "As soon as Mr. Runner and his guest are seated, we'll have opening devotions."

Jason took the handles of Runner's wheelchair and began maneuvering toward the vacant spots at Table Six. They weren't together, but there was no need to create an additional fuss. He pushed Runner into the spot where the other wheelchair had been and took the empty seat two places to the right.

Several of the ladies had snorted as Runner had been pushed to the table, and Jason thought he heard someone say "heathen" under their breath. But he wasn't sure what he heard or who said it. From their faces, it could have been any one of them.

An elderly man wearing a white shirt and tie had approached a microphone with a Bible in his hand. He read a Psalm and then asked if there were any prayer requests. A man at a nearby table launched into what amounted to a sermon about the need for the Holy Spirit to spread its fire in their midst and requested a prayer for the Holy Spirit. A lady at their table asked for a prayer for her arthritis.

Jason was amazed to hear Howard Runner address the man at the mike. "Chaplain, I believe it would be appropriate for you to pray for the insight to see ourselves as others see us."

Someone at Table Two harrumphed. One of the ladies Jason suspected of having uttered the word "heathen" sniffed and rolled her eyes. Runner's dart had found its mark.

After a short prayer which included a petition for the Holy Spirit, a request for healing of all the vicissitudes of growing old, and a request for self-examination, the meal was served. It came out on tall carts that carried two table's worth of standard cafeteria trays. Servers bustled about placing trays in front of the residents. The fare was thinly sliced beef, mashed potatoes and gravy, green beans, and dark chocolate cake with white frosting, and a roll tightly wrapped in cellophane.

The lady sitting between Runner and Jason gave her tray a quick look over and said to the server, "This is not my tray. I'm a diabetic, you know. I'm not supposed to have any sugar." She said it with pride as if being a diabetic made her very special.

The server looked at the lady as if to double-check her identity and then looked over the lady's tray. "All your exchanges are there, Mrs. Boersma," she said in a sweet syrupy voice that one might have used to address a kindergarten student. "You just don't have any butter for your roll, and that's as it should be. Enjoy your lunch."

"This isn't my tray," Mrs. Boersma muttered under her breath.

"*Bon appetite, mon ami,*" Runner said and Jason began to eat.

The meat and the beans were overcooked. The mashed

potatoes were . . . well . . . they had set up. The gravy was tasty, as one might expect from overcooked meat. The roll was very good. Jason didn't have an appetite for the cake. He had wondered what Runner had referred to when he described the beef as "Rainbow Beef." Now he could see. The meat had cooled enough so that there was a refraction of light on its surface, and you could see a rainbow on the surface of the meat.

There was little talk at the table. Some folks ate with apparent relish, some picked at the food, some complained about this or that. Some needed help to cut their meat or reach their cake and one of the servers went from table to table seeing to the special needs of the diners.

Mrs. Douma's physical limitations would not allow her to make the spoon go on a direct line from the plate to her mouth, and the result was similar to what might happen if a two-year-old tried to feed herself. Mrs. Boersma, the diabetic, ate her cake first, then licked her platter clean, literally, and there were others who showed varying degrees of dementia. Runner's grapes had been placed in a bowl at each table and Jason enjoyed a bunch of them.

After the meal, the Administrator, Dirk Van Dam, came by to see if all Jason's questions were being answered. "Actually I'd like to see the kitchen and visit with the dietary staff, if they're available." As they walked toward the kitchen, Jason clicked his pocket tape recorder to the "Record" position.

The cook and the dietitian were the same. A short, rotund lady with a jolly laugh who knew "what was good for these people." The weekly menu that was posted on a bulletin board was dog-eared. "Mrs. Rudder has been with us for seventeen years and has never missed a day. She's one of our most valuable employees," said Van Dam and the cook beamed.

"How do you accommodate special dietary needs, like a diabetic, for example?" Jason asked.

"We have all the residents classified as Rs, Cs or Ds. Regular diets, Caloric restrictive or Diabetic. That way when the trays are prepared, we prepare by exception and each C or D tray is prepared by portion restrictions or by substitutions."

"I sat next to a Mrs. Boersma who claimed she was a diabetic, yet her tray appeared to be the same as mine."

"Let's see, Mrs. Boersma is a C and a D. She is limited to twelve hundred calories per day. Her portions would have been smaller and she would have gotten the sugar-free Jell-O dessert instead of the cake and no butter."

Jason observed that with the exception of a new walk-in cooler, the equipment was not new, but seemed to be clean and functional. The discussion continued and Mrs. Rudder talked about her wish list for new and more modern equipment. This wish list was being made a reality by a women's group called the "Sarah Circle" that held bake sales and bazaars to raise money for improvements to the kitchen. The most recent purchase was the walk-in cooler. The conversation ended with Mrs. Rudder exclaiming, "We come a long way in sixteen years, but, yeah, there's always something you could use."

When they got back to his room, Runner switched on some classical music, and the conversation began with Runner's critique of the dietary fare. "The good Mrs. Rudder's R, C, and D categories are good in theory, but you saw the system fall down in front of your eyes. The D tray I was supposed to get was placed on Table Two in my regular spot. I ate from an R tray. I'm a brittle diabetic. But I know what my exchanges are supposed to be. No butter and I didn't eat my cake, but had some grapes instead. No damage done. But if I were suffering from dementia like Mrs. Boersma and ate what was put in front of me, I'd very likely be having a sugar reaction right now, which could very well kill me.

"Because you were there, the server got confused and gave Mrs. Boersma a regular tray also. Mrs. Boersma has enough acumen to recognize that and she told the server. The server is essentially ignorant and doesn't understand the food exchanges on a controlled diet. She assumed Mrs. Boersma didn't know what she was talking about because few of 'em do here. Fortunately, Mrs. Boersma's diabetes isn't brittle. So the cake she scarfed down before her meal is not what she should be eating, it'll elevate her blood sugar some but won't kill her. She put my uneaten piece in a napkin and is squirreling it away in her room as we speak. That might throw her for a loop, but I doubt it'll do her any real harm."

Jason was taking notes.

"The problem is they don't have either the money or the will to hire competent help. Mrs. Rudder has no training as an institutional cook. She had a large family—six boys I believe—and her husband died about the time their youngest left the nest, leaving her without means. Their selection of her for the job was more because she needed it than because she was qualified. They felt they were "ministering" to her. To their credit, they had her take some night courses at the community college on nutrition, but I think most of that's been forgotten. But she's a fine Christian lady." The sarcasm dripped from his voice.

Runner paused until Jason finished writing then continued.

"Which leads me to another point. This crowd thinks that to honor the Sabbath, which is the fourth of the Ten Commandments, you shouldn't do any work. It's also their tradition to have a big dinner after church on Sunday. So we get a big dinner on Sunday noon, then the kitchen help gets the rest of the day off, to keep the Sabbath, I suppose. A group of volunteers from a local Christian college comes in to fix the Sunday evening meal."

The old man paused. When Jason looked up, Runner was shaking his head as if in disbelief.

Runner began again. "If the regular kitchen help have a hard time figuring out the food exchanges, what do you suppose happens on Sunday night?" Runner rolled his eyes. "Blood sugar levels go higher than their expectation of getting to heaven for their good works."

He continued, "The operative philosophy seems to be that it's better to be accidentally poisoned by a fine Christian than enjoy good health by the hand of a heathen."

"Poisoned?"

"That piece of cake on my tray at lunch—under the right circumstances—could lead to my untimely passing into the great beyond if there is one. It's poison to me." Runner paused and he squinted as if he were trying to look back into himself. The intensity of the gaze let Jason know Runner had not yielded the privilege of the floor.

After a moment Runner continued. "Speaking of philosophy, I want to apologize to you for any discomfort I may have caused you by raising questions about your faith structure. This study you're doing could be a good thing for the Home; although frankly, I have grave doubts that they'll take your report seriously. You don't need any distractions. I promise not to feed your head with any more theological mush."

Jason sensed the discussion of the inadequacies of the food service of the Christian Arbor Home was over and Runner was changing gears.

"No need to apologize. Truth is, you've given me pause to think through some things I've taken for granted. Frankly, my studies have occupied most of my time. I had assumed my faith structure was cemented by the time I left high school, and I could concentrate my energies on my studies. Your questions made me think. My faith should be growing along with my vocation, and it hasn't.

"Your questions forced me to look at my faith critically and it *was* unsettling. I confess I've struggled a bit. And I've changed. I don't know yet if it's for the better, but my faith structure *has* changed a bit."

"Well, if you *have* changed, you're in good company. One of the most prolific writers in the Bible changed his theology as new revelations came to light. It's unfortunate that his role model as a theologian whose paradigms change as new information or new experience comes to light doesn't serve as a model for the Christian Church."

Jason stared at into the sparkling blue eyes that begged to continue. He reflected on whether he needed any more theological disquietude in this life. What the hell, I might as well be broke as badly bent, Jason thought. "Okay, who is this prolific biblical writer whose theology changed as new evidence revealed itself?"

"Paul."

"Paul?"

"The Apostle Paul." He pointed to the blue dust-jacketed Bible on his bookshelves.

"Look up the first Pauline book to the Thessalonians, chapter four, verse thirteen to about verse eighteen."

Jason thumbed through the back of the New Testament until he found the passage. "'*We wish you not to remain in ignorance, brothers, about those who sleep in death; you shall not grieve like the rest of men, who have no hope. We believe that Jesus died and rose again; and so it will be for those who died as Christians, God will bring them to life with Jesus. For this we tell you as the Lord's word . . .*'"

"Stop right there," Runner interrupted. "Remember when Paul said, 'Of this I have no inspiration of the Lord'? Well apparently, on this point, he feels he has some authority from God to say what's to follow. Please read on."

Suddenly Jason was aware of an approaching presence. He

turned to see Sharon Veeringa, the head nurse. He had not heard footsteps, and it occurred to Jason that she had appeared rather suddenly. Listening outside Runner's open door, perhaps, he wondered.

"Mr. Runner, I understand there was a mix up of the luncheon trays. I think we should do a blood sugar on you. We wouldn't want you to have a reaction, now would we?" She approached Runner with an alcohol swab and a lance.

"Is that your pretense for interrupting us?"

"Now Mr. Runner, I'm only interested in your health. I've given up on your soul a long time ago. But you're not trying to lead this nice young man astray are you?" Her voice was loud and her tone was typical of one who is used to talking to the elderly or children. She went about her business of taking a blood sample.

"Just doing a little Bible reading together. I'd welcome you to join us, but you insist on wearing your sixteenth-century hearing aids. I don't understand you, Veeringa. You practice sixteenth-century theology and nineteenth-century health care. When are you going to allow yourself to think about your theological system?"

"This is the twenty-first century, Mr. Runner, the twenty-first century," she replied in a tone of voice that clearly implied Runner wasn't as mentally with it as he thought he was.

"I am aware of the present century, Ms. Veeringa, and I was deliberately specific. If you practiced twenty-first century health care, I would've gotten the proper tray at lunch and you wouldn't need to prick my finger. I suggest you leave us to our discussions and go directly to Mrs. Boersma's room. If she's still alive, she'll be the one needing the additional insulin. About forty units, I'd guess, twenty for each piece of cake she's filched."

Ms. Veeringa looked at Runner as if to decide whether or not to believe him and then moved to leave. As she passed Jason, their eyes met and the head nurse clearly communicated the warning,

"Be careful."

"If she were as concerned for the welfare of the residents as she is for the welfare of their souls, this place would be . . . ah, but that's another story. Let's see, you were reading from Thessalonians. Do you have your place?"

Jason continued reading where he had left off. "*For this we tell you as the Lord's word: we who are left alive until the Lord comes shall not forestall those who have died; because at the word of command, at the sound of the archangel's voice and God's trumpet-call, the Lord himself will descend from heaven; first the Christian dead will rise, then we who are left alive shall join them, caught up in the clouds to meet the Lord in the air. Thus, we shall always be with the Lord. Console one another, then, with these words.*" Jason stopped and looked up at Runner, who was peering over his reading glasses at Jason.

Runner began to speak as if he was musing. "A reading of this passage would seem to indicate that Paul believed, indeed he even hints, of direct revelation from God, that Christ would be returning to set up the Kingdom of God on earth soon. The coming was imminent. Certainly within his lifetime and the lifetime of his readers, people would be taken up alive into heaven.

"As a result, people were apparently quitting their jobs and sitting around twiddling their thumbs waiting for the sound of the archangel's voice. If you turn to the second letter to the Thessalonians, you'll find Paul admonishing—I think he orders them—not to fall into idle habits, to work quietly for their living. And the man who will not work should not eat.

"Paul was obviously mistaken as to the timing, if not the reality of the second coming. His comments about taking what he said as God's words notwithstanding.

"The evidence—the failure of the second coming of Christ to happen as soon as he thought it would—caused him to change his understanding, his interpretation of the life and ministry of Christ, that is, his theology."

"As the church has had to do with their stand on the geocentric universe, the issue of slavery, and so forth?" asked Jason.

"Exactly. In fact, the way I read the Gospel of John, Jesus himself changed the way he thought of his ministry. Prior to his meditation in the wilderness, he was the hard-charging, feisty, fire breather that John the Baptist envisioned the Messiah should be. That was the Jesus who threw the tradesmen out of the temple. After the wilderness experience, he followed Isaiah's model of the suffering servant.

"It occurs to me that if it was acceptable for Jesus to change his vision of ministry—his theology—and it was okay for Paul to modify his vision, change is not only permissible, but it's the only intellectually honest road to take. And if you take this road as a Christian, you'll be in good company—the likes of Jesus and Paul— but lonely. Because, in spite of the mountains of new evidence and insights, most of the mainstream Christian Church has had trouble changing its position on any theological issue. Witness the evangelical Church's struggle with evolution with a universe full of evidence to the contrary."

That was a struggle Jason identified with.

Runner went on. "What this comes down to is another bit of proof that some of the notions the Church has held on to regarding inspiration and inerrancy put them in an untenable box. And instead of examining the box, they close it around themselves and the existence of the box becomes the proof of its correctness.

"Reminds me of a story about a professional football player who was cheating on his wife and who covered up his absence from the house by lying about playing cards with his teammates. After one of his trysts, he was sneaking home at six o'clock in the morning, only to be met at the door by his suspicious wife. 'And where have you been?' she asked.

"'Playing cards at Sam's' was his reply.

"'Until six o'clock in the morning?'

"'I didn't want to disturb you, so I've been sleeping in the hammock on the porch.'

"'That's a good story,' the wife replied, 'but I put the hammock in the attic yesterday!'

"The husband thought for a moment and replied, 'I played cards at Sam's. I didn't want to disturb you when I came home, so I slept on the hammock. That's my story and I'm sticking to it.'"

Jason chuckled. "One thing that bothers me, though, is when you share these thoughts with me, it all seems so logical. Why don't I read these ideas in the church papers or hear them from the pulpit?"

Runner sat back in the wheelchair and took a deep breath. "This is where the real dishonesty comes in. These ideas are not original with me, they've been and are being discussed, debated, and written about in the academic circles of mainstream Christian denominations throughout the world. But they rarely get out of the academic circles to pulpit preachers and thereby to the laity. The result is an academic intellectual elite and a laity that hasn't been exposed to the latest and best thought when theological issues surface.

"It's typically the greater governing body of the Church—made up of laity and ministers who've been out of seminary for a while—that decides the fate of professors who teach something other than the seven-day creation story. The new thinking stays within the academic circles. Academicians talking to academicians. Ordinary people aren't being drawn into the discussions for fear of their reaction and what may happen to the academicians' jobs.

"So the pulpits of the land preach a message that is not the best theological thought, sometimes not relevant, and often not communicative to the Post-Modern Age. As a result, Christianity has not exactly been a growth industry of late. Membership numbers in nearly every mainstream denomination are declining in spite of population growth. It's the equivalent of the medical profession practicing bloodletting and leeches and ignoring modern medical advancements while the patients die or are off seeking self-treatment."

"Or like running the Indy 500 in a Model A?" Jason asked. "But then, to what do you attribute the resurgence of so-called 'spiritualism' today, the growth of the 'New Age' religions?"

"I believe it's the natural hunger of the human heart for an understanding of the ultimate reality of life. The pity is, it's a hunger that the traditional Church should be filling, but much of the Church refuses to admit that their creedal statements are historically conditioned and to re-state them to be relevant to today's audience or evidence. New Age religions are flourishing in a void left by the traditional Church.

"Further, their refusal to restate their creeds has always been an enigma to me. Their Bible and all of their cherished doctrines and creeds to which they tenaciously cling are, irrefutably, historically conditioned documents. That seems to me to be a *prima facie* case for re-statement. By that I mean their Bible and their creeds were written by the best wisdom of that day, and spoken to the people of that day regarding current issues or reactions to doctrines or practices they thought were in error. We're different people, with different knowledge, and different questions. But these good people here and the fundamentalists and evangelicals prefer to stake their souls on sixteenth-century questions and answers . . ."

Jason raised his hand to interrupt. "But what of the contention that the Truth is changeless. God doesn't change. There is no need to rewrite the changeless Truth."

"First of all, my young friend, God changes, and He changes his mind. The story of God debating with Abram over the destruction of Sodom and Gomorrah is a proof text if you need one. Christianity hangs its hypothesis on a changing God. They believe God's plan to reconcile the world to Himself through the Jews failed, so He changed His plans and attempted the reconcilement through Christ. And further, it is important to distinguish Truth from our perception of Truth."

Runner squinted his left eye, which seemed to make his blue eyes ever so piercing. "Tell me, what absolutes are there that don't depend on our ability to comprehend, formulate a description of the absolute, then communicate the absolute? Is there a God that can be comprehended; and can you pass along your comprehension so I have the same understanding? Is your comprehension accurate, your description complete, and my understanding total? Will the words you use even paint the same images in my mind that your mind sees? Not a chance. Do you agree?

Jason nodded assent and thought to speak, but Runner was continuing.

"I'm reminded of the story of six blind men who were commissioned to describe an elephant. One felt the trunk, one the tusk, one the ears, one the legs, one the tail, and one the underbelly. Their descriptions were not recognizable as an elephant. But importantly, the blind men's lack of a consistent description does not belie the fact that there was an elephant. Our failing human attempts to describe the Truth in no way diminishes the Truth or our need to pursue it.

"The Christian Church and their Bible and creeds and hymns are not unlike the blind men's report. Each writer sees the Truth from his educational, historical, and experiential perspective. As time passes and the blind men die, or our ability to treat blindness improves, the Church should appoint six new men to re-examine the elephant instead of insisting the historical perceptions of the Truth are adequate, once for all.

"The Jewish faith doesn't have these problems. The rabbinical tradition has been re-interpreting the Scriptures and re-defining the faith from the time the Scriptures were written. They revel in the inconsistencies in the Scriptures, using them as the source for endless debate. For the Jewish faith, their scriptures have an ongoing life, which I think is far healthier than Islam's—and I think most Protestant Christian's belief—that the Scriptures were cast in stone when written." Runner paused and put his chin on his hands that were balancing his cane between his legs.

Jason did not let the pause linger. "What do you say to those people all around us like my brother, and to some extent myself, who love the old doctrines and creeds? They seem to be content where they are in their pilgrimage of faith. Is it necessary to upset them like you've upset me?" Jason said through a wry smile.

Runner smiled with his lips together, pulling his striking blue eyes into a squint that radiated wrinkles in all directions. "Creating a belief structure is our imperfect attempt to explain the unexplainable and it is a human, therefore, flawed endeavor. This endeavor doesn't result in knowledge that can be proven by a trail of evidence, or by logic, or the scientific method—it is accepted in faith.

"Faith, by definition, is not concrete. Hopefully, one's faith understanding will develop by new experiences and by new insights into a clearer understanding, fully aware it will never be perfect.

"If you believe in life after death and the possibility of either a heavenly or hellish existence, we're all betting our souls on imperfect, or, if you prefer, limited understandings. Each of us should be entitled to place his own bet. That is, come to his own understanding. My fundamentalist Christian friends here do not allow me that entitlement. I allow them theirs.

"They do not forgive me for my desire to find answers to new questions that come in the light of new understandings gained from the natural and social sciences every day. I forgive them their arrogant belief that they have complete answers out of the sixteenth century when they haven't yet come to understand the questions of the twenty-first. Let each of us find our own peace. I allow myself intolerance for those who make defining a new question, or seeking a new answer, a cardinal sin for which I'm supposed to seek atonement. Especially if, as I suspect, their concept of atonement is a paradigm that may no longer serve them on even a cursory examination."

There was a loud click as Jason's pocket recorder automatically shut off, having reached the limit of the memory card. It reminded both Jason and Runner of the real purpose of his visit. He inserted a fresh card in the recorder and the discussion returned to the menu, the diet, the monotony of it, and of the residents getting around their dietary restrictions by smuggling forbidden sweets in from the outside or from other residents.

Runner had said that the room of the diabetic, Mrs. Boersma, was a stash of chocolates, cookies and other sweets and that the staff turned a blind eye to it. Jason questioned whether the Home was potentially liable should an oversight or turning a blind eye result in a tragedy. Runner rejoined that for some of the residents, the family would be hard pressed to demonstrate damages, considering the residents' advanced dementia.

When the recorder clicked off for the second time, they talked about what Jason should investigate the following week. Runner indicated that an examination of the physical plant would take a couple of weeks and suggested they get into the building maintenance next, mechanical systems the following week. Jason agreed and collected his notes, shook hands with Runner warmly and took his leave, promising to return the next Friday.

He headed down the hall and the beginning of the weekend, wondering if his report would be akin to that of the blind men describing the elephant. Absolutely, he thought. And what of his theology? At this point, the only thing he was sure about was the existence of the elephant. But there would be time enough to explore the elephant. He had a fellowship to complete.

As he passed Van Dam's office, he remembered that he needed

a copy of the Home's financial statements for his report. He rapped on Van Dam's open door.

"Yes?" Van Dam asked absently and then he looked up and his look of preoccupation with the paper in front of him dissolved into recognition. "Ah, Mr. Richards! What can I do for you?" And without looking down, he put the paper he had been absorbed in into a folder that was on his desk.

"Mr. Van Dam, it's customary for these research papers to include an analysis of the Home's financial condition. I was wondering if I could obtain a copy of your most recent financial statements?"

Van Dam looked at him for a moment as if he were trying to assess Jason's motives for asking. Finally, he said, "I'm not authorized to give out the Home's financial statement without Board approval. If it's absolutely necessary, I could make a request of the Board. I know they've been reluctant to give out that kind of information in the past. We're a private institution as you know." Then he added, almost as an afterthought, "Not that we have anything to hide, you understand."

"Most of the research papers that preceded me on other homes have done an extensive study of the home's income to expense ratios in comparison to the other homes we've studied. You might find that sort of analysis helpful."

"Actually, we get that kind of analysis in the trade publications we subscribe to, so I'm not sure another study would provide us with any information we don't already have access to. But if it's necessary, prepare a letter requesting the financials, and I'll submit it to the Board. They don't meet again until, let's see…" Van Dam made a production out of consulting his calendar which was apparently not very well organized because he spent a considerable time leafing back and forth through its pages. "December 20. That's six weeks from now. If it's necessary…."

"I'll prepare a letter that you can use as a formal request. I'll include a promise to maintain their confidentiality."

"All right then, is there anything else?" The tone bordered on a dismissal.

"Not for the moment. I appreciate your willingness to be cooperative. Have a good weekend."

Cooperative? Like a pig's ass, Jason thought as he headed for his car. December 20 gave him about no time to include anything meaningful in his report. Thanks a lot, Van Dam.

# Chapter Nine

It was local lore that it never rained in Ann Arbor on a football Saturday. On Saturday, it poured as Michigan hosted Purdue in what was forecast to be a yawner. The betting line was Michigan by three and a half touchdowns. It was a typical Big Ten game, three yards and a cloud of dust, except for Michigan, it was four or five yards, and for Purdue, it was one or two. There was no dust coming up from the floor of the Stadium but plenty of splashes as the rain could not run off fast enough to prevent puddles here and there.

Jason wore a plastic poncho, which kept out the rain but not the chill. He wondered if going to a Big Ten game at The Big House under those conditions qualified him for having experienced the "Big Chill."

He was in a serious funk. He couldn't get Runner, Lipscomb, Head Nurse Veeringa, his brother—none of them or any of them out of his mind. At a time in his life when he seemingly had the world by the tail and should have been enjoying himself and relishing the outstanding prospects for his future, he was in serious turmoil, emotionally.

The score of the game was 21-0 in favor of Michigan. The score in his life was 3-1-1. Three for his orthodox tradition, one for a different and intellectually intriguing alternative, and one for himself who didn't quite know where he belonged. His emotions and his heart called him to embrace his tradition and forget Runner. His mind and questions that had been festering beneath and around his subconscious were attempting to induce him to at least give Runner an audience.

How does one know, how does one arrive at one's faith? Jason had arrived at his by being spoon fed by his tradition, but that begged the question, how did *they* arrive at their faith? Was the tradition just plain good enough? Should the faith as imbibed through the tradition be taken on faith? And if it should, could it then become his faith, as if by adoption, or was it still their faith into which he could be substituted? Could he face the Ultimate Reality and say "I believe just like my father" or "I believe just like Pastor so-and-so"? Jason didn't think so.

Michigan's halfback fumbled the football on his own 30-yard line and in the ensuing scramble, the ball was recovered by Purdue on the 11. Purdue scored on an end-around. Michigan 21, Purdue 7. The rain continued unabated. Baseball is a sensible game, Jason thought, they don't play in downpours.

Had he fumbled on his own thirty? He had had the game of life in hand. No doubts, no fears, no worries. Now he wasn't sure who had the ball and what the goal was, or where it was. He was a product of the Modern Period and the Enlightenment before that. Emanuel Kant had said that if you cannot define something by empirical means, it could not be proved to exist. Runner had forced him to think in empirical terms about the underpinnings of his faith. Should one do that?

Kant left room for accepting the reality of something on faith, but did that mean one just accepted on faith without thinking about it, without questioning it? Didn't it have to be reasonable? And when theology came into conflict with experience, which would yield? Would one change the faith, that is, reformulate the theology, or would one deny the experience?

Was his tradition "The Truth" or a systematic explanation of "The Truth"? Was the explanation itself as sacred as that to which it sought to give expression? How sacred was the tradition?

Jason recalled that one of his past ministers had spoken of "the weight of the Scriptures." That meant that if you stacked up all the verses that seemed to indicate a certain theological position and put them up against all the verses that seemed to indicate a contrary opinion, you were to hang your theological hat on the biggest stack, the stack with the most weight.

That mental image had begun to have new meaning in Jason's mind. Previously, he had concluded that the weight of the Scriptures equated with Truth. Now he wondered if the opposite was also true: that those Scriptures of lesser weight, those that led to a contrary or conflicting conclusion did not represent Truth. Did that mean that there was Scripture that did not represent Truth? Or did all Scripture represent Truth in some way or another and one was left to choose which was important? Or, did one leave the choosing of what is important to others more knowledgeable in matters theological? And if one did that, whose faith resulted?

Michigan scored on the second play from scrimmage after Purdue kicked off. A seventy-two-yard run up the middle. Michigan 28, Purdue 7. A roar went up from the crowd to Jason's right, the middle of the students' section. Someone was being passed up the rows by the outstretched hands of the tightly packed spectators. The guy was trying to protect his private parts as groping hands assisted him up and up to the top row. Security personnel were rushing to his assistance. He would be ejected from the stadium for his part in the prank. Strange, the victim pays for the offense. The students around the victim were cheering. Many of them were glassy-eyed and having a rip-roaring good time enjoying the prank, enjoying their schnapps, and enjoying the game. And Jason was struggling with theology. What had happened to him? His funk continued. He had no schnapps with which to dull his pain, and it continued unabated like the rain.

Perhaps the Scriptures were meant to be, as Runner had indicated, an account of those who had encountered the activity of God in history and were inspired to commit that account to writing. That was a big jump for Jason. He had been taught that the Bible *was* a revelation; Runner held that the Bible was a *witness* to revelation. Perhaps the writers' task was not so much writing instruments as to be witnesses and theologians. Perhaps they said, "This is what I saw and how I saw it and how I felt about it."

When they said Jesus said this or that, they were indicating nothing more than at that moment Jesus said these words to those people about that situation. This is what Jason thought Runner's position would be. On the other hand, his tradition had taught that the words of Jesus were timeless words of instruction from his deity, and further that the words had universal application. There was not a problem that could not be solved with a proof text. Indeed, if you couldn't find a proof text, it was not a problem worth solving.

Michigan was threatening to score again, but Purdue held, and the Big Blue was forced to try for a field goal. It was good: Michigan 31-7.

The problem with proof text kind of faith was what did one do when another was found that appeared to contradict the tradition. One of those not in the "weight of the Scriptures," but in the . . . the measure. That was a good way to put it, Jason decided, the weight and measure of the Scriptures. And the tradition had the weight of the Scriptures; Runner had the measure. Runner also had the measure of the orthodox evangelical Christians at the Home, including the head nurse.

A roar went up from the crowd as a greased pig had been released onto the field and the officials were trying unsuccessfully to corral it. Michigan 31, Purdue 7, Greased Pig 1. That's the way the game ended. Similar to the score of his life. Still 3-1-1 and he—or rather his elusive faith structure—was the greased pig. The rain continued, as did his ruminations, throughout the slosh back to his apartment.

That night he had trouble sleeping and when sleep did come, he had the dream again. But this time, the fisherman in the shiny black waders who chased after him, spewing obscenities, turned out to be the head nurse.

For the remainder of the weekend, Jason tried as best he could to push the faith conundrum to the back of his consciousness by attacking the requirements of the Fellowship with a vengeance. There were the preps for the Intro Ad 301 recitations and he was in the middle of a large study of cost containment on hip replacement surgeries for the University Hospital Controller.

All the while, he knew that Friday and his visit to the Christian Arbor Home was coming. He would have to decide whether he would allow his tradition to dictate his faith or continue to explore his intellectual curiosity with Howard Runner. Of course, how he framed the question in his mind provided the answer for him. As stated, he would explore his curiosity with Runner. He could also ask the question in terms of "would he stand by the tradition passed along to him through countless Christians before him, or would he chuck the tradition and listen to this man-devil whom he did not know nor did he know what the man-devil believed—if anything."

✟

A clear, crisp October Friday began with a touch of frost visible here and there. Jason organized his Interrelation Report notes and re-read what Visser's report had said about the building maintenance. Visser had noted the building and grounds manager—a Mr. Schuring—had no formal training in buildings management or in energy efficiency. He found the building needed some general repair to forestall long-term damage. There were things like leaks around windows, decaying eaves. Jason remembered the water damage he had seen in the lobby.

On the positive side, Visser's report noted the facility was spotless except for the kitchen, where deficiencies written up on a recent Washtenaw County Health Inspector had not yet been addressed some nine months after the citations.

Jason jotted some questions to ask Mr. Schuring. He dug out the letter he had prepared formally requesting the financial statements from the Board of the Home and left the apartment in time to enjoy a big breakfast at Denny's. As it was mid-morning, the restaurant was not busy and he picked up a copy of *USA Today*, the national newspaper, to read while eating. A teaser on the front page caught his eye. "Religion Professor Strikes Back at Jesus Seminar. Pg. A6."

Jason turned to page A6. "New Book examines the 'true' historical Jesus." Jason read with fascination of a Professor of Divinity, Luke Timothy Johnson, who had published a book on Jesus proclaiming that Jesus is not the Jesus of history. He went on to be quoted as saying that who Jesus was cannot be discerned with empirical reasoning. Jesus, he explained, is the Jesus of faith. He was answering those who were publishing out of the experience of the Jesus Seminar. A nineteenth-century theologian, Ernst Troelsch, whose name was not familiar to Jason, was identified as the one who first explored the historical Jesus and who was way ahead of his time. Troelsch's time had now come and the quest for the historical Jesus had come full circle.

Jason had read about the Jesus Seminar. It was a large group of mostly Christian scholars who met to ascertain how much of what Jesus said and did as reported in the Gospels was actually the words and actions of Jesus and how much of it was hyperbole or exaggeration, even myth. They voted with colored beads.

Jason pulled the page out of the paper and put it into his notebook. He decided over his pancakes that he could not hide from Runner. As a scholar, if he had any intellectual integrity at all, he must face him and expose his tradition to the light of scrutiny. Otherwise, how could he place the wager of his soul intelligently? He would confront Runner with the article in the paper and see where the discussion might go. He finished his pancakes, paid the check, and left for his meeting with Runner.

As he found a parking place, he saw the familiar wheelchair with Runner manipulating a long handled tool with a claw device. Runner appeared to be using the tool to pull up some plants. Jason parked and approached the wheelchair. It was the once verdant tomato plants, now hanging as if without life, apparent victims of the frost, that were being pulled up.

"Apparently the season's over, Mr. Runner?"

"Oh? Jason! Yes, it is. Nice to see you, Jason."

"I'm looking forward to our visit. Have you made arrangements to visit with the building superintendent?"

"Yes. Name's Marvin Schuring. Nice man, gets good grades in my book for not trying to save my soul. But he only wears short pants in the building maintenance field. If you would be so kind as to push me down this sidewalk, we can get to Schuring's office 'round the back and avoid the hens in the lobby."

"I'll be happy to if you'll be so kind as to allow me to put my notebook on your lap. Jason took the handles of the wheelchair and began pushing it away from the front door of the home. "After we meet with Mr. Schuring, I've got a *USA Today* article I'd like you to read."

"The one in today's paper about Ernst Troelsch?"

Jason was taken aback. "That's the one."

"Ernst Troelsch is an interesting story. Do you know why his work went unnoticed until now?"

"The article indicated he was ahead of his time."

"Well, I don't think he was so much ahead of his time as he was overshadowed by another giant of his day, Karl Barth, who went from being an obscure preacher from Switzerland to become one of the most influential theologians of all time. He was the theological rage. And Troelsch's work went unheard in the clamor. That entrance next to the loading dock is where we'll find Schuring."

Jason pushed the wheelchair toward the door Runner had indicated, then went ahead to open the door and held it for Runner to wheel himself into a closet-size office. It was furnished with old schoolroom-style oak furniture and it smelled of wax, like furniture or floor polish.

Mr. Schuring wasn't in the office or in the workshop adjacent to the office, but the whirring sound of a floor polisher could be heard nearby and Runner directed Jason to look about the corridors. "Schuring's jockeying that floor polisher we hear. See if you can find him and tell him we're here."

A tall, curly-haired man with glasses was guiding a floor polisher in wide strokes down the adjoining corridor. He was pulling the machine as he walked backward with a slow but deliberate pace. He appeared to be oblivious to everything but the sheen that the machine was coaxing out of the tiled floor. He started when Jason, who had approached undetected, touched him on the shoulder.

The tall man turned the polisher off and, displaying a toothy grin, stuck out a huge hand. "I'm Marve Schuring. You must be Jason Richards."

"Pleased to meet you, Mr. Schuring. Thank you for agreeing to talk with me for a short while. Mr. Runner is waiting for us in your work area. Is that a good place to talk?"

"As good as I've got," and Schuring opened the door to the workroom and held it for Jason to enter, after which he followed, talking all the while. "I unnerstand yer doing a survey of the Home like that other fella, Visser I b'lieve was his name. Nice fella, though near's I could figure, nothing ever come of his report. Least ways, I didn't see no changes.

"Not that things is bad, don't get me wrong. I rightly think we do a good job with what we got here, but we got a thing or two that needs tendin' to, ya unnerstand.

"It's jest that there's only so much money and it's got to go around. Van Dam and them state inspectors don't seem to care if the place is falling down, jest so's it's all spit and polished like. So I give 'em spit and polish and they're happy."

"In your mind, what sort of things need tending to?" Jason asked.

"Well like, I don't know if you noticed the water damage to the windows aside the front door in the lobby. When the building was built, they capped the walls with a cee-ment cap. Now that's one way a' doin' it, all right. But by rights, there shoulda been a copper cap atop the cee-ment cap."

"What would a copper cap accomplish?"

"A copper cap woulda kept the water outa the wall. A cee-ment cap absorbs some'a the rain. It freezes and gets a crack. Now the water can enter the cap through the crack and trickle down the course of blocks until it hits a barrier, like the transom over the door. Now it gots no place to go, it collects, it freezes, mebbe makes more cracks, and finds its way into the plaster 'round the windows."

"Do you know why a copper cap wasn't used?"

"At the time the buildin' was built, there weren't money for the proper caps or the folks didn't exactly know what they was doin'. Lots'a this buildin' was built with donated materials and labor. Now, after forty years of drippin' and freezin' and thawin', we got cracks eatin' away at the window and door frames and the buildin's lost its proof to the weather, so to say. Cost more extra money to heat the place each year than it would've to put proper caps on in the first place. Course, back in the twenties, weren't much thought put to the cost to heatin' the place. But that's another story."

There was a pause in Schuring's narrative. Jason referred to his notes. He looked up and asked, "Mr. Visser noted that there had been a scare when a Mrs. Batts died from an unknown virus. There was some thought that it may have been from Legionnaires' disease and the health department looked into the possibility of stagnant water in some of the air handling systems. Did anything come of that?"

"Naw, course we heat with steam here. Truth be knowed, we got very few ducts where there could be standin' water. But they's some shafting that the hot water pipes run through. They're a pickle to get into and so a feller's hard pressed to clean in there if'n he don't hafta. They paid for some fancy cleaning company to come in and give the place a good cleaning in what ducts we got. There was a directive that we was to have that type of cleaning at least once ever two years. Somethin' to do with mold spoors or somethin'. But they's no money in the budget for that and it ain't on the annual inspection list by the State, so we're able to slide by on that one. The Chairman of the Building and Grounds Committee—that'd be Claude Vander Plats—says if'n you can't see it to clean it and it ain't on the State's inspection list, don't spend time nor money on it. Mostly, he means money.

"Now don't get me wrong, I'm not saying we're violators. Not that we don't get wrote up a time or two, but some of our folks are on Social Security and Medicaid. You cain't run a country club on Social Security and Medicaid. We ain't got much money. But we got a lot of love and that's free, so that we give a'plenty of."

Jason asked a few more questions and when he was satisfied that he would get fewer and fewer facts and more and more homespun philosophy on the tender loving care of aging nursing homes, he thanked Mr. Schuring and pushed Runner back to his room.

"Have you time for a few questions?" Jason asked Runner when they had reached Runner's suite of rooms and had settled in.

"Fire away."

"How do you see the maintenance of the Home?"

"Schuring's right. They either don't have the money to spend or they're too tight to spend it. They'll spend as much as it takes to keep it clean because cleanliness is next to Godliness. And they're well intentioned. But I think one of the reasons Schuring is secure in his job is because he is neither bright nor ambitious, but he runs a mean floor polisher. So the place looks good and there's no pressure on Van Dam to make improvements from Schuring. Schuring's happy to give it just enough of a lick and a promise to keep the inspectors happy.

"The maintenance is indicative of the operational philosophy of the whole Home. Appearances are important, form versus substance. The place may be crumbling but the pieces will be clean and they will watch it crumble with loving care and great pride."

Jason had one more question on his notepad. "What about the personal services—like laundry, a barber shop, the library?"

"Frankly, the laundry service is poor. They're always losing someone's clothes, or there are buttons missing. I pay about thirty dollars per month to have my laundry picked up and delivered by a commercial firm. The Home charges twenty-eight dollars for substandard service. But in the literature, it looks good to be able to say 'In house, full-service laundry.'

"The barber is a beautician who's lost if she can't put your hair in pin curls, and the library's great if you like love stories where no one ever winds up on their back with their knees in the air and everyone is saved by Grace in the end. That would be Grace as in Grace Livingston Hill. They have at least two copies of every title she's ever written."

"Grace Livingston Hill?"

"She was the 1950's Christian equivalent of Danielle Steel. Of course, my library's off limits because the four letter words aren't blacked out of my novels and there's philosophy and theology books written by nihilists such as Nietzsche and heretics like Karl Barth. I even have Troelsch's book, the author referred to in the article in *USA Today*. He was an interesting fellow, Troelsch. He was the first theologian to apply historical thinking to what were accepted absolutes.

"Troelsch thought it appropriate to ask the question, 'What was the historical context in which this biblical statement was made or this theological understanding developed.' He thought it appropriate to understand the customs, the politics, the bias—to get into the skin of the speaker or the writer in an attempt to understand what the speaker meant.

"We all are inclined to think that things never change, that the way the world is now is the way it has always been and always will be. Troelsch urged a reading of the Scripture and an understanding of the development of the early Christian theology, which recognized its historical condition-ness. He said it was important to get an understanding of the time in which it was written and the audience to which it was intended.

"Now, a hundred years later, Troelsch is getting an audience far beyond what he had when he published. Now we have the big to-do over the historical Jesus. That is, trying to discover who Jesus might have been by understanding the customs, the politics, and the bias of the Gospel writers."

"Why did it take one hundred years for the Christian world to discover this Mr. Troelsch?" Jason wondered out loud.

"Herr Troelsch. A good Swiss preacher. It took a hundred years because he published about the same time as Karl Barth. And Karl Barth took the Christian world by storm. Suddenly, there was Barth and only Barth. The Protestant world was struggling with the effects of Kant and Nietzsche. They needed a *raison d'être* and Barth was it. Troelsch was lost in the fervor over Barth. It took a hundred years for Christian scholars to come again to the questions Troelsch raised. The Jesus Seminar is essentially trying to ascertain who Jesus of history was from the context in which he taught.

"I believe if Troelsch had been given a fair hearing, the Christian Church would be far different today. The Church could accept the diverse witness of the gospels and the Pauline Epistles and rejoice in what there is to learn from it, instead of trying to defend a unity that can't be supported with intellectual integrity."

Jason heard a small voice in the back of his head saying, Diverse witness? Let it go, Jason, let it go. There's trouble just around that bend, trouble you don't need. Let it go."

There was a knock at the open door and a young man presented himself in the hall. "Hello, Mr. Runner. I have your order from Izzy's."

"Bring it right on in," Runner responded to the young delivery boy. Then he turned to Jason, "I took the liberty of saving you from another meal in the dining room." Runner addressed himself to the delivery boy. "Put it on the secretary there. The money is in that white envelope marked IZZY'S. Yes, that's it, and thanks."

"Thank you, Mr. Runner."

"You're welcome, son." Runner paused as the young man took his leave, then he continued with Jason, "I don't know the extent to which you are willing to subject yourself to rainbow beef for the sake of your research paper, but Izzy's makes a Kaiser Killer that beats anything we'll get in the dining room. I hope you'll join me?"

"Smells good. What's a Kaiser Killer?"

"Stacked turkey on a very fresh Kaiser roll with tomato and lettuce and secret ingredients known only to Izzy. There's a TV tray in the closet there, help yourself while I pull myself up to the secretary."

Runner opened the bag and took out two large sandwiches wrapped in cellophane and two packages of chips. "I've ordered some iced tea from the dining room which should be here any minute." He distributed one of the sandwiches and a bag of potato chips and began opening his sandwich.

Jason heard the tinkle of ice cubes in a glass and turned to see Head Nurse Veeringa with a small decanter of iced tea and two tall glasses filled with ice. "I believe you ordered ice tea, Mr. Runner. So, it's Kaiser Killers again, is it?"

"In good conscience, I couldn't subject Mr. Richards to another meal of our famous rainbow beef, nor to any more of the scintillating prayers for his or my conversion, now could I?"

"I'm not sure the roast beef is any worse for his health than your humanistic philosophy is for his soul, if you want my opinion."

"You know, Veeringa, it occurs to me that using a head nurse to deliver iced tea isn't a very effective use of personnel. It would've been nice if you were showing your Christian love by just bringing us a cup of cold tea, as it were. But your motives are showing, Ms. Veeringa. Now, perhaps you could show us some common courtesy by allowing us some privacy."

"Actually, I'm checking to be sure you're counting your exchanges and brought the tea to save some steps."

"If you're truly concerned about counting exchanges, check the larder of sweets in Mrs. Boersma's room and do her blood sugar. Disingenuousness does not become you. Have a nice day and please close the door behind you as you leave. Thank you."

Having been summarily dismissed, Ms. Veeringa turned to leave and her eyes locked onto Jason's with a you-were-forewarned-yet-you-jeopardize-your-soul-with-this-man look, and it was withering. She left but she did not close the door behind her.

"She's concerned for your soul, Jason. Make no mistake about it, she delivered the tea to warn you. She couldn't care less for my blood sugar and whether or not I got my iced tea." Runner had turned to look at Jason over the rims of his half-glasses and his eyebrows were arched in a question mark.

What was Veeringa afraid of? Was it any of her business? What did she know that Jason had not yet found out? The questions piqued Jason's curiosity about Runner more that it frightened him. Piqued so much so that he forgot the small voice that had been warning him just a moment before. "What did you mean by the disparity of the Gospels? Isn't it generally held that there is unity in the Gospels? At least, that's what I remember from my tradition?"

Runner returned to his lunch and spoke between bites of his Kaiser Killer. "Yes, the unity of the witness of the Scriptures is important to most orthodox Christian faith systems. But even a cursory reading of the Scriptures shows a great diversity, especially in the New Testament.

"First, there's the differing backgrounds of the writers. Matthew was a tax collector, a position not held in high regard by his contemporaries. Luke was a physician and seemed fascinated by the miracles of Jesus. John was a fisherman. Paul was a Jew with Roman citizenship and a Greek education. It would be unlikely that these writers would see and interpret the events surrounding the life of Jesus in a unified way.

"Second, there is the differing biases of the narrators. Matthew is writing to the Jews, trying to convince them that Jesus is the long-awaited Messiah. Mark and Luke appear to be interested in only chronicling the events surrounding the life of Jesus. John, on the other hand, is constructing a Christology—that is, a theory of who Jesus was—and he often wrote in metaphors. Paul was trying to explain a singularly Jewish event to a world that understood things in the classic Greek philosophical paradigm.

"Third, there's the difference in the time the Gospels were thought to have been written, with Mark being the earliest and John the last, probably written some sixty years after the death of Jesus. Which raises the question as to whether John was around to write a Gospel at that time."

At that moment, Jason was wondering how he could possibly be calmly eating a deli sandwich in the swirl of heresy that was going on about him. Why did the concept of the diversity of the Gospels seem ripe for intellectual scrutiny when this kindly old man with the white beard and the clear blue eyes talked about it? Why don't I get upset during these sessions? That would come later, he thought.

Runner was continuing. "To be sure, these factors are not *ipso facto* reasons to conclude that the Scriptures must be a diverse witness, but given these factors, one shouldn't be surprised that the narratives don't speak with one voice.

"So, Matthew and Luke are the only writers to include the Sermon on the Mount. Mark, the earliest and, remarkably, John, the Christology Gospel, respectively, make no reference to the virgin birth. You need all the Gospels to glean all the words of the cross. John's words on the Cross depict a person in control, a God subjecting himself to crucifixion. Mark's words are those of a man out of control, alone and rejected by the God who he had served so faithfully. Oh, let's see, what are some others? Ah, John doesn't record a single parable in the whole of his Gospel. Then there is the discrepancy as to Andrew and Peter's calling to be disciples in Matthew and John, and the differing accounts as to the death of Judas we discussed before."

Runner paused. He broke off a piece of the sandwich and looked at it as he spoke. "Take the Gospel of John. It is the Gospel with the most pronounced differences. First, the chronology if the events as recorded by John is nothing like the chronology of the other Gospels, which admittedly have similar chronologies. In John, the ministry of Jesus is divided into two distinct parts without apparent regard to the actual sequence of events.

Runner put the piece of sandwich in his mouth and talked between chews. "In the first chapter, the writers set forth what may be the last Christology by an Apostle or his followers. The book begins, 'In the beginning was the word, and the word was with God, and the word was God.'

"That is interpreted by many fundamentalists to imply that Jesus was with God from the beginning of time, that he was the Word or the Truth, that he co-existed with God and he was God. It's a familiar passage. Quite in contrast to the opening verses of Paul's letter to the Romans. Read the first few verses for me, will you, Jason, while I have a bite or two of my Kaiser Killer here."

Jason put his sandwich down and fetched the New English Bible from it's now familiar place. He returned to his chair and turned to the first chapter of the letter of Paul to the Romans and began to read. "*From Paul, servant of Christ Jesus, apostle by God's call, set apart for the service of the Gospel. This gospel God announced beforehand in sacred scriptures through his prophets. It is about his Son; on the human level, he was born of David's stock, but on the level of the spirit—the Holy Spirit—he was declared Son of God by a mighty act in that he rose from the dead.*"

Runner was chewing and peering over his half-frame glasses. "Now read the footnote to that passage at the bottom of the page," he said with a mouthful of sandwich.

"*Or 'declared Son of God with full powers from the time when he rose from the dead.'*"

Runner was nodding his head as he listened and chewed. "Peter seemed to agree with Paul's idea of who Jesus was. Read Acts two verse twenty-two, then skip to verse thirty-three to thirty-five," and he took another bite of his Kaiser Killer.

Jason found Acts 2:22 and began to read, "'*Men of Israel, listen to me: I speak of Jesus of Nazareth, a man singled out by God and made known to you through miracles, portents, and signs, which God worked among you through him, as you well know. Let all Israel then accept as certain that God has made this Jesus, whom you crucified, both Lord and Messiah.*'"

Runner swallowed his food and wiped his mouth with a napkin before he continued. "Tell me, Jason, is there unity in those three statements? Cannot one get two distinct and different opinions as to who this Jesus fellow was? Wouldn't the Apostle John's Christology have you believe that this Jesus was a deity or God or some part of God from the beginning of time who was interjected into history? And having completed his work, returned to his anticipated reward on the right hand of God? Peter and Paul's Christology, on the other hand, would say that Jesus was a man, born of certain lineage, and became a deity upon his resurrection. Assuming you buy into his resurrection.

"Our friend Ernst Troelsch would say that one must come to an understanding of these passages from the historical context in which they were written and the intended audience. They both might be true, or one or the other or both might be the writer's articulation of what they have come to perceive as 'the Truth' and neither perception was perfect. That's where the Jesus Seminar comes in. And who can blame current scholars for trying to determine the truth of the matter? Would you mind pouring me a little more iced tea? Some more of that ice, too, if you don't mind."

Jason reached for the carafe and poured tea for Runner and topped off his own glass.

"The 'Truth' that Mrs. Veeringa keeps yapping about is only apparent to her and her ilk. It's not apparent to me and a good many others. On the other hand, a Professor of New Testament at Emory University, Luke Timothy Johnson, I believe—makes an understandable point in a book he wrote as a reaction to the Jesus Seminar. I have the book, if you're interested. Johnson says no amount of study will find the historical Jesus because he is the Jesus of faith. That would be the Apostle John's Jesus, while the Jesus Seminar looks for the Jesus of Matthew, Mark, and Luke.

"John's Jesus was the Jesus of faith, not of history. John's narration chronicles the first part of Jesus' ministry, from its inception to the contemplation in the wilderness, as modeling his ministry after his cousin, John the Baptist. This Jesus was a fire breather who threw the money-changers out of the temple; an incident, by the way, that's recorded in the last week of Jesus' life by all the other gospel writers. After his stay in the wilderness, his ministry takes on the model of Isaiah's suffering servant and he becomes a healer.

"This change in his ministry was so dramatic that John the Baptist sent some of his followers to Jesus asking him if he was the Messiah, or if John was to look for another. Jesus told the disciples of John the Baptist to report back that he had become a healer.

"Interesting to me that John was willing to scramble the

chronology of the events of Jesus' life—the history of it—to portray the Jesus of his faith. He…" Runner was interrupted by the entrance of Mrs. Veeringa.

"I've come to recover the glasses, if you're finished with them." The tone of her voice was as icy as the tea. Jason couldn't tell if she was angry or exasperated or both.

"Does the kitchen have such a shortage of glasses that you need be concerned with these two? Actually, Mrs. Veeringa, even a casual observer could conclude that since both our glasses contain iced tea we're still using them." Runner paused and sighed as if out of patience, then continued, peering over his half glasses, "Veeringa, instead of making up excuses for intruding, why don't you just come in and state your purpose. You've been standing outside the door eavesdropping now for some time, since just before I mentioned your name, in fact. It would be a refreshing change if you'd have the integrity to say what's bothering you or sit down and participate in the discussion. You might even learn something."

"I have more important things to do than eavesdrop on you, Mr. Runner. I'll be back for the glasses when you're finished. Don't forget your O.T. appointment at one thirty."

"Seriously, Mrs. Veeringa," Runner said sarcastically, "we were just about to discuss the proof text for the Gospel of God being revealed in the Old Testament, an interesting bit of the New Testament that evangelical Christians often ignore. You wouldn't ignore any part of the Bible now would you, Veeringa?"

Veeringa was at the door. She turned, "There's no point in discussing religion with someone who doesn't have any. Just remember, Mr. Runner, there's a judgment day coming. Probably sooner for you than for me." With that, she was gone.

"A righteous woman in her own mind. Righteous but dishonest. She's been outside the door for about . . ." Runner checked his watch. ". . . four or five minutes. I could see her reflection in the glass on the picture frame by the door. She *is* worried about your soul, Jason. You can expect her to collar you when you leave.

"She's right about one thing: it's nearly time for my appointment, and I'll be needing to get rid of some of that iced tea before I go. O.T.'s a worthless exercise, but they give you trouble if you don't follow the regimen. Apparently, they get the equivalent of demerits if enough people aren't active in their program. So I'll do my part for their accreditation. This has been a one-sided discussion. You save that article and we'll talk further next week. Until then?"

"Until then. Thanks for your continued help. Next week, I'll want to discuss the physical plant. Same time?"

"Same time."

"Thanks for the Killers. Next week, why don't I come around lunchtime, and I'll treat. Is there anything special I should avoid?"

"Desserts, the rest I can work around. It'd be helpful if I knew what you had in mind."

"How about steamed shrimp from Dominic's"

"That would be a wonderful treat!"

"See you about noon, then."

Jason left and headed for the front door. He thought about leaving through Schuring's maintenance door, mindful of Runner's warning that Veeringa would be waiting for him. But he had to deliver his letter requesting the Home's financial statements to Van Dam. Since the head nurse's office was just off the lobby, she would find him if she wanted to. He hoped she was busy or didn't want to see him.

She was in the lobby talking in loud tones to one of the ladies who was sitting on the overstuffed furniture waiting. Every time Jason saw these ladies, it gave him the chills.

Veeringa saw him approach and said, in an even louder voice,

"That's something we'll have to look into, Mrs. Baker. I have to go now, okay?" drawing out the "okay" as if she knew it wasn't. She quietly intercepted Jason. "Excuse me, Mr. Richards, I know your discussions with Mr. Runner are none of my business, but could you spare a few moments?"

Trapped. Jason didn't want to talk to this lady right now. He had problems enough with all he was contemplating without hearing from the other side. Wait, what was the other side? Wasn't it his side a few weeks ago? What was he doing to himself? What was Runner doing to him? "Certainly," he said.

"My office is just around the corner, here." They entered a small office adorned with pictures of small children in various activities.

"Mr. Richards, as I said, your discussions with Mr. Runner are none of my business. But I've been around Mr. Runner for quite a period of time and I believe him to be dangerous. If you keep talking religion with him, you'll most assuredly lose whatever faith you have. I did hear some of what he was talking about. He believes nothing and will not stop until you believe nothing as well. He doesn't believe that Jesus was the son of God and the Bible is very clear on that point." She reached for an open Bible that was laying on her credenza. She was prepared.

"The reference is First John, chapter two and verse twenty-two and following, *'Who is a liar, but he that denieth that Jesus is the Christ? He is antichrist, that denieth the Father and the Son. Whosoever denieth the Son, the same hath not the Father . . .'*

"Runner is an antichrist and he'll work you over and turn you every which way but loose. If you value your faith, you best confine your inquiries to your research paper, because *'what doth it profit a man if he gain the whole world and lose his soul?'*"

"That, I believe is almost a direct quote from the Gospel according to St. Matthew." It was Runner's voice coming from behind them. "I believe it goes on to say *'For the Son of Man . . .'* Note that Jesus does not refer to himself as 'the Son of God,' *'shall come in the glory of his Father with his angels, and then he shall reward every man according to his works.'* Shame on you, Mrs. Veeringa, preaching salvation by works. That's not the message of this sixteenth-century tradition of yours. But if that is the message of your gospel, there may be hope for me yet!" The voice was challenging but mischievous.

"Mr. Runner!" Veeringa's voice was angry and reproving. "You have no business . . ."

"Eavesdropping? Turnabout's fair play. So I'm the antichrist, am I? As this young man is my witness, we have only discussed what's in this Bible of yours. Examined it for what it says. You're the one who claims it's the very Words of God and infallible. If that's true, what can harm us from studying it? If examining and quoting the Scriptures is indicative of the work of an antichrist, who are you and what are you doing? Mmmh? Good day, Mrs. Veeringa. As you know, I have an O.T. appointment—that's Occupational Therapy, not Old Testament—and I shouldn't keep the therapist waiting. Jason." With that, Runner continued wheeling his chair down the hall.

The look of exasperation on Veeringa's face was almost pitiable. Jason tried to assuage her. "I appreciate your concern for me, Mrs. Veeringa. Please don't worry. Mr. Runner's is right about one thing. If he is trying to convert me to the side of the Devil, he's using the Bible to do it. So I don't think we have anything to worry about. But thank you for your concern."

Veeringa bit her lip and Jason could see she was fighting back tears. Her face didn't give away whether it was from frustration or anger. Finally, she shook her head as if to shake the hair from around her face and in a low tone of voice said, "Like I said, it's none of my business. But you be careful. He's the Devil incarnate."

Jason turned and left the home through the lobby, passing through the ever-present gaggle of overdressed ladies, waiting. One of the ladies was the one with the purple hat and purse, the "And I

Shall Wear Purple" lady he had seen in the lobby on a previous visit, waiting. Their conversation stopped as he went through the lobby and he could feel their collective eyes on him. He dropped his letter to the Board at the front desk and turned to leave.

When he reached the door, he stopped to examine the water damage. It looked as if Schuring's explanation was correct. The water was not coming in from the outside as Jason had first thought. The damage was from within.

He moved to the door, stopped, turned around, and met as many eyes as he could. "Good Day, ladies!" he said with a slight bow and as cheerfully as he could, and he turned and went through the door into the autumn sunshine.

Dirk Van Dam watched until the graduate student pulled out of the parking lot. He had overheard part of the exchange between Veeringa, Runner, and the student. And he had read the young man's request for the financials. Veeringa had rushed right in to fill in the details and get some succor, perhaps more succor than he should have passed out. On the one hand, this was going according to plan. On the other, it was time for some damage control. He picked up the phone and placed two calls.

# Chapter Ten

Lord 'a Mercy! What was he into here? His thoughts raced as he drove back to his apartment. He had decided to inquire of Runner about an article he had seen in *USA Today*. Runner not only had read the article but read the books of the people being quoted in the article, one of them having been written over one hundred years ago. And it all led to a discussion, no, a lecture, on issues ranging from the Scriptures being influenced by the times in which they were written, the Jesus Seminar, the diversity of the Scriptures, and an eavesdropping nurse who was determined to blunt what she sees as Runner's efforts to disengage Jason from his faith.

Who is this man Runner, this resident in a Christian nursing home who is reportedly not a Christian, and with a personal library in his bedroom? He has both obscure and current theology books, is obviously a very intelligent and insightful biblical scholar, and very well read. For not being a Christian, he certainly knew the Bible forward and backward. But if he wasn't a Christian, why bother knowing the Bible forward and backward?

Perhaps Runner was bored, and tormenting the evangelicals at the home was a diversion that gave him a distorted sense of pleasure. He did a good job if that was his goal, but Jason discounted that explanation.

Jason remembered some remarks his grandfather had made at a party given to honor his retirement. His grandfather had said that he looked forward to retirement because he would be able to do some things that he had wanted to do for a long time. He went on to regale the attendees with examples of these things. He was going to ride down the busiest two-lane street he could find at ten miles-per-hour below the speed limit during rush hour. Also, he had said he was going to go to the bank at the rush hour on Friday afternoon and tie up the teller with counting out rolled coins. He had been inconvenienced by retired people doing these things when he was in a hurry, and now that he had the time, he said he was going to carry on the tradition.

Jason didn't think this was Runner's way of going ten miles below the speed limit. Jason sensed Runner was a good person. He had only reacted negatively when he was put upon by those who were condemning him to Hell.

A loud horn blowing right behind Jason jolted him into realizing he was waiting for a red light to change that had already changed. He waved an apology to the driver behind him and resumed his drive and his thoughts.

The nurse, Veeringa, thought Runner was the Devil incarnate. Actually, she called him the antichrist. Is that what she meant when she said he was not what he appeared to be? And why did she care for Jason? Did she take him aside out of a concern for the welfare of the home or a concern for his soul? She barely knew him.

If she was concerned for a soul she barely knew, should the owner of that soul be at least as concerned? That was the dilemma, wasn't it? Strangely, Jason wasn't as bothered by the morning's events as he expected he would be. Runner had raised some interesting points, but Jason realized he had dealt with them on an intellectual and not an emotional level.

There were several things of which Jason had made mental note. He had not thought much about whether the Scriptures presented a unified or a diverse witness. He had been taught that the Scriptures were the inspired word of God, actually words of God, and therefore were infallible. There was a presumption on his part that the witness was of one voice. The idea that the Scriptures were a collection of the works of persons who had been inspired by an encounter with God as He interacted in history was a new one to Jason, but it made intellectual sense. And if the Scriptures were a human creation, by different people with different knowledge, experiences, biases, and agendas, the accounts could be expected to be different. Nonetheless, Jason expected the witness to be unified. That is, the message of the Scriptures would be singular, pointing to a singular Truth.

But, of course, there were significant differences in the interpretations of the Truth. Witness the vast number of different denominations in the Protestant tradition, some twenty thousand, Jason seemed to remember. Jason had been convinced that the particular denomination to which he belonged had . . . well . . . *The* Truth. It suddenly occurred to Jason how arrogant he had been to assume he had *The* Truth and that the members of all the other denominations had . . . well . . . less than *The* Truth. And they were equally as convinced, Jason was sure, that they had *The* Truth. An inappropriate arrogance if, as Runner had said, all any of us has is a human—therefore imperfect—perception of *The* Truth.

Runner. Jason's thoughts returned to the man, the antichrist, the Devil incarnate. Or was he an innocent, saintly-looking old man with remarkable blue eyes? Was he someone to be feared? It was true, as Runner had told the nurse, that all he had done was to cause Jason to think about what he had read from the Bible. Runner had challenged some of Jason's beliefs, but as Jason had complained to Lipscomb, he had used the Bible to do it.

Interesting that a non-Christian would have such a complete knowledge of the Bible. Or was he a non-Christian? He had made veiled references to "this Christ of yours," and "this Bible of yours,' and "the resurrection, if you buy into that." All of which implied that he wasn't. Yet Runner had this vast knowledge of the Bible and apparently was widely read in the Christian tradition. He was an enigma, to be sure.

Then there was the matter of what to do with the diversity of the Scriptures. Was Jesus a deity from the beginning, apparently miraculously inserted into history and resurrected to return to his heavenly home as John 1:1 would indicate? Or was Paul's version that Jesus was a fully human being who was deified by God through the resurrection? Did it matter? Was Jason concerned? Should he be? Wasn't all this getting out of hand? He had an education to get busy with, and it seemed all he thought about lately was his faith or lack thereof, or this point of theology or that. Surely, whether Jesus existed from the beginning of time or was deified by God at this resurrection was a question that could wait for its answer until his Fellowship was concluded. Yes, it could, and that was that.

He pulled his car into his assigned space at his apartment complex, gathered his notes and got out. He made a determined effort to leave the questions with which he had been wrestling in the car. If he had turned around to see if the questions had remained in the car, he would have seen them following like smoke roils after a car that drives close to a curbside pile of burning leaves.

Once in the building, he checked his mailbox before going to the apartment. There was a newsletter from Christ's Gospel Church which reminded him he hadn't attended services since his lunch with Reverend Lipscomb, a Consumers Power bill, and a square, hard Kraft paper mailer from FACULTY ON-LINE which read, "AS A COLLEGE EDUCATOR, YOU CAN EXPERIENCE THE POWER OF FACULTY ON-LINE FREE!"

Rank did have its privileges, he thought as he continued to his apartment. He tore open the small square folder.

"To start your free connection to FACULTY ON-LINE, insert the disk or CD into your computer," the package said. "*Roam* the Internet and World Wide Web with point and click ease. *Swap* tips and ideas with people who share your hobbies and interests."

Why not? He fired up his computer and followed the prompts. He was asked to enter his name, which he did. It was rejected as already assigned. He tried JasonR, JRichards, JasonRich; all rejected. In a whim, he tried RichJason and to the World Wide Web he was born again as RichJason.

The main menu screen came up and the topics from which he

could pick: Today's News, Personal Finance, Clubs and Interests, Computing, Travel, Education, Sports, Marketplace, People Connection, Entertainment, The Internet, Kids Only. He clicked on sports and then football, then college, then Big Ten, then Michigan and read some stories on the team and the game against Purdue and the upcoming game with Minnesota. Interesting.

He used the search engine to look up "nursing homes." In groups of twenty-five, over 18,000 websites were listed. Nursing Home directories, articles, ads for Homes by location. Fascinated, Jason browsed through some of the sites that attracted his attention. Most of the information was of little value or interest unless you needed to find a nursing home for your mother, who lived in Miami. If you did, there were websites for over twenty homes with their mission statements and pictures of their rooms, their administrators, their nursing staff, their food, their gardens and a list of their rates with whether or not they accepted Medicaid patients.

Jason then clicked on "Clubs and Interests." "Religion and Ethics" was a topic. Jason clicked on the "Religion and Ethics" icon, then "Christianity," then "Discussion Groups," then "Theology." The subjects ranged from "Creation vs. Evolution" to "Revelations" with a host of topics in between. One topic caught his eye, "Is Jesus God?" He highlighted and clicked on this topic. There were sixty-seven postings, the last one bore today's date. He started near the most recent postings and began to read at a posting from someone who called himself SASeller:

> Jesus was not God. Why? First of all, he prayed. A God wouldn't pray. To whom? Second, he died. God cannot die. God REVEALED Himself to some as "the FATHER," to others as a SPIRIT at work in them, and He revealed Himself THROUGH Jesus but not AS Jesus.

Then a response had been posted from JEFF C3592:

> I don't understand all of HIS book; my finite mind can only hope to approach the understanding of His infinite Word. I do read some every day, and every day I learn more—it's like panning for gold. It never fails to amaze me that His words are

simple words, yet they are brimming with meaning.

- I am the Way.

- I am the Truth.

- I am the Life.

For example, did you know "I am" is the very name of God? So that not only is Jesus saying that He is the Way [to the Father], but He is also saying "God" is the Way; "God" is Truth; "God" is Life.

If the Way is Jesus and the Way is God, then if follows by substitution that Jesus is God. These nuggets are buried all over God's handiwork of Scriptures and are a reflection of His Goodness. All we need to do is search and we will find.

## And PastorPete responded:

Jesus never says he is God. To the contrary, many times he distinguishes himself from God. To the rich young ruler he says, 'Why callest me good? There is none good but one, that is God.' And he claimed he did not know the hour of the coming of the Kingdom of God, only the Father knew.

His disciples didn't think he was God. They didn't believe he was resurrected at first. And then they thought he was the Messiah. The deification of Jesus is a construction of the Church in the early formation of Christology.

Jesus thought of himself as the pointer to God and the Church has turned the pointer into more of a god than God.

## Then JdanGray posted this note:

We are given two clear and unequivocal choices. One is that the claims of Jesus to be God are true and he is Lord in which case you can either accept him as such or reject him; or his claims were false in which case he either knew his claims were false which makes him liar and a hypocrite and a fool, for he died for it, or he did not know his claims about himself were false and thereby he was a sincerely deluded lunatic.

## The next was from Musicks4me:

To JdanGray:

RE << the claims of Jesus to be God>>

Please cite one place in the Bible where Jesus says he is God! One, just one, that's all I ask.

**JdanGrey responded:**

To Musicks4me:

RE<< One verse, just one, that's all I ask>>

John 8:58 "In very truth I tell you, before Abraham was born, I am."

**From PastorPete:**

RE<<John 8:58>>

I find it interesting that such an important theological construction, i.e. that Jesus proclaimed himself God, is only recorded in one of the Gospels, and, it should surprise no one that the writer that records is John. John of John 1:1. Does anyone else think that if Jesus had proclaimed himself as deity it would have been recorded up and down the Gospels? Wouldn't that have been the news of the decade, century, millennium? And, that the disciples would have caught on to it?

**From SFJames:**

To PastorPete. How can you call yourself a Christian if you don't believe Jesus is God? If you ARE a pastor and you don't believe that and don't preach that, you are leading your flock astray. Perhaps it would be better if a millstone would be hanged around your neck . . .

**From PastorPete:**

<< better if a millstone . . . >>

Many of my fellow pastors have suggested just such a solution. Please know that I do not diminish the role of Jesus in God's plan for the salvation of the world. My only point is that Jesus did not proclaim himself to be God and many of the things he said and did would lead me to believe he did not think of himself as God, just as his disciples didn't believe it at the time of his ministry. I think I'm in good company, Matthew, Mark, Luke, James, Paul to name a few. As to John, I'm anxious to talk this over with him when I see him.

Jason could have predicted the next posting. It was from a new respondent, Sonflower:

> To Pastor Pete. <<I'm anxious to talk this over with him when I see him>>
>
> If you don't believe that Jesus was God from the beginning, how do you think you will get to see him in heaven? I don't think you will get there.

Jason was fascinated. Here, on the Internet, people from all around the world were talking about the very things he was thinking about. He decided to pose Runner's question. He clicked on the "REPLY" button and began to write to JDanGrey:

> I have a question for you or anyone else who would care to respond. Did Jesus exist from the beginning of time, then was miraculously interposed into history, resurrected, and returned to heaven—God all the while as it would seem from reading the passage in John 1:1, or, was Jesus a fully human being who was deified by God at his resurrection as Paul would seem to indicate in Romans 1:1ff.
>
> RichJason

He clicked on the send button and a "Message Sent" message came up to indicate the communication was sent and was available for the world to see. The world, the whole world. The anonymity of a *nom de plume* or "handle" was of some comfort. It occurred to Jason that the backyard fence had become a circle. A conversation with a neighbor to the south could be joined by the neighbor to the north, the conversation coming full circle around the world and being enjoined by any one of millions of people. The question posed to Jesus by the lawyer, "Who is my neighbor?" came to mind. Was the answer today, "Anyone on the Internet?"

He did not log back on to the Internet until the next morning. When he clicked onto the Theology topic, his computer startled him by saying, "You have new mail." Sure enough, there were two responses addressed to his posting. From someone who identified himself as 1st Horseman:

PMFJI Perhaps I can help.

<< Was Jesus God from the beginning>>

Reading of Christ being declared the Son of God in the chronology as it is presented in Romans 1:4 might give the impression that He was deified at his resurrection, but He was not declared the Son of God at His resurrection. He was declared the Son of God before he was born in prophecy: Psalms 2:7. He was born God. He was conceived by the Holy Spirit: Matthew 1:19.

The clearest example of Christ's divinity is found in Isaiah 11:10-16, compare: Romans 15:12, Revelations 5:5, and Revelation 22:16. He returns to an already built temple: Malachi 3:1, see also Matthew 24:25, 2 Thessalonians 2:4, and Daniel 9:27.

Compare Him to the one who builds the temple to which He will return (and who is one of the two witnesses in Revelation 11:15 and Isaiah 11:4) in Isaiah 11:1-19: see Isaiah 11:1 and Zechariah 6:12. You will note that lesser one is a man, who is given spiritual powers, including the spirit of the Fear of the Lord. The greater One is not given any spiritual powers, He is God and already has all those powers.

His in Christ.

Jason noted that all the references to Jesus were capitalized. He also wondered what PMFJI meant. Internet jargon?

The other posting was to the 1st Horseman from a Philip Henson:

<< he was declared the son of God in prophecy: Psalm 2:27. He was born God. He was conceived by the Holy Spirit: Matthew 1:19>>

I don't know why you think the passages you quoted prove your point. You undermine your own point in the first of them by saying that it was a prophecy. The writer of the Psalm was speaking of a time then future—the fulfillment of which was spoken about by Paul in Rom. 1. Jesus was indeed declared to the son of God after his resurrection—he did not exist before his birth.

Matthew 1:19 (I presume you mean v.18) only says that

Mary was with child by the power of God. I don't know why you think this makes Jesus God? If miraculous birth marks the one born as God himself, then what about Isaac, Samson, Samuel, John the Baptist, etc.

So Jason had one response from one who believed in the John Christology, one who liked Paul's understanding. Good. It would be interesting to see why or how each one discounted the other's proof text. He crafted and sent a message to each. To 1st Horseman he wrote:

> Thank you for your response. Please translate PMFJI.
>
> If I grant for the moment that the passages you cite are proof texts for the existence of Jesus as Deity prior to the resurrection, how do you deal with (honor, acknowledge) the initial opening (can we say the underlying assumption?) on which Paul bases his Christology in the Book of Romans?
>
> Which begs a larger question. Assuming you have read the posting of Philip Henson, are your two Christologies, which appear to me to be far apart, close enough so that you and Mr. Henson can say you have faith in the same Jesus/God?
>
> RichJason

To Philip Henson:

> I take the liberty to respond to your response to 1st Horseman's response to my posting regarding the nature of the origin of the deity of Jesus.
>
> Your response did not address John 1:1. I would be pleased to hear how the Christology of John, that Jesus was from the beginning, fits into your faith system. If you read my posting to 1st Horseman of today, this all begs a bigger question and an important one. If I am correct in suggesting that align yourself with Paul's Christology and dismiss John's and can the three of us find a common ground as it relates to just who this Jesus was?
>
> RichJason

"Good-bye," the computer voice said as Jason disconnected from FACULTY ON-LINE. He checked on the weather. It was hazy and warm. It would be a great day for a football game. Michigan was hosting Minnesota for the Little Brown Jug, and it was homecoming. He looked forward to a relaxing day.

Michigan 28—Minnesota 14. The Little Brown Jug—an old crockery water jar which was the traveling trophy that was awarded to the winner—would remain in Ann Arbor for another year. The Michigan Glee Club and many of its alumni were part of a spectacular halftime show. They sang some of the songs that were uniquely University of Michigan songs. "College Days," "The Bum Army," "The Friars' Song," as well as "The Victors" and the "Yellow and Blue." The Glee Club had been on a world tour the summer past and had competed successfully in a competition in Scotland.

Jason had tried out for the Glee Club when he first came to Michigan. He had made it through the first tryout but then learned that he would need to purchase a tuxedo, the cost of which was three hundred dollars, which he didn't have. He didn't return for the second audition and had been sorry ever since.

During the game, it was typical for the stadium announcer to report scores of interest, including the score of the Slippery Rock Teachers' College game. The fans in the stadium broke into the biggest cheer of the afternoon when, amidst other scores, the announcer said, "A final score from East Lansing; "Michigan State Ten, Central Michigan Fourteen." Central Michigan was a member of the Mid-West Athletic Conference, which was made up of smaller schools that couldn't attract the best football talent, while Michigan State was a member of the Big Ten Conference, the biggest schools in the country with arguably some of the best talent in the country. Central wasn't thought to be in the same league as State, either actually or figuratively. Jason thought of his brother. Poor Willard, he would take this hard. And Jason's "sympathy" would compound the pain like iodine on a bad cut!

It wasn't until the walk home that it occurred to Jason that he had sat through the whole game without thinking about theology. Perhaps this part of his life was settling into its proper role. It was important, perhaps more important than he had acknowledged it to be before he met Runner—but not consuming.

He spent the rest of the day working on the "Length of Stay—Total Hip Replacements" study for the Controller's Office of the U of M Hospital. Because of his faculty status, he could dial into the University's network and call up the records he needed to work on the study from his apartment.

When he logged off the University's network, he remembered his posting on the Internet. He dialed into FACULTY ON-LINE and when he clicked onto the Theology topic. The now familiar voice said, "You have new mail." There was a numeral two in the mailbox icon. He clicked on the mailbox icon, and a response from 1st Horseman was displayed:

>   RichJason:

>   PMFJI stands for Pardon Me For Jumping In and is probably one of the more common abbreviations or "smileys" (which came about when modems were slower and access time was more expensive). G stands for grin, VBG for Very Big Grin, LOL for Lots of Laugh or Laugh Out Loud—used for making sure your reader knows your trying to be funny. IOW is "I Often Wonder." BTW is "By The Way." IMHO is "In My Humble Opinion" and my personal favorite, YOAPA which stands for "You Overly Affected Pompous Ass."

>   << the existence of Jesus as Deity prior to the resurrection, how do you deal with in initial opening (can we say the underlying assumption) upon which Paul bases his Christology in the Book of Romans>> Romans 1:4 refers to His resurrection as a declaration of His being the Son of God, not His being declared the Son of God at his resurrection. Since the wording of the verse could be read either way, I pointed to Psalms 2:7 to show that it wasn't at His resurrection He became the Son of God.

>   << Assuming you read the posting of Philip Henson, are your two Christologies close enough so that it could be said you have faith in the same Jesus/God>>

I don't know. I don't know if he was rejecting John 1:1 or merely thinking of Jesus in the flesh. It wasn't germane to His being the Son of God; so I didn't deal with it. If you would prefer to discuss this further, may I suggest Email for some privacy?

His in Christ.

## The other posting piece was from Philip Henson:

RichJason,

I reject that Psalms 2:7 has anything to do with proving the deity of Jesus.

As to John 1:1, it is commonly held that the Gospel of John was the latest of the Gospels, and was written toward the end of the first century, probably by John's disciples as indicated by the first person plural in John 21:24. It was written at a time when the Jewish followers of Jesus were in disrepute because He hadn't returned as promised and were being kicked out of the temple. John is written in reaction to this and therefore its Christology is, well... reactionary.

I believe the Christologies in John 1:1 and Romans 1:4 are in direct conflict. I believe Romans 1:4 is the Christology as developed by the early Church up to the time of Paul. I believe there is much scriptural evidence that the disciples were surprised by the resurrection, didn't expect it, and from it concluded that God was at work in this life, this man, Jesus.

Just who was Jesus was not clear to those who walked and talked with him. Some of the disciples (followers of James) kept the Jewish traditions thinking Jesus was the Messiah and the Messianic Age was at hand. Others clearly needed him to be God incarnate—the Jesus of John 1:1. Others believed Jesus was a human deified by God as Paul did.

With this divergence of opinion by those who were in the first century, I fail to see how anyone in our time can be absolutely certain who and what Jesus was by reading the writings of these same people.

I believe that the resurrection of Jesus was God's "YES" to the world's "NO," and, that Jesus' way and his teachings were affirmed by God by the resurrection. A pre-existent deity? No! None the less my God now? Yes!

Regards,

Philip Henson

Jason had two new unseen friends. Well, his Internet alter ego, RichJason, had two new friends. He decided to explore the mind of someone who would call himself "1st Horseman." He worked on a reply, which he sent off. It read:

1st Horseman:

I would prefer Email. Responses in the Forum postings are often not on point, less than well thought out, and sometimes downright vitriolic (and sometimes I suspect alcoholic).

I'm not sure your response to my question about Paul's Christology was answered fully. If you believe Scripture to be the literal word of God, why would God inspire Paul to make this statement in Romans 1:4?

It has been pointed out to me that often Christians collect all the proof text they can find for a certain position, as you seem to have done by quoting several verses that indicate a pre-existing deity, call that "the weight of the Scriptures," and then dismiss the verses that seem to indicate that at least one of the writers had a contrarian or varying understanding. We hang our systems on the "weight of the Scriptures" but dismiss the "measure" of the Scriptures.

Regards,

RichJason

Jason logged off FACULTY ON-LINE and logged on to the rest of the week.

On Monday, Jason had a progress meeting with Professor Playdon, his mentor on the Interrelational Report Requirement. He had printed up his outline and he assembled his notes and the paper that Visser had submitted several years earlier and showed up at Playdon's office on the tenth floor of the Business Administration tower at the appointed time.

Playdon was dressed as if he were headed for the golf course after their meeting, and it was in sharp contrast to Jason's khaki slacks and navy blue blazer. Jason was pleased that he had chosen not to wear a tie.

"Jason, nice you could come by. Please, take a chair. So, how are you coming on your research paper?" Playdon's bushy white eyebrows were arched and he had a knowing smile as if he knew something the whole world didn't and wished they did.

Jason began by giving Playdon a copy of his outline and began to present what he thought was important to a person in institutional living, his progress in interviewing his contact, and verifying the information he was being told by interviewing operational personnel at the home. Playdon was sitting on the edge of his desk in front of Jason and his eyes went from the outline to Jason and back as Jason talked.

When Jason finished, Playdon cleared his throat and lowered the paper. "How are you getting along with your Mr. Runner?" There was that knowing smile again. Did he know something? Jason guessed he did.

"Famously, I'd say. He's very widely read and I'm actually enjoying my visits. This has turned out to be a very interesting assignment."

"So I'm told." Playdon stood up and went around to the chair behind his desk. When he turned back toward Jason he was smiling. "The administrator from Christian Arbor phoned me. Apparently the staff there is concerned that you may be coming under some kind of spell. Is this man a witch?" Playdon was smiling broadly.

"Van Dam, the administrator, called you with concern for me?"

"Yes. I must say this kind of concern has never been expressed for any of our Fellows before. I also noted that this Friday is the full moon and, well, I wouldn't know how to explain to the Dean if we lost you. I decided to offer to accompany you if you think you're in any danger." Playdon's eyes were all a-twinkle and he appeared as if he was trying to keep from laughing.

"Well, you're certainly welcome to join me. But I hardly think I'm in any danger. I'm just so taken aback that Van Dam would call. I mean, I don't . . . did he really call? I'm sorry they bothered you about this. I'm, well . . . I don't know what to say."

"I'm not bothered at all. Just amused and more than a little curious as to who this Runner fellow is."

"He's a non-Christian biblical scholar or philosopher, or, well, I don't really know what he is, except that he's very well read and thoughtful, and an articulate man for his or any age.

"He occupies two rooms, one a sitting room and the other apparently a bedroom that is jammed with books. Physically, he is wheelchair-bound and a severe diabetic, which is why he's in the Home. As you know, the Home is owned and operated by a group of evangelical Protestant churches, and its residents and staff are drawn from these churches. I'm told that Runner's daughter was able to place him here because of her church affiliation, not his.

"The staff is nonplused by him. They see a responsibility to take care of him as well as save his soul, the latter a responsibility apparently shared by the other residents as well. I judge him to be a serious biblical scholar and a very intelligent man. Their difficulty is that he is able to use their Bible to refute their brand of orthodoxy."

"That's a unique twist. Using the Bible to refute orthodoxy. Interesting. But why do you suppose Van Dam has a fear for you?"

"There's a nursing supervisor who thinks Runner is the antichrist or the Devil incarnate. She knows I'm from the same evangelical tradition and she has demonstrated a concern—actually, she took me aside and warned me—that Runner is tempting me to fall from my faith."

"So how is the conversion or proselytizing of Jason Richards by the Devil incarnate coming along?"

"Well, ah . . ." Jason paused. This was getting altogether too personal and the whole thing was now blown way out of proportion. "It's true that Runner has challenged me to evaluate some of the tenants of my personal faith. But, frankly, my faith is my business and none of theirs. I'm too polite to tell her to butt out. Dr. Playdon, I . . ."

"Bill, remember?"

"Ah . . . yes. Jason paused. "Ah, no offense, Professor Playdon, but, frankly, I'm uncomfortable calling you 'Bill'."

"I'll not tolerate insubordination on this matter. As I said, Dr. Playdon makes me feel as old as I look, and I prefer to be thought of as young as I feel. Do we have an understanding, *Mister* Richards?"

Jason broke into a grin, "Yes, *Dr.* Playdon."

Dr. Playdon smiled knowingly, cocked his head, and thrust out his chin. "This is fascinating. If you don't mind, I'd like to meet this Mr. Runner. Besides, it's been some time since I've met with Van Dam and it would be good P.R. for the program and the school to stroke him. From what you say, Mr. Runner and I will get along just fine. Just fine . . . ."

This was an unexpected turn of events. "You're certainly more than welcome to come along. But, if you don't mind my asking, why do you think you'll have an affinity with Mr. Runner?"

Playdon folded his hands and put the pads of the forefingers of each hand together. He used them to prop up his chin as he thought for a moment. Jason intuitively felt the question had been invasive and wished he had not asked it. But Playdon began to speak.

"I too, consider myself to be a very thoughtful spiritual person. But I haven't been to a church service, other than the obligatory weddings and funerals, for over twenty years."

Playdon paused for a moment as if reaching back into ancient history. Then, looking away from Jason into space, he continued.

"I had been on the Vestry or Board of Trustees of my church for quite a period of time. Served as the treasurer for over fifteen years. But one day it occurred to me that what this particular church did was practice religion every Sunday, Sunday in and Sunday out. They practiced but they never got it right. I can still remember the sermon that woke me up, as it were. The minister was preaching an Advent sermon on the Song of Simeon and the Magnificat. It dawned on me that these two prognostications of the life and ministry of Christ foretold of a social gospel. Freeing the enslaved, sustenance to the poor, justice for the humble, and so forth. And Jesus' gospel was a loving the unloved, feeding the hungry, healing the sick, forgiving the transgressor, freedom from political bondage—ministry that bespoke of the grace of God to all humankind, but especially to the disenfranchised. In Jesus, the common folk could see the face and the heart of the eternal God who had interacted in history.

"In the early centuries, Christianity proclaimed this wonderful message. In his book *The Passion of the Western Mind*, Richard Tarnas calls it 'exultant Christianity.' Over the years, the Church turned that wonderfully uplifting vision of the role of Jesus into a message of Jesus' death as the vehicle to save wretched mankind—a creature incapable of any good thing—from the wrath of an avenging God. I hold Augustine to account for that. Nothing like a reformed drunken womanizer to turn sociability and the expression of love in sex into sinful debauchery.

"In order to hold their power over the laity, the Church dangled the keys of the door to Heaven. They bartered salvation for good behavior, their version of social order, and tithes. And my former church was no different. From my understanding of the Scriptures, I judged that we talked about Christianity and practiced religion when we should have been talking about religion and practicing Christianity.

"Just at that time, it happened one of my colleagues—an Ancient History Professor who specialized in the Roman Empire—who went to the same church, sought counseling from the senior pastor because he came to believe he was struggling with homosexuality. He was a married man but felt attraction toward a male graduate student." Playdon's gaze returned to the direction of Jason. "Do you know what the Mennonite practice of 'shunning' is?"

"Isn't that where a whole community is not allowed to communicate with a person who was fallen out of favor with the Church or community?"

"That's right. That's what happened to my friend. This was a mainline Protestant denomination, mind you." Playdon's gaze returned to somewhere in space. "The senior pastor violated the privilege of the confessional, spread the word that my dear friend was of questionable sexual preference and he was, well . . . 'shunned.' When I figured out what was going on, I paid a call on the minister and challenged him on it. He made two points with me. He asked me by what authority I questioned a man of God, and did I not believe the Scripture when it taught that homosexuality was an abomination?

"It was the opinion of this 'man of God' that my friend had fallen from God's grace and was no longer worthy of the church's concern. And all along, I had thought that those who were deemed to be outside of God's grace *were* the concern of the church. We spent a considerable portion of our annual budget supporting missionaries to save the souls of heathens around the world. But a long-time member of the church who may have been a homosexual was not worthy of our concern, and moreover, was to be scorned. I walked out of his study, out of that church building, and out of the Church. For all practical purposes, I haven't been back.

Playdon's gaze returned to Jason. "I believe I'm a deeply spiritual person. I believe I have a close, personal relationship with God as revealed through Jesus Christ. But I no longer practice religion as I once did, and I cannot abide those whose professions of faith are justifications for their brand of intolerance."

"What ever happened to your friend," Jason asked.

"My dear friend had more problems with the rumors about his sexuality spread by his good Christian friends than he did about his identity. He told me that he was able to shed any guilt he felt about his struggle when he learned the servant of the Centurion that Jesus healed in the New Testament was described as 'very special friend.' From his academic discipline, he knew that many Roman Centurions were homosexuals. He felt that if Jesus did not condemn the Centurion, and further went out of his way to heal his 'very special friend', this minister, this 'man of God' had no business condemning him for the questions he had."

Jason wondered how many of Professor Emeritus William A Playdon's students or associates had heard that story. Better yet, why did he choose to tell it to me, Jason thought. He caught himself pressing his lips together in a half-grimace and nodding his head as if he were approving. Runner would like Playdon very much, he guessed.

"I think you and Howard Runner will get along just fine. And I'd be honored if you'd accompany me. It's my turn to spring for lunch, and we've decided it would be steamed shrimp from Dominic's. Does that suit you?"

"Lord have mercy, that's a religious experience all by itself. I'll be honored to commune with you, your Mr. Runner, and Joe Dominic's steamed shrimp."

"Can I pick you up here, say eleven forty-five on Friday next?"

"I look forward to it. By the way, have you had any luck in getting a peek at the Home's financial statements?"

"Van Dam said he had to get Board permission. They don't meet until just before Christmas. Frankly, I won't have time to do much with them, and I got the distinct impression that that would sit just as well with Van Dam."

"Mmmh. He's being true to form, if I recall correctly. That's the tactic he used with your predecessor. I'll call Van Dam back and ask to see him during our visit. Maybe we can get those financials with an end run, what do you say?"

# Chapter Eleven

It wasn't until Wednesday that Jason received an email from the 1st Horseman. It read:

> RichJason:
>
> < I'm not sure your response to my question about Paul's Christology was answered fully. If, as you say, Scripture is the literal word of God, why would God inspire Paul to make this statement in Romans 1:4>>
>
> Until now, I didn't really understand your question, but I think I do now. In which case I hadn't answered it. I see Scripture to say He was and is God, not that He became God at some point in his ministry.
>
> I see Romans 1:4 as "a" declaration, and I think you see it as "the" declaration. Another declaration is recorded in Matthew 3:17 where the voice of God from heaven declares, "This is My Beloved Son, in whom I am well pleased," which some read to say He became the Son of God as the Holy Spirit rested on Him. John 1:1 tells us He was God at the beginning.
>
> <<call that "the weight of the Scriptures," and then dismiss the verses that seem to indicate that at least one of the writers had a contrarian or varying understanding. We hang our systems on the "weight of the Scriptures" but dismiss the "measure" of the Scriptures>>
>
> More often a number of Scriptures together provide limits and bounds to what is being presented to us where what is being presented is limited by all of them. If Romans 1:4 stood alone, it would seem that Christ became the Son of God upon his resurrection. But often the Scriptures are repetitive for clarification or to emphasize a point. In the case of Romans 1:4, the repetitive declarations show that is was "a" declaration, not "the" declaration.
>
> In short, I feel that using multiple scriptures isn't applying the "weight" of the Scripture but applying the "measure" of each of the Scriptures, but when scriptures

are identical it appears that the extra "measures" carry more "weight."

His,

Well, well, thought Jason, you chose not to answer the question as to what do you do with the verses that seem to be in contradiction. You don't think contradictions are additive. His thoughts were interrupted by the ringing of the telephone.

"Hello."

"Jason? Willard. I'm concerned about you. You must be busy not to call and hassle me about State's losing to Central Michigan."

"Will, if I thought there was anything I could say to make you feel worse, I would've called."

"Nice, real nice."

"Were you there? Did you get to live through it play-by-play?"

"Play by agonizing play. We were pathetic and they played their hearts out. Actually, it was hard not to root for Central. It was David and Goliath all over again."

"I thought about you, believe me!"

"I'm sure you did. Listen, I have a line on two free tickets to see the Red Wings this Saturday afternoon. Karen has a bridal shower for one of her nieces. Care to go?"

"Where are the tickets?"

"What do you mean, where are the tickets? If they're in nose bleed heaven, you gonna turn 'em down?"

"Oh, I don't care where the tickets are located, I just don't want you to have to sit next to some Central Michigan graduate who'd be all over your green-and-white case. I know how you feel and I'd hate to have to sit next to you if you're going to be blubbering all through the game. Can you check out who's sitting next to us?"

"Yeah, right. These happen to be in the Security First Underwriter's suite. We'll be with some big hitters in the insurance industry. Think you can behave? Be sure to bring a handkerchief."

"A handkerchief?"

"Yeah, I don't want you to embarrass me by picking your nose or sneezing into your hand. I heard lots of U of M grads do that."

"I think it's just a passing fancy. It was nice of you to notice, though. Willard, jealousy doesn't become you. You should get some counseling so you can wear your academic inferiority complex with a little more grace. Is that all or am I going to have to listen to your jealous ranklings the whole trip?"

"I'll be by your place about ten in the morning."

"I'll be ready."

"Bring your Bible?"

"To a hockey game?"

"I thought you would be more comfortable with it. You brought it to the last football game we went to. Seriously, there *is* something I want to talk about."

"Okay, see you at ten on Saturday."

"Good, and get a couple of Mrs. Langfurd's sticky buns for a pre-game snack."

"It's Mrs. Lundsaford's, and consider it done."

"See you Saturday."

"Bye."

Jason hung up the phone. Bring my Bible? To a hockey game? Damn! Religion to the right of him, religion to the left of him. Right religion, left religion. He didn't think he could be more involved in theology if he were in seminary. Was this his retribution for not going into what his minister had called "kingdom service"?

✣

The week went by quickly and Jason had little time to give much thought to the Friday meeting with Howard Runner and Professor Playdon. The purpose of the visit from Jason's point of view was to review the functionality of the physical plant with Runner, have Playdon meet Runner, and have a short visit with the Administrator, Van Dam. Jason called Runner to say he would be bringing his mentoring professor along for the Friday luncheon meeting.

While Jason was sure Runner and Playdon would get along, he wondered about Playdon and Van Dam, especially about Van Dam's call to Playdon. Strange he would call unless he was dissatisfied somehow with Jason's interaction with Runner or Head Nurse Veeringa. But Jason reviewed his conversations and unless the Head Nurse was being obtuse, there was nothing unseemly about her except her exasperation with Runner. Jason sensed that had been going on for some time before his arrival on the scene and would go on long after he left.

He ordered two and a half pounds of steamed shrimp, two loaves of garlic bread, and three individual salads to go and picked them up just after 11:30. The aroma filled his car before he went the half-block to the Bus. Ad. Building. He parked in the faculty ramp and headed for the tower that held the office of the faculty. Professor Playdon was in the lobby talking to Dean Nixon when Jason entered the building.

Dean Nixon saw Jason enter and waved him over to where he and Playdon were standing. "Good morning, Jason. So the two of you are off to visit one of our Interrelational institutions. Do they have any idea of the horsepower the two of you represent?"

"Jason's all the horsepower we need. I'm just going along for the ride. I might sneak in a question or two for their administrator for the article that Jason and I are corroborating on for the *Hospital Administration Monthly*. This program's generated a considerable interest in our field. It's unique, you know, and the Davidson Fellows who have left have distinguished themselves. David Pott over at Cleveland General, and Sam Greenberg at Mount Sinai, and I believe Roger Reyburn was just promoted at St. Judes'. I believe we have a warm lunch to pick up, so we best be going, right, Jason? Dean Nixon."

Dean Nixon was all polish and politeness, "Good luck, gentlemen. I'll be interested in your article when it comes to the publication committee."

When they got to Jason's car and opened the doors, the pungent smell of the spicy steamed shrimp and the warm garlic bread hit them. "Ah, you picked our lunch up already! Isn't that a wonderful aroma," Playdon said. "A person could improve his fluency in Italian by just ingesting the smell."

"We'll hurry over to the nursing home before they get cold."

When they got to the Christian Arbor Home, Jason carried the bags and boxes containing the lunch. Playdon carried Jason's briefcase and a small leather-bound notepad, which appeared to contain a legal pad.

As they entered the Home, they were greeted by the usual women in waiting, including the woman wearing purple. They stared as one at Professor Playdon. A new resident perhaps?

Jason led the way to Howard Runner's suite. The door was open, and there was a round table in the middle of the room set with a tablecloth and three place settings. Pachelbel's Fugue in D Minor being played by a harpist was softly coming out of the sound system in the room. Runner looked up when Jason knocked on the door casing.

"Jason, Jason, come right in. Well, well, well. Professor Playdon, this is a pleasant surprise. Ah . . ." Runner was clearly surprised by the appearance of Playdon. "Ah . . . please come in. Come in. Jason indicated his mentor was coming along, but I had no idea it would be you. Here, set your things on the end table there. Jason, you can put lunch on the table here."

Jason was startled. "Mr. Runner, you know Professor Playdon?"

"One doesn't attend the U of M Business School and not know of Professor William A. Playdon. Many years ago, I had the distinct honor of sitting under your tutelage in Accounting . . . uh . . . 501 and 502." Runner had paused as if he were confused about the course numbers or something. Then, "You'll forgive me, Professor. Accounting was not my strong suit, but it was one of those degree requirements, and I had a devil of a time with it. I think the trouble I had was that your text had no pictures or diagrams and few examples. Electrical Engineers need diagrams and pictures or they're lost. But you got me through it and the understanding I received held me in good stead later when I needed to be able to read and understand my own company's financial statements."

Jason had been watching Runner at first, astounded that he knew Professor Playdon. And when he looked back at Playdon, he noticed that Playdon appeared puzzled.

"Mr. Runner?" Playdon came around the table and extend his hand. "I apologize, but I don't remember that we've met. You were a graduate student at the Bus. Ad. School?"

"For a time beginning in the late fifties, the Engine School had a program where you could get a combined Master's Degree in Engineering and Business. I went through the first class on that track. Received my Masters in Electrical and Business in 1964."

Jason busied himself setting up the lunch while Runner and Playdon reminisced.

Runner continued, "I remember sitting in a large classroom along Tappan Avenue with about a hundred other students—about twenty of us graduate students, the rest juniors in undergraduate school. One of the most memorable experiences was sitting in the room waiting to take the final exam and Gerald O. Dykstra poking his head in the door. He looked around and mounted the raised platform at the front, went to the board and wrote, 'Good luck, fellows. Signed GOD.' As I recall, it didn't help me much."

Playdon's demeanor still seemed to be one of puzzlement. "I remember the incident. Dykstra was Business Law, as you know. His Hamburger lectures on bailments were legendary. So . . . you were once a student of mine? I confess I don't remember you, but those 301/501 sections were large." Playdon paused, his puzzlement seemed to have passed. He continued, "So, how are you getting along with my young associate, Mr. Richards here?"

"I look forward to his visits. If one has one's wits about oneself, these are damnable places in which to live. I read a fair amount, but there are few here with whom one can talk about anything but the Detroit Tigers or the Lions if it's fall. If you're unfortunate enough to be accosted by a woman, have your list of aches and pains at the ready for discussion.

"Jason has been a refreshing change. He doesn't talk about the Tigers, and I don't have to talk about his aches and pains. But enough talk for the moment. We should attack these shrimp before they get cold. Help yourselves to iced tea or I have a pot of hot tea here if you prefer?"

Jason portioned out the shrimp and the garlic bread and poured iced tea around. "*Bon appetite*, gentlemen."

They all began to peel and eat. Runner was the first to pause and speak. "Professor Playdon, I feel . . ."

"Could we agree," Playdon interrupted, "that communion over the Joe Dominic's shrimp should be done on a first name basis? Our young friend here cannot seem to make his mouth formulate the word 'Bill', but, please, call me Bill."

"Yes. Bill. As I was saying, I feel it necessary to warn you, if

Jason hasn't, that this institution is infested with well-meaning souls who feel incumbent to save your soul. Most likely, we'll be set upon by one or more of these whose pretense will be to empty the trash or fluff the pillow. They'll then warn you that I'm the First Wheelman of the Apocalypse and conversation with me will surely damn your soul to Hell. If you engage them, they will be encouraged. Do so at your own risk."

"Interesting that you should bring that up. Actually Mr. Van Dam, the administrator, phoned me to indicate some concern for Jason's well-being. There was an implication that Jason's study was involving him with a cultist at best and perhaps witchcraft. In as much I have never seen a witch or an exorcism, it piqued my intellectual curiosity. I must say, I'm disappointed in you, Howard. I expected to see smoke coming out of your ears when you spoke and the room to smell of sulfur. Instead, I find you were a student of mine and, perhaps, by association, I can be accused of filling your head with whatever tripe they're accusing you of espousing. You said you had a *devil* of a time with accounting, didn't you?"

Runner was amused. "In that phone call you have the sum and substance of what's fundamentally wrong here. They concern themselves with externals and ignore that the place crumbles in about them. I don't suppose Van Dam asked you to help them with their antiquated accounting system? Would you believe I have the only computer in the building? I've offered to buy the home a computer and an accounting software package so they could better track their costs and revenues.

"Van Dam says he has his own system and he doesn't need any of these newfangled systems. In the meantime, I believe they forego thousands of dollars of potential revenue because they can't differentiate their costs between residents in supportive care, like myself, and those who require skilled nursing. I can look at the rates they charge and count the number of employees per resident and see their billing rates are not matched to their costs. It doesn't make sense. Then Van Dam has the world's foremost accounting authority on the phone, and he consults as to whether young Jason here is being bewitched."

Playdon chuckled, "Sounds like more than a little of the accounting I threw at you stuck. Jason, would you mind pouring me more iced tea? These shrimp are delicious, but they make a man thirsty."

"I believe our meeting today was to discuss the physical plant, was it not?"

"That's on my agenda, if you care to talk about it," Jason said.

"Well, the mechanical systems in this place are a pet peeve of mine. The heating in the building is a circulating hot water system fed by a gas-fired boiler. The system was designed so that the individual room controls were operated by a hand-turned valve located at the heating unit in each room. Jason, would you please pass the bread? Thank you. Anyone else for bread?"

Runner continued, "Individual room controls. Good in theory. But they didn't invest in a water purifying system and the water delivered by the city comes out of the Huron River. It contains a high amount of ferric oxide. Rust. These pipes have become clogged with rust and other mineral deposits to the point where they have to increase the pressure to get hot water to all the rooms. Open the valve a little bit and high pressure generates a large volume into the heater with the consequence that the system overheats the room.

"In addition, the valves are old. Many of them are permanently stuck in the open position. Others, like mine, are placed where I can't reach them even if it did work, because I can't get to it from the chair. When I first came here, the ambient temperature was eighty-six degrees in this room, sixty-nine in the other room. I bought a small fan and circulated the warm air to the cool room. But if I only had one room, I'd either be hot or cold.

"Then there's the problem of the seasons. The boiler requires a three-day start-up and a three-day shutdown period. So, if there's either a warm spell in the winter or a cold spell in the summer, it's handled with iced tea or long underwear."

Runner paused and offered more iced tea, which was accepted.

It was Playdon who spoke next. "I notice you have a thermostat near your heating element, what does it do?"

Jason had not noticed a small box that looked like a small alarm clock with large red LED numbers mounted to the wall above the heating element until Playdon directed their attention to it. Its numbers read "70."

"Aha! The first time the system was shut down, I had a plumber come in and install an electronically controlled valve and hooked it up to that thermostat. He first had to install a larger pipe to act as a manifold so that it would be easier to control the volume of water entering the heating element under this higher pressure. Gentlemen, I'm proud to say this is the closest thing to climate control you'll find in this building."

"But how do you reach that thermostat from your chair?"

Runner got a glint in those blue eyes as he pushed his wheelchair back and spun toward the cherry secretary and picked up what Jason had thought was Runner's remote control TV changer. He held it in the direction of the CD player and clicked a button and the CD player shut off. Another click and the player came back on. He turned it toward the thermostat and clicked it again and the LED display changed from seventy to seventy-one to seventy-two. He clicked another button and the display returned to seventy-one, then seventy.

"I've adapted the same technology used in a TV remote control to control my thermostat," Runner said matter-of-factly, as if he were showing someone a No. 2 lead pencil.

"I think Van Dam may be right about you Howard. That *is* witchcraft!" There was a note of awe in Playdon's voice. "Have you thought to market this?"

"My company looked into it but our market research indicated people didn't change the temperature setting often enough for one thing. For another, the thermostat was being accidentally activated too often. In addition, the technology isn't proprietary, so if it proved successful in the marketplace, you'd find yourself competing with inexpensive imitations before you could say your name twice. It wasn't worth it, but it has brought me a measure of comfort."

Jason asked the obvious question, "So why doesn't the Home install these regulators in all the rooms."

"They say they can't afford it, and it's not a state licensing requirement to have individual temperature controls in every room. I suggested they could raise the entry fee by two hundred dollars and convert the valves as new people came in. The Board's response was they thought that would be unfair for those people who were already here."

They had finished the last of the shrimp and garlic bread and Runner began to clear the table by piling plates atop one another. Playdon had leaned back in his chair and spoke. "Tell me, Howard, overall, how do you like it here?"

"Overall . . . I don't. The atmosphere is oppressive, almost mean-spirited, unless you're one of the elect, that is—chosen of God for salvation. The food is prepared with little or no concern for its nutritional value, the recreation revolves around hymn sings and their definition of bible study. I love to play bridge, but playing bridge requires the use of bridge decks, which are referred to in this place as 'devil cards', so Rook and Uno are the card games of choice here. Then of course there is 'Bible Lotto', which is the Home's equivalent to Bingo. But, sadly, when you're in my position, your lifestyle choices are limited."

"Have you thought about seeking a place that might be more amenable, less parochial?"

"Ah, but this Home needs money. I have a little. I can afford to rent the second room in which to house my library. This is the only Home in the area I can do this. I gladly trade the oppressive atmosphere for the freedom to retain my library."

"That I understand. I can see through the door you have an extensive collection. Not all accounting books, I presume," Playdon said with a chuckle.

"Mostly witchcraft." Runner's grin crinkled up his face and the blue eyes fairly danced. "A few philosophy books and some works of note in the field of theoretical electronics. But mostly witchcraft."

"From what Jason has told me and from what you've said, apparently you're at some odds with whatever brand of orthodoxy this tradition espouses. In as much as religious beliefs are usually somewhat personal, how did your, ah, brand of witchcraft come to be commonly known here."

Runner shifted in his wheelchair before beginning. "Interesting tale. The first week the recreational director saw it as her responsibility to push me to get involved and the first recreational opportunity that presented itself was Wednesday night bible study, led by a local minister who is nearing retirement, a Reverend Werkman. And while these folks claim to read and interpret the Bible literally, I didn't feel he was interpreting the particular passage we were studying literally or honestly. Unfortunately, he made the mistake of asking my opinion about the unity of the Scriptures. I said I thought the Scriptures had a wax nose."

Playdon laughed out loud.

"Reverend Werkman was taken aback at first. Asked what I meant. I explained that I found the Scriptures to be a diverse witness. Often unclear and sometimes opposing viewpoints could be supported from the Scriptures. You see, I had the mistaken notion that this gathering was to be what it claimed to be—a bible study, with study meaning the search for knowledge and understanding.

Perhaps even truth, maybe even *The* Truth."

"The only truth was in that I was *truly* mistaken. The Right Reverend Werkman was gravely offended, and there was righteous indignation in his voice. He called my comment about the Bible having a wax nose into serious question. He labeled the statement 'offensive to right-thinking Christians', as I remember his words.

"I indicated his quarrel was not with me, but with Martin Luther. Those were Luther's words. I merely borrowed them for the evening. He questioned my source; I questioned his scholarship. My reputation as the Devil incarnate—as the Head Nurse here calls me—was born and, as you know, seeds well-planted need little encouragement. I later learned that his credentials *were* questionable. He had passed through the seminary on C-plus grace. I had unwittingly touched a sensitive nerve. But, in spite of his questionable scholarship and the pap he preaches, he continues to be the chaplain here and pastor a small congregation nearby—largely because he is sincere and with this crowd, sincerity goes a long way. A lot farther than scholarship."

"To what do you attribute that?"

"The theology of this particular tradition harkens back to the sixteenth century, and the great statements of the reformation. The Heidelberg Catechism, the Canons of Dordt, the Belgic Confession, were all wonderful defining statements of faith for their time. They spoke eloquently and with great clarity of the principles of the reformation. And if the world had not changed in the five centuries since, they would still be operative. But the world has changed and this tradition, by and large, does not acknowledge the change.

"For them, it's as if the Enlightenment happened in a different culture. They do not acknowledge that Nietzsche, Hume, Marx, or Descartes existed or that their questions were ever asked. Modern man, however, thinks with a post-Enlightenment mind. The Enlightenment has influenced our culture, whether we acknowledge it or not. This is the culture into which the present day Church must witness and be an influence. But their answers are to sixteenth century questions."

"And not many people have sixteenth century questions?" Playdon rejoined.

"Exactly. So year after year, the Church's membership numbers dwindle. They wring their collective hands and wonder how they can influence the world. Their evangelistic endeavors increase, but they don't realize that they are trying to feed fish to horses and the horses aren't eating." Runner paused to take a long draft of his iced tea. He savored it, then he continued.

"At the moment, one of the nurses and I are going round and round on the question of whether salvation is only available through a personal reliance on the mediation of Jesus Christ. This tradition maintains a very exclusivist position that there is no other way to attain a heavenly reward in life after death.

"These discussions, if one can call them that, came about after her repeated and unsuccessful attempts to save my soul and make me religious. They can't figure me out, and the fact that I don't think like they do and question their beliefs is a burden they carry like a great weight. They wish they could unload me.

"She was not at all pleased when I asked her if it was her mission to get me into heaven, wouldn't she welcome the idea that there might be more people in heaven than her exclusivist position allowed for?" Runner paused to shift his weight in the wheelchair again.

Salvation by Christ alone was one of the tenants of the tradition from which Jason came. A number of bible verses came to mind that clearly indicated that. He decided this was not a moment he could let pass without some rejoinder. "There are a number of bible verses that would seem to be on this point. How do you read, 'There is no other name under heaven given among men whereby we must be saved'?"

Runner turned as Jason asked the question. "That's taken from Peter's speech to the Sanhedrin, shortly after Pentecost, I believe. Peter and John had healed a lame man and the Sanhedrin had arrested them and asked them by what power or by what name they had healed the man. I think Peter's statement is quite true. There *is* no other name given among men, that is, no other human being, through which humanity can see the face of God.

"My question to you is, does Peter's proclamation preempt God from saving souls directly through His own love and grace—His devout followers who call on His name? As I said, this passage would seem to indicate that Jesus was unique on the human scene and that through this life Christians have a window to see into the heart of God. But, again, does God give up His prerogative to love and save other of His devout children who may not have heard of Christ? Does God owe obeisance to Peter's pronouncement?"

Jason hesitated but was not deterred. "What about the account of Jesus saying, 'I am the way, the truth, and the life. No man cometh unto the Father but by me'?" As he spoke, he sneaked a glance at Playdon, who was listening intently, hand clasping his chin like Rodin's *Thinker*.

"Ah, yes! Three things about that verse. First, in that passage, which I believe is in the Book of John, chapter fourteen, verse six, Jesus is having an intimate discussion with his disciples. A particular discussion, with particular people, at a particular time. I think it's a fallacy to draw a *universal* conclusion from a *particular*. I would say, therefore, it is dangerous to conclude that these particular words apply universally, to all people, for all time.

"Second, in the next few verses, Jesus seems to indicate a more inclusive salvation and not one gained by belief in Jesus as redeemer, but by doing the will of the Father and obeying the commandments. Get the New English Bible there, Jason. But wait," Runner held up his hand to restrain Jason from getting up. "I fear we're boring our distinguished guest with this discussion. Are we Bill?"

Playdon straightened a bit in his chair. "Not at all! I'm fascinated by this particular brand of witchcraft. A witch that quotes Scripture? No, please go on, I'm interested in where you're going with this."

"Good! Jason, read the part beginning after Jesus rebukes Thomas," Runner said.

Jason had gotten the Bible from its customary position and found the passage. "*In truth, in very truth I tell you, he who has faith in me will do what I am doing; and he will do greater things still because I am going to the Father. Indeed anything you ask in my name I will do so that the Father may be glorified in the Son. If you ask anything in my name I will do it . . .*"

"See!" Runner interrupted. "There's an indication that to be a follower of Jesus, you're not a believer, you're a doer. One must follow the example, the way of Jesus, not the theology. Read on, Jason, if you will."

"*If you love me, you will obey my commandments . . .*"

"There it is again. What is it to love Jesus? Obey his commandments. Now, Jason, skip to the place where Judas asks Jesus a question. It's five or six verses farther."

"*Judas asked him—the other Judas, not Iscariot—Lord, what can have happened, that you mean to disclose yourself to us alone and not to the whole world . . .*"

"Stop. Can you hear the question? Judas is asking whether this good news is just for Jesus' acquaintances. Continue reading, if you please." Runner was acting as if he couldn't wait for the next verse, like it contained some new and startling revelation never before heard.

"*Jesus replied, 'Anyone who loves me will heed what I say, and my Father will love him, and we will come to him . . .*"

Runner had interrupted again. "There. Who is it that loves Jesus? From the earlier verse, one who does his commandments.

And what is the reward for doing the commandments? Anyone in the world that obeys the commandments will be loved by the Father. From Jesus' own words, the Father loves a doer, anyone who does or keeps his commandments. It raises a question in my mind whether it's one's belief in Jesus' death as a mediation for sins or is it one's obedience to the commandments of God that is the means of attaining the blessing of eternal life?

"Third, earlier, in the same chapter, mind you, Jesus says, '*In my father's house are many mansions . . . I go to prepare a place for you.*' That indicates to me that Jesus thought there were mansions for other folks than those whose understandings were based on Jesus' way.

"I don't denigrate the nurse's concept of salvation through a belief in Christ. But while her tradition demands it, her scriptures do not. This same Peter that you quoted a moment ago, when he was called to Cornelius the centurion said, '*I now see how true it is that God has no favorites, but that in every nation the man who is godfearing and does what is right is acceptable to him.*' I believe that the possibility that God's grace is much broader than the exclusivist position the Church postulated in the sixteenth century is raised in their scriptures.

"And a further point, these folks hold that God doesn't change, they say one of His attributes is that He is immutable, changeless. Then it seems to me an interesting question is did He revoke His covenant with the Jews? Could He revoke it? Are the promises of God revocable? Can God change? And an even more distasteful contemplation to these folk regards the recognition that the descendants of Hagar and Ishmael may be included in those descendants to whom God promised Abram to be a God.

"Paul was quite clear in the eleventh chapter of his letter to the Romans that the whole of Israel will be saved because they are God's friends for the sake of the patriarchs. Paul says, '*For the gracious gifts of God and his calling are irrevocable.*' My nurse argues if anyone believes that the door to heaven can be opened just a crack farther than salvation through Christ alone, that person is evil and condemned to Hell. That's a logic that I cannot, for the life of me, follow, and which, I believe, condemns both Peter and Paul to the same end to which they condemn me.

"I find this particularly troublesome as we approach the end of the twentieth century when mankind has become a global family. We wonder why governments cannot get along in peace when many in the Church cannot find it in their hearts to talk to those of other faith traditions. They condemn them to Hell, regardless of their devotion to the same God.

"In the sixteenth century, the question of a global community wasn't an issue. In fact, it wasn't given serious consideration until a Fordham University professor, Cousins was his name, wrote a book called *Christ of the Twenty-First Century*. I have it somewhere in there. He was the first serious Christian scholar to talk about global consciousness. But because the issue wasn't addressed in the sixteenth century, this brand of orthodoxy feels it's of no importance. They will not be dragged into the twentieth century."

Playdon had been sitting back, listening intently. He leaned forward and said, "Your description of this kind of orthodoxy reminds me of something I read several years ago. I think it was Marshall McLuhan, a thinker who was the first social commentator to recognize the importance the media would play in our lives. He said, 'we are rushing headlong into the future with our eyes firmly fixed on the rear-view mirror.'"

"*That* is it exactly," Runner responded, smiling broadly.

Playdon continued, "I'm old enough to remember the split up of the Presbyterian Church in the early 1920s. I don't remember all the reasons for the split. There was a controversy over the virgin birth and the infallibility of the Scriptures. And I don't remember *all* the leaders, but I remember William Jennings Bryan and a fellow by the name of Machen, I think it was. But what I do remember is that before the split up, the Presbyterian Church was a very powerful force on the American scene. It's no exaggeration to say that presidents consulted with the leadership of the Presbyterian Church before making decisions that affected the moral standards of society. They were influential in the passage of prohibition and blue laws.

"After the breakup, their influence was gone. They were powerless to stop the repeal of prohibition, for example. Some say they lost their influence because they were fractionalized, others postulated that their inability to settle their theological differences rendered them unfit to stand as a social conscience.

"In some measure, that breakup was the precursor to the erosion of the influence of the Church—to the point where now we have no societal moral standards and nowhere to go to look for standards. Society has lost confidence in the fractious Protestant Church and the Roman Church doesn't address many of the issues we face today.

"There was a time, not so many years ago, when a philanderer would not be considered fit for the presidency. I point to Gary Hart, whose dalliance put him out of the running as a candidate for the Democratic Party. These days it would appear to be politically incorrect to hold a candidate to any standard of character, need I call William Jefferson Clinton to mind? But enough of the ruminations of an old man." Playdon put his hands on the arms of his chair and leaned forward as if to rise. "Howard, this has truly been my pleasure. A great lunch, good company, stimulating conversation, I hope we can do this again some time." And with that, Playdon pushed himself to his feet and leaned over the table to shake Runner's hand.

"I'm happy you could accompany my young friend," Runner returned. "I hope I didn't bore you with my disenchantment with those who brand me a witch. They're well-meaning folk, and I don't cast aspersions on their intentions, only their persistence and their unwillingness to consider the possibility that others may find their joy in a different understanding of the Truth."

Playdon moved to go. "I quite agree. Jason, why don't you finish up with Mr. Runner here while I pay my respects to Mr. Van Dam and assure him that Davidson Fellows were selected for their ability to withstand the effects of witchcraft? Stop by and fetch me from Van Dam's office on your way out, would you? Good day to you, Howard," and he disappeared in the direction of the lobby and Van Dam's office.

"Well, well, Jason, you didn't tell me you would be accompanied the esteemed Professor William A. Playdon. He was a legend thirty-five years ago. I suspect he's attained the accounting equivalent of sainthood by now."

"I can't tell you how honored I am to have him as my mentor on this project. I confess to being more than a little apprehensive, but he is, well, grandfatherly. He's writing an article for the *Hospital Administration Monthly* about the Interreactional Requirement Program, which is the research paper that brings me here. Apparently, researching a care facility from the perspective of the patient has attracted national attention in the discipline. He's using some of the material I'm generating for the article, so I may get a footnote mention."

"Well, good for you. I'd like to see a copy of that article when it gets published."

They talked more about the physical plant, the lack of proper return air ventilation and some structural problems that prevented installing the proper exhaust systems in the kitchen. After about fifteen minutes, his questions satisfied, Jason bid good-bye and headed in the direction of the lobby and Van Dam's office. He could hear the lobby was abuzz until he entered and the talking and whispering stopped. Again, Jason felt as if he were the entertainment for the day. The purple lady was still there along with several others. He went to the matronly lady at the reception desk and asked for Mr. Van Dam.

The receptionist struggled to her feet and made her way to the connecting door to Van Dam's office. She went partway in and announced, "The young man is here."

Van Dam and Playdon came through Van Dam's door that opened onto the lobby. They were both smiling like they had just sealed a lucrative business deal. Van Dam's bigger-than-life voice was saying, " . . . any time at all. We're pleased to have you and be a part of this program. Our Board is looking forward to Mr. Richard's report."

"It's purely advisory, you understand, but most of the institutions find the report of interest. On behalf of the Bus. Ad. School, we are pleased for your continued participation in the plan. Thanks again for your time," Playdon said as they shook hands.

The ladies in waiting spoke not a word but took it all in as if they were watching a stage play. In that case, Jason thought, exit stage right, Professor Playdon, to what I'm sure will be a sitting ovation from a grateful audience. You may be the only entertainment offered today.

The sun was shining brightly, and it lit up the blazing fall colors as they exited the building.

Jason was the first to speak, as Playdon seemed to be engrossed in thought as they walked toward the parking lot. "Well, I hope this was as profitable a visit as you hoped for."

"Very profitable for the School, and very interesting." He offered nothing more.

"Did you get around to asking about the financial statements?"

"I got the same chapter of the run-around you got, only the second verse."

"At least you and Runner seemed to have some things in common."

"Yes, Jason. Yes, we did. But his name is not Howard Runner."

# Chapter Twelve

It took a few steps for what Playdon said to register with Jason. Runner's name is not Runner? What? "I beg your pardon?" The bewilderment came out of Jason's mouth in a blurt.

Playdon kept a steady pace toward the car, walking with his hands in his pockets and his head down, as if he were in deep thought. "I don't know who he is, but his name is not Runner. I judge this man to be about my age, plus or minus five years. I've had master's degree students that were my age, but not that many. I don't pretend to remember every student I've had in forty years of teaching, but my mother's maiden name was Runner. I would have taken note of a student my age whose name was Runner. This man's name, when he took my class, if he took my class, wasn't Runner."

Playdon stopped and looked at Jason. "How does that strike you?"

Right between the eyes? Jason thought he sensed a headache coming on. "*If* he took your class? You think perhaps he didn't?"

"Oh, on reflection I think he did. Lectures for Intro 501 were usually in one of the large lecture halls along Tappan Avenue and the 'Good Luck from GOD' was something that Gerry Dykstra was known to do from time to time. But I can assure this man's name was not Runner at the time."

They were approaching Jason's Honda. Jason punched the key fob to unlock the passenger door for Playdon and went around to his side of the car. Judas Priest, he thought, what have I gotten myself into? Jason got in and buckled up, but he didn't start the car. There was an obvious question. "What does this do for the validity of my paper?" What it might do for his fellowship went unasked for the time being.

"What do you mean?"

"If Runner's not who he says he is, how much can I rely on what he says? Further, is the research done with him as the contact or control valid?"

"What have you done to validate what he's told you about the Home?"

Jason thought for a moment. He mentally reviewed what he had done so far: conversations Van Dam; with the maintenance man, Schuring; he had eaten a meal and talked to the woman who was the Home's nutritionist/cook; and he had seen Runner's interaction with both the residents and the staff. Almost everything Runner, or whoever he was, had told him had been validated by someone else on the staff or in the Home. His answer to Playdon was, "Virtually everything. And there has been nothing, absolutely nothing, to cause me to question his integrity until now."

Playdon smiled benevolently. "That's good. I'm not sure changing one's name indicates a lack of integrity or nefarious intent. Consider where Marion Michael Morrison's career in the movies would have gone if he had not changed his name to John Wayne. None the less, it piques one's curiosity, does it not?"

"That's an understatement." Jason started the car and began to maneuver out of the lot. As he did, he noted that Runner's grape vines had lost their leaves. Victims of the frost, he supposed.

"How did your meeting with Van Dam go?" Jason asked after they had gotten into traffic. "Was he really concerned about my soul?"

Playdon chuckled. "Actually, I think he was a little embarrassed that he had called. His real concern was that he didn't want Runner's agnosticism to antagonize you and reflect poorly on the Home. He hinted that you might be negatively biased against the Home because of Runner."

"Really."

"Do you have a take on that?"

"Yes I do. It's a validation of something Runner—or whoever he is, told me. He said that the administration did whatever it could to keep up appearances while the mission of the Home was neglected. Van Dam's concern apparently is not the impression I get of the operation of the Home, but rather the theology of its constituents."

"Form versus substance?"

"Exactly. I'm curious as to your reaction to Runner himself."

"We might expect the Devil incarnate to have a *nom de plume*. Interesting fellow. Well read and a serious thinker. My guess is that he's not as far from the orthodoxy of the Home as they and you might think. My guess is that at one time or another he was one of them."

"You think Runner is or was from the same Protestant tradition as the Home?" No way, Jason thought.

"You told me his daughter was able to get him admitted there because of her church affiliation, didn't you?"

"Yes, that's what Van Dam told me."

"Well, it's possible that the daughter got religion in general, and this brand of orthodoxy in particular, on her own. It's more likely that she got it from him. Religion is most often imbibed from the family structure, 'the apple not falling far from the tree' sort of thing. I'm guessing, but I'd be willing to wager my week's wages against yours that there's a story worth repeating in there somewhere."

"I am not yet to the point of receiving a week's wages."

"I'm past that point, so we can both afford the stakes. Philosopher turned electrical engineer? An agnostic biblical scholar? A retirement home resident with a library full of theology books who has invented a thermostat controlled by his TV remote? Not your typical nursing home resident, eh?" Playdon pronounced the "eh" like a Canadian, as a combination question mark and exclamation point.

Playdon continued, "However, the most telling indication to me was his passion when he expressed his concern that the Church wasn't addressing itself to a needy world in a way the world could understand. That's a point I would most heartily agree with, as you know. That much passion is usually reserved for something someone cares very deeply about. An agnostic or an atheist wouldn't care a fiddle or a fig for the Church's failure at anything.

"I'd say you should stay with your Mr. Runner, and let him be Mr. Runner or whoever he wants to be. He may even get comfortable enough with you to favor you with his story. Which, I suspect, you'll find more interesting than my own. And when you hear it—if you hear it—satisfy my curiosity as soon as you can and pay off on the wager."

Playdon paused. They were pulling up to the front entrance to the Bus. Ad. School. The events of the morning had Jason in somewhat of a dither, which Jason felt Playdon sensed. And he *was* getting a headache and it felt like it was going to be a whopper. Playdon pulled himself out of the car and turned back. He ducked his head down enough so that he could see into Jason's face. There was a grin on his face and a twinkle in his eye. "Carry on. You're doing just fine. But pay attention to the lunar phases. I'd hate to lose you before you get the full scoop on our friend Mr. Runner. I'm going to go back into the records and see if I can figure out who he was back when. If I'm able to pin it down, I'll give you a call. Meantime, thanks for the lunch and allowing me to tag along."

"Thanks for going along. I'll certainly keep you posted. Have a good weekend."

Playdon closed the car door and ambled off toward the entrance. Jason sat in the car for a moment before starting off to his apartment. This was one of those times in his life when, as his father would say, he didn't know whether one was afoot or horseback. The same old question kept coming back, over and over: who was the man who called himself Howard Runner?

Then there was another frustration. Here he was in the presence of two great minds—at least one great one and one good one—and he had the same feeling he would get if he started watching a movie long after it began. He could see what was happening but was unable to grasp its significance.

Runner's not really Runner? Runner was once an orthodox evangelical Christian? And Playdon had postulated this after a one-hour conversation. Jason had been oblivious to these possibilities after meeting with Runner for . . . how many weeks now? He had taken the staff and the Home's assessment of Runner as a reprobate at face value and hadn't questioned it. It may turn out that that had been a mistake. But all things considered, he did not think the mistake would jeopardize the Fellowship. He eased the car away from the curb with his mind turning almost as fast as his tires. He needed some aspirin for his head and an answer or two for his soul. He thought he could feel some of the shrimp in his stomach exercise legs they no longer had.

His angst continued into the night, and it was the early hours of the morning before his mind was blessed with the peace of sleep. He began to dream of fishing on the Pere Marquette river, but he willed himself awake. He didn't want to encounter the TV evangelist again or the Head Nurse. When sleep overtook him, his slumber was so deep that when the alarm jangled his bliss, he was sure he had just fallen asleep. It was the day to spend with Willard at the hockey game and Jason welcomed it with feelings of good expectations. The "Playdon/Runner/Who is Runner Really" story would surely be one of the topics of the day.

He dressed and drove over to Mrs. Lundsaford's house and the bakery she operated from her back room. The warm environment of that back room gave him the impression that calories and fat grams were being imbibed even as he inhaled the wonderful smells. Little wonder that the Lundsaford daughters were stout women with rosy cheeks and big bosoms.

Jason bought a couple of several varieties of sticky buns for the trip and a Long John for breakfast. Try as he might, he could not eat one of Mrs. Lundsaford's Long Johns without spilling the filling on him. Novice Long John eaters were well advised to wear bibs. Veterans ate with practiced care. How she was able to stuff four ounces of custard into a two-ounce Long John was one of the great scientific mysteries of all time. It was breakfast enough and before the Long John was consumed, Jason had a dollop of custard on his jacket.

When he returned home, Willard was already there, waiting in his minivan. Jason parked and waved and made a clockwise circular motion with this forefinger. Willard understood and rolled down his window.

"Be right out," Jason called. He spent a few minutes trying to get the custard out of the front of his jacket and packing the sticky buns into a suitable travel container.

He locked up the apartment and Willard started the minivan as Jason got in.

"Hey, little brother, How's by you?" Willard said as he eased away from the curb.

"I'm doin', big brother. You're early. Sorry, I wasn't quite ready. How's the Deiter Man?"

"Bummin'. He thinks it's every six-year-old's right to attend at least one hockey game a year. As it turns out, he had a low-grade fever this morning. Karen wouldn't have let him go to Detroit with a fever. He couldn't have gone along anyway."

"Well, if he had a father that loved him and wasn't too tight to spend some money on the poor kid, he'd get to see a game or two. My father used to take me all the time."

"Yeah, right. Our father didn't know ice hockey existed in the

U. S. of A."

"What? Didn't Michigan State have hockey then? I seem to recall Michigan winning a national ice hockey championship or two back in the early fifties."

"Big talk for someone going to a hockey game but depending on someone else's generosity for his ticket. I think a little more respect is due here, little brother."

"Mmmh, I see feelings are still a little tender from Michigan State's defeat at the hands of one of their big interstate rivals. Was it Hillsdale or Hope College? No, that's right, it was Central, and we all know what a Division I powerhouse they are. Please forgive my insensitivity."

"Be careful little brother. What goes around comes around." It was the good-natured banter they had enjoyed since Jason could remember. At this point Willard made a right turn where Jason expected him to turn left.

"Where are you going?" Jason asked.

"To the Joe Louis Arena in Detroit, Michigan."

"How do you expect to get there going this way?"

"I'm going take Main Street to US-23, north to I-96 to I-696 to the Lodge Freeway to downtown Detroit. Relax, little brother, I know the way to 'the Joe.'"

"That'll take us twenty miles out of the way. When you get to Main, turn left and take Stadium to State and State south to I-94. I-94 goes right past the Joe."

"There is a lot more traffic on I-94, especially around Detroit Metro. Trust me, this way is faster."

"Trust you? You get the birthright and you think you're always right. Give you an inch and you think you're a ruler."

The banter continued for a time, then they rode in silence.

Jason wanted to tell Willard about Runner and was thinking about how he could introduce the subject when Willard broke the silence.

"How are you doing with your Fellowship?"

"Great! I'm about half way through the study I'm doing for the U. Hospital on the length of stay for total hip replacements. The statistics show that the success rate for total hips has no correlation to length of stay. If anything, the folks who stay in longer have a longer recovery time."

"And all of this means?"

"It means that the number of days your insurance will pay for you to recuperate in the hospital will be shortened from the current seven days to five or less. Reduction in length of stay is happening for nearly every medical procedure. Normal deliveries for a live birth have come down from five days to two-and-two-tenths days in the last twenty years."

"Why do the hospitals want you out so soon? It would seem to me the longer you stayed, the more revenue."

"Partially true. But the rising costs of medical expenses have caused insurance companies to cut whatever cost they can. Getting you out sooner saves them big money."

"How are you coming on the paper you need to write?"

"Are you really asking about the paper or the person I'm interacting with in the nursing home?"

"Actually, little brother, I assume the paper, as with all your scholastic endeavors, is coming along just fine. It's your interaction I have an interest in."

"An interest in?"

"Frankly, when we were at the picnic before the State U of M game, you scared me to death. I mean, when is the last time we talked theology? Ever? And you come to the picnic with Bibles in your basket and take off challenging the inspiration of the Scriptures and the infallibility of God's word. Yes, I'd say I have an interest. I have an interest in the destiny of your soul."

"What if I tell you that was just a passing fancy, that I don't have any questions anymore? I merely raised the questions as an academic exercise?"

"And I'll ask you 'why the sea is boiling hot, and whether pigs have wings.'"

"So you think 'the time has come to speak of many things?'"

"Yes, and more than 'sailing ships and sealing wax and cabbages and kings.'"

"Well, I have a lot to tell you. But why does my changing my view of the way Scriptures were inspired and whether the Biblical record may contain scientific errors or errors of fact cause you to be concerned about the destiny of my soul?"

"Because those views are in error."

"I'm not sure they're in error. They may be different than yours, but that doesn't make them in error. And it certainly doesn't put my soul in jeopardy."

"That's not what we believe. You start to deviate and where do you go from there?"

"On to question the deification of Christ and salvation by Jesus Christ alone."

"Oh, my God! See? What did I say? You mess around with these things and now you're off the deep end. Now you don't think Jesus is God? What . . ." The veins in Willard's neck were bulging as they did when he became agitated.

"Apoplexy does not become you, big brother. Before you *drive* us off the deep end, let me tell you what's been going on."

For a half an hour, Jason brought Willard up do date on his

meetings with Runner, the conversation with Playdon, the meeting with Runner and Playdon, and finally Playdon's revelation that Runner was not his name and his speculation that Runner was from the same tradition.

They were approaching downtown Detroit before Jason had finished. A large Wonder Bread sign reminded him of his container of Mrs. Lundsaford's sticky buns. "You want a sticky bun?"

"Not while I'm negotiating this traffic and my mind's pudding. How in the world did you get yourself mixed up in this? You're crazy ya' know. You know as much about theology as you do about banking. And believe me, I wouldn't let you run a piggy bank. You'd hurt yourself. And I think you've hurt yourself trying to run around doing theology."

"Well let me be sure the record's straight. I believe the Scriptures are inspired, I believe in the deity of Jesus, and I believe in salvation through Christ."

"Now you're playing with words. You don't believe these things like you're supposed to."

"So now there's a right and wrong way to believe that Jesus is God?"

"I'm not going to argue with you. These views are heresy. There was a time when you could have burned at the stake for these views. And not to mix a metaphor, but you've become a flaming liberal. And ya' know what they say about liberals."

"No, what do *they* say?"

"That the religious left is a non-sequitur."

"That's a mean-spirited thing to say."

"May be mean spirited, but it's true."

"Do you have some clever little saying about moderates?"

"The moderate middle is muddled."

"Very cute. I don't think I'm a liberal, and you have to get into the right-hand lane. The turn to the Joe is the next right, Jefferson Avenue."

"What would you call yourself?"

"A modified conservative. There's the turn-off. The ramp to the garage is the next right."

"The ramp to the garage? You know what it cost to park in the garage?"

"Yes, and I also know what it cost to leave your car on the street in downtown Detroit. Six bucks is cheap insurance. I'll pay it, you tight wad."

"You're as liberal with your money as you are with your theology. I can't wait for Christmas."

"They say you can't take it with you, and I assume that is true regardless of your destination. And are you sure I still celebrate Christmas?"

"It ain't funny, little brother. If your mother knew of your views, oh, I hate to think—"

"What's funny is you, clown man. I see things a little differently than you and you're ready to condemn me to Hell."

"It ain't funny, little brother!"

"It's hilarious!"

It was a great game and a great time. The Security First Underwriters had a suite to which a red-coated usher escorted them. John Carpenter, that would be "Mr. Carpenter" to the Richards boys, the president of the company, was a handsome man of about fifty-five with white hair and a tanned complexion. He welcomed the two brothers to the suite with a polish that oozed out like it had been practiced for a long time. He introduced Jason and Willard to a very attractive woman, his wife, Mary Lou, who appeared to be the same age as her husband, and another man, Justin Richter, the company accountant. Jason thought Mary Lou Carpenter was a bit overdressed and over-jeweled for a hockey game.

Carpenter proudly showed them around the suite which had a large L-shaped overstuffed sofa, two large upholstered chairs, a television set, a wet bar, a large refrigerator stocked with soft drinks and beer, a serving counter on which was a platter of finger foods, and a chafing dish with hot chicken wings. There were bottles of liquor, all with pricey labels that graduate assistants rarely saw.

One wall of the suite was glass with sliding doors that opened out into the arena where there were two rows of seats ahead of a countertop behind which were several bar stools. The suites in the Joe Louis Arena were at the top of the seating area. The ice surface was far below. It occurred to Jason that the television in the suite was a necessity.

"So, gentlemen, please make yourselves at home. Help yourself to the refrigerator or the bar. There is a selection of decent wines in the cooler under the bar." Carpenter's hand swept the serving counter. "This is the *hors d'oeuvres* course. During the first period intermission, they'll come with an assortment of salads. The bratwurst and hot dogs come during the second period intermission. If you have any questions or need anything, just ask. There are programs on the bar out in the arena seating area.

"You have three choices to watch the game. You can sit in the seats, or if you are eating, you can use the bar stools here. Or, you can watch the game on the closed circuit in here. After the game, we're invited to visit the Red Wing Room where the players come after they've dressed. Enjoy gentlemen. Can I start you with something to drink and some chicken wings?"

Caesar salads, sapphires, and Chivas Regal at a hockey game? It was so incongruous that Jason was sure Willard was fighting off an urge to say, "No, thank you, I just had a booger." Jason had seen the distinctive green bottles in the refrigerator and asked for a Heineken and a napkin and caught a knowing look from Willard. Willard seconded the order. They each took their beers and a plate of chicken wings to the bar.

When Jason was sure he could not be overheard he said, "I hate when this happens."

"Hate what?"

"Slumming like this. Just to make you look good I took a napkin, so's I wouldn't have to wipe the foam off my mouth with my shirt sleeve. To be honest, I would feel like an interloper, except for one thing."

"Mffswhat's that?" Willard said as he stripped the meat off a chicken wing by pulling it through clenched teeth.

"Carpenter is a U of M grad, and these tickets are in nosebleed heaven."

"That's two things, but you're right on both counts. How could you tell he was a Michigan grad?" Willard's look toward Jason was incredulous.

"The polished elegance, the good taste in liquors, the wine selection. He has an air of intelligence. Signs of just another successful Michigan grad."

"Yeah, right." Willard rolled his eyes in disdain.

"As a fellow Michigan grad, I can discern these things, Willard. Richter, on the other hand, is a State grad."

"Really. How could you tell?" Willard asked and took a swig of his Heineken.

"I noticed his class ring when he reached up to pick his nose."

"Pppnnhh!" Willard nearly choked in reaction and in the process had snorted beer and chicken pieces through his nose.

"Handkerchief," he snorted.

"You're a State grad, you can wipe your nose on your sleeve. It's expected."

"Damn it! I need something to wipe my nose!" Willard rasped between snickers and sputters.

"So, it's 'Damn it', now is it? Nice talk. Here's a napkin. Very nice talk indeed. So the liberal left is a non-sequitur, is it? The moderate middle is a muddle? Sounds to me like 'the religious right is neither' is applicable here. Does your mother condone your profanity? And look at your shirt, there's enough chicken wing on there to feed a hungry family in India. You're disgusting, Willard. Quite frankly, I don't think showing off by passing half a bottle of Heineken's through your nose is a good career move."

Willard didn't know whether to laugh or cry through his coughing and sputtering, and the more Jason heaped ridicule on his head, the more he sputtered. When he gained control, he headed for the bathroom to clean up. When he passed by the accountant, Richter, he noticed that Richter was wearing a class ring. It had a green stone. The giggles started all over again.

The Red Wings won over the Maple Leafs or "Maple Loafs" as Carpenter called them. Pavel Datsyuk scored twice and Henrik Zetterberg had two power-play goals to lead the Wings. This, Jason decided during his second bratwurst, was the way to watch a hockey game—sitting at the bar with a plate of food and the beverage of choice and when the Red Wings scored, you went inside of the suite to watch the instant replay or, from time to time you could check on the Piston's game which was in progress over at the Palace.

They declined the invitation to go to the Red Wing Room after the game, Willard explaining that he had to negotiate the ride back to Grand Rapids and wanted to make the trip before he became too tired. They thanked the Carpenters for their hospitality and made their way back to their car, elbow to elbow with the "other" fans, the ones who had paid for five-dollar hot dogs, ten dollars for beers and sixty dollars for their tickets. The "other" fans were also distinguished by their Red Wing paraphernalia. Jackets, T-shirts, sweatshirts, caps, blankets with the winged wheel insignia of the team. It was in sharp contrast to the Carpenters and their Caesar salads, sapphires, and Chivas Regal.

Jason tried unsuccessfully to persuade Willard that the I-94 route to Ann Arbor was faster and shorter than the way they came. As they retraced their route, they talked for some time about the game, Carpenter's relationship to the bank, how Willard came to get the tickets. It wasn't until they turned off I-96 onto US-23 that the subject came around to theology and Jason's relationship to Runner, or whoever he was.

There had been a stretch of silence before Willard brought the subject up. Jason had sensed that Willard was tense and that something was bothering him. When he began to talk, there was a catch in his voice.

"I want you to know that I care for you a great deal. I don't want to meddle in your life. You're a big boy now, but I'm really concerned when you talk about leaving the tradition we were raised in."

"Will, I haven't left the tradition. I believe in the same things I did before. A different perspective, perhaps, but I arrive at the same place as you do. Creator God, revealed in history as recorded in the Scriptures but more fully in Jesus Christ, who was raised from the dead and is the cornerstone of the Christian Church. What, of substance, has changed? The fact that I have come to my beliefs by a different understanding?"

"I just don't think there's anything to be gained and a great deal to lose by questioning the great doctrines of the Church."

"I haven't questioned any of the great doctrines of the Church, Will. How many times do I have to say it?"

"You're different and it makes me nervous. I have a feeling

that the people at the Home are right. This man Runner is a liberal Christian at best and an atheist at worst, and there's nothing to be gained by fraternizing with the enemy."

"What's it going to take to convince you that I'm okay and you're okay? What great doctrine of the Church would you like me to test Mr. Runner on?"

Willard thought for a moment, then he turned to Jason and with a smirk said, "Ask him about the virgin birth! That one usually separates the saints from the sinners."

"I'll ask him, Willard. Just for you, I'll ask him."

They were passing over the Huron River on the north entrance to Ann Arbor. Jason repeated the lines of a nursery rhyme that their father often quoted when returning home from a trip of some distance: "Home again, home again, jiggety jig."

They had taken the long way, but the journey had been trouble-free. And a thought came to Jason. "I still say this way is fifteen-to-twenty minutes longer than to go I-94."

"I've never gone that way, and I'm comfortable with I-96. When you drive, we can go your way."

"So you admit it's a matter of preference, and whether one takes I-96, your way, or I-94, my way one can still get home from The Joe?"

"Yeah, so what's your point?"

"My point is that while you continue to feel more comfortable following our religious tradition to your eternal reward, and I may wish to follow a slightly different way, we can both get home, so to speak."

Willard didn't respond, which was his way of agreeing in principle. He turned off Washtenaw and passed the few houses to Jason's apartment. "It's been great, little brother. Hey, don't forget Mrs. Langeford's sticky buns. Sorry. We were so busy talking I forgot all about them."

"It's Mrs. Lundsaford. That's okay, it's breakfast. Thanks for thinking of me for the tickets. Glad I could go. Say 'Hi' to the Deiter Man for me and give my love to Karen."

"I will. See-ya'-later-Bye."

"Bye, and thanks again."

Jason turned and went up the walk, unlocked the door to the apartment and switched on the lights. He went to put the sticky buns in the cupboard when he noticed the message light flashing on his answering machine. He pressed the "Play Messages" button and listened as the tape rewound and the message began to play.

"Jason, Karen at five-thirty on Saturday. Tell Willard to come right home. I can't seem to get Deiter's fever down . . ." Jason didn't wait for the end of the message. He bolted for the door, in time to see the taillights of Willard's minivan turning onto Washtenaw Avenue.

He returned to the phone and dialed Willard and Karen's number.

Hello?"

"Karen? Jason. I'm sorry, but Willard just left and I couldn't give him the message. He just dropped me off. Didn't even get out of the car. He should be home in about two hours."

"Oh, that's okay, Jason. Thanks for calling. It's probably nothing. Deiter fell asleep on the davenport about a half-hour ago. It's probably a touch of the flu or something, but he has no symptoms except the fever. And he's not complaining. He'll probably be fine in the morning. Was it a good game?"

"Who cares about the game when you can sit in the lap of luxury like that. Willard can tell you all about it. Ask him about the smooth career move he made with about two ounces of Heinekens."

"I will. Thanks for calling."

"Happy to do it. Hope the Deiter Man feels better. See you later."

"Bye."

Jason hung up his jacket. He went to put the sticky buns away, but his taste buds overcame good intentions and he opened the container and took one. He placed it upside down on a paper plate and slathered butter over the exposed bottom. From long experience, he knew butter didn't stick to the frosting on the top. He put the bun into the microwave oven for twenty seconds. While he was waiting for the oven, he poured himself a glass of milk and clicked on the TV. The sports report was on, and he was able to watch the Datsyuk and Zetterberg goals again. The microwave's bell sounded, and he removed the now-warm sticky bun. The butter had melted into the warm dough. It was a bedtime snack to stop time for.

# Chapter Thirteen

At first, the jangling of the telephone blended into his dream, then it didn't quite fit into the storyline and was confusing, then he awoke to the ringing's reality. It was still dark. The red numbers on the alarm clock read 4:16.

"Hello?"

"Jason! Willard . . ."

The distress in Willard's voice brought Jason into full consciousness immediately and with one motion, he swept the blankets back and sat up on the edge of the bed as he said, "Will? What is it?"

"It's Deiter. He has a serious infection. Something called gas gangrene. God, Jason, they have to amputate his leg at the knee to save his life . . ." There was a pause and Jason knew Willard could not speak further. There was a lump welling up in his own throat, as well.

"What happened? I mean, how'd he get it?"

"They don't know, but it could take him . . ." there was a pause and the words then came in a rush as if between sobs. "I can't think of losing him."

"I'll be there as soon as I can get to Grand Rapids. What hospital?"

"Spectrum . . . Butterworth campus."

"Is there anyone I should call for you? Anything I can do?"

There was another pause, then, "No."

"I'll be there in two hours. Hang in there big brother."

"Thanks, Jason."

✝

The clock on the dash of the Honda read 6:25 as Jason swung past the front entrance of Spectrum Hospital and went down into the parking ramp. It was virtually empty, and he was able to park near the entrance, which made for a short walk to the entrance of the hospital. A woman in a volunteer's smock smiled at him as he approached the information counter through an empty lobby. "Can I help you?" she asked.

"Do you know where I might find the Richards family? My brother's little boy is having some sort of emergency surgery."

"Would that be Deiter Richards? He's been assigned to room thirty-one fourteen, but the surgery waiting room is on the second floor. If you take the first set of elevators down the corridor through those doors and to the left; and get off on the second floor, you'll see a set of doors marked, Surgery Waiting Room. There is an information desk just inside the doors. The receptionist there should be able to help . . ." Jason had started down the corridor before she had finished.

He didn't need the receptionist in the Surgery Waiting Room. The Richard's family was one of only a few spread-out in a very large room full of chairs and sofas. They all looked up as he pushed the door open. They all looked haunted. They all looked as if they were expecting someone else, but when they recognized him they all started walking to meet him: Willard, Karen, his dad and stepmother, Karen's mother, and behind them, Jason recognized Wayne Wright, the minister at Willard's church.

As Willard approached, he held out his arms and as he got closer, he appeared to Jason as if he had cried the health out of himself. They clenched for a moment. Jason was about to ask about Deiter's condition when a voice behind him began speaking. Willard and Jason drew apart.

The speaker was a short man of about fifty, dressed in a green scrub suit with a green surgical hat and a white mask that had been pushed down over his chin so it was being worn like a scarf. He looked like a man who didn't like to bear bad news but had a job to do.

"First, he came through the surgery very well. All his vital signs are very strong. We elected to amputate a little below the knee. The most important thing is that we have to be above the necrotic tissue. We think we are and while it's better to be safe than sorry, it'll be much easier for him to deal with a prosthesis if we can save the knee joint.

"As I indicated to you before the surgery, we're dealing with a very deadly organism. I think we've excised it. If we have, his prognosis is good. We've elected not to close off the wound and treat the open area aggressively with antibiotics. We're fortunate to have a hyperbaric chamber here at the hospital. This is a chamber in which we can control the environment and particularly the oxygen content of the air. We have found that if a patient ingests high levels of oxygen, the blood becomes oxygen enriched and can fight off infections more efficiently. In addition, we know that the body absorbs oxygen directly from the air, especially in open wounds. While leaving the wound open will be unsightly, it will give us a better opportunity to administer the antibiotic therapy aggressively and expose the wound to the oxygen. We're going to use this aggressive treatment for a few days until we're sure we've eliminated all the diseased tissue.

"He'll be in surgery for about another thirty minutes, but it'll be a while before we'll be able to get him into the chamber. I suggest you get some breakfast. By that time, he should be in Recovery and in the chamber and beginning to come out of anesthesia. We like to have the parents around for these little guys when they start coming around. Moms and dads can have a great settling effect. Any questions?"

"Did you find the entrance site?" Karen, always the nurse, asked.

The doctor turned to Karen. "I had asked Dr. McMaster, the pathologist, to be in attendance for consultation to help us decide whether we were ahead of the necrotic tissue when we cut. He examined the limb visually and thought there was as small puncture wound in the instep. He'll be able to make a more complete determination when he gets to the lab."

"Did he concur that you were ahead of the necrotic tissue?" Karen, still the nurse.

"I think we are. He thinks we are. But, frankly, it's difficult to be absolutely certain. There were no signs that we could see. He'll be conducting tests on the limb in the lab to help us be absolutely sure."

"And if he finds the incision was too low?"

"We hope it won't be necessary, but if it was too low, and the antibiotic and oxygen therapy hasn't arrested the bacteria, we'll have to go higher. There's no choice. If it gets to his groin area, it will be a matter of hours before it becomes fatal."

It was surreal. The doctor's words had come out of his mouth in a connected stream of large, one-dimensional letters that had mass. They were heavy, but they didn't fall to the carpeted floor. They hung in the air around chest level and were oppressive. Big H's and B's and F's. It didn't matter that they were spoken just above a whisper.

"Thank you, Doctor."

"I'll be making rounds and I'll check in at his room to see how he's coming. I'll see you then."

They stood in silence for a moment, each dealing with the puncture wound in their hearts as best they could. Jason's father interrupted the silence, "I think we should get something to eat.

We're all going to need our strength. The coffee shop is on the main floor just off the lobby. Shall we?" With that, he held his arms out from his side and moved forward toward the door, herding his little family group as he went. Reverend Wright followed.

The coffee shop was not busy and they pushed two tables together to accommodate the seven of them. When they had seated themselves, a waitress appeared. Apparently no one felt like eating, as they ordered light: toast, bagels, English muffins, cold cereal, etc.

Jason felt the need to be brought up to date, "How did the Dieter Man get gangrene?"

Willard sucked in a deep breath, which seemed to shutter into his lungs and he exhaled. "*Gas* gangrene. From what they told us, it comes from a very toxic bacterium that is present in soils and somehow gets into the system through a wound. It begins destroying healthy tissue creating a gas that the bacteria thrive in, and it literally races through the body. Apparently, he stepped on a nail or something and the organism got into his system."

"How'd you discover it?"

"Well, he had this fever that didn't go away. At about 6:30 last night, he fell asleep watching TV on the sofa in his play clothes and Karen decided to let him sleep. When I got home, we carried him up to his bed and put his pajamas on. When we took off his socks and sweats, the skin on his foot and ankle was puffy and crackly to the touch. Karen looked up at me with kind of a puzzled look and then said, 'We're on our way to the ER.' In ER, they diagnosed it as gas gangrene and operated as soon as they could get an orthopedic surgeon out of bed. I called you after he had been taken to surgery."

"Was there any pain?"

"No." Karen was answering. "Only the fever."

Perhaps Dieter had no pain, but there was plenty around the table. Her eyes were hollow from the crying and the lack of sleep.

Her voice was as hollow as her eyes.

"How come I've never heard of gas gangrene?"

Their father answered, "Because you didn't fight in the Civil War. Most of the casualties of the Civil War who weren't killed outright died from gas gangrene, also known as moist gangrene. At that time, they would close up wounds trapping this bacterium the wound. It's highly toxic, and most often, it was deadly. When they learned to allow wounds to heal from the inside out, and with the onset of antibiotics, it virtually wiped out gas gangrene. But occasionally . . ." his voice trailed off.

There was another heavy moment like the other heavy moments before Reverend Wright spoke in a quiet voice. "As you know, I have a service to conduct at ten o'clock and I'll need to get home and freshen up a bit before I go to the church. Before the breakfast comes, I'd like to ask you to join me in asking for God's help for Deiter and for all of us."

The heads automatically bowed.

"Dear Heavenly Father, those of us present who know and love little Deiter place him before you. You are the Great Healer; we ask you for your healing touch. You are the source of all wisdom; we ask for your blessing on the medical decisions that are being made on his behalf. You are the source of all strength; we ask you for the strength that we need to be a support to Deiter and to each other. This little life, your gift to us means so much to us . . ." Wright's voice broke and he took a deep breath. He continued and the sounds came forced and as if he did not have enough breath to speak. "Spare him to us. His life has so enriched ours. And . . . we have so much left to give him and he to us. We pray again for your healing touch for this little one . . . and your strength for our bodies . . . and your peace for our souls. In Christ's name we pray, Amen."

For Jason, the pain in his chest was so constricting he could hardly breathe. Until now, all through the drive from Ann Arbor, the possibility of losing Deiter was ethereal. Now the Deiter Man had lost a part of his leg and the possibility of losing this little life was concrete to Jason. Through his tears, he could see they were all wiping the tears from their eyes and the snot from their noses. This wasn't right. This just wasn't right.

The breakfast came. Institutional food lived up to its reputation. They all picked it over while they talked. Karen's pain was laced with guilt for not diagnosing the problem earlier. As a nurse, she felt she had been lax in not questioning the persistence of the fever. Their consolations were futile. Jason understood she would carry a personal hell that would be revisited every time she saw Deiter limp.

They had not been in the coffee shop long enough to get refills before Karen, the mother, couldn't stand it any longer and announced she needed to go back to the Surgery Waiting Room. They all followed except Reverend Wright, who hugged Karen and Willard and indicated they were in his prayers and those of the congregation of their church. He promised to stop back on the way home from services and left.

Jason had a new appreciation for ministers and priests and their role of consoling their parishioners through the difficulties of life, the valleys of the shadow of death. This is where the rubber of one's faith structure hits the road, and right now, it was leaving skid marks in the form of the fear of evil.

☦

Six years and forty-two days from the first time he was placed in his mother's arms, Deiter Richards died there.

He never regained consciousness from the first surgery. Diseased tissue was discovered in the amputation site by the pathologist. They took him back into surgery to amputate the leg at the hip but discovered necrotic tissue when they made the incision. It was then, as the doctor had said, just a matter of time. They brought him to a private room and his family gathered around, helpless, speechless, hopeless.

Deiter's breathing became labored at about twelve o'clock. Karen asked for a rocking chair. When it came, Karen, the mother, gathered the little boy up in her arms, sat in the rocker, and rocked him. His breathing stopped once, she kept rocking and looked up and simply said, "I get a steady pulse." Karen the nurse. The breathing began again, only more labored.

Several minutes later, the breathing stopped again. She kept rocking. The breathing began again. When the breathing stopped again, she rocked for a few minutes longer, and then she stopped, turned to the nurse who was attending, and said in a whisper, "He's gone." Then Karen, the mother, led the grieving.

The funeral was on Wednesday. There was a small, private service at the cemetery in the morning and a public memorial service held in Willard and Karen's church in the afternoon, followed by a luncheon in the activity room of the church. Jason left for Ann Arbor after the luncheon. There was nothing left to do, nothing left to say, no tears left to cry.

As Jason drove the two-hour trip to Ann Arbor, there was time to reflect on people's actions and reactions. His heart went out most of all to Karen. This was going down hard on her. She felt a heavy responsibility for not responding earlier to the persistent fever. There was no consoling her. This was going to take therapy, Jason thought. A lot of therapy.

Many of their friends and family had tried to support her and the rest of the family—some by just being there, some by expressing their love for the couple by soft words and an embrace, others in rather strange ways to Jason's way of thinking. They had said that there was nothing she could have done, that this was God's will. By implication, if she had diagnosed the problem earlier and had done something that would have changed the course of events, she would have been working against God. And it implied that somehow God deliberately caused this little one to die. Intellectually, Jason could accept neither. It could not be, that to work to save a life could be going against God's will. Neither could he accept that God would instigate the evil tragedy that was this little one's death.

Some tried consoling the family by quoting the "all things work together for good to those who love God" passage from the Bible. Jason could not accept that as an answer either. There was no good that could be ascribed to this evil. There were wounds that would leave visible scars, if they ever healed at all.

Willard had taken little time to grieve. He took care of all the arrangements and took care of Karen and took care of Karen's mother. Only for a short time on Monday evening at a time when Willard and Jason had stayed on after everyone had left the visitation did he tend to his own grief, and then only briefly. As they stood there, alone with the open, little white casket containing the remains of the Deiter Man, Willard said, "Damn it, Jason, why? Why?"

Jason had no answer and was so choked up that he couldn't have spoken if he had something to say. So was silent. The well-intentioned Christians who had all the answers were no longer there, so the room was silent. Heaven was silent. Willard gave up on trying to control the grief, and he wept bitterly in Jason's arms.

The faculty of the Bus. Ad. School had sent a floral arrangement, no doubt because of the thoughtfulness of Professor Playdon, who Jason had called to ask for leave of his Monday meeting and the Tuesday Intro Ad recitation. Playdon had only said, "Be there for your brother and sister-in-law, Jason. We'll tend to things here." Jason had not called Runner and wondered what his reaction to this tragedy would be.

Wayne Wright had conducted the committal service at the cemetery. There was a young preacher with *cajones*, Jason thought. He had a brief meditation that was not what Jason had expected from one so steeped in the tradition. He had said that none of us knew God and none had experienced God's love directly. The only way we experienced God's love was through the love of another. Our comfort was to be found in that we were the instruments of God's love to this little one, and Deiter's unquestioning love for us was what the love of God for us was like.

The prayer he closed with was beautiful. As Jason remembered it, it went,

> O God, in the intimate circle of family, we experience a unique bonding, made the more poignant because we gather in the presence of an open grave, and there is no denying the reality of loss, of separation, and thus, honest grief . . .
>
> Loss is proportionate to love . . .
>
> Pain is measured by what the one removed from us meant to us.
>
> And this little one meant so much.
>
> Amazingly, O God, these are bittersweet moments.
>
> There is no denying the loss . . . but there is no denying the joy either.
>
> The beauty of this moment overwhelms us.
>
> Things come into focus . . .
>
> We gain perspective . . .
>
> We know in tangible experience what we thought we knew before . . . but find we didn't know at all . . .
>
> That what really matters finally is the love we've known . . . love received . . . and love given.
>
> It wells up within us, so that it seems our

*hearts might burst.*

*In Your presence we offer our Thanksgiving for this son, this grandson, this nephew.*

*This one in whom we invested our lives, for whom we tried to model out what is to live well, to love deeply and faithfully, to walk humbly before Your face.*

*And he, with childlike faith, returned that investment hundred fold.*

*What a gift he was!*

*From our depths we give You thanks, that the light of his life shined on us and brightened our way even for so short a time:*

*By his confident portrayal of a shepherd in the Sunday School play.*

*By his complete trust as he prayed nightly, "Now I lay me down to sleep . . ."*

*By his unbridled love for all things small and helpless.*

*With his winsome, toothless grin and his ability to giggle and laugh in peals.*

*The images tumble through our minds. We remember and we laugh and cry at the same time.*

*We would have kept him here and yet would not. We celebrate his life.*

*We say not Goodbye, but* auf Wiedersehn *. . . until we see him again . . .*

*For with him, we do not believe this is all*

> *there is.*
>
> *In the end, it is not death, but life. It is not the grave, but glory.*
>
> *Receive our worship, our thanksgiving through Jesus Christ our Lord who taught us to pray saying, Our Father who art in heaven . . .*

Jason's chest became tight as he recalled the prayer, delivered passionately in a clear, confident tone. Wright's was an honest theology that acknowledged the pain but pointed beyond the pain to a celebration of the life and its glorious transition. A bittersweet prayer for a bittersweet moment. Jason recalled the moment at the end of Dostoevsky's classic novel "The Brothers Karamazov" where Alyosha Karamazov finally came to learn what love was in the death of little Ilyusha. In reading it for his Russian Literature class, Jason knew intellectually what Alyosha had come to learn. Now in the death of his little nephew he came to know experientially what love was.

It was just as Wright had prayed:

> *"We know in tangible experience what we thought we knew before . . . but find we didn't know at all . . .*
>
> *"That what really matters finally is the love we've known . . . love received . . . and love given."*

Wright's theology was in sharp contrast to that contained in the memorial service message delivered by the pastor from Karen's home church, a Reverend Arnold Edge. Edge was a man with the stern demeanor of a pilgrim preacher. He had intoned, "Deiter's death was according to God's plan for their lives. A plan we do not understand but which will work out for our good and a plan that we must accept in faith. You have no right to grieve. The only appropriate emotion is joy because little Deiter is in heaven with

Jesus, a far better existence than we could have afforded him here on earth."

So not only did the Richards feel devastated by the loss, they now felt guilty for feeling devastated.

And this by God who, of course, did this for their own good. Jason couldn't help take that theology to its logical conclusion and wondered if this was God's way of doing things for his devoted and supposedly beloved children's "own good." Why didn't God do things to people who were evil for their detriment? Experience taught him that bad things, like Deiter's death, happened to good people in equal measure as to bad people. Further, good things often happened to bad people.

Could the evil in the world; gas gangrene, gas warfare, the gas ovens of the Third Reich be a part of God's plan? God's design? Was all this evil God's doing, ". . . working together for good to those who love him?" That's what Jason's tradition held for him. The stern Reverend Edge even chastised the Richards for feeling anything other than joy. Would he have them celebrate this death as one would celebrate a birth or a wedding?

Jason's experience—his grief, his pain, and witnessing the pain of his dear brother and sister-in-law—was in conflict with the answers of his tradition, with the theology of respected ministers of his Church. My God, what are the answers? Where are the answers? Are there answers? He wondered.

He consciously stopped thinking and listened. All he could hear was the hum of the engine of the Honda and the rush of the air coming out of its heater. Heaven, once again, was silent.

What did come to him was a line out of Wright's prayer at the graveside. "Things come into focus . . . We gain perspective . . . We know in tangible experience what we thought we knew before, but we find we didn't know at all."

Jason thought, we thought we had all the answers, but the

experience exposes the flaws in some of those answers. We are shaped as much by our experience as by our knowledge. Our theology has to hold up in the light of the tangible. Or, perhaps it's that the tangible experience has a role in shaping our theology. The tangible does not change God, but our explanations of how God interacts in our lives do change and may change in the light of the tangible experience. It was what Howard Runner has been saying all along about the tradition! And it was what the head nurse, Veeringa, was denying.

Veeringa. She was at the funeral home visitation. Not her exactly, but her ilk, quoting scripture verses for the sake of quoting Scripture. Scripture verses that didn't work. Scripture verses that increased the hurt. And all with good intention. She had answers for questions that were no longer relevant and no answers for the questions that were searing their souls. The questions of "How could He?" and "Why?" were not satisfied with "Just because this is God's plan," and the ever-popular "Some day we'll understand."

"Things come into focus . . . We gain perspective . . . We know in tangible experience what we thought we knew before but we find we didn't know at all."

Heaven was not silent, after all.

☦

When he arrived at his apartment, there were three greeting card-size envelopes and a standard business envelope with the Bus. Ad. School's return address in his mailbox. The first one he opened was a sympathy card. On the outside cover, the card read, "With deepest sympathy on your loss," and the message on the inside read, "Earth hath no sorrow that Heaven cannot heal," and it contained the calling card of Reverend Lipscomb. Once again Jason was reminded he had not been to church for some time.

He opened the second envelope to find another sympathy card. On the outside cover were the words "With Love and Sympathy."

And the message in the inside was handwritten. It read, "Jesus loved him, this I know, for the Bible tells me so." It was signed "Howard Runner."

The third card was also a sympathy card, this one signed "Bill Playdon," and it had an additional message. "Sorry to hear about the tragedy of your nephew. Call or stop in when you get a chance—I have news on the identity of H. Runner."

The large envelope contained a personal letter from Dean Nixon formally expressing the condolences of the entire faculty and granting leave from his duties for whatever time was appropriate.

☦

Thursday brought the regimen of the Davidson Fellow back into full focus. When he got to the Intro Ad 301 recitation, he was greeted by Professor Miller himself, who insisted that he would be handling the class and Jason was free to sit in or leave if he had better things to do. With good humor, Miller added that it was time he took some responsibility for the organization of the lectures he was giving instead of having all the fun and leaving the hard work to his grad asses. He extended his sympathy for the loss of Jason's nephew and added, "A real tragedy when you lose a little one like that, eh?"

Jason stayed to hear Miller, who was notorious for his rambling and disjointed lectures, try to impart his vast knowledge in an orderly fashion in the recitation. The wisdom of the lecture-by-Miller/recitation-by-others was soon apparent. Miller's brilliant mind did not function in an orderly manner and he jumped from idea to example to funny story to another idea and perhaps then back to the original idea and then an example for the second idea. Several times Jason caught the eyes of students who would raise their eyebrows and roll their eyes signaling their frustration at trying to organize the thoughts of the respected, but disorganized, educator. After the lecture, several students expressed their hope privately to Jason that he would be back in action next week. He assured them he would and that he would include today's recitation in his presentation.

After a brief discussion with Miller, Jason set off toward the elevator that would take him to William A. Playdon's office and punched the button for the tenth floor.

As the door of the elevator opened to the tenth floor, Playdon was standing there, waiting to get on. When Playdon saw it was Jason, he said, "Jason! I was on my way to Miller's office to see if you had taken the recitation this morning. It's good to see you." He backed away from the elevator. "Come into my office and tell me all about what happened to your nephew."

Jason started at the beginning and told the story to the kindly gentleman, a giant in his field and a good and gentle soul.

When Jason was finished, Playdon said, "A terrible thing! Terrible thing. When you think of the strides medical technology has made in the past few years and yet in many things, we're at the mercy of the created order. Well, I want you and your family to know that you have our sincere condolences."

"Thank you. And thank you for your card."

"You're welcome. Now . . ." Playdon paused as he took a file folder from his desk, "I've asked the Records Office to check into those individuals who graduated from the University with a combined Engineering and Business Degree. This was a program that the University inaugurated after the launch of 'Sputnik' when it was discovered to our national horror that we were not graduating enough engineers. There were only 182 individuals who were in that program who graduated in 1964, the year Runner said he graduated.

"As I suspected, none were named 'Runner.' And there were eleven who were over the age of thirty-five. One was a woman, leaving ten possibilities. Here is a list of the ten."

Playdon removed a sheet of paper and handed it to Jason. He continued. "For obvious reasons, we can eliminate Hung Liang,

Maseo Ishiwata, and Phillipe Servas, all of whom were not US citizens. Of the seven that are left, four have kept in touch with the Alumni office and their current status is known. By the way, Stanley Wesfall is the retired president of Wesfall Aviation and a big supporter of the University. That leaves three. Norman P. Prince, Richard A. Mehr, and Robert A. Davis. Of these three, my money is on Richard A. Mehr."

"Because . . . ?"

"He did his undergraduate work at Hope College and listed his major as Philosophy. Hope College is an excellent liberal arts college with an affiliation with the Dutch Reformed Church, the same tradition as those churches that support the Christian Arbor Home."

"Bingo!"

"I think so. Tell me," Playdon paused as he put the folder back on his desk, "what are you going to do with this information?"

"I don't know. But it has my curiosity piqued. For the moment, I think I'll just continue to work on my paper with Howard Runner and see if Richard A. Mehr shows up. I have several more sessions with him. I see no reason to press him. Still, why does someone change their name? Interesting."

"Keep in touch."

"I will. And thanks for this time. I appreciate your . . . friendship."

"Any time, Jason. Any time."

On Friday at eleven o'clock, Jason knocked on Howard Runner's half-opened door at the Christian Arbor Home.

"Jason! Jason. Come in, come in. I was so sorry to hear about your nephew. What a terrible tragedy. So sudden! Such a young life to be snuffed out. Sit down, tell me about it."

It was a catharsis to tell the story from beginning to end again, to get it out of himself, to make an attempt to expunge it from his soul. Throughout, the man who called himself Howard Runner sat in his wheelchair with his cane between his legs and his mouth resting on his hands, which were resting on the crook of the cane. The blue eyes peered intently at Jason over the rims of the half-frame reading glasses as if he were seeing to it that Jason told the whole story and left out not a word.

When Jason was finished, there was a moment before Runner raised his mouth away from his hands and spoke. "Playdon called me on Monday morning with the news. I wondered if you would be back for today's session. I'm glad you came. Now, for what it's worth from an old man who has seen his share of tragedy, don't be too hard on the Nurse Veeringas of the world. When you go to a funeral home, it's not what you say that matters, it's that you are there. Your physical presence is enough support. But we feel compelled to say something when nothing is going to assuage the pain even a little bit.

"And if the Veeringas feel the need to place everything to the account of God, let them. It's the faith structure they need to make what little sense there is to be made of the vagaries of life. Even the great C.S. Lewis postulated that pain was the chisel that God used to shape us. When the love of his later life contracted cancer and died, you might have seen that story in the recent movie 'Shadowland', I think he changed his mind. But these are great mysteries, Jason. Great mysteries. The great Whys of life are properly capitalized, so to speak," and the blue eyes sparkled.

"And what do you think of it?"

"I wish I could lay all of the evil in the world, all of the tragedy, at the feet of God. Then I wouldn't need to hold myself accountable for any of the ills of the human condition. But that's not rational. I think that just as we're given free will or freedom to choose, we're given the human condition. Just as the possibility of free choice allows us to choose either good or evil, the human condition contains the possibility of accident, of disease, of pestilence, of war, as well as the possibility of love, joy, and peace. I'm certain that when your little nephew died, God wept right along with you, just as God weeps when we make the wrong choices in life.

"And as for this being in God's plan, that's not scriptural. If you need a proof text, I have a Bible open here . . ." Runner reached for the writing top of the cherry secretary and lifted off the now familiar Bible with the blue dust jacket, "*Jeremiah says, 'These are the words of the Lord . . . I alone know my purpose for you, says the Lord: prosperity and not misfortune, and a long line of children after you.'*"

Runner lowered the book and looked at Jason over the reading glasses perched on his nose. "These words would indicate to me that God has a plan for us. A plan for good and not for evil. And as for the good Reverend Edge, what you tell me he said makes me cringe. He would practice theology on you when he should be the healing touch of God. I say 'practice' because I don't believe he has it right yet. From what you say, he would benefit from instruction at the feet of young Mr. Wright. I'm curious as to why Wright had the committal service and Edge had the memorial service. What was his connection?"

"A long-standing member of Wright's congregation had passed away on Saturday. The service was postponed until Wednesday to accommodate relatives who were vacationing in Australia. Wright had committed to that service before my nephew died. Edge was Karen's pastor before she married Will. In fact, he married them. So Edge was asked to pitch hit, so to speak."

"And struck out, so to speak?"

"So to speak. Would you say that the words from Jeremiah you read are inspired?" Jason asked good-naturedly.

"It says right here that they are. 'These are the words of the

Lord . . .' Now then, tell me, Jason, how are *you* doing?"

"I'm doing okay. I didn't realize how much the little guy was a part of us. Separate but like, almost indivisible. It's painful to see the agony caused by his death. Karen, Willard,—none of us will ever be the same.

"Intellectually, I had all the answers. Experientially, some of those answers are inadequate. Something you said to me on my first visit is appropriate. You said that a belief structure based on other people's misconceptions may not serve me well. I understood that intellectually. Now I've experienced it concretely. Reverend Wright said the same thing in a different way in the prayer he offered at the graveside. He said, 'We know in tangible experience what we thought we knew before, but we find we didn't know at all."

"We'd all do well to sit at this Reverend Wright's feet."

There was a pause in the conversation and then they got down to what had become the secondary reasons for today's visit—the I.R.R. paper and the topic of the day, how the Board of Directors of the Home was selected and how the Home handled its certification audits with the State of Michigan. Runner expressed his opinion that at least one seat on the Board should be reserved for a resident, but he allowed that finding one who could pass his test of twos might be difficult on an ongoing basis. Runner deferred to Van Dam, and Jason sought out Van Dam to get the answers that Runner could not provide.

It was clear from the conversation with Van Dam that the control systems necessary to assure certification with a high degree of certainty had not been improved upon since the time of Douglas Visser's I.R.R. report some years ago. Van Dam indicated the Board was unwilling to spend money for the type of systems and administrative help that was necessary to implement and maintain the kind of documentation that would be desirable.

Jason asked about Runner's offer to buy the Home a computer

and the software to at least upgrade their accounting systems.

Van Dam joked that he knew nothing about computers, including how to turn them on, and he hoped to go to his grave without ever learning about them. With reluctance, Van Dam admitted they were trusting in the providence of God that no incident happened that would cause them to have a problem with their certification or their finances. The risk, of course, was that without certification, they would not be a Medicaid approved facility and would lose the revenue for their Medicaid residents.

Jason could not help seeing the correlation. Be careful, Mr. Van Dam, he thought. Bad things do happen to good people.

When the session with Van Dam was over and Jason was on the way out, he half-expected to encounter Nurse Veeringa. She was nowhere to be seen, but the lobby fixtures, the ladies-in-waiting, were still waiting.

# Chapter Fourteen

Saturday was the last game of the football season, and as it was for so many times in the past, it was against Ohio State and it was for the Big-Ten championship with the winner going to the Rose Bowl. It was an apple cider and donuts kind of a day. But the bright sunshine and crisp air could not erase the replay of the previous week's events in Jason's head.

Ohio State, the 'Oh how I hate Ohio State' school from Columbus, was a huge favorite and a win for them would give them legitimate standing as the national champion. It was an exciting game, made all the more so by Michigan gaining an early lead and building on it to pull off a 28-14 upset. Actually, Ohio State was never in the game. Michigan's halfback with the unpronounceable name went wild and Ohio State's candidate for the Heisman Trophy was ineffective against a strong Michigan run-prevent defense.

While there was no inclination to wrestle with theology during the game, Jason could not help but remember that a few short weeks before, the Deiter Man had sat in these very seats, all dressed up in his green and white garb. Wright was right . . . the images tumble through the mind and we laugh and cry at the same time.

On Sunday afternoon, the phone rang. It was Willard.

"Jason. Listen. I called to tell you how much it meant to Karen and I to have you there for everything."

"Thank you, Will, but I didn't do anything."

"You were there, man. You were there. That's all you needed to be."

"Anytime, big brother, only never again. Okay?"

"Not if I can help it."

"How's Karen doing?"

"She's taking it hard, Jason. Right now, she's sleeping. She feels guilty for not diagnosing the thing sooner."

"That may take some therapy to get over that."

"She's a strong woman. She'll get over it with our help. Everyone's been so good to us. Supper's been brought in every night by ladies from the Church and our friends have made sure we've been included. It helps, but it doesn't cover it."

"I was impressed with your minister. He's got some stones. You'd be interested to know that I told Runner about his service and Edge's message. His comment was that Edge should take lessons from Wright."

"Wasn't Wright great? I've asked him for a copy of the prayer he prayed at the cemetery. I'm going to have it printed up and framed."

"Wright was in sharp contrast to Edge."

"Say that again. That turkey tried to make us feel guilty for not rejoicing over the Man's death. I was having trouble holding it together before he said that, but that made me so mad I had no problems after that. Can you believe he said that?"

"No, it's a perspective on grieving that hadn't occurred to me before. When you get Wright's prayer printed, I'd like a copy."

"See you get one, little brother. Speaking of Runner, or whoever he is, did you ask him whether he believes in the virgin birth?"

"Actually, it seemed inappropriate to break into his consoling me to find out if he's an atheist. Give me a break, Will. I'll ask him and you will be the first to know."

"Just askin'. Listen, I just called to say how much we appreciated you being there and all. You don't think of this very often, but family means a lot, ya know?"

"I think I know."

"Well, I gotta run. Other calls to make."

"See you later."

"Bye."

The virgin birth. Jason wondered what Runner would have to say about the virgin birth. As he thought about it, he wondered what his Internet friend would think about the virgin birth. He went to his computer and posted a note to the 1st Horseman:

> 1st Horseman:
>
> Have a curiosity about your understanding of the doctrine of the virgin birth of Jesus.
>
> RichJason

As the days went by, Deiter's death occupied less and less of Jason's conscious thoughts. By the following Friday, he realized that he had thought about the events of the previous week but a few times. He was reminded when he assembled his things to see Runner—or whoever Runner really was—and he saw a note to remind him of Willard's question about the virgin birth. Then the images tumbled through his mind, again.

He had planned to stop at Izzy's Deli to pick up some Kaiser Killers for lunch because he had arranged to attend a physical therapy session, which was scheduled for one o'clock. Physical therapy was to be the topic of his inquiry today.

Strains of the aria "I Know That My Redeemer Liveth" from Handel's *Messiah* was coming from the sound system in Runner's room. Runner was sitting in his wheelchair with his eyes closed. Jason could see he was not sleeping as his head moved almost imperceptibly with the music. "And because he lives, / and because he lives, / and because he lives, I know, I too shall live . . ." the rich soprano voice triumphantly sang. Not your typical music for a reprobate, Jason thought.

As the notes died, Runner opened his eyes, "Oh, Jason, come on in." He directed the remote at the player and the music volume was reduced to little more than background music. "Put the offering from Izzy's there on the table. I have some iced tea and some hot tea coming from the kitchen. We'll eat when it comes, if you don't mind. In these places you live your life around their schedule. You can't make up your own.

"I was just enjoying a little of Handel's *Messiah* as you might recognize. Did you know Handel wrote that when he got to the 'Hallelujah Chorus,' he saw the curtains of heaven open and heard the choirs of heaven singing and wrote down the music and the words as he heard them? If anything was ever inspired, Jason, it's the 'Hallelujah Chorus.' I'm not sure about some parts of the Bible, but I'm sure about that. And who can dispute that when they experience that marvelous work? Again, experience shaping theology, mmh?"

Jason was settling into the leather wing-backed chair. "I couldn't agree more. Every year around Christmas time, they have a 'Walk-in Messiah' over at Hill auditorium, and I try to make it just to sing the 'Hallelujah Chorus.' It's a wonderful experience every time I can make it."

"You sing, Jason?"

"I tried out for the Michigan Glee Club but couldn't afford the tuxedo."

"There's a pity. Me with all my money and no place to spend it and you with the chance of a lifetime are denied for the price of a monkey suit. Life isn't fair, Jason. It's not fair. Speaking of not fair, tell me, how is your family doing?"

"Time heals. They're good people. They'll recover. It'll take some longer than others, but life goes on. It doesn't wait for you to get the answers."

"True enough. And how are *you* doing?"

"Well enough. I'm busy and that keeps my mind off it. Before we get into the paperwork, I have a question I'd be pleased if you'd answer. Actually, I've been talking to my brother about some of the things we've been discussing . . ."

"And he is a little more traditional in his approach to his faith, I presume?"

"Yes, well, yes, and . . ."

"And he is concerned that you're not as traditional, or are you?"

"Well, yes, again."

"What was his question?"

"Well, he wanted to know how you felt about the concept of the virgin birth."

There was the rustle of a starched uniform and the tinkle of glassware and Nurse

Veeringa came through the door with a tray containing a carafe of iced tea and a teapot and cups and glasses of ice. "I'd like to answer that, if you don't mind. The virgin birth is not a concept, it is a necessary fact." Her voice was as icy as the tea in the carafe.

"Ah, Ms. Veeringa," Runner said, lowering his head to enable him to peer over his half-frame glasses. "Again you appear at the exact moment you're most unwelcome. But in this case, won't you join us for a discussion. I'd be interested in your insights. Why do you think the concept of the virgin birth is necessary?"

Veeringa had put the tea down and appeared as if she was leaving but the challenge from Runner must have been too much for her to reject. She set her jaw and joined in as if it were a fray. "The virgin birth is necessary for Christ to avoid the contamination of original sin that is passed on through human conception."

"Interesting. Why must he avoid the contamination of original sin?"

"So he could be the perfect sacrifice for our sins on the cross. His death atones for the sins of the world. And to claim that for yourself, *you* must accept Christ as *your* savior so that He can mediate *your* sins before a righteous God." It was clear from her emphasis who Veeringa thought was the unrepentant sinner in the room.

"So, if there is no virgin birth, the rest of God's redemptive plan falls apart. Is that your understanding?"

"It all fits together. I don't know of a single Christian who doesn't believe in the virgin birth. It's part of the Bible, it's part of the creeds."

"Tell me, Ms. Veeringa. If all I ever read of the Bible was the Gospel of Mark, could I come to a saving knowledge of your Jesus Christ?"

There was some hesitation; Jason could see she was leery of where this was going. "Yes, I suppose so."

"Well, if all I had were the Gospel According to Saint John, could I come to a saving knowledge of Christ?"

More hesitation, but, "Yes, I believe so."

"What about the letters of Paul?"

"Yes, I think you could, so what?"

"These are men who, you would agree, were Christians. Founders of the Christian Church? If in fact they wrote the books ascribed to them, some of them actually walked with Jesus and were taught by Jesus?"

"Yes, so what? What's your point?" She was growing impatient.

"I don't think they believed in the concept of the virgin birth. Or if they did, they didn't think it important enough to mention it in their writings. Not any of them. Not once. Or, if you insist on a divine intervention understanding of the inspiration of the Scriptures, the

Holy Spirit did not think the concept of the virgin birth important enough to have inspired these writers to include it in their writings.

"So, you'll forgive me if I take issue with your assertion that the virgin birth is *necessary* for Christ's atonement to work. Further, if one does not believe in the virgin birth, one might be in good company: the likes of Mark, John, Paul, and Peter and by some definitions of inspiration, the Holy Spirit itself at times."

Veeringa had become angry and tears were welling up in her eyes. Her lower lip quivered. Runner didn't wait for her to respond. He lowered his voice and it became compassionate. "Now listen, I have no intention of upsetting you. I ask you now, as I have asked you many times before, to sit down and discuss this or any other issue. I can see this issue is of great importance to you, and I have suggested an alternative understanding. Discuss it with us. Please."

"What's to discuss? You think you have all the answers."

"That's a charge I lay at your feet. You overheard Jason's question and you came forth with the answer, uninvited I might add. Your belief in the virgin birth is not without foundation. The creeds of your tradition were not written without scriptural basis. You imbibed the concept of the virgin birth from your mother's milk. I have no intention to take it away from you. But don't dismiss another, equally well-meaning child of God, if he or she questions—I said *questions*, not denies, *questions*—the concept of the virgin birth."

Veeringa didn't back down. "The whole point is these things are not to be questioned. The Church, the reformers, the creeds, have settled these things long ago. Either you believe it or you don't, to your eternal damnation. It's as simple as that. There's no reason to question. If Matthew and Luke say Jesus was born of a virgin, that's good enough for me and should be good enough for everyone."

"My whole point to you is that your systematic theology should be good enough for you, and mine should be good enough for me without your damning me to Hell. You would denigrate every understanding of the Truth that does not exactly agree with your tradition's very narrow understanding of the Truth. Not only denigrate, but label it apostasy." Runner paused but didn't yield the floor. "Will you grant me that your understanding of the things eternal is a human understanding and, therefore, limited; dare I say imperfect?"

"Of course."

"Will you grant me further that what we are trying to understand, with our admittedly human limitations, is God—who cannot be understood?"

"Yes."

"Are we not then discussing degrees of imperfection in understanding what we have just now agreed is beyond the limits of our comprehension?"

"I suppose so."

"Then by what standard do either of us have the right to condemn the other to Hell?"

There was a hesitation, as if she knew the answer but was reluctant to say it. "The Standards of Unity."

"So we digress to the sixteenth century? Well then, Mrs. Veeringa, on that we agree to disagree. I was hoping to hear that the standard was the Bible or the Book of Mormon or the Koran. Some founding document."

She drew herself up to her full height. "Mr. Runner, I would have said the Bible, but you don't believe in the Bible except to quote it when it suits your purpose. I *believe* in the Bible, all of it, not selected passages. Now if you'll excuse me, I have work to do." Having delivered this pronouncement with strident tones, she turned on her heel and was off.

Runner was silent and continued staring at the space where Veeringa had been standing.

"Sorry I asked." Jason broke the silence.

Runner continued staring at the space. He was resting his mouth on his hands, which were crossed over the handle of his cane. Then he spoke to the space. "The tragedy is that *she*," he said, raising one finger to point at the space, "is the one who only accepts selected passages. The ones that suit *her* purposes. And she doesn't realize it. She thinks the only Bible there is are the verses she knows. It gives one pause that perhaps Henry VII was right to cause William Tyndale to be put to death for translating the Newer Testament into English. 'The Bible will just confuse the people' was the mantra of the day." He paused, still staring into the space.

"I shouldn't fault her," he continued. "It takes courage to read the whole book. Courage, and integrity, and an openness to the fact that not all the answers to life's questions are in there and sometimes it contains different answers to the same questions. Jesus Christ is not the Great Placebo. Interesting, the human lot. Interesting the desperate need for certainty in an uncertain world. Interesting . . ."

Runner's voice trailed off. At that moment, the majestic strains of the opening chords of the Hallelujah chorus were audible from the CD player. "Ah, Jason! The 'Hallelujah Chorus'! Handel brings us from the ridiculous to the sublime, from the doorstep of Hell to the throne room of Heaven." He picked up the remote and pointed it at the player to raise the volume. "Let's eat lunch before all the ice in the tea melts. I don't want us to be late for my therapy appointment."

"You don't want to be late for your therapy appointment? I thought I remember you as having nothing good to say about the therapy program here. Didn't you call the physical therapist a physical terrorist?"

"We have a new therapist and I have an ulterior motive for your visit there. A motive I think you'll find most pleasant."

The P.T. Department of the Christian Arbor Home was

contained in a twenty-by-twenty-foot room located in the basement of the facility. The equipment consisted of floor mats, padded tables, parallel bars, a Hoyer lift for transferring people from a table to a chair, and other paraphernalia. The therapist was a young woman named Annie who greeted them as Jason pushed Runner's wheelchair into the room.

"Mr. *Runnerrrr*. I see you have a *friend* todaaaaay." Annie was obviously in the habit of addressing her patients as if they were either four years old or senile.

Runner shook his head. "Ah, Miss Skelvan. You sweet young thing. Your presumption that all of your patients are as intellectually reactive as a stump doesn't serve you well in my case. Despite my advanced physical limitations, I assure you I am not senile and I can still process reasonably well. I'd like you to meet Jason Richards. Jason, Annie Skelvan."

"Miss Skelvan." Runner could process, all right. She *was* a sweet young thing. She was blonde and attractive and would have made a knockout kindergarten teacher. Jason instinctively looked for the wedding ring. Missing. This meeting was Runner's ulterior motive.

"Mr. Richards. Welcome to our physical therapy department such as it is. So you're a friend of Mr. Runner?"

"Yes. Actually, I am doing a graduate research paper on institutional health care facilities from the care recipient's perspective. Mr. Runner has graciously consented to be my . . ." Jason fumbled for the right words. She was pretty. And perky. "My study person."

"Guinea pig is more like it. And he's heard rumors about the human torture that passes for therapy in this room. He's here to substantiate the truth of what I have to endure at your hands. Don't be fooled by this innocent exterior, Jason. Therapist Jeckel and Miss Hyde are alive and well and living in Ann Arbor, Michigan. Let's get going. The quicker we're done, the quicker I can start healing."

A Certified Occupational Therapist's Assistant or, as Annie referred to herself, a C.O.T.A. which she pronounced as "coat ah," was concerned with enabling patients to take care of themselves, get dressed, eat, manipulate wheelchairs, get out of the bathtub and so forth. A Physical Therapist, she informed Jason, was concerned with the rehabilitation of joints.

"What's the difference between a therapist and a therapist's assistant?"

"Essentially two years of college and fifteen thousand dollars a year. After a few years of experience, we can do the same kinds of rehab but I need a therapist to sign off on my charts. But it's cheaper for the Home to have a C.O.T.A. on staff and an O.T. or P.T. come in once a week to sign the charts and review the case work.

"Okay, Mr. Runner, it's transferring for you today. Wheelchair to passenger car seat."

For the next fifty minutes, sweet, perky Miss Annie Skelvan put Howard Runner through a demanding regimen of transferring from the wheelchair to a seat that was rigged to simulate getting in and out of an automobile seat.

"Shuffle your right foot, pivot the left, shuffle right foot, pivot your left, good! A little more . . ." She was oblivious to Jason. Jason was not oblivious to her.

At the end of the hour, Runner was perspiring like someone who had jogged for the hour. "See what I mean, Jason? There's no pity taken on an old man. No matter that the therapy may well be the cause of my death. This woman will come to my wake and cackle that it's a pity I died, I was just getting good at getting in and out of the car. Now at the risk of embarrassing both of you, I have a little surprise for you." He paused, looking at both of them to see he had their attention. "I have arranged for the two of you to have dinner as my guests at the Weller Inn tomorrow evening."

"But—"

"I'll not take 'no' for an answer. You both are deserving of a night out in some good company. Miss Skelvan for putting up with an old curmudgeon like me with such a good spirit and Mr. Richards here for what he's been through in the past few weeks. Reservations are for seven o'clock. I'm only sorry that I can't join you, but as you can see, I couldn't get out of your car before the dinner got cold."

"Mr. Runn—"

"Tut, tut... protest all you will. But please respect the wishes of an old man. The two of you will find that you have plenty to talk about. Besides, I've rather come to enjoy people talking behind my back. It's settled then. I'll expect a full report, well, almost a full report, from each of you next week."

Jason was as taken aback as was the C.O.T.A., but intrigued at the possibility of a break in what admittedly was a hectic schedule. It was, after all, a dinner date at Ann Arbor's finest restaurant with the lovely Ms. Skelvan. "Perhaps we should do it just to humor him and, on reflection, it may be good therapy for him. You're a therapist, are you not?"

Annie Skelvan blushed, but—Jason was pleased to see—was not objecting. "Well, it beats microwave popcorn and a video with my Sheltie. And a good therapist always puts the progress of her patients before her own well-being, so I guess I'm duty-bound to accept, on the basis that I'm only accepting because this will be good therapy for Mr. Runner."

Jason was quick to reply. "Of course. It's the only condition under which I would expect you to accept."

Runner was elated. "Good, I'm pleased that you're able to see the wisdom in this little arrangement. Now, Jason, if you would be so kind as to assist me to my room, I think I need a bath in Ben Gay and an injection of extra strength Tylenol. I only have six days to recover from this session until the next one begins, I best be getting started. Good day, Therapist Jeckel."

"Miss Skelvan. Can I pick you up at six thirty?" Jason asked.

"Please, call me Annie. I live in the Island Drive Apartments." She gave him the number and address.

"I'm in the book if you come to your senses and think the better of this ridiculous setup." Jason lowered his voice and added, "And he said he wasn't senile."

"See you at six-thirty."

When they were out of earshot of the therapy room, Jason hissed, "You *are* the Devil incarnate. Veeringa's right about you. I suppose you have a Bible verse appropriate to this occasion as well?"

"I think the lovely Miss Skelvan can be found aptly described within the Song of Solomon. A comely lass that, but more importantly, she's a real solid young woman, and she's the only one of the help with whom I interact that does not try to save my soul."

"I meant a verse to justify your actions back there."

"The only thing that comes to mind is that you're braying like Balaam's ass and it doesn't hide your pleasure. I was able to arrange for you what you were contemplating yourself, but weren't clever enough to pull off unassisted."

"Not only are you a devil, but you're a presumptuous devil."

"You act as if I had arranged for violinist or jeweler to be present. It's only a dinner at Weller's for two of my favorite people. If it turns out to be an intimate dinner for two, that's not my fault."

"What if she falls all over me, as she's likely to do?"

"You say I'm presumptuous? Listen to you. I'm more worried what happens if you fall all over *her*. If I judge correctly, you're the one with the testosterone. I have a reputation to uphold, unsavory as it is here. So try to control yourself. The last thing I need is for these hens to be clucking that I was responsible for the lovely Miss Annie

Skelvan losing her innocence."

"You needn't worry about Miss Skelvan losing her innocence at my hand."

"See to it. Ah, here we are. I have my key right here. So . . . best of luck tomorrow evening. I hope you have a wonderful time. I've recommended a *Piesporter Goldtröpfchen Riesling Spätlese* to the sommelier. I think you'll like it. Thank you for lunch. You saved me from the rainbow beef and the ambiance of the Home dining room again. That in itself is worth the dinner at Weller's."

"Thank *you* for your time, and thank you for the dinner. You're right, I could use a night out. I only regret that I'm forced to spend it with a beautiful young woman and fine wine and cuisine instead of microwave popcorn and a video with her Sheltie. But if you insist and if—and only if—it'll be good therapy for you, I suppose it's my Christian duty to do what I can for my Guinea Pig, as you call yourself. As I see it, this is part of the required research for my paper. An in-depth interview with one of the key personnel of the Home would be not only appropriate but essential, don't you agree?"

"Quite, heh, heh. That's the spirit. Enjoy! And take notes. I want a full report. Next week. Say, that reminds me. Next week is the Thanksgiving weekend. I expect my daughter will be in town, so if you don't mind, I won't be here next Friday."

"I expect to go home for the holiday as well. How about Wednesday, instead. I'd like to talk about the Home's system for medication distribution. It was an area of some criticism in Visser's report."

"Wednesday would be just fine. Can we make it in the afternoon, say one thirty or two o'clock?"

"Suits me fine."

"I'll look forward to it. And don't forget, I want a full report on the dinner."

# Chapter Fifteen

"Let's see if I have this right. You have a dinner date with a therapist from the Home that was arranged by Runner, or whoever he is?" It was Willard on the phone.

"Implausible as it is, you got it."

"Who is this really, and why are you impersonating my brother Jason?"

"You watch too much TV. What's the big deal? You act as if I never date."

"When was the last time, little brother? I'll bet you can't remember her name."

"Last summer. I took Kelly Sheenan to see the Circle in the Park's production of *Annie Get Your Gun*."

"Oonnh! Are you sure it wasn't Shelley Keenan and you went parking in the Circle and you produced—"

"Colonel Mustard, you're a crude son of a gun and you don't have a clue. How does a refined lady like Karen put up with you and your talk?"

Willard took the reprimand in stride. "Dad and Mom will be thrilled. They're a little concerned about you. All work and no play makes Jack and so forth. Weller's, eh? Remember not to put the palate cleanser on your baked potato."

"If I remember correctly, that's your stunt. Wasn't that your way to impress Karen's parents the first time they took you to dinner at their country club, Mr. M.S.U. Smoothie?"

"I thought they colored the sour cream. How was I supposed to know? They didn't serve raspberry sorbet palate cleansers at Ponderosa, which was our family's big night out."

"I would have thought you'd pick up on palate cleansers in one of your cooking classes at M.S.U. Didn't you pledge that culinary fraternity, Eta Pi?"

"I didn't rush any . . . Eta Pi. Very funny. You treat Ms. What's-Her-Face like you treat me and you'll go another four months before anyone will go out with you. You should listen to your big brother and show a little respect."

"That's all I ever show you, Willard. A little respect. Listen, how are you doing?"

"We're getting along. The people from the Church have been great and Pastor Wright's been super. He's been trying to help Karen to see it wasn't her fault. She's having the toughest time. God, how I wish I could help ease her pain."

"I'm sure you are, big brother. Just be there for her."

"I am. I am. Well, good luck on your date. Call me if you need me."

"Right, I don't know how I'll get along without you."

"Just trying to help out my little brother. What did your man Runner, or whoever he is, say about the virgin birth?"

"He didn't deny it"

"But did he affirm it?"

"No, but as he pointed out, neither did Mark, John, Peter, or Paul. He asked the question, 'If these New Testament writers didn't think it important enough to mention it, should it be a big concern to you?"

"He's a heretic Jason."

"Who? Mark, John, Peter, Paul, or Runner? Think before you answer."

"I don't have to think. I just believe, okay?"

"Exactly, you don't think. And as I said before. Two different roads leading to the same destination."

"You better be sure of that. A mistake here could be more than fatal."

"I genuinely appreciate your concern."

"Listen, I gotta run. Keep in touch. I want to hear how your date comes out."

"You'll be the first one I call if she proposes."

"Yeah right, you should get so lucky."

"Say hello to Karen, and give her my best."

"I will. Talk to you later."

"Bye."

Jason wondered if he had a reply to his posting to his Internet friend yet.

He turned on the computer and dialed into FACULTY ON-LINE. "You have mail waiting." came the familiar voice. Jason clicked on the mailbox and opened the posting:

>RichJason:
>
>I am aware that the concept of the virgin birth of our Lord does not appear in the much of the early writings of the Christian movement. Mark and Paul, for example, do not mention it. There is some scholarly speculation that the idea of human sexual intercourse with the gods and resurrection (which is quite common in Greek mythology) and was a concept that was borrowed by the early proclaimers of the Gospel to give credibility to their claim for the uniqueness of Christ to the culture of the time. On the other hand, could not a wise God use these tools to effect a miracle that could be readily understood by the culture into which Jesus was sent?
>
>For me, the *doctrine* of the virgin birth is not as important as the *fact* of the resurrection. For me, these two

miracles **do** set apart this life as the one through whom we see to the very heart of God. However, grant me the resurrection and the rest, all the rest, is negotiable.

    Not what you expected from some on the right fringe of the religious right, right? <VBG>

    His,

    1st Horseman

Interesting. Give the 1st Horseman the resurrection as a fact and the rest, the doctrines, the creeds—or as Runner would characterize them, the historically conditioned human constructions—are negotiable, Jason thought.

✝

Jason bummed about that Saturday. He cleaned up the Honda, picked up his laundry and worked on the project for the hospital Controller.

At five-thirty, he showered and shaved and got dressed. He chose his best khaki slacks and a light blue, button-down Oxford cloth shirt, the one with 'JMR' monogrammed on the sleeve. He selected his Campbell Plaid wool knit tie. It would be a subtle accent with the navy blazer.

✝

Annie Skelvan was ready to go when Jason knocked on the door of Apartment 103. As soon as she answered the door, they both started to laugh. She was wearing a Campbell Plaid skirt with a light blue Oxford cloth blouse and a navy blazer. "So you shop at Ann Taylor's too?" she asked.

She . . . well . . . cleaned up nicely, so to speak. Her blonde hair had been swept back away from her face and gathered in the back of her head in a French twist. Her short plaid skirt had a large gold safety pin worn vertically in such a way so as to appear to be holding the skirt from unwrapping which, to Jason's mind, was gawd-awful sexy. The ensemble accentuated her figure in a way her white uniform had not. She was several steps above 'not unattractive'; she was a stunner.

Jason felt a bit out of his league and a warning went off in his head. Why did a beautiful, professional, young woman like this one just happen to have a Saturday night free of social commitments? Why wasn't she married or engaged or dating steadily? Why worry about it? This is just one evening; enjoy it, Jason advised himself.

"So, how long have you known our benefactor," Jason asked as they headed toward Weller's.

"Only about a month, which is just as long as I've been at the home as the C.O.T.A."

"Where did you work before you took this job at the Home?"

"I'm fresh out of O.T. school, Grand Valley State U. in Grand Rapids. Actually, I graduated last spring, but I had a Practical Ap. course to finish up. But after that, I moved to Ann Arbor to take this job and here I am."

"Were you from Grand Rapids?"

"Grandville, actually, just on the southwest side of Grand Rapids. And you?"

"Next door in the fine city of Wyoming."

"Really! Where did you go high school?"

"South Christian."

"*Calvin* Christian."

Interesting, thought Jason. Same age, same tradition, same hometown, same Campbell Plaid, same blue blazer. He had heard once that coincidence was God's way of remaining anonymous. "Enough talk of our pasts or we'll find out we're related and that Runner's guilty of fostering incestuous relationships."

"That sweet man couldn't be guilty of anything. He takes a

bad rap from some of the staff, but I think he's a dear man and a refreshing change from most of my clients at the Home. Like he says, he's about the only resident who can pass the test of twos."

"String two sentences together and remember them for more than two minutes. But he's guilty, all right. Guilty of being widely read and very insightful, as well as having a great sense of humor. I've come to gain a great respect for his knowledge and his wit. Let's see . . . Weller's has valet parking I believe . . . so . . ." Jason said as he pulled the Honda under the canopy leading to the front door, ". . . here we are."

The reservations were under Richards.

"Ah, yes! Mr. Richards, your table is ready. If you would be so good as to follow me, please." The large, jolly man with silver hair looked as if he might be the owner and he led them to a table in an out-of-the-way corner of the restaurant. Jason noticed that reservations apparently weren't necessary as there were several empty tables in the vicinity of the one to which they were being led.

Their waiter was a handsome, middle-aged black man whose nametag read "Curtis." He announced that he understood that some of the details for their dinner had been pre-arranged. The wine steward would be along presently and that he, Curtis, would be back shortly with a sampling of what he called, "the *hors d'oeuvres* of the house."

"He didn't leave us with menus," Jason remarked as Curtis left.

"Maybe pre-arranged means more than the wine and *hors d'oeuvres.*"

"It wouldn't surprise me. But for a man who can't get in and out of a car, how does Runner know about Weller's?"

"Oh, I can answer that. When his daughter is in town, he arranges for Ambu-Cab to pick him up and take him whenever he wants to go out with her. Frankly, the O.T. regimen is just to enable him to get in and out of a car in case Ambu-Cab isn't available or in an emergency."

"Being able to get in and out of a car would be a big advantage. Ambu-Cab must cost a fortune," Jason said.

"I don't think Mr. Runner needs to worry about money. From the scuttlebutt at the Home, he's very well off financially. Although, I don't know how he made his money."

At that moment, the wine steward arrived carrying a green bottle and a sterling silver ice bucket and, with great ceremony, removed the cork and presented it to Jason. The aroma was outstanding. The steward poured a small amount in Jason's glass and said, "For your discernment, sir."

Once again, Jason felt out of his league, but he had been to the movies. He swirled the wine around in the glass without sending it sloshing onto his lap. He sniffed it and then tried it. It tasted like very, very rich apple juice. "It's excellent."

"Very good, sir." And the wine steward filled Annie's glass and then Jason's and put the bottle in the ice bucket. "Enjoy!"

Jason held up his glass. "I'd like to propose a toast to our benefactor and friend, Howard Runner."

Annie had held up her glass as Jason was speaking and then added, "To his good health and ours."

After they drank the toast, Annie was the first to speak. "Mmmh. *This* is good wine."

"It's German and I'd tell you what it is but I can't pronounce vowels with the funny little marks over them."

"Umlauts. I can handle the odd umlaut or two, let me see . . . *Piesporter Goldtröpfchen Riesling Spätlese*," she said, reading the label. "I believe *Piesporter* is the town, *Goldtröpfchen* is the vineyard, and *Spätlese* means late harvest. Our mutual friend knows his wines."

"I suppose we should have expected that. My, my, what have we here?"

Curtis had appeared with a sectioned serving dish. "These are deep fried cheese balls; an assortment of veggies and cheeses; this is marinated herring; these are miniature crab cakes; and these are the house specialty—mushroom caps stuffed with crab meat which, I might add, is Mr. Runner's personal favorite." Curtis placed the dish on the table. *"Bon Appetite!"*

"This is dinner enough," Annie exclaimed. "No need to ask for the menu."

"Did he say Mr. Runner's personal favorite? Do you get the feeling Runner is a regular here? Speaking of menus, here they come."

Curtis was approaching the table with two leather folders, which he placed open and upright on the table. "Take your time, enjoy the wine and *the hors d'oeuvres*, and when I notice the menus lying on the table I'll stop by to take your order."

The *hors d'oeuvres* were excellent, the wine was outstanding, and the conversation was comfortable. Annie was open and apparently at ease with herself and the surroundings. They found they knew some of the same people and, to neither of their surprise, they discovered that they were related—almost. A nephew of Jason's stepmother's sister's husband was a second cousin to Annie by marriage and coincidentally, both their parents had attended that wedding. It was a memorable wedding because, at the reception, the groom's minister had taken the microphone and had, incredibly, asked that the dinner musicians be stopped because they were playing secular love songs and the music was, therefore, " . . . not to the glory of God."

When Jason opened his menu, he discovered that the entrees were listed but there were no prices. Annie noticed too and wondered out loud about the prices.

"I believe it's our friend Runner's way of saying we should enjoy ourselves and not worry about how much of his money we're spending."

Annie ordered the Shrimp Amerousse and Jason the Prime Rib.

The conversation continued about the things they had in common—Grand Rapids, their respective educations, and of course, Howard Runner.

"This thing with his atheism is a big issue with some of the staff and some of the residents," Annie offered after affirming that her marinated shrimp was outstanding.

Jason was effusive over the prime rib. "I don't think he's an atheist or even an agnostic," he said, returning to the conversation about Runner.

"Really! Actually, I don't discuss it with him. I think a person's religion ought to be his own business. I know this much; what a person believes doesn't help him dress himself or get into a car. But your views aren't shared by the staff." She paused to savor another of the succulent shrimp.

"You can say that without fear of contradiction. I've been present with he's had a theological skirmish with the head nurse. She wasn't afraid to condemn his soul to Hell, more or less out of hand."

At that, Annie stopped chewing and tilted her head in puzzlement. "Veeringa?" she said covering her mouth, embarrassed that she had blurted it out with her mouth full of Shrimp Amerousse.

Jason's antennae went up. "Why not Veeringa?"

"I'll bet it wasn't over the relative ethics of the seventh commandment."

"Come on. That woman's so religious, she wouldn't say 'Sex' if she had it on her plate."

"Sometimes they're the hottest. Unless I miss my bet and the gossip mill is a mile off, she's got her sights set on Van Dam."

"The administrator."

"None other than."

"Isn't he married?"

"So is she."

Jason could tell by her tone that she was both serious and disapproving. "What do the residents think of Runner?"

"Most of the women think he's some sort of devil. And some of the residents have rather pointedly told me they think he should be made to go live somewhere else."

"My mentor, Professor Playdon—who accompanied me on one of my visits—speculated that Runner's actually from our tradition."

"A closet Calvinist? No way!"

"In fact . . ." Jason paused. He was going to share that Runner had changed his name when an idea came to him as to how he might find out for sure who Howard Runner was.

"In fact what?"

"In fact . . ." What the hell, why not? "In fact, Howard Runner is not his real name."

"Is not his . . . Jason Richards! Who . . . ? What are you saying?" she sputtered. Her fork had stopped in midair.

Jason commanded her full attention and a lovely attention it was.

"When Professor Playdon met Mr. Runner, Runner indicated he was in one of Playdon's graduate accounting classes. They're about the same age, so Playdon thought he should remember anyone in one of his classes that was about his own age, but he couldn't remember our friend. But the clincher is that Playdon's mother's maiden name was Runner. Playdon would have remembered someone his own age whose name was Runner. He checked with the Records Department of the University and no one named Runner graduated from the Engine School from 1962 to 1966, a two-year window on either side of 1964, the year Runner said he got his degree. Given all we know about Runner, Playdon narrowed it down to three possible candidates. He believes Runner's given name was Richard Mehr."

"Why would a person change his name, especially a successful person, a good person?"

"I don't know. But there are other things about Runner, or Mr. Mehr—that gives one pause. For example, how many nursing or retirement home residents have a second room full of theology and philosophy books? And that's another thing. One of the three people on the list of possibilities—the one named Mehr—graduated from Hope with a degree in Philosophy."

"Hope College? In Holland, Michigan? It's hard to believe that a Hope graduate would be an atheist."

"I don't think he's atheist. I think he's a widely read biblical scholar. Just a few weeks ago, there was an article in *USA Today* about an obscure theologian from the turn of the century named Troelsch. Not only had Runner heard of him, he had read his book, which was printed in the late 19th century. And had a copy of it in his library."

"Sounds more like he's a theologian than an engineer. Do you know how he made his money?"

"By inventing some kind of light-emitting diode used in hand-held calculators. But you can help solve the mystery of who Howard Runner is, if you're willing."

"Me? How?"

"I don't have access to his records and no reason to ask to see them. You do. His real name or his last place of employment should be somewhere in the records. There may be something in his file or on his application for admission, something that could help track down who Runner is."

"Gee, I don't know. What difference does it make what his name used to be?"

"No difference. But I think there's a story behind our benefactor. An interesting story. And frankly, my curiosity has been piqued."

"Isn't that a way to euphemistically say that you're just plain nosy?"

"You should be a *psycho*therapist."

"If I *were* a psychotherapist, I'd have discovered his dark secret by now. Well . . . ," she paused as if contemplating whether she should get involved, "Okay, I'll see if there's anything in the records. What're you going to do if we find out something?"

Aha! The first person plural "we" had crept into her speech usage. Good long-range sign. "Depends on what we find out, I suppose. Perhaps nothing. On the other hand, if his name change was necessary to give him some measure of peace and quiet in the Home, that would be important enough to rate a mention in my I.R.R."

"I.R.R.?"

"It stands for Interrelational Report Requirement. My research paper."

Curtis had been clearing the table and now presented them each with a heavenly looking dessert. "This is our famous Death by Chocolate. It's a favorite of Mr. Runner's except his diabetes limits his enjoyment of it. He wants you to enjoy it for him, and he will enjoy it by substitution. Can I get either of you a coffee or tea?"

When Jason got back to his apartment, he reflected it had been a perfect evening. Runner was right. Annie Skelvan seemed like a good person, not to mention that she was very good looking and could handle a German umlaut or two. He wondered if he could muster the courage to ask her out again. He felt she was out of his league what with her blond French twists, knockout looks, and a great figure.

But wait a minute. He was the Davidson Fellow, wasn't he? Wasn't that a league of its own? But then there was the haunting question, why was a good-looking young professional woman like her unattached? Perhaps in another date or two, he would find out. That is, if there was another date or two.

In Apartment 103 at 1106 Island Drive Apartments, Annie Skelvan was getting ready for bed. It had been a perfect evening. Jason Richards was a good-enough looking guy with fantastic prospects for his future. He had been a fun date. But . . . she wondered as she brushed the French twist out of her hair . . . why is a guy like him unattached? He had been warm and genuine and a perfect gentleman. A real treat. The few guys she had dated since she had come to Ann Arbor thought that her price to get bedded was a few draft beers and whirl on the dance floor. Wrong!

She knew what her mother would be saying at this moment if she were present. "Annie, you're getting older! Annie, you shouldn't be so particular! Who do you think you are, Annie?! A career is nice to fall back on but it's time you settled down and started a family! We were married and had two kids when I was your age! He seems like such a nice young man! Does he go to church?!"

Even the questions had exclamation points when her mother was haranguing her about the lack of visible marriage prospects.

Actually, Jason had come into her life at an opportune moment. She was planning to get up early in the morning and drive home to Grandville for the day. There was to be a celebration of her father's fiftieth birthday. Her mother would ask if she was seeing anyone and Jason Richards would be a handy foil to fend off her mother's well-meaning but tiresome concerns. "This one has possibilities, Mother," she could say.

But, why was he unattached? Perhaps in a few more dates, she would find out. There would be more dates. She knew just how to finagle that. Howard Runner. Jason was obsessed with Howard Runner and this crazy idea that he was someone or something other than represented. Oh yes, Mr. Jason Richards, there would be a few more dates. You can count on that, big guy, she thought.

☦

Sunday was a lollygag kind of day. Jason slept in, blew off going to church, and went out and got a copy of the Sunday *New York Times* and a thank you card with some small blue flowers on the cover to send to Runner. He penned a little note on it: "Angels rushed in where fools had feared to tread. The night was wonderful, the wine was excellent, the food was superb, and the company better than the wine or the food. Thanks for being the angel."

He returned to the apartment to enjoy the *Times* and watch the Lions beat the Giants 35—14. He then paid attention to the requirements of his Fellowship. He was immersed in some serious statistical analysis for the "Length of Stay for Hip Replacement" study when the ringing of the phone startled him. The experience of the past few weeks had left him with a dread of late night phone calls. This one was coming at nine-thirty on a Sunday night.

"Hello?"

"Jason?" It was a female voice, familiar but not immediately identifiable.

"Yes?"

"This is Annie. Annie Skelvan."

"Annie! To what do I owe the honor of this call?"

"You're not going to believe this but . . . I know who Howard Runner is."

"You what? How did you . . . I mean . . . did you check the records?" She had his undivided attention.

"No, I went home for the day for my dad's birthday. I just got back. Listen, Jason, you were right, it *is* a very interesting story and I know it's kind of late, but I think you'll want to hear this and it's too long to tell you over the phone. If you're not busy and you could come over, I'll make some hot mulled cider and tell you the whole story."

Judas Priest! "I'll be right over."

He checked what he was wearing and decided something a little more dressy would be appropriate. He decided on clean jeans and a green Polo turtleneck top.

For the second time in as many nights, Jason pulled his Honda into the visitors' parking spot in the Island Drive Apartments. He was trying to think of something clever to say to her when she opened the door of the apartment and decided to ask if this was where the cider lady lived.

When he knocked on the door, the knock was greeted by the muffled yapping of a small dog. The Sheltie. Then he heard "Skippy! To your cage." The barking stopped and a moment later the door opened and Annie Skelvan stood there grinning. The grin broke into a hearty laugh before he could ask if she was the cider lady when she saw what he was wearing. Jeans and a dark green Polo turtleneck top. Exactly what she was wearing.

"I don't believe in omens," she said, "but for the record, where *do* you shop? Come in and make yourself comfortable. I'll get the hot cider."

He sat on one corner of a large over-stuffed sofa. When she came back and had served the cider, she sat on the other end of the sofa facing him with her back to the armrest and she pulled her knees to her chin and said, "You, Jason Richards, will not believe what you are about to hear."

"Let's have it, cider lady."

"It was my father's fiftieth birthday today so I went home this morning. Of course, my mother, being the good Dutch mother that she is, wants to hear every detail about my life. Especially my marriage prospects. This time I could tell her I had this date last night and how it came about with Mr. Runner and all, and I told her about your idea that our benefactor was living under an assumed name.

"Well, one thing led to another and my aunt, who was there for the celebration, heard me tell about Runner. She asked me about who we thought Runner might be, and when I mentioned the name Mehr, she about came out of her skin. '*Richard* Mehr?' she asked.

"My aunt knew Richard Mehr, and get *this*: he was a well-known minister in a Dutch Reformed Church in Spring Lake, Michigan, who resigned because he was going to be put up for a heresy trial. This happened back in 1958, and she was a member of that church at the time." Annie couldn't control her enthusiasm for the story she was telling. She hadn't touched her cider since she started it.

"Incredible! So did your aunt know how Richard Mehr changed into Howard Runner?"

"She didn't know what happened to him. He just sort of left town, left the church, and apparently only a few people knew what happened to him. The only thing those in the know would say is that he left to begin a different life. She said the whole affair was a huge tragedy. His congregation loved him but the local denominational governing body—called the Classis—wanted him out, and out he went. Apparently, he had published articles in the church papers that were controversial and there was some jealousy because his church in this little town of Spring Lake had become one of the largest in the whole denomination. She said he was even a professor in the seminary affiliated with Hope College for a while."

"But do we know that it was Richard Mehr that changed into Howard Runner?"

"You can change your name but you can't change your eye color. When I asked my aunt to describe the Richard Mehr she knew, the first words out of her mouth were 'he had these remarkable blue eyes' and Richard Mehr was bald already in 1958. It's him, Jason, I just know it is. Remember when I said Runner sounded more like a theologian than an engineer? My aunt said being a theologian was one of the things that got him into trouble. He was thinking and writing and preaching about things that were ahead of his time. She said that what really cooked his goose was that he had little patience for denominationalism and the politics of religious structures, whatever that means."

"Sounds like it could be Runner, Detective Skelvan. It certainly sounds like it could be."

"So, what are we going to do?"

"Well, Thanksgiving weekend's coming up. It occurs to me that something like this would have been reported in the local newspaper. There must be some record of it. I could spend some time in the library and see if there's been anything printed . . ."

"You don't have to go that far. My aunt said she kept a notebook with all that sort of stuff in it—newspaper clippings, memos, even minutes of meetings. She said I was welcome to borrow it if she could find it."

"That'd be great. If there are newspaper clippings there might be pictures that will confirm that Runner is Mehr, or it won't."

"But that still leaves the question, it if does confirm our suspicions, what are we going to do?"

"I don't know, cider lady. I don't know. On the one hand, I feel an obligation to protect his wish to be Howard Runner. On the other hand, I wonder if he put us together because he wanted us to know about Richard Mehr, and I hadn't been perceptive enough to figure it out myself. He sensed I needed help and so he sent in the Skelvan cavalry. Remember he said he thought we would talk about him behind his back?"

"I discount that. He had no way of knowing of your suspicions or that I had an aunt that knew him before his metamorphosis. I think he has a genuine concern for you and wanted to be sure you get to meet some really nice girl to round out your life."

Bells rang off in Jason's head. He hoped his surprise at that comment didn't show. "Do nice girls ply their intended victims with hot mulled cider?"

"They do if they don't happen to have anything dandy or quicker in the house."

He couldn't get to sleep after he went to bed. His mind was abuzz. There was Annie Skelvan who had entered his life unexpectedly and with more of a presence than he was sure he wanted right now. He had gone from wondering if she was out of his league to wondering how long it was going to take to get to first base, or was he there and already on his way to second? Her take off on the Ogden Nash poem was hilarious if a bit unexpected.

> Candy
>
> is dandy,
>
> but liquor
>
> is quicker.

On an impulse, he had extended his arms to hug her when he was saying good night and she had snuggled her lovely figure right in and stayed there until he broke it off. Runner was right, a comely lass that, and a real solid young woman, so to speak. She was gorgeous.

Then there was Howard Runner. Regardless of what his name was, who was he and what was his story? Jason would try to see Annie's aunt's notebook. There was a two-fold purpose there; see the notebook and see the notebook with Annie Skelvan—and see Annie. Let's see, that would be a threefold purpose then, wouldn't it? A trinity of purpose. That had a nice ring to it. Ring. It was amazing all the double-entendres that made an appearance when you liked someone. Liked? Loved? Liked. Liked a lot. Liked a whole lot!

But all of this would be in the name of research for his I.R.R., right? Plus, there was now more than one Interrelational Research going on. Research was research, was it not? Then there remained the nagging question, why was a bright, young, attractive, professional thing like that unattached? Why?

Then there was also the question of his understanding of his faith tradition. The more he explored with Runner, the more he felt he was going out on a limb. But strangely, on reflection, he was more at ease on the limb. It seemed there was less apology to make, less blind trust needed, and more honesty with the fact that he did not have God under his intellectual control. If Runner was Mehr, it answered a lot of questions about his alleged heresy at the Home. Perhaps the same questions Runner raised with him were the ones that got Runner into trouble with his denomination.

He had a meeting with Playdon in the morning, who would be interested to learn what Jason had found out through Annie. Annie. It was more pleasant to think about Annie. Especially the two or three seconds she had been in his arms less than an hour earlier.

Annie Skelvan couldn't sleep either. She was sure she had blown it. She had been way too aggressive with the "they do if they don't happen to have anything dandy or quicker in the house" line. The poor boy's head had nearly snapped off his neck. And the thing of it was, she really didn't mean it to sound as forward as he seemed to have heard it. Well, she wished she had thought of a less blunt way of saying it. Darn! It had come out all wrong.

On the other hand, they were both grown-ups. Why beat around the bush? If you like somebody, why pussyfoot about? On reflection, he must be a real gentleman or a stump not to have come on to her after that invitation. He had no way of knowing it was unintentional. Or was it?

Besides, he had hugged her when he said good-bye. No kiss, but a hug. Funny how much can be communicated with a two or three-second hug. Funny how much cannot be communicated with a two or three-second hug. It was more than an I-like-you-like-a-sister-and-I-want-to-show-you-some-brotherly-affection hug. There was more contact than that and it was a little too long for that. It was more of an I'm-glad-to-have-met-you-and-I'm-glad-you're-a-female type hug.

Actually, one could stretch it and interpret it as an you're-really-nice-and-I-like-you-a-lot type hug. He *had* put his arms all the way around her and pulled her in tightly. Perhaps it was only her imagination, but on reflection, she thought she had felt him feeling her body with his body as they hugged which made it a combination "you're-really-nice-and-I-like-you-a-lot and, oh,-you-*are*-a-female-and-I'm-glad-of-that type hug. It was close enough and long enough for that. To be sure, he initiated and certainly hadn't resisted the encounters.

It didn't matter, now she had two holds on him. Howard Runner and her aunt's notebook. God, how she hoped her aunt could find that notebook. If she could, there would be more hugs. Hugs whose communication would be unmistakable unless he was a stump. Her mother had a point—she wasn't getting any younger and finding candidates with whom to spend the rest of one's life was like finding a parking place: the good ones were usually taken or handicapped.

# Chapter Sixteen

It was raining steadily the next morning as Jason wheeled his Honda into the staff parking ramp. The privileges of rank manifest themselves once again, he thought. He was a little early for his appointment with Playdon so he stopped into the Bus. Ad. School's lounge for a cup of hot tea. By force of habit, he headed for the student's area to enjoy his tea and read the sections of the *Wall Street Journal* that were spread about the lounge when he heard his name called out.

Playdon and Dean Nixon were at a table in the section where the faculty usually sat and were motioning for him to join them.

"Ah, Professor Playdon. Dean Nixon."

Dean Nixon was beckoning him with both hands, "Jason, join us here, will you? I have to leave in just a moment. As it happens I have a ten o'clock appointment. But first, tell me, how is your family getting along. Terrible tragedy about your nephew, eh?"

"Yes it was, thank you for asking. They're doing as well as one might expect. My sister-in-law has some guilt feelings but she's seeing someone. The reports I have is that time is healing."

"Sometimes time's the only thing that ameliorates the pain. I know my brother's boy drowned in Torch Lake back in the fifties when he was eight years old. My brother says not a day goes by but what he doesn't think of that boy. I recently asked how he was doing with the loss and he said he hoped one day to be close enough to the hole in his heart to be able to look into it. Such a pity when one of the little ones goes like that and us old farts hang on forever. Well, gentlemen, I have to run. Good day to you and if I don't see you again, have a great Thanksgiving holiday." And he was off.

"So Jason, I ask you the same question. How are things going with our Davidson Fellow, mmh?"

"Great, just great. I think before long I will be able to confirm that our Mr. Runner is actually Richard Mehr as you suspected."

"Oh my." Playdon expressed some surprise. "What have you learned?"

"I'm dating this girl . . ." Oh, now I'm dating her am I? ". . . who's an occupational therapist at the Home. I told her about our suspicions that Howard Runner may actually be Richard Mehr. It turns out that she was talking to her family about it and one of her aunts knew a Richard Mehr, a very popular preacher in Spring Lake, Michigan, who got into some trouble with his denomination. This Mehr resigned the ministry to avoid a heresy trial. He later dropped out of sight and was reputed to be starting a new life somewhere."

Playdon had turned his face away from Jason as if to hear better but kept his eyes on him and furrowed his brow in a quizzical expression. "When was this?"

"1958, I think she said."

"I remember that. It was in the papers. As I recall, it was over the literal interpretation of the Bible and he said that the grace of God may not be limited just to born-again Christians. It caused a hell of a hubbub at the time. There hadn't been a heresy trial around here for a long time.

"I remember it because there were several Jewish faculty members at the School at the time and one of them asked me if mainline Christians actually thought that they would be the only ones in God's good graces in the hereafter. He was a good friend. I told him that I couldn't speak for other Christians, but I was sure he wouldn't make heaven but that his wife certainly would because she had her hell on earth living with him." He laughed a little.

"We had a good laugh over it. So you think that reprobate pastor was, is, Richard Mehr, now appearing at the Christian Arbor Home as Howard Runner?"

"Strong possibility. This girl's aunt went to Mehr's church and kept a scrapbook, which I'm hoping to get a look at over the holiday break. If there are newspaper clippings, there should be photos which will either confirm it or it won't. I thought to do an Internet search on both Howard Runner and Richard Mehr, but with the requirements of the Fellowship I haven't had the time."

"If it is confirmed, what will you do then?"

"I've been thinking about that. I'm of a mind to respect his privacy and his decision to change his identity. If I'm right about this, it answers a lot of questions about Runner and his interaction with the other residents and the staff and why he has such a broad knowledge about theology and philosophy. But unless I hear better wisdom, I don't think it plays a role in my Report and I see no need to bring it up with him."

"I think that's the best wisdom. If he wants you to know, he'll tell you." Playdon was sitting back in his chair fiddling with the handle of his coffee cup for a moment, thinking. Then he straightened up and slowly crossed his arms and placed his elbows on the table. "Jason, I think he knows that we know."

"How so?"

"Thinking back, when he told us that he had been in my class, he got a peculiar look on his face, as if he had started to say something that he didn't want to finish. I assumed, as he said at the time, that he didn't do well in the class and he was embarrassed that I would remember him as a poor student. That explanation doesn't make sense now because when I looked at Mehr's records, I had given him straight A's. I think he got caught off guard and said some things that he knows might have revealed his identity."

"I remember that happening. I thought he was confused about the course numbers or something. And I distinctly remember him saying he didn't do well in the course because you didn't have any illustrations in your textbook."

"Well, my best wisdom is no better than yours. Leave it alone. And I'll put the wager on your bill," Playdon said with sly smile.

"Wager?"

"A week's wages that Runner was from the same tradition as the Home."

Then Jason remembered. "You were right. Well, don't spend it all in one place."

"I'll try. By the way, that's quite a lovely young lady you're squiring about town."

Jason raised his eyebrows in question. How did Playdon know about Annie? His question was answered before he could ask it. "I had dinner at Weller's on Saturday night as well. In fact, I couldn't get a table for over half an hour because of you."

"That's funny, I noticed the place wasn't very busy. There were empty tables all around us."

"I know. Runner bought out the seating in that corner of the restaurant. Stanley Weller's a friend of mine and, unbeknownst to me, knows Runner as well. Apparently, Runner wanted no distractions for the two of you. He needn't have bothered," Playdon said with a twinkle in his eye, "you were so engrossed in the charms of that young lady that you wouldn't have noticed if the President had been seated at the next table."

Jason felt his face flush. "Was it that obvious?"

"Yes, and not without good reason, I might add. Mrs. Playdon thought you made a very attractive couple. When are you scheduled to go out to the Home next?"

"Because of the holidays, I'm scheduled on Wednesday."

"Good. There's only ten weeks before the paper's due. It's best to stay on top of it. By the way, could you stop up to my office some time before the holiday? I have a first draft of the article we're co-authoring. Maybe you could review it over the weekend?"

"Isn't co-authoring a bit of a stretch here? I haven't put one word to paper."

"Not at all. I'm writing about your experience. You're doing the research. I'm just a scrivener."

Yeah, right, and the check's in the mail, Jason thought. He said, "I'll stop up and get it before I leave today."

"Good. I'll have it in a large manila envelope with your name on it at the receptionist's desk if I'm not there."

☩

The light on his answering machine was flashing when he got back to his apartment.

"Jason? Annie! My mother phoned. My aunt found the scrapbook or notebook—whatever you want to call it—and we're welcome to take a look at it over the weekend. Call me. See ya later. Bye."

He looked at his watch—5:30. She should be home. He dialed her number.

"Hello?"

"Annie, this is Jason. I just got your message. That's great about the notebook."

"Isn't it? I can hardly wait. Listen, sometimes the holidays are busy. Why don't you give me a call when you see how your weekend shapes up, and we can make something more definite when we know what our families have planned for us?"

"That sounds good. I was tentatively thinking about Friday evening. Dinner somewhere? Something light like a burrito at the Beltline Bar."

"That's your idea of eating light? Actually, it sounds great. I'll be hungry by Friday night. And they have great sangria. You'll call me with the time? Do you want me to meet you there?"

"I'd be honored to escort you portal to portal."

"Good! I like to be squired by a sailor. I'll wait to hear from you."

"See you later."

"Bye."

Squired by a sailor? What did that mean . . . ? Ah, Calvin Christian High School's athletic participants were known as the Squires, South Christian's were known as the Sailors.

✜

Jason made his way to the Christian Arbor Home after lunch on Wednesday. It was the day before Thanksgiving and this was the last thing he had scheduled before leaving for home for the weekend. As he came toward Runner's room, he could see the door was open and could hear conversation coming from the room. He slowed and strained to hear who Runner's visitor might be. Perhaps Runner had forgotten about the appointment. It was a female voice and it was unfamiliar.

He kept walking until he was in the hallway opposite the open door when Runner spotted him. "There you are! Come in, come in. There's someone here I'd like you to meet. Jason, my daughter, Susan DeLong. Susan, my young friend, Jason Richards."

Susan rose from the sofa to greet Jason. "I'm so pleased to meet you, Jason. Papa has told me so much about you. It's nice to put a face with the stories."

"It's nice to meet you. I can say that meeting your father has been *my* pleasure. I look forward to our weekly sessions."

"Okay, okay, enough of the obligatory small talk. Sit down you two. Jason and I have business to discuss. I received your thank you card in the mail yesterday. It wasn't necessary, but it was a nice gesture. Tell me, did the two of you pick out the cards together?"

"No, I wasn't aware that she sent you a card . . ." As Jason was touting his disclaimer Runner held up two cards. Each one had the same small blue flower design. "That's scary," he acknowledged out loud. "Did she tell you we showed up with the same clothes on?"

"Yes, and she told me she had a good time with a little more enthusiasm than was necessary. Tell me, *did* you have a good time?"

"Wonderful."

"Good." Runner lowered his head to peer more directly over the half frame glasses. "And you were able to control your testosterone . . ."

"Papa!" Susan interrupted her father. "Mind your manners." There was mock horror in her voice. She turned to Jason, "Forgive my father. There was a time when he could control himself, and knew what was appropriate to say in mixed company. But as he's aged, the control's been slipping."

"She's been accusing me of losing control ever since I used to challenge the young swains that would come calling for her. But enough of that, how'd the evening go? Tell me all about it."

"It was a perfect evening. I think I handled the three-fork issue correctly and didn't spill any soup on my tie. And the Death by Chocolate was just out of this world."

"Is that what Curtis called it? Death by Chocolate? That's not the name of that dessert, it's called Climax by Chocolate."

"Father! Please! Forgive him, Jason, he . . ."

"I gave Stan Weller that recipe, Susan. I think I know what the name of it is. Great isn't it, Jason? I always get a small taste of it when I go to Weller's. So what if it kills me, eh? What a way to go. And if it kills me, they can rightfully change the name of it to Death by Chocolate, eh? Stanley is a dear friend. He's a devout Jew, by the way. Conservative. Keeps a kosher kitchen. He claims that his mother, who died at ninety-six, recited the book of Psalms twice a week from memory right up until her death. Think of that. Most Two-Pound Bible Christians don't read the Psalms twice through in a lifetime."

"That is quite a feat considering you can't remember the name of a recipe at age seventy-six," Susan responded with mock seriousness.

"Maybe it's the kosher food keeps her mind sharp. Maybe it's the respect she gets from her children that keeps her going, eh, Susan?"

Susan just rolled her eyes as if her father were too much to bear.

"Stanley worked for a while for Ford and then went to work for his dad at the restaurant. We had a wonderful French chef in the dining room at my company at the time. Henri was his name." Runner pronounced his name "Onh-RHEE." "Henri had these wonderful original dessert recipes. Stanley was on my Board of Directors and every time we had a Board meeting, we served lunch complete with one of Henri's desserts. Stan would beg Henri for the recipe. Most of the desserts on the menu at Weller's, including Climax by Chocolate came from when Henri was the chef at the company.

"How did you come to have a restaurateur on your Board?"

"Oh, we were at Michigan together. He's one of the brightest men I know. We sat together in a couple of classes, and he introduced me to the game of squash. We got into some marvelous religious discussions. I had been introduced to a vision of pluralism that held that the different major religions are man's attempt to give expression to his understanding of the Truth, or as you would say, God. The image used was groups of people standing in a cathedral of stained glass windows with the sunlight streaming through. My group stands and sees the light through a particular window. Your group, standing in the light of a different window, will see the light differently. A different group, different light. Light from the same source, but seen differently through different windows. I postulated that different faith traditions; Christians, Jews, Muslims, Hindus, and so forth—all see Truth or God, in different ways because they were standing in different traditions as represented by the different windows diffusing the same light differently.

"This image gave Stanley Weller a place to stand as a Jew in a Christian culture at a time in his life when the Christian culture seemed oppressive to him. We've been fast friends ever since. I joke that I was the one who enabled him to take Christian money at his fine restaurant with a clear conscience. I've attended synagogue with him. I've heard Elie Wiesel, Chaim Potok, and Rabbi Kushner of *When Bad Things Happen to Good People* speak there. It is a wonderfully talented congregation with such good humor. There's no question the spirit of God is present in that congregation.

"For forty years now Stanley and I have been speculating whether it'd be possible for Christianity and Islam—which are both spin-offs of Judaism—to spin back into one great religion. He refers to it as Christianity and Islam coming home.

"We've concluded that it won't be in our lifetime. But Jason, think of the terror and carnage that's been perpetrated over the course of human history, essentially because of one seemingly insignificant event—Sarah's jealousy causing Hagar and Ishmael to get thrown out of Abraham's tent. From that moment on, the sons of Isaac and the sons of Ishmael have been wreaking havoc on each other continuing to this day. The only difference between nineteen hundred B.C. and two thousand A.D. is the sophistication of the weapons. And all the bloodshed and terror in the name of the same God, which seems to be ramping up these days to acts of unspeakable horror—stonings and beheadings and the like.

"Further, you'll allow that the Christian record against the

Jews is perhaps more unconscionable. Again, in the name of the same God. Is it any wonder that religion has been a turnoff for most of modern mankind? Or as Stanley said, 'With the kind of treatment the Christians have given my people, who could be afraid of Hell?'"

"Well," Jason offered, "Hell's eternal."

The blue eyes bore right in on Jason. "Is it longer than two thousand years?"

"*Touché*. But Jesus is the cornerstone of Christianity. Would the Jews accept him as the Messiah or, even more to the point, as God?"

"There's the rub. Even the early Christians began to doubt that Jesus was the Messiah when the Messianic age failed to materialize as Jesus himself prophesied and Paul seconded. That would be an even harder sell now. But perhaps more to the point, do you have to insist that Jesus was God? It's a claim of the Church that he was God. He didn't make that claim for himself. He clearly thought of himself as the *proclaimer* of the way to God. The Church has proclaimed the proclaimer.

"I would say emphasizing Paul's Christology as opposed to insisting on John's idea that Jesus was God and with God from the beginning of time could give Christianity the wriggle room it needed if the leadership wanted it. But realistically, we're not going to unwind two thousand years of the serious theological striving Christianity has gone through to justify its existence and its crimes. Unless it's good business or expedient politics to do so."

"Papa." Susan chimed in. "You're so cynical. In one sentence you would bring the religions together theologically and the next, you say it would take a secular miracle."

"Would you have me propose that the church leadership would accomplish this reunion? Remember it was less than four hundred years ago that Europe was engaged in a bloody thirty-year-long war to settle what was truly in the communion cup—a conflict that remains unresolved to this day, albeit with less violence. Pragmatism, my darling daughter, starts with the letter 'P.' So do the words 'perks', 'perches', 'power', and 'preachers.' Do you really think that those who are feeding at the trough of organized religion will give up their place for the glory of God? You're quite right! I'm a cynic and justifiably so. Do you deny they have had the chance for two thousand years and we've not seen a hint of it? Not a sniff?"

Throughout this discourse, Jason could feel that Susan Delong never took her eyes off him. She was watching intently, so much so that Jason could hardly refrain from returning the look. He suspected she was watching for some acknowledgment that he knew the secret. He felt like a player in a game. It was as if there was an elephant in the room and they were making small talk about this and that, but no one acknowledged the presence of the elephant. When we leave, we will wonder if anyone else saw the elephant. The emperor has no clothes, Jason thought.

Susan was speaking and edging forward on the sofa as if getting ready to stand, "I have a few things to pick up for Thanksgiving dinner tomorrow before the stores close, so I think I'll run along. You're being picked up at five thirty and you need to eat by six thirty, right? I'll see you then."

She rose to leave. "Jason, it was nice to meet you and again, thank you for choosing my father for your study project. You've been a nice change in his routine. If he gives you any trouble . . ." she went fishing in her purse and came up with a business card, "you call me. Have a nice Thanksgiving and I hope to see you again."

The business card gave her name as Susan Runner-Delong, Major Account Representative with Techtronics, Ltd. and listed her phone numbers.

"Is this your company?" Jason asked after she left, referring to the card.

"I don't have much to do with it anymore. I go for Board

meetings and occasionally when the mood strikes me I'll go over and work on an idea or two in the lab. But technology in the field of electronics moves so rapidly, if you miss a week, you miss a lot.

"And that, my young friend, is why I am enamored with philosophy. Ideas about the creation, the soul, the heart of man, our ties to the Eternal, our strivings for *raisons d'etre* are as ancient as the written word and as fresh as what you haven't yet read. I came up with an improvement on the light emitting diode and within one week, others in my firm had made my original one nearly obsolete. All the while, Socrates is as germane today as he was when he was forced to drink his cup of hemlock.

"I've come to believe that the secret to great wealth in America is to find a way to make Socrates commercially popular. Americans spend millions on pet rocks and sequins on their jeans and die without a consciousness of the great ideas of Western and Eastern civilization. Your tradition knows something about total depravity and believes it's a ticket to Hell. What about cultural and moral depravity? Aren't they an equal, if not eternal hell? The hell of the here and now? Ah, Jason, we get so soon old and so late smart, if we ever get smart at all. But enough of the ruminations of an old man. What is it we're to talk about today, you and I? Medication distribution, if my memory serves me."

You *are* a closet philosopher, a closet theologian. Will you come out of the closet? thought Jason. But he said, "Yes. Visser's report—and I brought a copy of it with me—came down hard on what he thought were some less-than-careful procedures for handing out medications. I would like to follow up on that. He included the written procedures as an exhibit in his report . . ."

At that moment, as if on cue, a rotund young woman dressed in white interrupted Jason, coming into the room carrying a small paper cup. "Good afternoon, Mr. Runner. It's time for your two o'clock pills."

"Good afternoon, Maizie. This is Mr. Richards, a friend of

mine. Maizie, would you please tell Mr. Richards what it is you have for me to take this afternoon?"

The girl was taken aback by the question. "Your pills."

"Well, we hope they're my pills. But what are the pills, what kind of medication?"

Her eyes darted between Jason and Runner as if she were guilty of something. She was getting uncomfortable. "I don't know what they are, but they're your pills."

"What are these pills for; what kind of condition or illness?"

"I don't know, I'm sorry. No one ever told me what's wrong with you."

At that Runner laughed. "And how do you know these are my pills and not Mrs. Boersma's pills, for example."

"Because they're in your slot on the tray. Yours is the fourth room, your name is on the door. These are the pills on the fourth slot. The fourth slot has your name on it. Come to the hall, I'll show you."

"That's not necessary, Maizie. How do you know I'm Mr. Runner?"

Maizie got a funny look on her face and then started to giggle. "Well, I can tell you're not Mrs. Boersma!"

Runner laughed at that as well. "Let me see the pills that are supposed to be for me. Yes, these are my Glucotrol pills. Very good, Maizie. Thank you. You get an A."

"Thank you, Mr. Runner." She scurried out the open door, surely wondering what that was all about.

"The residents are the best control this place has for proper medication distribution. The person passing them out knows nothing about medication. For me, I can check. For most of the residents, they don't know the difference between the pills they take and M&M candies. The mistakes are rare. In three years, I've been passed the wrong medication only twice. But once can be fatal."

"What can the Home do to improve the system?"

"Spend more money on better help. That young woman has no formal training in pharmacology, and she couldn't tell the difference between a coated aspirin and an M&M. But getting better help is not as easy as it sounds. Because many of the residents are on Medicaid, it means a larger deficit or raising the fees of those on private pay. Raising the fees means the Home prices itself out of a competitive market. In addition, good help's very hard to come by for nursing homes. These conditions aren't the best and cleaning up after old men and women is not the same as changing a baby's diaper. You don't see candy stripers in a nursing home. It's not glamorous work.

"Ah . . . look who comes to see us! Come on in Annie! Jason, I believe you know Miss Skelvan, the therapist Jeckel and Miss Hyde of the Christian Arbor Home?"

"Miss Hyde and I are on a first name basis, I believe. How are you Annie?" From the look on her face it was not a good day.

"I brought my car to the garage this morning and I just called to see if it was ready, and they say it won't be done until Friday." She turned to Jason. "I hate to impose, but I'm here to see if I can hitch a ride to Grandville with you this afternoon or tonight. Whenever you're leaving, if you have room."

"Absolutely! When are you off work?"

"Right now, as a matter of fact. And I'm all packed and ready to rock and roll. I just need to stop at my apartment and change and pick up my bag."

"I have a few minutes more here with Mr. Runner and I'll be ready to go. Should I come to the P.T. Room?"

"I'll be in the front reception room. I have to punch out yet and pick up my check."

"I'll see you in a few moments."

Jason finished up with Runner, who had gotten a copy of the Home's written medication distribution policy, which they discussed at some length. The procedures didn't always follow the policy but there was an honest attempt to do the best they could with the resources they had. In the final analysis, the Home depended more on Christian concern and caring for the people they served than on written policies, and they had kept incidents to a remarkable minimum.

"Well, that's that. Now, be off with you. You have a beautiful young lady in waiting in the lobby. Do I need to come with you so we can be certain you pick up the right one? I'd hate to see you have Mrs. Kaufmann on your hands for the weekend."

"And who's Mrs. Kaufmann?"

"I affectionately refer to her as 'Our Lady of the Purple Heart.'"

"The one who wears the purple clothes?"

"The one and only. And there's no charge for the little arrangement I made with the mechanic who's fixing Annie's car."

Jason stopped dead in his tracks. "You arranged for the garage to delay fixing her car so she would need a ride home? You are the Devil incarnate."

"No, no, I didn't. But I might have if I'd thought of it." His blue eyes were all a-twinkle, "I didn't know her car was in the garage, *if* it's in the garage. Have you thought about that, Jason? This may just be a ploy on her part to further your interest in her. Be careful, Jason, be very careful," he said with mock seriousness.

"Be careful? Now you tell me! You're the one who got me into this."

"That's like saying God made mankind, so he's responsible for the mess mankind is in. I admit to playing god in fixing you up with her, but I absolve myself from whatever mess you make of it. Listen, travel safely, and have a good Thanksgiving."

"The same to you. See you next week Friday? I want to talk about how Medicare and Medicaid works."

"I'll be looking forward to it."

# Chapter Seventeen

"Do you think about your faith much?"

They were between Ann Arbor and Grand Rapids on I-96. The conversation had centered around the problems Annie was having with her car and then their respective family's traditions for celebrating Thanksgiving. Then the conversation turned to Runner, or Mehr and the theological discussions in which Runner had engaged Jason over the past several weeks.

"No," she answered. "Not seriously since high school, I suppose. Life got busy and I'm comfortable with my beliefs. There hasn't been any challenges, which is fine with me."

"That's where I was, P.R."

"P.R.?"

"Pre-Runner. I had a place for everything and had everything in its place. And I had nothing to change or challenge that. Until I met Howard Runner."

"You've really been into it with him then, I gather?"

"The man has caused me to have nightmares."

"Nightmares? That seems a little extreme. I'm glad I don't discuss theology with him, then. What do you talk about that gives you bad dreams?"

"Pretty much everything. It started with the inspiration of the Scriptures, then the inerrancy of the Bible, then the deity of Christ, the possibility of salvation apart from Christ, the virgin birth, and yesterday, it was the possibility that all religions are man's attempt to understand the same God. He called it pluralism."

"Heavy stuff. Is there any question in your mind that he's a theologian? Engineers don't talk about pluralism and the virgin birth. Speaking of which, what does he say about the virgin birth?"

"You want nightmares?"

"Come on, I'm not going to get nightmares by discussing the virgin birth. You think I'm a Jesus groupie or something?"

"No, but when you think someone's taken away one of the important tenants of your faith, you start to worry that the whole thing may be a house of cards. Then you get nightmares."

She was silent for a few miles and Jason did not interrupt her thoughts.

Then she turned to him and said, "I don't think I want to hear what he had to say about the virgin birth."

The death of Deiter Richards cast a shadow over the Thanksgiving festivities. Not a cloud but a shadow. It was the first time they gathered as a family since the funeral. For a long time, it was like the presence of the elephant that everyone saw but no one mentioned.

Finally it was Karen who mentioned how hard it was not to have Deiter around on holidays when there was so much attention given to family. Karen, the mother, was indicating in her own way that she was healthier than the rest of them.

Then they talked about it. They remembered, they laughed, they were silent, they were healing. It didn't bring back the physical presence of Deiter, but the elephant disappeared. The shadow, however, remained, although now only a shadow of its former self.

On the ride from Ann Arbor, Jason and Annie had agreed to meet to review the scrapbook on Friday evening over burritos at the Beltline Bar. When Jason arrived at the Skelvan home to pick her up, he was invited in to meet her parents. These were awkward moments. Intellectually he knew they were as nervous as he was. But he felt as if he were on the witness stand and they were cross-examining him.

"Annie tells us you're going to be a hospital administrator."

"I hope to be someday," which were polite words meaning, if I do decide to ask your daughter to marry me, I will be able to provide for her financially.

"I understand you went to South Christian High?"

"Yes, I did," meaning, I'm a nice Christian young man and I promise to go to church every Sunday and have your grandchildren properly baptized.

"So you were born and raised around here?"

"Yes, in Wyoming, just a mile or two from here," meaning, yes, I'm from the right side of the tracks and there are no known criminals in my family.

"Are there many hospital administration jobs around?"

"A few come up from time to time," meaning, if I do marry your daughter, we probably won't be living in Grandville.

Until Annie appeared and rescued him. This time it was in a navy cardigan sweater over a white oxford cloth blouse and navy wool slacks. No matter the bow or the wrapping, the package kept looking better and better. It was hard to know where to look—not to gape, for that matter. It took a moment for Jason to notice she was carrying a black box the size of a scrapbook.

In the car she said, "My, my! A navy V-neck over a white turtleneck. I guessed wrong. Close, you'll allow, but wrong."

"Did you know we both sent Runner the same Thank You note?"

"First thing he showed me. Listen, really, I'm willing to go back in and change, if you feel more comfortable dressing alike."

"That's okay. I thought about the navy cardigan, but my grandfather was wearing it."

"Am I to suppose that V-neck's not his as well?"

"Ouch, ooh. That hurt."

"Don't play with dogs you can't run with."

"I heard V-necks are coming back."

"How soon?"

He gave up. "Hey! I was dressed well enough to drive you home from an Ann Arbor. Are you like all the rest? Use me and lose me? Tell me now. I may not want to go through with this date."

"You'll go through with it. I've decided the only way you'll get your hands on the scrapbook is after I've had my fill of burritos and sangria. Come to think of it, it'll quite likely take two pitchers of sangria, what with what's in my little black box here and all," she said tapping the box that was resting on her lap.

He resisted the urge to jump all over something that two weeks ago would have not even occurred to him. Instead, he said, "Well, tell me. Is it him?"

"All in good time, Mr. Richards, all in good time," she said, grinning wickedly.

At the Beltline Bar, they didn't have to wait to be seated.

"Table or booth?"

"Booth." Annie offered, "Non-smoking if you have it."

After they were seated, they ordered chips and cheese and burritos and a pitcher of sangria. When the waitress left, Annie opened the box and withdrew a thick, beige scrapbook. She put the empty box on the bench beside her. Then she opened the scrapbook slightly to determine its orientation. Upside down, Jason could see the banner of the *New York Times*. She closed the cover and turned the book around, and then reopened the cover. It was a slightly yellowed copy of a newspaper. The banner proclaimed that it was indeed the *New York Times*. It was dated August 22, 1958. There was a large picture under a headline that read, CHRISTIANS SPLIT: CAN NON-BELIEVERS BE SAVED? The likeness in the picture was unmistakable. It was Howard Runner forty-odd years ago.

"Judas H. Priest!" He looked at the picture. He studied it. It didn't change. It was Howard Runner, or as the caption said, Richard A. Mehr. He looked up to find her grinning at him.

"Have you read all this?" he asked, indicating the whole scrapbook.

"Cover to cover."

"And your impression?"

"You were right. It's a remarkable story. And our friend Mr. Runner is a remarkable man. Come sit on this side. I'd like to be able to see what you're looking at as you go through it," she said as she picked up the box and slid to the corner of the booth to make room. Just enough room.

As Jason got situated and opened the book, she said, "If you start from the back of the book and work forward, you can get a feel for the chronology."

It was a remarkable record. Newspaper articles from the *Grand Haven Tribune*, *Grand Rapids Press*, *Muskegon Chronicle*, *Detroit Free Press*, *Holland Sentinel*, *The Dallas Star*, *The Los Angeles Times*, the *Herald Tribune*, this story had gone around the world! There were transcripts of radio talk shows, personal letters from around the world, official letters from church officials, minutes of meetings, letters to the editors of the local newspapers. This was more information than an internet search would have provided. Who needs Google when Annie has her aunt?

Essentially, the controversy came down to two issues: was the Bible the only authority for faith and life, and, was salvation possible other than through Jesus Christ, or, as Mehr expressed it, was the grace of God available to the devout of other faiths?

Mehr's position was that the Bible was the Church's founding document and was very important as an authority for faith and life, but that experience also played a role throughout history in changing the theology of the Church—specifically in understanding the creation process, in the Church's understanding of slavery, and in the role of women in the Church. In each of these issues, Mehr had argued that our human understanding of what the Bible teaches changed in the light of natural or societal revelation. Further, Mehr argued that every doctrinal construction was historically conditioned and that for the Church to be relevant to the times, it had to speak in the language and in paradigms that could be understood by contemporary society. He called on the Church to be true to its stated motto, "Re-formed and always re-forming according to the Word."

The Church's position was that the Bible was the only standard for faith and life and that human experience didn't play any part in the formulation of theology or as an authority for faith or life. The sixteenth century doctrines were as relevant to our day as they were to the sixteenth century. Truth doesn't change.

As to salvation apart from Christ, Mehr's position was that; to the Jew's for example—the covenant promises made to the patriarchs were irrevocable, a position he believed was confirmed by Paul's writings in Romans 11. As to the other religions, he held that for anyone to claim to know the mind of God as it related to the extent of His grace to the devout of other faiths who called on His name was presumptuous and arrogant. This was especially true, Mehr said, in a time when the globe was shrinking and we would soon be forced to deal with other nations and cultures as our neighbors, if not family, and we would come to experience the devout of other faiths.

The Church's position was that salvation was through Jesus Christ alone, that there was "no other name under heaven given to men by which we must be saved" (Acts 4:12), and that Jesus was "the way, the truth and the life. No one comes to the Father but by (him)." (John 14:6).

Mehr's answers were that he agreed that there was no other human in the history of the world through whom God's grace was mediated and for him; Jesus was the way through which we see the heart of God. But to say that the grace of God could not be mediated directly to His devout followers or that Jesus' death somehow pre-empted God's grace exclusively for the followers of Jesus was to read something into the verse that was not there. As for the John 14 verse, to take that statement—made to his intimate circle of friends—which was a *particular* in the logic sense, and to make it a *universal* statement to exclude everyone else from God's grace was first of all a fallacy and, secondly, not a faithful interpretation in the light of all that was known about God's grace.

The Church leaders responded that Mr. Mehr's interpretations were not those that the Church traditionally accepted as being faithful to the doctrines and creeds of the Church. Mehr agreed with that.

Jason could not help but remark that if the picture did not confirm that Howard Runner was Richard A. Mehr, the theology certainly did.

The cheese was no longer soft by the time they got around to nibbling on the chips. Jason was skimming the articles as fast as he could to get the gist of the controversy, until he got to one piece over which Annie stopped him.

"Take your time on this one," she said. "This is a copy of a presentation Mehr made to the Classis at an early meeting. They were calling on him to recant his views."

# THE CLASSIS OF MUSKEGON

February 29

Sisters and Brothers,

You have before you a recommendation of your Executive Committee stating its conclusion that on two of the three questions put to me:

- Salvation apart from Jesus Christ, and

- The authority of Scripture,

my understanding is unacceptable and thus a process of separation should be undertaken—separation of myself from ordination.

And, to the best of my knowledge, judging the nearly unanimous voice of my people, separation of Christ Community Church, which I now pastor, from the denomination, as well.

I regret the recommendation. I had hoped the conclusion would be reached that there was room within the denomination, particularly within our local Classis for the posture and perspective that is Christ Community's, the largest of the churches in the Classis and one of the largest in the denomination.

While I regret their conclusion, I must say that my encounter with the Executive Committee has been cordial and gracious. I have a sense that they have genuinely tried to hear me and represent my views. They have labored long and struggled seriously and have treated me with respect. For that I am grateful.

It is not my purpose at this time to defend or explain my views on the specific issues raised.

Let me, however, say to you all what I said to the Executive Committee at the close of the session in which I addressed the three questions put to me. I think the real question has to do with a fundamental perspective on the theological task of the Church—is there room in the Muskegon Classis for one like myself who is—by inclination, passion, and education a wrestler with Scripture, with 2,000 years of Christian tradition, with finding a way to express the reality of God, of Grace, of the wind of God's Spirit—nudging this cosmic drama toward the Shalom of God's Rule?

This has been and is my life. My theological study has never been an intellectual game or a speculative charade. Were that the case, I could have accepted the contract offered me by Hope College some ten years ago, or managed to salvage my teaching position at Western Theological Seminary some five years ago now, or pursued an academic career at any point over the course of my ministry.

I have not done that. Rather, I have for the period of my ministry, with the exception of a six-month sabbatical, averaged forty-seven Sundays per year in my own pulpit with my own people, preaching never once without a biblical text. I have honestly, before the face of God, sought to understand and explain. And between Sundays I have been a pastor visiting my people, being with them in joy and sorrow, in struggles of living and the loneliness of dying.

And if you would know me most intimately you must know that there is no more sacred time for me to be the presence of God's love and grace than at the passing of my people and no time in which I *delight* more in the privilege of preaching than at the funeral of those I've loved and served.

I relate this because I want you to know that my theological reflection is pursued in the interest of my pastoral calling. My heart is in the congregation.

But, I have worked in the larger Church as well. If you will check the records, I have served some years in leadership within this Classis. In the past decade, I served as Chair of the denomination's Task Force of Evangelism and Renewal, on the Task Force founding the Dallas churches on a new model, on the Leadership Task Force under the old General Program Council, and on the Task Force that established and implemented the Theological Education Agency. And for seven years I was on the Board of Theological Education, serving the last couple of years as its Chair. At one time I was serving the denomination five assignments beyond Christ Community Church.

Some ten years ago now, I was invited to be one of the founding members of the Board of Editors of *Perspectives*, a journal of Reformed thought established by the RCA to stimulate theological discussion within the Church, and I served for these ten years.

I mention that because it is germane to the matter before us this evening. I was the one among the editors who more than any other addressed the entire denomination on key theological questions. We determined the contents of the respective issues in a bi-annual, three-day meeting and I seemed to be the point man in what was at the heart of our effort—to stimulate theological reflection and discussion. Why me?

In large part that fell to me because I was based in a congregation that had flourished in an environment of theological inquiry. There are not many in the Church who can risk openly raising and discussing questions that challenge traditional thinking. My beloved people have afforded me that rare freedom and thus I attempted over the decade of my writing to address the whole Church.

And again, why?

Because with deep conviction I believe the theological task belongs to every generation and a living Church will always be working at the fresh translation of the faith in order that theological expression and ongoing human experience stay connected. It is because I believe the grace of God—come to expression in Jesus Christ—is the news this world needs to hear, that I work tirelessly at finding a way to say it that will bring God's judgment and grace to bear on the human situation.

The biblical story is the founding story, the record of the revealing God encountering the human person in Israel and in Jesus and the Apostolic witnesses.

The Christian tradition is the record of the development of that story and its ongoing interpretation.

Present human experience in the cultural context in which we live—the explosion of human knowledge in the respective disciplines of human thought—must be taken into account.

Out of that mix emerges the preached Word—and here is the incredible claim of the Reformed tradition: the preached Word which becomes the Word of God.

I have suggested that the fundamental question before you is whether one who conceived of the task of preacher, pastor, theologian such as I do has a place in your midst. I have given account of myself by answering the why of my mode of ministry in two respects: My theological work is for the end of doing my pastoral work with authenticity and integrity and, secondly, to be a gadfly in the whole Church to stimulate the fresh expression of God's grace in our time.

What will you do with me? As you consider that, let me point you to my people. Paul wrote,

"Are we beginning to commend ourselves again? Surely we do not need, as some do, letters of recommendations to you or from you, do we? You yourselves are our letter, written on our heart to be known and read by all."

Read my people. Judge my theology by the lives of my people. Is that not a valid test? Is there a pastor among you that would not rejoice to have such a people?

And then more personally, in my mailbox this morning, I found a note from my daughter Susan, who is a member of one of your churches.

The second sheet read:

Dear Dad,

We love you and support you!!

All our love. Your Family!!!

And there were the signatures of six children and five grandchildren, even four-year-old Markie, in his own hand. The signatures came together on one sheet from Minnesota to Florida and back to Michigan. I do not apologize for the tears that came to my eyes.

Dear friends, I share this with you to lift up what ought not to be lost sight of—those who over many years have been pastored by me and lived with me intimately have surrounded me with love and solidarity such as I can hardly take in.

I am truly humbled for no one knows as well as I how flawed I am, how far I fall short of my own ideals, how limited my insight, how partial my understanding. But, beyond all the weaknesses that I share with the common lot of humankind, there is Grace—God's grace—grace present, amazing and abounding.

Let me appeal to you to defeat the recommendation before you. Let me appeal to you to end this investigation. Let us all then get on with our respective ministries.

That is not to deny a wide diversity of understanding among us. But, a broad spectrum of views is not a detriment to ministry. Rather, it gives us broader appeal to our community as together we bear witness to the grace of God in

Jesus Christ.

Grant me the privilege of being at your left, of pushing the limits, of stretching the parameters and trust me that I do it in Jesus' name for God's sake and the well-being of the human family. I do not fault you if you cannot live on the edge with me. In my Christian experience, I have traversed the whole spectrum from far right to far left but I have my eyes still on Jesus in whose face I see into the heart of God.

In December last, my mentor and dear friend, Hank Berkhof, died. In November of the previous year, Leiden University honored him and I was invited to bring a tribute. That weekend I visited with him; for two hours I wrung every ounce of energy out of him. I told him how near I stood with him, yet I said I sense I am facing a new direction. He affirmed that and said it must always be thus. On my first visit to him, there was pinned to the drape his study Tennyson's words:

*Our little systems have their day,*

*They have their day and cease to be.*

*They are but broken lights of Thee,*

*And Thou, O Lord, art more than they.*

I loved him immediately and over the years our friendship had grown. Finally on that Saturday, I took his hand and prayed with him, commending him to the God of all mercy, he uttering softly his own, "Ja." "Ja."

He taught me that our little systems shatter, but the Eternal God moves on with us. What a

> grand and glorious work this is in which we are all engaged.
>
> Let's get on with the work.
>
> Richard A. Mehr
>
> 2-29

"Very moving," Jason said softly with a catch in his voice. "It's Howard Runner, all right."

"It wasn't moving enough. The meeting ended by their voting thirty-eight to nineteen to move toward a peaceful separation."

"But from what I've read so far, the separation was anything but peaceful."

"The rub came when Mehr's church voted to stand by him and separate from the Classis as well, and by a nine-to-one majority. But listen, I have a suggestion. The burritos are getting cold and the sangria's getting warm. Let's put the book away. You can take it with you. It deserves to be read rather than scanned. Besides, I'm authorized to make you an offer you can't refuse."

He closed the book, although reluctantly, and handed it off to her, careful not to let anything fall out. "And what kind of an offer would that be?"

"My Aunt Maria Jean would like to talk to us and tell us the whole story. Turns out she was on the Board of Governance at Mehr's church and the church's delegate to all these Classis meetings. That's how she comes to have copies of some of these letters and things."

They talked through the burritos and the first pitcher of sangria, and the second, and a pitcher of Diet Coke. And it continued on the way back to her home. They questioned, they conversed, they speculated, they wondered about it all and the man who they had come to know and love and who was in the middle of such a big controversy in the Church so long ago, and had dropped out. And all the while they wondered about each other.

Jason continued to wonder why someone like her was unattached and wondered if she liked him at all or whether this whole episode was just about her curiosity over their mutual friend. He would find that out before the night was over, he decided.

At the same time, Annie was wondering what her friends would think. Some of them would think of him as being a little too scholarly; actually, the word "nerdy" might come to their mind. And if nerdy wasn't a word, she had just coined it. So be it, this one had substance. This one thought beyond the end of tonight. He could not be so sweet and unpretentious for this long if he was faking it. And while sweet and unpretentious were desirable qualities, she wondered if he had a romantic bone in his body. That would be put to the test shortly, she decided.

In the silence that ensued after Jason had turned onto her driveway and had switched the Honda's engine off, she sighed and remarked about how it was too bad they didn't make cars like they used to.

"How's that? Now there's something wrong with my car?"

"There certainly is, Mr. Richards."

"And what might that be."

"It's impossible for you to play Sailor and me to play Squire and do some of the sweet things Sailors and Squires are wont to do at the end of nice evenings, what with the gear shift between these bucket seats and all."

Bells rang off in his head again. And they played just the music he wanted to hear. "Where there's a will . . . Let me show you just one of the ways the Japanese automobile designers envisioned how this might happen."

It wasn't impossible to play Sailors and Squires in an '08 Honda after all. Something Jason realized she knew all along.

# Chapter Eighteen

"So last night was the fourth time you've seen her in a week?" It was Saturday morning and Karen was pouring tea in their comfortable kitchen.

"Yes, and I'll be seeing her again this afternoon. We're invited over to her Aunt's house for tea and to get her Aunt's take on my nursing home friend. Apparently she was one of the lay-leaders of that church at the time of this fracas."

"I was right. Will you admit I was right? The man's a heretic." Willard could not contain his satisfaction.

"I don't think he was ever adjudged to be a heretic. Besides, do you want to hear about this girl or talk religion?"

Karen, the sister-in-law, jumped in, "I want to hear about the girl. She's an O.T.?"

"She calls herself a C.O.T.A. That's a certified O.T. assistant."

"There's a lot of demand for that right now. You can pretty much work when and where you want to and no weekends, which are the scourge of the nursing profession."

Willard couldn't allow the conversation to remain civil. "I want to know if this relationship has possibilities. Is she a hot enough number to overcome your innate shyness and inexperience in matters of sexual encounters?"

"Willard! Mind your tongue!" Karen said it with less than the appropriate seriousness, revealing her curiosity as well.

"I haven't needed to tell her about my inexperience. I don't plan to try to bed her, but if I do, I'll confess that I'm a bumbling virgin and go for the sympathy angle. Good plan? What do you think?"

"It lacks, but it's the only chance you have. Maybe I should come along, see to it that you get it right."

"Actually, I referred to you last night. As a matter of fact, the only time I could think to bring your name up was in the heat of passion."

"Naturally, but I'll bite."

"She remarked that it must be impossible to make out in a '08 Honda. I said where there was a will there was a way."

There was a silence as both Karen and Willard looked at him with blank expressions.

"It's such a pity when I have to explain 'em to you, O Experienced One. Where there's a *Will* . . . there's a way."

"I guess you had to be there." Will tried to recover.

"I'm glad you weren't."

"When are you going to bring her over?" asked Karen.

"When are you going to be home alone?"

"Good point," she said casting a scornful eye at Willard.

"If she's everything you said she is and you like her, I hope this works out for you."

"It's a little early to tell, but thanks."

"Me too, little brother. And I'll be interested in what more you find out about our nursing home friend."

☦

Annie's Aunt Maria was a seventy-five-year-old widow who lived with a golden retriever named Digger in a small but lovely year-around home on the beach south of Grand Haven, another small town that was adjacent to Spring Lake. The two towns together had no more than twenty-five thousand souls. Hardly the kind of place where one would expect to find a heresy trial, especially years earlier.

It was a pleasant forty-minute drive from Grandville through farmlands and fields of blueberry bushes and growing nursery stock. The home was at the end of a long drive that wound through a magic land of virgin white pines, fiddle-back ferns, and sand dunes until the road opened to the house and a spectacular vista of the blue waters of Lake Michigan.

The house was nestled atop a dune and its western exposure was two-story glass with balconies overlooking the lake. The late afternoon sun shining from the west made the water dance with diamonds in the swath of the sunlight. There was a fieldstone fireplace with a blazing fire to make the place snug and cozy against the November afternoon.

To look at Maria Jean Van Dyken, she appeared to be an average person, like anyone's idea of an older aunt. What wasn't immediately clear, but didn't take long to find out, was that she had a keen mind. After the introductions and Aunt Maria's inquiry about who knitted the handsome, wide-knit wool turtlenecked sweater Annie was wearing, she served tea and homemade chocolate chip cookies with nuts. The cookies were soft and still warm, and they were wonderful.

"Before we begin, how *is* Dick? We haven't corresponded for four or five years. Actually since his last hip surgery, the one that didn't work out so well."

Annie answered. "He's fine. He's bound to a wheelchair and right now I'm working to help him keep what leg motion he has retained. But there's almost no hope that his condition will improve. More surgery is apparently out of the question. He's a joy to have as a patient, although the nursing home staff, as a group, are a bit disgruntled with him. They think he is an atheist or something and are constantly trying to save his soul."

"I don't think they need to be concerned about his soul. Do any of them know who he is?"

"We don't think so."

"Jason, if I may ask, why did you even think to question who he was? His whereabouts have been such a well-kept secret over the years. Even I had no idea where he was. All the correspondence goes through his daughter, Susan. And for you two to be asking questions was so . . . well, I was so shocked when I figured out who it was you were talking about last Sunday at your father's party."

"Actually, Mrs. Van Dyken . . ."

"Please, Jason! Call me Maria Jean or Aunt Maria, if you like. Mrs. Van Dyken sounds so old when someone as young as you says it out loud."

"Very well, Aunt Maria." Jason recounted the story. "For me, the tip-off was that while it was clear that he was an electrical engineer, all he ever wanted to talk about was philosophy and theology. He has a second room in the nursing home crammed with philosophy and theology books."

"So Annie tells me. He was never very far from his library and a stack of unread books. That extra room is no surprise to me. Well, tell me, do you have questions or would you like me to tell the story? What's your pleasure?"

"I'd like to hear the story from the beginning, if you don't mind. But first, there is one question that's been bothering me."

"Certainly."

"How did a church in such a small village get to be one of the largest churches in a mainline Protestant denomination?"

"That's not the half of it. There were five or six other churches from the same denomination in this area at the time. What happened was that from the time he arrived in Spring Lake, there was an excitement at that church that was tangible. It grew from one service on Sunday morning to two services to three in a sanctuary that sat three hundred fifty. Finally, we built a sanctuary to hold eleven hundred and we still held two services. And why did the church grow? Dick Mehr. He was a powerful preacher who pulled up a stool and addressed the issues of the day and the struggles of life in such a way that you felt blessed by having been in worship. And you wanted to come back, and you missed it if you couldn't be there. He could move you like no other preacher I've ever experienced."

"He preached from a stool?"

"He was having trouble with his hips at that time already and couldn't take standing for three services. One time a member of the congregation said that he thought Dick could preach from a bar stool, meaning of course from a stool in a bar. Dick told him if he got one, he would do it and he did it from then on.

"Essentially, I believe the growth came from his preaching but the worship services were enhanced by great music and exchanges with the local Roman Catholic church and the Jewish synagogue and eminent theologians. Easter Sundays were to die for. You just wouldn't miss them. And there were party Sundays with Dixieland bands playing and there was sacred dancing. It was something else for a Dutch Reformed Church at that time, let me tell you. Worship was celebrative. We made a joyful noise.

"And I must say, Dick didn't appeal to everyone. But he attracted seekers and questioners for whom the Church had been a turn off for some reason or other. Some people came from other churches in the denomination, which didn't help Dick's popularity with his fellow ministers. Some came from other traditions, all the way from lapsed Lutherans to Eastern Orthodox. The best of these traditions blended and there was an acceptance and an inclusivity that was tangible. And the church grew dramatically.

"But let me start at the beginning. The First Dutch Reformed Church of Spring Lake, Michigan, was ninety years old when Dick first arrived. He was fresh out of college and was the intellectual hope of the right wing of the denomination."

"Excuse me, did you say the right wing?"

"The *far* right wing. He left after a time and went to Europe to study for his Ph.D. When he returned to this country, he was divorced and a broken man and had lost some of the dogmatic certainty for which the far right is sometimes noted. The church was without a minister then and they asked him back at a time when a divorced preacher was synonymous with an unemployed preacher.

"That's when things began to happen. We changed the name of the Church to Christ Community . . ."

The story was a fascinating one, interrupted more than once to freshen the tea or pass the chocolate chip cookies.

"It's my opinion what really got Dick in trouble was his tireless efforts to push the denomination into the next century before they had had gotten out of the last one. First, we called a divorced man into our pulpit—strike one. Then we changed the name of the church, omitting any denominational references because Dick thought that denominational references had lost their meaning to the average Joe on the street—strike two. We allowed Dick to remarry—strike three. Dick pushed for women to be elders, not a popular position at the time—strike four. He pushed for the ordination of women ministers which some folks thought was unbiblical—strike five. He got the position on the editorial Board of *Perspectives* and wrote articles that some called thought provoking, others called heresy. The heresy charges didn't seem to faze him. I can still hear him saying 'the heresy of one generation is the dogma of the next. If I live long enough, I'll be old news.'

"He was given the position of Professor of Preaching at the seminary when it was coveted by others—strike seven or eight. He refused to partake in the politics of the local Classis and go to their meetings on a regular basis. And I think there was a measure of professional jealousy that Christ Community had become a mega-church—although they weren't called mega-churches at that time—while by-and-large the other churches in the Classis grew slowly, if at all.

"In fairness to the other side, there was blame to be laid at our feet as well. Some of our members made statements that the theology of the other side was out of the dark ages and that the other ministers in the Classis hadn't thought a new thought since they left seminary. There was the clear implication by some that we were the enlightened ones and they were naïve. We also caused trouble for them because our church refused to pay assessments for the denominational news magazine.

"I remember one of our associate ministers likened the situation to us being the successful child who had not shown proper deference for the parent, and they were the parent who could not bless the success of the child.

"So while the presenting problem was Dick's theological views, the politics of the situation was such that some his peers were fed up with his success and his perceived arrogance. They didn't stand up for him when the heat came. They were glad to be rid of him and said so among themselves."

"Arrogance? That's the last word I would think to use to describe him now," Jason offered.

"What not many people knew was that he was very shy. His shyness was often mistaken for arrogance because he wasn't outgoing and gregarious, except to his congregation where he felt comfortable. He almost always refused invitations for guest appearances.

"His congregation loved him and stood by him in a remarkable show of solidarity. That's what kept him going. But at the same time, he was deeply pained by some of the ministers from the Classis and others from the seminary or the larger denomination who would call him and support him privately, but would either remain silent or speak in favor of his being separated in public."

"Why would they do that? For fear of losing their jobs or financial support for their ministries. These were people of national repute, people of influence in the denomination."

"So from what little I've had a chance to read, there was an initiative for a peaceful separation. But the separation was anything but that. What happened?"

"The Classis had no leadership. Their Executive Committee bumbled and fumbled their way through this mess like men trying to push a rope. One of my fellow elders joked at the time that he felt their bumbling was reason enough to ordain women. He said it was the only way to get someone with *cajones* into our pulpits."

Both Jason and Annie snickered. Aunt Maria paused and smiled at her little joke, then pressed on with the story.

"For example, there would be a separation agreement struck between the Church and the Classis negotiating committee and they'd fail to bring it to the Classis for approval, or they would bring the agreement to Classis and tell Classis they thought they got a bad deal, or they . . ."

"What do you mean, a bad deal?" Annie asked.

"A lot of the wrangling was over money. The Classis wanted compensation for the loss of the Church property and the dues the Church was paying. When presenting the agreements for approval they wouldn't bring the most up-to-date versions. The body would ask questions the leadership couldn't answer.

"And the Classis was not of one mind. Dick had a few supporters in the group, but the Classis executives would lessen their influence by not telling them of important committee meetings. It wasn't pretty and frankly, we felt there was a lack of competence or integrity on the part of their executive committee, and maybe it was some of both.

"Some members of Classis sabotaged Dick. There was one in particular I remember. Herman Wurst was his name, a minister who retired from a quite successful ministry in the area but didn't get the recognition his efforts deserved, probably because Dick was getting all the notice. He had been pastured into some capacity in the denominational offices. He would come to the meetings with a personal agenda and ask questions—not to get answers—but for the purpose of raising straw men and confusing the issues.

"We suspected he saw a chance to further his standing in the greater church. He wasn't above standing on Dick's fallen body to do it. He was a self-perceived champion of 'doing what was painful but was necessary and right' and lobbied behind the scenes for Dick's separation—all with the obligatory piety and appropriate self-righteousness, of course. We irreverently nicknamed him 'The Right Reverend Hot Dog.'

"And remember, their *only* concern was for the purity of the gospel and the furtherance of the Kingdom of God. The evidence that the Kingdom of God advanced further at Christ Community Church under the leadership of Dick Mehr than at most of the other churches in the Classis combined was somehow lost in the debate.

"But I haven't answered your question, have I? Things became mean-spirited when they realized the Church was going to follow Dick out of the denomination if the Classis forced him out. This was the third largest church in the denomination and represented a significant portion of the financial support of the Classis. They didn't understand that the membership grew because of the ministry of Dick Mehr, not because it was a church of their particular denomination.

"Actually, few of the members felt a strong allegiance to the denomination. The allegiance of vast majority was to Dick, the minister who was marrying them and burying them and helping them through the struggles in their life. It was pressure from the community and pressure from the denomination that forced them to back off and let us go into independence.

"Having won the battle—apparently anyway—why did he finally then resign and take on a new life?"

"Some said that finally the fight just wasn't worth it. Others said what triggered his leaving was someone on the playground told his granddaughter that she was going to Hell because she went to Christ Community Church, and the child who said it was the daughter of a lay-leader of another church in the Classis. Others speculated that the last straw was the hateful letters in the newspaper saying we should take the name 'Christ' out of the name of the Church. There were calls on the telephone calling him a heretic and a devil and an apostate. Finally, he hung up from one of those callers and walked away from it all. I think he did it for health reasons, both physical and mental. Remember, this group of his peers acknowledged on the one hand and in writing that Dick had a work and ministry through which many had been blessed, but they wanted to "hold him in disrepute before Christ, the church, and the community."

"He didn't walk away from it all. He took a lot of it with him. I can testify to that," said Jason quietly.

"I can tell you that we've all taken it with us. There are wounds that have never healed on both sides of this fence. It changed the face of the denomination. Many good pastors took early retirement rather than have to take a stand that might be unpopular. Hope College took a turn to the right and lost some of its standing in the wider academic community. My grandchildren were bred into Hope, that's where their parents were educated. But when the time came, they chose to go elsewhere because of some of its shift to the right and the loss of some of its academic freedom. They used to try to hire the best educators they could, regardless of faith profession. Very near this time, statements affirming a belief in Christ's atonement became a hiring prerequisite for faculty. And I'm told that life was made to be uncomfortable for a tenured professor of biology who happened to be Jewish."

Aunt Maria was silent for a moment and they were left with the hiss and occasional crackle of the fire in the fireplace and the sleeping Digger's heavy breathing. She spoke softly when she started again. "It's a time in my life I wish I could excise but can't. From time to time I'll get out the scrapbook or come across a sermon reprint and all the memories come flooding back, with all the good ones tinged by the bitterness of the brouhaha. I don't know whether to pray for it to happen again or to help me forget it happened. What a tragedy it was . . . such a tragedy . . . and all for what? An exclusivist claim for God's grace for just me and my little group—grace for which the best of us are undeserving—and the rest of His children be damned? And in their view, heaven became closed to me because I suggested that its doors may be opened wider than just wide enough to let me squeeze in."

When the story was over and the questions were answered, Annie and Jason took Digger for a walk on the beach. Actually, as it turned out, Digger took them for a walk as he insisted on playing an endless game of "Fetch the Drift Wood." They talked a lot at first, about what they had heard and what it had meant when it happened and what it meant to them now. They spoke less as they became enthralled with the beauty of a majestic sunset that slathered up the whole western half of the sky with reds and oranges and purples.

Observing that magnificent scene, Annie caught her breath and said, "Such beauty! Do you think it's His way of telling us that no matter how bad we screw things up in His name, He still paints 'His footsteps in the sky . . . ?'"

"'And rides upon the storm!' It's clear to me that God maintains and supports his Church, because if the Church were dependent on man's efforts alone, it would have self-destructed long ago."

There were periods of time when they didn't talk, when the only sounds were the waves washing up on the shore and rushing back to join the lake and the scrunching of the sand as they walked. When they didn't talk they wondered as they walked.

Jason wondered if the beautiful young woman he had his arm around and who had her arm around him was one that he liked a lot or loved and whether she liked him or loved him.

Annie wondered if this serious young man who had his fingers wrapped around her waist about one inch below where the curve of her breast started liked her a lot or if she was merely a tool to help him learn about his nursing home friend and complete the requirements of his degree.

Jason stopped and faced her. He was holding her with one hand on each side of her torso. He looked at her intently, and then slowly bent over and kissed her. Then he gathered her into his arms and hugged her. And there was no mistaking what kind of a hug he intended it to be. His brother Willard would have called it the vertical prelude to the horizontal symphony.

She pressed into him with the full length of her body so that he could not mistake what kind of a hug she intended it to be. Actually, later she would feel better about the look than the kiss and the hug. She had kissed and hugged a lot of guys but none of them had looked at her like that, either before or after the kisses and hugs. He was a very serious young man and that had been a very serious look. If her perception of the meaning of that look was correct, it was no longer a question of whether but a question of enough.

Maria Van Dyken stood in the doorway as she watched the young couple drive back through her part of the magic forest. Young people in love were so full of hope and promise. And full of questions. The questions don't go away, do they? Each generation may phrase them a little differently, but essentially, they are the same questions, "What is the Ultimate Reality? Who or What, finally, can I believe in?" And through the corridors of her memory came one of the answers that Dick Mehr had given her many years ago, "That I am not my own, but belong, body and soul, to my faithful Savior, Jesus Christ." That was her answer. She wondered if it would still be Dick's answer. She wondered if it would become the answer for these young kids. She prayed they would find their answers.

When she could no longer see the taillights of the nice young man's Honda she called Digger into the house and closed the door. She sat down at her writing desk, picked up the phone, and punched the numbers for long distance information for the eastern part of the State of Michigan.

"Thank you for calling AT&T. What city please?"

"Ann Arbor, for a listing for Howard Runner?"

"Please hold for the number," said the human voice.

The familiar computerized voice followed and gave her the number.

Without a moment's hesitation after getting a dial tone, she punched the buttons. It rang twice and when the connection was made, an unmistakably familiar voice said, "Hello?"

Now she hesitated, uncertain of the wisdom of the call . . . then made her voice reach out over the years and over the miles and said expectantly, "Dick . . . This is Maria Jean Van Dyken . . . ."

# Chapter Nineteen

On Sunday evening, Jason drove back to Ann Arbor alone. Annie had an armchair that needed to get to Ann Arbor but was too big to fit into his Honda. Her father and mother brought her back in their Suburban.

During the drive to Ann Arbor, he decided two things: that he better find out soon why Annie Skelvan, this intelligent, charming, witty, beautiful young professional woman he was seeing was not already attached, because before too long he would be past caring what the reason was, and, in spite of—or maybe because of—what he had found out over the weekend, he would continue to respect Runner's privacy.

He had spent the afternoon reading over the contents of the scrapbook. The historical record was fairly complete. There were the minutes of meetings from both sides of the controversy, copies of letters from all over the world, many expressing support, some condemnation. There were newspaper editorials for and against; letters to the editors that went both ways, but mostly in condemnation; articles from religious publications and position papers. Throughout the controversy, except for the comments from some of the lay-leaders of the Classis, the debate was handled with dignity and compassion by the parties involved.

Runner and his Church exhibited a particularly noticeable grace and a singular purpose, as if they were well advised and under good leadership. Their position was usually articulated very well. The Classis seemed to flounder here and stumble a bit there. It was apparent that, as Maria Jean Van Dyken has said, they lacked leadership or a defining purpose.

The one connection that Jason could not make in his mind was how the opposition condemned Runner to Hell. Runner proclaimed Jesus as Savior and Lord and affirmed Jesus was the Christian's way to reconcilement with the Father. Runner also believed that God's grace may be extended to the devout of other faiths that called on God's name.

The opposition believed that salvation was attainable only through Christ; therefore, many of the opposition claimed Runner was going to Hell and was leading his flock to Hell as well. It was that "therefore" that didn't connect. As Mrs. Van Dyken had said, "If I open the door of heaven wider than for me to squeeze in, it somehow shuts for me." And while that might not compute for him, Jason knew it computed for his brother even now, some forty years later. Had he, Jason, changed so much, or was he never really there?

He wondered where his Internet friend was on these issues. When he attempted to turn on his computer, he was surprised to find it already turned on. He reached for the mouse only to find it on the left side of the keyboard instead of on the right where he always used it. The screen lit up as soon as he touched the mouse. It had been on, but in the "sleeping mode." He distinctly remembered he had shut it off when he left for the weekend. Or had he? He was almost positive he had turned it off. And he had no reason to leave the mouse on the left side of the keyboard. Unsettled, he logged onto the Internet and crafted an e-mail message:

>1st Horseman:
>
>Thank you for your response re: the virgin birth.
>
>&lt;&lt; . . . what you expect from the religious right, right?&gt;&gt;
>
>Right!
>
>&lt;&lt; . . . grant me the resurrection and the rest, all the rest, is negotiable.&gt;&gt; Bold statement, but I understand, grant me this historical fact and all the rest is human interpretation. This understanding is quite different from my tradition of systematic theology where there is an accepted interpretation for EVERYTHING, outside of which it is dangerous to wander.
>
>Your answer emboldens me to ask your understanding

on yet another issue: where do you stand on the issue of salvation through Christ alone vis a vis the devout of other faiths i.e. Jews and Muslims?

Regards,

RichJason

Jason had also reviewed Professor Playdon's draft of the magazine article on which he made a few notes in the margins. He didn't think someone of his caliber should rework an article written by someone of Playdon's caliber. And the mystery of the off again—on again computer lingered in his subconscious.

☦

The article was the initial subject of their weekly Monday morning meeting. But before long the conversation turned to the Christian Rest Home and then to Runner. Jason told Playdon about the notebook and the conversation in the beachside home.

"Did this aunt of your young friend know where Runner was before now?"

"No, she said his whereabouts was a closely kept secret."

"Do you think she has been in touch with him since you left her?"

"I don't know. I didn't think of that possibility. Do you think she has?"

"I shouldn't wonder. They were up to their eyeballs in some pretty heavy stuff. That kind of involvement usually engenders strong relationships. If you were her and knowing Runner as you do now, and you found out where your long lost friend and former pastor was, would you call him?"

"I probably would."

"You'll know soon enough. Friday I'd wager. Interesting. Very interesting. If he does know that you know, this may become all the more interesting."

"How so?"

"He'll be able to talk to you as Richard Moore or Mehr or whatever. Things won't have to be filtered through his alter ego. Besides, it's not often one gets to engage a real honest-to-goodness internationally known heretic. I'm envious. Let me know how it comes out."

☦

Jason felt a growing angst as the week moved inexorably toward eleven o'clock on Friday. On the one hand, the discovery had been accidental. One the other hand, he had left no stone unturned when the mystery presented itself. Runner's true identity was none of his business. But perhaps Runner had set him up with Annie so they would piece the whole thing together. Then again Runner wouldn't need to do that, he could have just told Jason who he was. Or Playdon.

He had become certain—as Playdon had suggested—that Runner knew that Jason knew. But then, why hadn't Annie called. Surely Runner would tell Annie if he had spoken with her Aunt. That would lead one to believe that Runner didn't know that they knew.

And what of all the things they had talked about? Was Willard on good ground when he implored Jason to forget about the understandings he had come to through Runner? Here was a man who was to be tried as a heretic in a mainline Protestant denomination. But he made so much sense and was so well read and intelligent.

But then wasn't it Pastor Lipscomb that had said that ". . . the Devil's work is most insidious and clever in academic circles were the ability of the mind and the power of reason is glorified." Lipscomb and Willard could walk in lockstep down his throat on this one.

Lipscomb, Jason had almost forgotten about Lipscomb. He made a mental to note to call him before the Christmas holidays. Perhaps he should make it a point to make it to Sunday worship services, Jason thought.

It was cold and blowy on Friday morning. A sharp contrast to the previous weekend when it was almost like summer when Jason and Annie had walked on the beach and watched the sun drop into Lake Michigan. Everything was either in contrast to Annie or about Annie these days. His feelings for her were getting out of hand, he thought as he pulled into the parking lot of the Christian Arbor Home.

Our Lady of the Purple Heart was holding court as usual in the lobby. "Good morning, Mrs. Kaufmann."

The lady was taken aback when he addressed her personally. "Good morning," she croaked in response and surprise.

The door to Runner's room was open as usual and he was sitting at his secretary writing when Jason tapped on the door frame.

Runner looked up over his half frame glasses and bellowed, "Jason, Jason, my young friend. Come in, come in and if you don't mind, close the door behind you." He lowered his head, the better to look directly at Jason. "Today, some privacy might be appropriate, neh?

"So," he said gently as he wheeled away from the secretary, "I understand you've had a busy weekend and now you know."

"Yes, now I know. Rather, now I'm certain."

"Well, Jason, you can take the theologian out of the pulpit, but I have come to learn that you can't take the theology out of the theologian. But tell me, what gave me away?"

"It was hard to believe that an electrical engineer would treasure a book by Ernst Troelsch."

"So! True enough. I thought I might have given it away when

I was surprised by Professor Playdon. At that time I hadn't changed my name yet. I was still Richard Mehr when I took his classes."

"That was another strong indication. He knew your name wasn't Howard Runner."

"How was that?"

"His mother's maiden name was Runner."

"So was my favorite Philosophy teacher in college. I had a wonderful talk with Maria Jean Van Dyken. We laughed, we cried, we caught up. She was such a trooper in those difficult times. But the way, I'm pleased to see that your relationship with Annie progresses."

"And just how do you know it progresses?"

"The lovely Mrs. Van Dyken has a genuine concern for her niece. She also has a very powerful telescope."

Runner watched in amusement as Jason blathered a weak attempt to defend himself before continuing. "Thou protesteth too much. It's clear my work in setting you two up has accomplished its purpose and your hormones have taken over. Don't apologize, that's how it's supposed to work. Now, about me, perhaps you have a question or two before we get down to the business of your visits?"

"More than a few. Most importantly, why, when it appeared that you had prevailed, did you decide to bag it?"

Runner paused a moment as if to consider his answer. "At the height of the controversy, there appeared to be two courses of action. One was to follow the urgings of several of my ecclesiastical colleagues and press the fray, rally those in the denomination who agreed with me, and force the discussion of the critical issues at the highest levels. The other was to back away as gracefully as possible. A fight would have split the denomination that had nurtured me, a fight in which the cause of Christ would not have been honored. And at my core, I'm not a fighter.

"One of my close friends and churchmen was a psychiatrist. He could see that my health was deteriorating under the strain of trying to hold it all together. He said I was borderline physical and mental breakdown and, if I didn't get out, my heresy trial might take place in the throne room of heaven. I responded that I was certain I would get a fairer hearing there. But for the sake of my health, my family, my children, my grandchildren, and to avoid an ecclesiastical bloodletting, some close friends engineered my removal from the situation. On reflection, it was probably harder to get out than it might have been to stay in.

"But it was clear that my presence was a lightning rod for this whole affair. When I was gone, those who would've defrocked me—and there were more than a few of those—lost interest in the fight. The denomination was able to squirrel the relevant issues away and they're now the subject of some debate in theology classes in the seminaries. But no one has since raised the issues in the greater Church for fear of the reaction I got. So honest inquiry on these issues and on others have been stifled. The winners lost. The key issues were lost, too."

"To your mind, what were the critical issues?"

"Not the authority of the Scriptures or salvation through Christ alone as was reported by the press, although the charges brought against me rightfully indicated my understanding of these doctrines was to the theological left of the majority of that Classis. Rather, the fundamental question was whether the Church would be true to its own motto which called on it to keep re-forming its doctrines to find a relevant expression of God's grace for our time.

"Help me out here," Jason interjected. "The motto of your denomination *was* to keep re-forming its doctrines. That was clear in the articles I read in Maria Jean Van Dyken's scrapbook. Given that, why didn't the Church allow for that to happen in your case?"

"On reflection, I think the Church has fallen into a trap. A trap to which most established denominations succumb. There's a time in their history when the fires of religious passion burned brightly. In most instances, that fire comes from some revelation, some experience, or a new understanding of the Scriptures. The experience is verbalized. The verbalization is then explained and the insights gained are codified to preserve the passion. Succeeding generations retain the dogmas, their creeds. Then times and perspectives change, the fires abate, but the dogma remains. The dogma becomes the defining standard; it becomes more important than experience that generated the passion and fueled the fire that forged the dogma, and it supersedes the Scriptures.

"Scriptures become the proof of the dogma. Scriptures are interpreted in the light of the dogma, instead of allowing the Scripture to shed its light on the dogma. I was never accused of being in disharmony with the Scriptures or denying the experience, only with the dogma, which in this case were the Standards of Unity—the Heidelberg Catechism, the Canons of Dordt and the Belgic Confession."

"What do you mean when you say the Scriptures are interpreted in the light of the dogma?"

"That means when you come to a passage of Scripture that would seem to be a contradiction of the creeds, you say, 'that passage cannot mean what it says, I must interpret this passage in the light of my creed, therefore, it must really mean such and so.' For example, the creeds hold that God's grace will be limited to only those who believe in Jesus. When you come to the first letter of John where he says that Jesus ' . . . is the atoning sacrifice for our sins, not only for ours but also for the sins of the whole world', you say, 'because the creeds only hold out hope for those who believe in Jesus, this passage doesn't *really* mean the *whole* world.'

"I believe with deep conviction that the theological task belongs to every generation and a living Church will always be working at a fresh translation of the faith so theological expression and ongoing human experience stay connected. The Classis and many in the

Church at large believe the statements made in the sixteenth century said it once and for all and deny the ongoing human experience. Therefore, the theology and the human experience do not stay connected and the theology lacks integrity and becomes irrelevant."

Runner paused for a moment, as if reflecting on those times so long ago when his little controversy became shouts heard around the world. Then he drew a deep breath and continued, "Now forty years have passed. The human experience has continued, knowledge has grown geometrically, human understanding in the physical sciences and the human sciences multiplies, and the Church remains in a cocoon spun in its larva stage in the sixteenth century. And it could emerge as the butterfly for which a hungry world waits."

"But, with all due respect," Jason jumped in again. "If I take your premise to its conclusion, in the past five hundred years, or in the past forty, the Church has been content with its sixteenth-century paradigm and many in the Church not only accept it but will defend it to the death, my brother included. Their theology *is* relevant to them."

"Good point. I would agree that the sixteenth-century paradigm is relevant to the Church and those born into it, but it's my contention that it's not the most effective way to proclaim the gospel to those outside the Church. For the most part, that proclamation isn't successful in its appeal to the man or woman on the street. In this country, church membership does not keep up with population growth. In Europe, the practice of religion is virtually dead.

"I think the example of Jesus can be relevant here. First, he was a good preacher and theologian in that he attempted to find a fresh expression of the faith and connect it to his contemporary scene. Second, he took his ministry to the streets, to the people. He didn't, for the most part, attempt to become a better churchman and work within the Church to improve the Church, which may have been his downfall as it was the established Church that did him in.

"The other thing I would say is that many in the Church have long held the untenable position that my different understanding somehow denigrates yours. For example, when I questioned the position of the Church of salvation by Christ alone and suggested there was another possibility allowed by the eleventh chapter of Romans and other scripture passages, I never once suggested that salvation *couldn't* be attained through Christ. That is to say, I never once denied salvation through Christ. In fact, I claimed it. I proclaimed it, every Sunday.

"But because I had come to an understanding of Romans that was broader than what was commonly and previously held, there was both the perception that I was wrong and that I had invalidated or cast aspersion on the sixteenth-century paradigm. I don't think either was the case. This idea that my understanding somehow denigrates yours has been so terribly fractious, as evidenced by the some twenty thousand different Protestant denominations in this country alone. What kind of a witness is that to a world that's coming together, becoming a global village?"

Runner paused to rub his mustache down with his thumb and forefinger.

"At the time, I thought I was merely an idea whose time had not yet come. I see now its time has not *yet* come. In fact, the politics and the state of religious thinking have moved even farther to the right than at the time of my little controversy. Now the religious right would be the politics."

"How do you feel about that?"

"Threatened." Runner paused and pursed his lips and nodded thoughtfully. "Threatened. The biblical tradition is that the prophetic voice spoke over against abuses of power by the state. If the religious gain power, who will be the prophetic voice over against *their* abuses. Lord Acton, a British historian said, 'Power tends to corrupt, and absolute power corrupts absolutely' which Eric Hoffer, an American philosopher, quite correctly expanded in a work that came out in the early 70s called *Reflections on the Human Condition* when he said,

301

'Absolute faith corrupts as absolutely as absolute power.' I saw that in action in my dealings with the Classis and it was scary. If you think the Inquisition isn't possible, witness present day fundamentalism in operation in Islam, Judaism, and Christianity."

"In Christianity?"

"Are shootings at abortion clinics in the name of God any different than the murder by ISIS of Iraqis because they are Christian or the murder of Israeli Prime Minister Yitzhak Rabin?"

"Not in principle, I suppose. I'd like to ask about one of the big issues raised by your critics. Salvation by Christ alone. Actually, I have two questions. If salvation is available without Christ, what's the point of his death and resurrection, and what was their authority to condemn you to Hell if you argued that the devout of other faiths may be the recipients of God's grace. I fail to see the logic in that argument."

"What's the point of Christ's death and resurrection? I would say this. First, God didn't need Christ to die to reconcile mankind to Himself. From what we learn in the Older and Newer Testaments, He was doing a perfectly good job of it B.C. The promises He made to his people—I'm speaking of Israel now—spoke of eternal rewards for the faithful. The ending of the twenty-third Psalm comes to mind. The poetry of the King James version says it best. '. . . *and I shall dwell in the house of the Lord for ever,*' and the end of Psalm 121, '. . . *The Lord shall preserve thee from all evil: he shall preserve thy soul. The Lord shall preserve thy going out and thy coming in from this time forth and for evermore.*' But in the fullness of time, the Pax Romana, common language, roads and means of travel paved the way for the event of Jesus, for the gospel to be spread to the Gentiles and through the gospel, the Gentiles could also be reconciled to the God of Creation.

"I would say further that the gospel, as wonderful as it is, did not preempt God's ability to accept those who lived a life of obeisance and humble devotion and faithfulness to Him and followed His commandments. There's no scriptural basis for such a preemption. That road to God is still open. Horace Bushnell in a wonderful book paints the metaphor of a flower being nurtured into opening to the sun without the radical disruptive necessity of being born again. And further, would God create His creatures, humankind, flawed and then condemn eternally because they could never live in perfect obedience? That I don't believe.

"One of the most meaningful parables Jesus told was the 'Parable of the Prodigal Son', which I believe was misnamed. It should be called the 'Parable of the Prodigal Love of the Father' for it's a parable about the Father. The image is one of a father with unconditional love who allows his children the freedom to stray or to stay at home and begrudgingly be obedient. Then, with joy in his heart, he welcomes even the most wayward of his children home and kills the fatted calf. Three things are often missed in this wonderful story. First, the Father does not wait for a confession from the wandering son to receive him home with compassion and kisses; the Father's love is unconditional. Second, the Father didn't wait for the son to come into the house and repent, he ran out to meet him. And third, the Father also went out to entreat the pouting elder brother. This is Jesus' metaphor for who he understood God to be. This is not the metaphor the Church most often uses.

"The Church uses the metaphor of a judgmental Father who demands perfection before grace is meted out. The death of Christ is an atonement for the sins of the world or, as some would say, the sins of those who believe in him. How did we come to that metaphor? Well, it wasn't always the commonly accepted metaphor.

"The early Church thought Jesus was the Messiah the Jews were looking for and the Messianic age would come soon. Well, it didn't come soon. It didn't come at all. The Jewish Jesus movement fell into disrepute. So what then did this death and resurrection mean? A very early church father by the name of Origen, who lived around two hundred AD, postulated that the role of Jesus was to lead the fight between the forces of good and the forces of evil who were led by Satan, and thereby save the world. His emphasis was on universal redemption as opposed to individual salvation. He was attempting to bring the principles of Greek philosophy, particularly Neoplatonism and Stoicism, together with the Christian theology of the day."

"So Origen would not have been welcome in your former Classis?" Jason asked.

"Ha! You have perceived rightly! He was trying to connect the theology to the human experience of the day. Well, Origen's metaphor served the Church for almost one thousand years until a fellow named Anselm came along in about eleven hundred AD.

"Anselm, who was the Archbishop of Canterbury, contrived a proof for the existence of God from man's idea of a perfect being. Origen's paradigm didn't fit into that proof or model. A perfect God, a less than perfect man. How are they to be reconciled? Anselm lived in the middle ages when there were serfs and feudal lords. He borrowed a metaphor that would be understood in his time. Just as the serf could never pay the price of his freedom, sinful mankind could not measure up to a perfect God. Jesus by his death paid the price to set the sinner free and we have the metaphor of the atonement." Runner lowered his voice. "I don't think Anselm would have been welcome in my former Classis either, eh? He was trying to connect theology to the human experience of his day, too.

"The Reformers adopted Anselm's paradigm for themselves and it continues in many parts of the Church to this day. Now, if you ask me if the commonly accepted concept of the atonement we have today is necessary for salvation, I ask you, what about all those folks who thought they were good Christians who lived before the time of Anselm? They didn't understand the concept of the death of Christ as an atonement for their sins as we do now. I hope it wasn't necessary for them.

"And I would say there is good scriptural basis for Anselm's paradigm. The passage in First Peter, chapter three, I believe, '. . .

*For Christ also died for our sins, once and for all. He, the just, suffered for the unjust, to bring us to God.'* But the same Peter in a later chapter fuels Origen's metaphor as well when he writes, *'. . . Awake! be on the alert! Your enemy the Devil, like a roaring lion, prowls round looking for someone to devour.'"*

"Excuse me for interrupting," Jason had to butt in to get Runner's attention. "But this 'forces of evil led by the Devil' metaphor, is that where a TV preacher I heard recently gets his theology whereby he has the Devil influencing the Supreme Court?"

"Most likely. I often think the technique of some of these TV evangelists is to *scare* the hell out of folks, literally. The image of the Devil as a roaring lion prowling around looking to eat you, or serving on the Supreme Court writing the opinion to keep prayer out of the public schools would serve that purpose very nicely."

"Do you believe in the Devil?"

"The Devil has been used as a convenient whipping boy on which to heap the blame mankind ought to accept for himself. Mankind is evil enough without the need of a superimposed evil persona. 'The Devil made me do it' is a good comedy line. I do not deny the possibility of a fallen angel, I'm just not sure he plays as important a role in mankind's evil bent as we have given him credit."

"On the other hand, Mark Twain is reputed to have said '. . . we may not pay Satan reverence, for that would be indiscreet, but we can at least respect his talents. A person who has for untold centuries maintained the imposing position of spiritual head of four-fifths of the human race, and the political head of the whole of it, must be granted the possession of executive abilities of the loftiest order.'"

Runner chuckled as he paused to shift his weight in the wheelchair. "But back to my point, I would also say there's good scriptural basis for believing that it's not the death of Christ that is the hinge point of Christianity. It's the resurrection of Jesus from the dead. The resurrection, whereby God singularly blessed the life and ministry of this Jesus and gave his teachings *force majeure* and further made him unique in all of history to date. And what was the life and ministry, the teachings of Jesus? He proclaimed the grace of God and modeled out a life of love for and obedience to the Father and service to mankind. This I preached, and preached with passion.

"But keep in mind, there is not, nor can there, be a completely accurate human metaphor or paradigm, all of which at their best are human constructions of what's impossible to understand, let alone define. Origen, Anselm, the Reformers, we in the twentieth century—all we can construct are stammering attempts to express the inexpressible."

Runner paused as if to think as to whether he had answered the question. Then he continued, "And your other question? Oh yes, how does it follow that if I allow God's grace to extend to others, I'm condemned to Hell? I've wrestled with that question more than once. My detractors would say that to deny the necessity of the redemptive act of Christ is to denigrate his life and purpose, and that would be a denial of Christ. And if Christ is the only way, to deny Christ is to be damned. The Classis claimed that salvation through Christ alone was a core issue. If you must have it as a core issue, and if I don't believe in a core issue, perhaps on that basis I am condemned.

"If course, to hold that I'm condemned is to have the arrogance to condemn someone else's imperfect understanding on the basis of your own imperfect understanding. And there was arrogance aplenty at the inquiries that were held by those who would have held me, as they said, '. . . in disrepute before God, the Church, and the community.'"

Runner paused and swept his hand across his forehead as if to wipe away a headache or a memory. "It's generally held that the more one studies and the more one comes to understand, the more one is confronted with his own lack of understanding. Or, as it is commonly expressed, 'the more you know, the more you know how much you don't know.' That knowledge gave me great comfort throughout that controversy when there were those who accused me with great certainty.

"And I acknowledge I'm not blameless. There was a time in my life when I knew all the answers. I would have led the charge against one such as I had become. But my own journey has taken me from having all the answers to not being sure what the questions are, and trusting that God is the final answer and the only one I need."

"So you moved from the right to the more liberal position you now espouse over the course of your ministry?"

"Moderate, Jason, moderate. I'm not sure a Calvinist can ever move far enough to the left to be a liberal. I can affirm the Apostles' Creed and could take my ordination vows today and mean them. Right and left, conservative and liberal, even denominational divisions are meaningless labels these days. The difference is one of emphasis. The conservative among us emphasize the judgmental side of our knowledge of who is God. There is good scriptural basis for that position and, frankly, it's a lot easier to control your parishioners and parishioners to control their children from that position. There are a lot of oughts and musts in the practice of religion in obeisance to a God of judgment.

"You must do this and you must do that. It becomes a musty religion. Heh. Heh." He looked over his glasses with an amused expression at his play on words. "As a pastor, you become the arbiter of God's grace and it's a great position in which to be.

"Those more moderate emphasize the unconditional love side of our understanding of who is God. Good scriptural basis exists for that position as well. As a pastor, it's not as easy to control your people—that is, their giving and their church attendance—because you are no longer the arbiter of grace. Grace that flows from One who loves unconditionally needs no arbiter. But their revelry in the grace of God frees them to sing and dance and delight in the gift of life."

"You just said you could affirm the Apostle's Creed, but you question the doctrine of the virgin birth."

Runner peered over his glasses in a quizzical look. "No, I don't believe I . . . ah, you refer to the discussion with the nurse? I believe all I said was that if you have trouble believing in the virgin birth, you may be in good company. The likes of Paul for example. I have no trouble with the virgin birth, but I got it at my mother's knee. My only point with Nurse Veeringa was that I questioned her whole construction as to the necessity for Christ to escape the taint of original sin for the atonement model to work to save her sins. No, I'm fine with the virgin birth."

"Do you miss the ministry?"

"With every fiber of my being. I couldn't leave theology alone. I continued to read. Since I am fluent in Dutch I write for religious periodicals in Europe under a *nom de plume*. The irony of it is that the articles get translated into English and printed in theological journals in the United States, journals that wouldn't think of publishing me if they knew who I really was," he said gleefully and with relish. He slapped his knee at the irony of it.

"Ah, Jason," he continued, "what games we play in organized religion. At the height of our little controversy, the *New York Times* sent a reporter to do a story. His name was Niebuhr and incidentally, his great uncle was the theologian Rhinehold Niebuhr and his grandfather, H. Richard, was a professor of divinity at Yale who advocated a restatement of Christianity in light of the developments of the twentieth century—a man after my own heart . . ."

"I saw the article in Mrs. Van Dyken's scrapbook. You made the front page," Jason interrupted.

"Yes, well the day after the article appeared, a man who represented himself as the editor of a monthly religious magazine phoned me and the good people from my congregation who were quoted in the article. He was obstreperous and rude and one of these folks took him on, so to speak. He asked the man if he thought his uncivil behavior reflected well on the Jesus he alleged to model his life after. His response, as it was reported to me, was snarled into the phone, "I may be rude and I may be uncivil, but I'm going to heaven, what do you think about that?" My congregant then asked the editor if he thought there was any possibility that they would meet in heaven. The editor responded, 'Not a chance.' To which my friend replied, 'Good! Because if people of your ilk are in heaven, it's not a place in which I aspire to spend eternity.'"

And it's not just us Protestants who malign each other. Arguably the most influential Roman Catholic theologian of our day is Hans Kung. But he's was disrepute with the Vatican so the classes he taught at Tübingen University weren't accredited by the Church, yet they're packed. When he toured the US several years ago, he lectured here at Michigan for several months. Standing room only at this, a secular university. And still his church holds him in disrepute.

"But enough about me. You have work to do. You asked me about Medicare and Medicaid. I have several booklets here . . ."

Runner was interrupted by a knock at the door. "Pizza delivery for a Mr. Runner."

It was Annie carrying a large pizza box and some cans of Diet Pepsi. "Come in, come in. I thought you'd never get here. Jason, tip the delivery lady, would you please."

Annie began to get the pizza ready for their consumption.

"Buy low, sell high," Jason said with a deadpan look and got a puzzled one in return.

"Buy low, sell high?"

"That's his tip for you. Buy when stocks are low, sell when the price goes higher."

"Be still my heart! You're such a romantic, Jason. See if I bother to get cleaned up and smell nice for our date tonight."

"Aha, you two are stepping out tonight?"

"The Friars are in concert tonight along with several other college groups at Hill Auditorium."

They bantered until the pizza and the sodas were gone, then Annie excused herself. "I've got a one o'clock," she explained. "See you at two, Mr. Runner?"

"Not if I can concoct the slimmest of excuses!"

She turned to Jason. "See you at seven? Is this thing hotsy-totsy formal or will sneakers and a tank top do?"

"Speaking of the slimmest of excuses. Do you *own* a tank top?"

"No, but 'R Fashions R U' is open until nine tonight."

"See if you can get two of the same color, something in teal or puce. Man's medium for me."

"Right! I'll get right on it. I'll see you two later, gotta go. I'm a working woman," she said as she disappeared down the hall.

"Well, Jason, do you want to talk about Medicaid now? Or should I say, can you talk about Medicaid now?"

"Is it that obvious?"

"It might not be if I were blind and deaf."

"Let's talk about Medicaid." Jason referred to his notes. "If a resident becomes destitute, does the Home have to keep the resident and accept the Medicaid reimbursement?"

"Not legally, but to their credit things are done here with a sense of doing what's compassionate. To a point, at least. Remember, a significant portion of the Home's operating revenue comes from the contributions of the supporting churches, which makes up the difference between operating cost and Medicaid reimbursement.

So no one is asked to leave if they run out of money.

"On the other hand, there are two waiting lists—one containing the names of those who are private pay and can afford the four thousand four hundred dollars per month and another list with those whose fees will be paid through Medicaid reimbursement which amounts to two thousand two hundred dollars. As long as there are private pays on the first waiting list, the second list is kept in the drawer.

"And frankly, it's a dilemma for the Home's administration. I'm glad I don't have to deal with it. Their operating costs are about four thousand two hundred dollars per month per resident. For every Medicaid resident, they have to raise an additional two thousand bucks per month to break even. If they do that by raising the rates for private pay to five thousand dollars per month, the Home prices itself out of the market and the ratio of private pays to Medicaid residents decreases and the Home is in deeper financial trouble."

"If there is a waiting list, is there any question about your keeping your other room there?" Jason asked, pointing to the library.

"Oh, I don't think so. I pay the full cost for both rooms and books don't eat. In addition, I typically give a gift at year-end that's too big for them to ignore. Once Van Dam hinted that they may need the room and I told him if I had to give up the library, there would be two rooms available. He hasn't mentioned it since. Also, there's usually only one waiting list—the Medicaid list—and Van Dam is pragmatic. He wouldn't give up eight thousand eight hundred dollars per month and one mouth to feed and take care of and substitute four thousand four hundred per month in Medicaid reimbursement and two mouths to feed and take care of. I'm a good deal to him and he knows it."

When Jason got back to his apartment, he punched up the number of the Bus. Ad. School and then Professor Playdon's extension.

"Hello?"

"Professor Playdon, this is Jason Richards."

"Jason. How did it go with Mr. Runner?"

"He acknowledged who he really was right up front and didn't seem too upset that I knew. You were right. He's more open than when he had to speak through his alter ego."

"Good. Well, I've been thinking about you and wondering how you came out. I'm glad you called. But the way, our article will be in the next issue of *Hospital Administration Monthly*. I have a release that you'll need to execute and a nice little honorarium for you."

"Really! That was unexpected. Do you need the release to be signed now?

"Monday will be soon enough, unless you want to pick up the check now."

"Thank you, but no. I'll see you Monday. Have a nice weekend."

"Good-bye."

# Chapter Twenty

"You're out on a limb little brother. I warned you this was going to happen. Didn't I warn you? Admit it. Go ahead, I'm waiting . . ."

"You warned me, Willard."

"But you wouldn't listen to your big brother and now you're in over your head. Now you're finally coming to your big brother for advice and it may be too late for me to help you. Do you think she loves you?"

"How do you ever know that for sure?"

"In my case it was easy. They threw themselves at me. They couldn't help themselves."

"What color is the sky in your world, Willard? For the record, I don't think three dates in three days is *prima facie* that we're in love. We're just very good friends and happen to enjoy each other's company."

"Yeah, and the moon is of green cheese made. Three dates in three days. What did you do, go to the Graduate School Library and make out in the stacks? What do U of M lovers do?"

"For your information, it was a night of culture followed by a Saturday Blockbuster Video new release with popcorn and her dog, and this morning it was church and Sunday brunch at the Marriott."

"Did she let you play with her schnauzer?"

"It's a Sheltie, potty mouth."

"Oonnh, I see! So what's holding you back? If you need money for a ring, I'm a banker you know. Speaking of banking, next week Saturday I have to take a one-day course at Wayne State. Karen's going to go along and shop in the outlet malls in Monroe. We'll be coming through Ann Arbor Saturday night. How about dinner, the four of us? Karen is more than a little curious to meet her potential sister-in-law."

"Judas H. Priest, Willard. I've known the girl for a total of three weeks. This isn't rush week at MSU is it?"

"So how about it, is it a date?"

"Is this an invitation or are we going to try to out-fumble each other for the check? You're as good at that as anyone in MSU's backfield."

"Real funny. If you were to ask me for a loan for the ring, that would be business and the bank would buy. Seriously, we'd like to get together. Tell me about our nursing home friend. Does he know that you know who he is?"

"Yes, Annie's aunt—who didn't know where he had gone—phoned him and it came out that we knew. He openly admitted it when I went to see him and we had a long talk about it. Very interesting."

"I spoke to Reverend Wright about him. He knew of the controversy."

"What did he say about it?"

"Uh…not much."

Willard's words were spoken with a strained casual, tone, a clear signal he was either hiding something or he didn't want to talk about it. Jason took a bold move. "So he's in agreement with Runner's theology, is he?"

"I didn't say that."

"I think you did. Come on, let's have an attempt at honesty here."

"Well, truth be known, he thought that some of the guy's ideas weren't so far off base."

"Well, well. What does this mean? Is Wright wrong or is Wright left of where you thought he was. Are we now not so sure Runner's damned to Hell?"

"Wright is right, and he's certainly not as left as you are. You have to admit you were on shaky ground yourself for a while."

"I'll admit I'm still on shaky ground, but I'm comfortable there."

☦

In his last comment on the phone to Willard, he had synthesized in one sentence his internal dilemma and his comfort. There had been a time in his life when he had a very well delineated and complete system of beliefs, a processing method with which all of life's questions and its complexities could be answered or explained; birth and death, joy and sorrow, peace and anxiety, love and hate, the sacred and the secular. There was a certainty to life, a certainty born out of a long tradition of this systematic understanding of the ultimate realities of life. This system, along with its certainties, had been infused into him by his parents, his church, his teachers, and he had taken it without pause, without question, and certainly without critical examination. And he was so sure of the certainties, that he was past thinking about the system. He would just apply its answers to whatever life situation came his way and life went on.

But from time to time, something would creep into his experience where the answer offered by the system did not match the evidence. Examples that came to mind were: the age of the universe; the assumption that alcoholism was a sin; that movies and dancing were inherently evil; that sickness—like AIDS was a punishment for a specific sin; that Roman Catholics were not really Christians; the death of his nephew and the minister's admonition that his family had no right to grieve.

When these anomalies arose, he would either dismiss the system—as he did with the question of the age of the earth—or he would suppress the question. Or as in the case of movies and dancing, he would participate and feel guilty. His spiritual mind told him the system was not to be questioned and his Kantian mind told him the evidence was irrefutable. So the trick was to compartmentalize the system apart from the evidence and not to hold one up to the light of the other.

Life in this mode had certainty, but an acknowledged discomfort existed because there were known parts of life that didn't fit into the system. For example, a man could sleep with his wife but couldn't dance with her. Or, Jason could not go to the movies but his parents saw nothing wrong with watching the same movies on television. The size of the anomalies was not important, they were like leaks in the dike. Jason took some measure of comfort in the assumption that everyone had some discomfort.

The discussions with Runner had slowly taken away his certainty but somehow had increased his comfort in direct proportion. He could comfortably admit he was on shaky ground and he was at ease with himself and the questions of the ultimate realities of life. He was still on a bridge over a cavernous void, and there were almost no props under the bridge now. But below the void there was God. And God was behind him and God was in front of him. He had come to realize that the bridge was of his own construction—it was man-made with borrowed material and it was subject to the ravages of experience. But fortunately the strength of the bridge was unimportant. There was God. A God standing with outstretched arms like the Father in the Parable of the Prodigal Son. Perhaps a God who would run toward him if his bridge gave way just as the father ran out to embrace the returning prodigal son.

He wasn't done with the System. It remained a good framework. In fact, it provided him with two important proof texts. He had to admit to himself that once a Calvinist, always a proof texter. He couldn't give the cite, but the verse went, *"Trust in the Lord with all your heart; and lean not unto thine own understanding. In all thy ways acknowledge him, and he shall direct thy path."* He read that, ". . . lean not unto thine own system."

The other was from Psalm 23, "*Yea, though I walk through the valley of the shadow of death, I will fear no evil. For thou are with me; they rod and thy staff they comfort me.*" Jason read that, ". . . yea, though I walk over the cavernous void on my shaky bridge with little support, I have comfort because I know I am in the presence of God."

He had been trusting a system. The words of the Tennyson poem kept meandering through his mind.

> *Our little systems have their day,*
>
> *They have their day and cease to be.*
>
> *They are but broken lights of Thee,*
>
> *And Thou, O Lord, art more than they.*

He also found there was comfort in the wrestling. It felt good to question, to search, much like it felt good to sweat during a good workout. He might never find all the answers but he allowed there must be some sanctification that came when struggling to understand what was the mystery of God—a God who, by the process of struggle, became nearer and more real. God had moved from the abstract to the palpable but certainly no easier to define. God remained inexpressible.

Jason's ruminations led him to wonder if the 1st Horseman had responded to his e-mail about salvation through Christ alone. When he logged on to FACULTY ON-LINE, the familiar voice said, "You have mail waiting." It was from the 1st Horseman and Jason called it up:

> RichJason:
>
> Greetings from the sunny South. Do you have snow yet? If you do, keep it!<g>
>
> <<where do you stand on the issue of salvation through Christ alone>>
>
> You picked a good one, as you'll see. Salvation does come

through Christ, but he is the Lamb on Mt. Zion (Revelation 14 & Obadiah 17) and He is the judge at the white throne judgment (Revelation 20) where there is an implication that some appear to have their names in the book of life. Psalm 14:2 and 53:2 says *"The Lord looks down from heaven on all mankind to see if any act wisely, if any seek God."* This passage in Psalms may be the basis of Peter's testimony to Cornelius the Centurion in Acts 10:34, *". . . of a truth I perceive that God is no respecter of persons. But in every nation he that feareth Him, and worketh righteousness, is accepted with Him."*

In the messianic section of FACULTY ON-LINE I received a post from an orthodox Jew telling me that the idea of a personal faith was foreign to Judaism and that all Jews had to do to be saved was to remain faithful, i.e. be 'God-fearers' and wait for the Lord to save them. He went on to say that he hoped I liked kosher, because heaven would be <g>. As I went to the Scripture to prepare a rebuttal, I got a surprise. Not only was the belief scriptural, it was in the New Testament! Romans 11.

I had really expected to find a misinterpretation of Old Testament scriptures. But it's hard to explain away verses 25ff, *"For there is a deep truth here, my brothers, of which I want you to take account, so that you may not be complacent about your own discernment: this partial blindness has come upon Israel only until the Gentiles have been admitted in full strength; when that has happened, the whole of Israel will be saved, in agreement with the text of the Scripture:*

> *'From Zion shall come the Deliverer;*
>
> *he shall remove wickedness from Jacob.*
>
> *And this is the covenant I will grant them,*
>
> *when I take away their sins,'*

*In the spreading of the Gospel they are treated as God's enemies for your sake; but God's choice stands, and they are His friends for the sake of the patriarchs. For the gracious gifts of God and His calling are irrevocable."*

Even the Pope said the covenant God made with the Jews was irrevocable. I'm with the Pope on this one! <VBG>

Regarding Muslims, assuming they are 'God-fearers', if the covenant was to Abraham and to his seed, what choice are you left with? Do you like the concept of a mutable God? Not I!

His,

1st Horseman

Runner wasn't not alone on this one either. This from a person who described himself as being from the far right of the Protestant spectrum, a person—judging from his screen name and his frequent references to Revelations—who believed in the thousand-year-reign of Christ. A pre-millennialist. Interesting. Very interesting.

✝

Monday's meeting with Playdon carried with it a surprise. They talked about the progress Jason was making on his I.R.R. and about his conversation with Runner. Before Jason left, Playdon reached for a folder on this desk and withdrew a legal-looking form. It was a release to publish an article entitled "Institutional Administration: A View From the Bottom" in the *Hospital Administration Monthly* which indicated co-authorship by Professor William A. Playdon and Jason Richards. There was a place for each to sign, which Playdon had already done. Jason added his signature to the document and handed it back to Playdon who was handing him a check in return. A check for one thousand dollars.

"One thousand dollars! One thousand dollars?"

"Jason, my young friend. The likes of us do not come cheaply."

"But I've done almost nothing. I . . ."

"Nonsense! You did the fieldwork, I wrote the report. They were willing to pay handsomely to get your experience and my name in their periodical. It's their standard fee."

"I got two hundred bucks from the Appraisers' journal and I thought I had taken advantage of them. That was paltry by comparison. I just have to continue to keep better company, I guess. This is certainly unexpected and very much appreciated. This is almost enough . . ." Jason stopped in mid-sentence and looked up feeling a bit sheepish.

"To buy a ring?"

Playdon didn't miss a trick, did he? Jason's sheepishness turned into embarrassment. "Well . . . yes. A very nice ring. When the time comes, of course."

"Of course," Playdon responded and then raised his arm to look at his watch. He looked back at Jason without lowering his arm as if to say, "Is now the time?"

✣

The week flew by. Jason found an excuse to call Annie almost every night and the nights he didn't call, she called him. At her suggestion, he was to arrange to have lunch brought in on Friday for the three of them. He decided to order the *hors d'oeuvres* of the house from Weller's for carryout. When he phoned Weller's, the receptionist told him they didn't do carry out, Jason indicated this was for a close personal friend of Mr. Weller's. Jason was put on hold before Stanley Weller himself came on the phone. Jason explained who he was and that the order was for Howard Runner.

"Are you the young man who was in here a few weeks back as Howie R's guest? The kid with the knockout girlfriend? You gonna deliver these to Howie R.?"

"Yes sir, that was my plan."

"You'll do no such-a-thing. I'll make this delivery personally. When do you want them?"

"It's for lunch this coming Friday."

"You just let me take care of it. I'm glad you called, we'll have some fun with this. Noon on Friday."

"Do you know where Mr. Runner . . ."

"Hell, kid. I've been there more times than you. I'll be there."

☦

The discussion with Runner on Friday was to be on medical services provided by the Home and Runner had mentioned something about Medicare/Medicaid fraud that Jason wanted to explore.

As Jason approached Runner's open door he could hear sounds of the Christmas season coming from the CD player. It was a unique sound with very close harmony. Jason didn't recognize the artists. Runner appeared to be busy over a yellow legal pad at his secretary but he put down his pen at the sound of Jason's knock.

"Jason! Come in, come in. Sit down." He reached for the CD changer, but Jason stopped him.

"That's lovely. Who is that?" he asked as he settled into the leather wing-backed chair.

"That group? They're called 'The Singers Unlimited.' It's a successor group to a very popular male quartet from the fifties called 'The Hi-Los', a group considered by some to be the best vocal ensemble ever. This group achieves that spectacular sound by very good arranging by their founder, Gene Perling, and by a technique whereby one singer sings more than one part and the recording takes are overlaid to create that phenomenal blend. It's a technique called 'overdubbing.' Unfortunately they cannot duplicate that technique on a live stage. I'm glad you like the sound. Listen . . ."

The strains of a Russian carol about little children anticipating the birth of the baby Jesus in a world of snowbound valleys and shaggy ponies came through the speakers. "It's beautiful," Jason acknowledged.

Runner pointed the changer at the CD player and lowered the sound level. "Well, my young friend, we talk of medical treatment today?"

"Yes, your perception of the level of medical care and treatment available from the Home. From your perspective, is the care adequate, good, substandard?"

"In most cases, I would have to say it's good. Sometimes it's better than it needs to be, sometimes, they stumble. First of all, most of us realize that the mortality rate in nursing homes is almost perfect. Having said that, the doctor on call here, a Doctor Johns, is semi-retired, and frankly, he's what my father used to call a *sawbones*.

"It's been said that medical knowledge expands itself every five years. This means that since our friend got out of medical school, the medical knowledge has expanded exponentially by a factor of seven, and I don't think we can expect he's stayed current. He's a good fellow, means well. And for the aches and pains and flu shots that need to be attended to, who can say he's not adequate.

"I would say that the nursing staff here's adequate. Perhaps I'm wrong, and this is certainly a generalization, but it seems to me that if you are bright and aggressive and all fired up about your profession, you'd be a surgical nurse or on an orthopedic ward somewhere. I think what we have here isn't necessarily the top two or three in the graduating class. To put it another way, geriatric nursing is not a specialty to which many nurses aspire.

"However, there is no faulting their tender loving concern or the devotion to their job. I even have to say the head nurse, Veeringa, for all the grief she tries to give me is overworked, and underpaid.

"In their defense, there's never been a time that I'm aware of that they haven't responded appropriately, even if they consider you to be the Devil himself. We're not about the saving of lives here or speedy recoveries. So again, the care is adequate and appropriate to the mission."

"But you said sometimes the care goes beyond what is necessary? What did you mean by that?"

"Two things. First, the state requires that all nursing home residents be seen by a primary care physician at least once every two months. Ostensibly, this is to prevent neglect and be certain there's proper nutrition and care. I've been here for nearly four years, so my doctor has seen me at least twenty times. It's 'Hi Howard. How you doing? Any complaints? No? Fine. Swell. Goodbye, and that'll be forty dollars, if you please.'

"I don't begrudge the man his forty dollars. It is an imposition on his time to come here. But it isn't necessary. And for those of our number who are on Medicaid, multiply all those visits times all those patients whose average stay is six years times forty dollars times all the nursing homes, and we shouldn't wonder why the system's bankrupt.

"The other thing is there are scam artists abounding in this field. Here, I saved this for you . . ." Runner wheeled to the secretary and retrieved a flyer printed in large letters on blue paper.

Jason took the flyer.

> The Ocular Clinic of Ann Arbor
> by special arrangement
> is able to offer complete and in-depth eye examinations
> by our trained professional staff.
> **AT NO COST TO YOU!**
> This examination includes vision testing
> as well as testing for common diseases of the eye,
> such as amaurosis, amblyopia, glaucoma, etc.
> These examinations will be completed
> in the comfort and privacy of your room on
> <u>**Tuesday**</u> and <u>**Wednesday, December 3 and 4.**</u>
>
> **THESE EXAMINATIONS ARE COMPLETELY
> COVERED BY MEDICARE**
> To make your appointment
> **CALL 618-3300**

"Frankly, how many nursing home residents are in need of this kind of eye examination? Not many. How many of the residents sign up for this 'Free' examination? Almost all of them. I was suspicious so I signed up.

"My 'trained professional' had no formal education past high school but had done thousands of these exams. She couldn't tell me what amblyopia was. She looked at my records before the exam and confirmed them to me verbally. She then gave me a quick eye exam to confirm that these glasses were the correct prescription for reading glasses.

"She told me my prescription was getting weak and she thought she could detect some astigmatism. She said it would be really important that I make an appointment right then and there with the Ocular Clinic for a more complete examination. I thanked her and sent her on her way. I found it strange that my ophthalmologist hadn't detected any problems in my annual visit some three weeks before.

"Medicare paid eighty dollars for an unnecessary and inadequate eye exam for fifty-two residents. That's over four thousand one hundred dollars in two days, not to mention the 'more complete' examinations that these folks were hustled into."

"But the Home wasn't a party to these exams, was it?"

"My question to Van Dam was, why let the charlatans come in in the first place?"

"And he said?"

"It can't hurt and it adds to the service the Home provides. I was suspicious, so I called this outfit and represented myself as the director of a nursing home and inquired about their program for my residents. The mystery was solved when I was advised that a fifteen-dollar referral fee for each examination would be paid to me directly if I signed my home up for their service. So we know why our pious Director chose to "provide this service to our residents"—to line his purse with seven hundred seventy dollars, his share of the scam."

Runner was interrupted by a knock on the doorframe. It was Annie who was grinning like the Cheshire Cat. "I think lunch as arrived gentlemen." She beckoned to an unseen person, who Jason expected would be Stanley Weller. "Come in, come in!"

It wasn't. It was a tall thin young man dressed in the waiter's attire that Jason remembered from their visit to Weller's—black pants, black vest and tie, and a formal white shirt. He was pushing a wheeled serving cart with three covered serving dishes. "Mr. Runner's room?"

"Yes it is, yes it is! Jason, what have you done here? Look at this!" Runner exclaimed.

"My name is Martin and I'll be your server." The waiter proceeded to arrange the table with a flourish—china, silver, linen napkins, then came the wine. He popped the cork and gave it to Jason. Jason sniffed it and was reminded of vinegar.

But before he could say anything the waiter said, "It's our best Chablis. I'm sure you'll enjoy it!" He proceeded to pour a small amount in a glass and handed it directly to Runner, who sniffed it and hesitated.

"Chablis?" Runner was puzzled. "I would have thought a *Piesporter* . . ." He paused as he took a small sip, which caused him to skewer up his face. "This is . . . bad. In fact, it's awful! It tastes like . . . like vinegar! With all apologies to your sommelier, I'm afraid this bottle is not palatable! I do hope you brought another."

"Oh, I'm so sorry Mr. Runner. It's the only bottle I brought. Perhaps the entrée will be more to your liking." Having said that he began removing the covers from the silver dishes he had placed in front of each of them. The plates contained . . . small sandwiches?

"Pate du almond and with a delicious all-fruit spread. As you ordered?" the waiter asked with mock seriousness.

The three of them looked at each other in disbelief. Peanut butter and jelly? Then Runner began to shake his head knowingly. "Stanley Weller, you schlep! I can see your handiwork in this. Show yourself if you dare," he bellowed and started to laugh.

From around the corner came a robust man of about sixty with silver hair and swarthy features, laughter forcing tears down his cheeks. "Howie R, how are we, eh? Ha, Ha. Schlep is it? So you're too good for peanut butter and jelly and my best vinegar, are you? Marty, get this outta here and bring us some real Weller food and wine, eh?" He pulled up a chair.

Amid introductions and much banter between the old friends, Martin set to the task with flank speed and soon there was a small bowl of seafood chowder and the *hors d'oeuvres* of the house set about in generous portions and a bottle of *Piesporter Goldtröpfchen Riesling Spätlese*. As it was being poured, Mr. Weller turned to

Jason, "I brought the wine for you kids and I. Howie here can't tell the difference between a good *Piesporter* and vinegar. It's so sad."

The food served, Runner asked Weller to say Grace. Weller held up his hands like a supplicant and said a prayer in Hebrew. Jason recognized but a few words; "Adonai" and "Shalom" and when the words stopped, it seemed appropriate to say "Amen" and Jason did, as did Runner.

Weller raised his glass in a toast and said, "To life . . . to good friends . . . and to lovers! *L'Chiam!*"

"*L'Chiam!*"

And the festivities began under Martin's watchful eye.

"Young lady, do you know what *L'Chiam* means?"

"To life?"

"Common Gentile mistake. It really means: 'let's eat!'" They all laughed.

"You laugh," Weller continued between mouthfuls of mushroom caps. "But before I went to Hebrew school I thought it meant 'let's drink' because my father would say it and everyone would empty their glass. How do you like the chowder? It's great isn't it? My mother's recipe, God rest her soul."

And so it went until Weller became serious. "Howie, don't let this go to your head, but we miss you at the lunch table. The other day there was a hell of an argument between Stevenson, the financial guy from Hoover, and the know-it-all from Associated Freight, oh, what's his name? . . . DePacter. Stevenson is an old shoe kind of guy, and apparently he's a Unitarian and DePacter is a tight-ass fundamentalist type. They got into it over who's going to heaven. Stevenson wouldn't keep the Devil himself out, and DePacter thinks he's going to sit down to a four topper in no-smoking.

"For a while, we had one of those text count wars like you used to instigate. We all said we should adjourn over to Howie's and get it settled, but I don't think DePacter and you are kosher. You're both Christians so you should be kosher. But then, you can't be kosher if you're Christian, if you know what I mean.

"Listen, I gotta run," Weller said, rising from his chair. "I got a big group of Japanese honchos coming in at twelve-thirty and I should be there to make sure the *sake* is heated properly. I got a Japanese cook in to do *tempura* for them. Marty! You take good care of my friends here and make sure Howie doesn't eat too much of the Death by Chocolate, eh?"

"It's not called Death by Cho—"

"Yeah, yeah. I know what it's called, but there's a lady present. Listen, Howie! I'm sure I'll see you soon. Try to get down there for lunch some day. It's pretty much the same old crowd and we all miss you." He turned to Jason and then Annie. "I wish you kids all the best, huh? And Weller's does the best job of wedding receptions in the area, and for Howie's sake, I'll give you a good deal. Marty, I leave my friends in your good hands!" And the whirlwind whirled out much as he had whirled in.

No one said anything for a moment, as if they were out of breath from being engaged by Weller. Then Runner spoke. "He's introverted, he's shy, he's quiet, he has no sense of humor, but that's my friend, Stanley Weller. I never could get an edge in wordwise with him. He's in his early sixties, and he hasn't slowed down one bit."

"What did he mean, the one guy would sit down to a four topper in no smoking?" Annie asked.

"A 'four topper' is restaurant speak for a table for four. He meant that Bob DePacter has such a narrow view of who's going to be in heaven that Stanley thinks that when Bob gets to heaven he expects to be seated at a table with four place settings—one each for God the Father, the Son, the Holy Spirit, and one for himself."

"Is there really a round table where local execs sit around and talk about religion?" Jason was incredulous.

"I don't know if you saw it, but Weller's has a section that reminds one of a club room. There's a large table where you could go for lunch and join friends. The discussions were usually about politics or business issues, but from time to time religion. It was an eclectic group, not just businessmen. There were several ministers and a rabbi, several profs from the U., a few doctors—one who had been a medical missionary to Afghanistan—and a psychiatrist. The discussions were lively, to say the least, and in the middle of the discussion you could usually find Stanley directing traffic."

"What's a text count war?" Jason asked.

"With your background, you'd have loved it. Someone would make a statement like, 'Fred's not going to see the pearly gates with an attitude like that'

"Someone else would say 'Fred's not going to see the pearly gates in any case.'

"Then another one would say, 'Everyone will see the pearly gates . . . and from the insides. There's enough hell on earth.'

"Another would chime in with, 'Oh, I don't think everyone's going to be there. I agree with Sam, Fred's going to have to play a different fiddle if he's going to be there.'

"'How can you say that?' someone would challenge.

"'The good book says, *"For God so loved the world that he gave his only begotten son, that whosoever believeth on him shall not perish, but have everlasting life."*'

"'Well, what about the next verse? *"For God sent not his son into the world to condemn the world but that the world through him might be saved."* Sounds to me like the whole world's going to make it. Even you and Fred!'

"'What about the verse that says, *"For I am not ashamed of the gospel of Christ: for it is the power of God unto salvation to every one that believeth."'*

"Still another would weigh in, 'I'm on Fred's side on this one and I offer First John 2:2, *"He (Jesus) is the atoning sacrifice for our sins, and not only for ours but also for the sins of the whole world."* I say it's very clear, Fred's in, we're all in.'

"Someone would agree. 'I hang my hat on First Corinthians 15:22. *"For as in Adam all die even so in Christ shall all be made alive."'*

"And so it would go. One verse after another. I called it 'Text Count Warfare', and may the most texts win. The laymen could usually carry the first few rounds and then the ministers, the heavies, would weigh in for the late innings. If it were a philosophical point, there would be quotes from Socrates, Plato, Hume, sometimes the Marx brothers—Karl and Groucho, and sometimes Casey Stengel. If you were a layman in one field, you might be a heavyweight in another. It was great fun." Runner paused as the waiter entered with a tray. "Oh, Martin. You're a good man. You bring in the Death by Chocolate."

Marty distributed the dessert and poured tea.

"And so theological issues were decided by who had the most texts to support their views?" Annie asked.

"Theological issues are almost never decided by text count warfare. Remember that Martin Luther said, 'The Bible has a wax nose.'"

"A wax nose?" Annie said as she took her first bite of the dessert. "Mmmmmh. This is so good," she moaned.

Jason and Runner exchanged knowing looks before Runner replied, "I'm glad you like it. Luther meant that you can usually make the Bible say whatever you need it to say at a given moment." Runner reached up and bent his nose over with his forefinger.

Annie had to swallow her mouthful of the dessert before replying, "I have heard it said the Bible is a like a puzzle, and that if you were to study it, the pieces would all fit together nicely to form a complete picture, and the words used to describe that were 'systematic theology.'"

"If that analogy were correct," Runner replied, "you would have to have wax pieces in your puzzle to make every verse fit. While some pieces fit together nicely to make one system work, there are often the same number of pieces that fit together to make other systems make sense."

Jason had formed a question in his mind. "Our tradition is one that espouses the concept of limited numbers of people being saved, a chosen few who accept Christ."

"Limited atonement. Yes."

"I'm curious, who wins the text count war on limited atonement vs. universal salvation?"

"It's about even, five or six clearly for one position and five or six for the other, and several that are unclear."

"That's not what our tradition has said."

"No, but here again we talk about the weight of the Scriptures. Calvinists and most evangelicals and fundamentalists have come down on the side of limiting God's grace to those accepting Christ as their mediator to God. There's very good scriptural basis for that and it fits very nicely into the whole of Calvin's systematic theology. On the other hand, the tradition has pretty much ignored the other side of the argument. And that's okay. However, I would take issue with those who say the Universalist's position is completely untenable. That's not to be honest with the Scriptures."

"Are you finished here?" Martin had entered holding a teapot. "More tea for anyone?"

"Oh my! It's nearly one o'clock. I've *got* to get back to my appointments," Annie said with some alarm. "I'll see you two heavyweights later." Then she turned on the sarcasm. "Oh, and by the way, not to make too much if it, but as to the wedding reception referred to earlier, let me know when it is and whether I'm invited. I may have to get a dress." Then came the charm. "And Marty, thank you! It was wonderful. We're here every Friday if you're free," and she was gone with a flounce.

"Mmh, Marty is it? I'm afraid that Martin's not free, rather comes dearly. Martin, you can go back and tell your profligate boss that he's outdone himself. Do you have a check for us?"

"I was instructed to tell you that there would be no check, and he also told me to tell you that the gratuity has also been taken care of. He mentioned something about your being parsimonious. Forgive me for asking, but is that a physical condition of some kind?"

"It cripples some folks for the whole of their lives, Martin. He said that about me, did he? You tell my good Jewish friend that I said it's not Christian to make sport of the handicapped."

"I'll tell him sir, and you all have a good day."

"Thank you, Martin."

When Martin was gone, Runner turned to Jason and lowered his face to peer over his half-frame glasses, "So, there's to be a wedding reception at Weller's, is there? Will it be soon?"

"I never mentioned a wedding reception. Your friend Stanley is a troublemaker."

"It's only one of his many talents. He's also very good at reading people."

# Chapter Twenty-One

The American Banking Institute conducted classes in the various aspects of the banking business. These classes enabled the employees of its member banks to obtain continuing education on what was new in the industry. Willard Richards had registered for a course in credit management offered that Saturday at Wayne State University, located in Detroit. Karen accompanied Willard and spent the day Christmas shopping at an outlet mall near Detroit. They made plans to stop in Ann Arbor on the way home that evening to have dinner with Jason and Annie at the Old German, a quaint *bierstube* that had seen generations of students enjoy its imported beers and hearty German cuisine.

Jason picked Annie up at her apartment and they were traveling the mile or so to the restaurant. Intellectually, Annie knew she was not on trial or display here. But then, why was she wearing the third outfit she had tried on and why had she worked for thirty minutes on her hair? She felt some apprehension and expressed it to Jason. "I think I know how a guy feels when he comes by the house to pick a girl up on the first date."

"Nothing to fear. This isn't a coming out ball, this is a casual dinner with my brother and his wife. She's the kind of person that takes stray kittens in out of the rain, and he proves the adage that you can't make a silk purse out of a sow's ear."

"So which one am I being compared to, the wet kitty or the sow?"

"*Please* don't set me up like that. The only awkward part will be when my brother makes some kind of an inappropriate remark about why I haven't asked you to marry me yet. And he will."

"And why is that?"

"Because that's the kind of slug he is."

That was not the question she wanted an answer to. "So you haven't asked me to marry you because your brother is a slug? Is that a genetic sort of thing that I should be concerned with?"

"No. I mean, yes. What I meant was . . ."

"Frankly, I think there's reason to be concerned about the gene pool here. This is the second case of hoof-in-mouth disease I think I've diagnosed in two days. And apparently your brother has a terminal case of it."

"Second case?"

"The wonderful Mr. Weller mentioned something about a wedding reception, to which I haven't received my invitation. At least not yet. Perhaps it's in the mail?"

"It's in the m-a-l-e."

"Ohhh. It's in the *male*, is it? So how are you going to answer your brother when he asks?"

"I'm going to ask him if he needs an ice pack."

"An ice pack?"

"For the kick he'll get under the table from Karen."

"I think I'm going to have fun tonight. I know I like Karen already."

"Frankly, you are more like sisters than we are like brothers."

"Is that how you think of us? Our relationship is like two *brothers*? Are you a stump? What do I have to do?"

"You're doing just fine. Here we are." Jason said as he turned the Honda into the parking lot of the Old German, "Try to make a good impression, will you. None of the double entendres stuff. Willard won't understand it anyway, and it may make him feel badly, what with his inferior education and all."

334

"I'll try to behave."

✝

They had a good time. Karen and Annie did get along as if they were sisters and Karen obviously had Willard on a very short leash.

It was not until the desserts came and the coffee and tea were poured that the discussion got around to Howard Runner. It was Karen who brought up the subject. "Did Willard tell you that Wayne Wright has a collection of Runner's sermons from before he left the ministry?"

"No, as a matter of fact he didn't mention that. I wonder why that might be, Willard?" Jason screwed up his mouth and cocked his head toward Willard who was conveniently drinking his coffee and looking into the cup as if nothing of significance was being said.

Karen continued, "Did he think to mention that the prayer that Wright offered at the committal service for Deiter was one that he found in a funeral sermon of Runner's?"

"Come to think of it," Jason replied, "our sanctimonious Brother Willard hasn't been very communicative about Mr. Runner lately. Of course, when he thought Runner was a flaming heretic, he had plenty to say. But, I suppose anything's difficult to articulate with a mouth full of crow."

"Crow is also a verb form, little brother, and your use of it doesn't become you. It's true that Wright has some of Runner's writings and it was a beautiful prayer, but I remain convinced that there was more than a little fire under all that smoke of several years ago. And as for me and my house, we will serve the Lord as we always have, to paraphrase Moses or Joshua or one of those guys."

"So," Karen said with a smirk, "You speak for the whole family, do you?"

"Well I, for one, am not ready to chuck a theological system that I'm comfortable with, and that's served hundreds of thousands of Christians for over four hundred years, on the basis of the liberal thinking of this friend of yours."

Jason interjected, "I don't think you should. I've never *asked* you to chuck your tradition or change your thinking. I've only asked you to allow me to travel on my own road and to respect that road. I-94 versus I-96."

"Sounds like a new proof text, I-94 verses I-96. By the way, and speaking of ways, I tried I-94 from Wayne State to Ann Arbor. I didn't like it."

"Did it get you here?"

"Yes, but I didn't like it."

"Do you think we should take I-94 off the map and plow it up because it's not your favorite way?"

"Okay, okay. I get your point. I-94 works for some people, I-96 for others."

"And my theological understanding works for me and is my connection to God, and if yours works for you, God and I bless yours and withhold not your favor from mine as well."

"Uncle already!"

☦

"That was a nice time. Karen's a sweetheart and Willard wasn't the ogre you made him out to be." They were back at Annie's apartment settling in to watch the late news.

"How much damage could he do with that choke chain around his neck? I'm surprised he could swallow his food."

"I didn't see that she reined him in all that much."

"Be sure there was a rein, or a threat, or a bribe of some kind for him to behave himself for that period of time. Trust me that as we speak, Karen's telling him he was a good boy and what a nice impression he made because he kept his mouth in check."

"And what a nice couple we make?"

"Don't flatter yourself too much. Remember I said she's the type to take in stray kittens out of the rain."

"Would you take me in out of the rain?"

"Are you a wet kitty?"

At that moment, the elder Richards' mini-van was turning off US-23 and onto I-96. "I think they make a very nice couple," Karen was saying.

"That pretty thing would make a very nice couple with anyone."

"Willard! You're incorrigible! Is that all you think about?"

"Hey! I was a very good boy while we were with them, now I'm with you."

"Yes, you were a good boy," Karen said seductively, "and for that you may have the lollipop I promised."

"Could you make it a couple?"

"M'mm. What flavor do you want?"

"Do you have a cherry one?" Willard asked with a grin.

"Not any more, but I've got the little box it came in."

And she knew what Willard's rejoinder would be before he said it. Intimacy of this magnitude was so satisfying it made her shiver for the joy of it.

Karen, the wife, was healing.

This was going to be a big week. The week before the Christmas break for the University and the end of the semester, and it was the week of the exit interview with Van Dam. During his weekly meeting with Playdon, Jason went over the highlights of what he would say to Van Dam.

"On the good side of the ledger, the Home serves a real need for a specific population, it's reasonably priced, it has availability, and it's adequately staffed by people who care a great deal.

"On the other side of the ledger, they operate close to the edge in many ways. They do not have a nutritionist trained in geriatric nutritional needs. They seem to cut corners that may jeopardize their accreditation. Their staff at the top is adequate but the non-professional staff is marginal . . ."

Playdon interrupted, "What do you mean by that? Before you said they were adequately staffed, did you not?"

"Well, for example, the cook attempts to individualize the meal trays according to dietary requirements, but the staff that delivers the trays doesn't understand the system or the resident's needs, so it's possible the trays don't get delivered to the right person. The person responsible for the medication distribution is a qualified professional with pharmacological training and she sets up the distribution of the medication. But often the person who passes out the medication, as Runner says, 'doesn't know a coated aspirin from an M&M.' These lower staff personnel are paid little more than minimum wage for what is sometimes messy work and often comes with life-or-death consequences."

"And they don't or won't fill these lower staff positions with better educated, more skilled staff because of cost? Is that what you mean by cutting corners?"

"That and availability. Working in a nursing home isn't very glamorous and turnover is a problem." Jason continued, touching on some of the other issues, including the fact that Van Dam had dodged him on the financial statements.

"What do you make of their not providing you with financials?"

"Well, his excuse about Board approval may be valid."

Playdon looked skeptical. "It's been my experience that executives that are proud of their financial management are eager to demonstrate the financial health of their organizations. People who are in financial trouble, or who are not proud of their management, or who have something to hide are more circumspect. My CPA training reminds me to be from Missouri. But, of course, we have no authority to demand anything. So for me it will remain as a cloud. I recall that Visser ran into the same stonewall."

Playdon made suggestions here and there to emphasize something positive or to rephrase something negative to make it more acceptable.

"As I see it," Jason summarized his findings, "they've been slow to adapt the latest care and management methods available, and little by little, they've let the physical facility decay. Eventually, the State licensing people are going to call them on it, and they'll have to get their act together or be out of business. From the perspective of the typical resident, he or she doesn't know better and accepts the conditions. The extra tender loving care that is clearly there goes a long way with a resident who doesn't know or care that the roof cap leaks."

"Very good. Will this Friday be your last visit with Runner as well?"

Jason was collecting his papers. "No, this is exit interview day because Van Dam's leaving to go home for Christmas and then taking a few weeks off for some skiing. I expect two or three more visits with Runner before I begin writing, and then I think I'm going to ask him to read the draft."

"Good idea! I presume you'll be going home for Christmas?"

"Yes, sir."

"Well, have a blessed season, and I'll see you when you get

back."

"Merry Christmas and a Happy New Year to you and your family as well!"

⁂

Jason set up the exit interview with Van Dam for the same time as his regularly scheduled Friday meeting with Runner. Because his report would be from the resident's perspective, he wanted the resident to be present. His uneasiness over the meeting grew exponentially as the time for the meeting grew near. His problem was that his report would not be as complimentary as he was sure Van Dam would want it. On reflection, that was Van Dam's problem, not his.

In preparation for the meeting, Jason re-read Douglas Visser's report from several years ago. Essentially the same conclusion, the Home was not updating its methods and facilities to keep pace with the current state of the art in nursing. The problems Visser pointed to were confirmed by Jason's inquiries. There was a tone in Visser's report that made Jason uncomfortable. In places, the report was almost vitriolic—as if Visser wanted to say more than was appropriate in a report of this nature. He had had this feeling about the report before. An idea occurred to him. Why not call Visser and find out from him firsthand how he felt about the Home?

Why not? He dialed the number for long distance information for the San Francisco area for the number for San Francisco General Hospital and dialed it.

"San Francisco General."

"Douglas Visser, please."

"I'll connect you."

"Mr. Visser's office, Miss Bennett speaking."

"Mr. Visser please, this is Jason Richards calling from the

University of Michigan."

"Can I tell Mr. Visser of the nature of your call?"

"Miss Bennett, I'm the current Davidson Fellow from the University of Michigan, and I hope to speak to Mr. Visser about a report he did on the Christian Arbor Home in Ann Arbor, Michigan when he was the Davidson Fellow."

"I'll see if he's available. One moment, please."

Jason twiddled his thumbs for about as long as it took Ms. Bennett to explain the nature of the call.

"Hello, Doug Visser speaking." It was a crisp voice that carried with it a sense of urgency or impatience—Jason couldn't tell which.

"Mr. Visser, my name's Jason Richards and I'm the current Davidson Fellow, and I happened to select the Christian Arbor Home for my Interreactional Report as did you. I wonder if you might have a few minutes to talk about your report."

"Jason, call me Doug. Tell me, is Van Dam still the administrator there?"

"Yes he is."

"That's too bad. I was hoping my report would get his sorry ass fired. Did he get his act together since or does that place still have its head in the sand?"

"I would have to say things haven't changed much."

"If any of the nursing homes in my system ran that way, I'd be out on the street so quick I wouldn't have time to grab my ass or my hat. You know why they don't get shut down, don't you?"

"I have no idea."

"They have several board members who are Mr. Bigs in each of the political parties. By the way, do you know if a Mrs. Kaufmann is still around there."

Our Lady of the Purple Heart! "Yes, she is."

"She was the person that I interviewed. Does she still wear those outlandish purple outfits?"

"Yes, and she's been sitting in the lobby every time I come and she's typically still there when I leave."

"Good for her. She is one sweet lady, formerly a school teacher. I fell in love with her. So what can I do for you?"

"My exit interview with Van Dam's on Friday, and I was afraid I might be too hard on him. I was calling for the benefit of your experience."

"What you should be calling for is that pecker-head's head. When I got there, of course, I was full of book learning and didn't know the woods from the world. But I got an eyeful real quick like. Half way through my report, Mrs. Kaufmann was suddenly taken to the U. Hospital. I went to see her and learned she was there because some minimum wage aide who was passing out medications gave her two fifty-grain tablets of something instead of two fifty-grain tablets of something else.

"That little mistake put Lizzy Kaufmann into cardiac arrest and in I.C.U. and with some permanent brain damage. Until the day I left, there hadn't been an incident report made out. 'Just a little mix-up that caused Lizzy to have one of her spells.'"

"And here I was concerned that I was going to be too hard on Van Dam."

"You can't be too hard on that son of a bitch. Unfortunately, his type is all too common in private, church-affiliated nursing facilities. For your money, you get pretty smiles and civility but little substance. Is he still making it with the Head Nurse?"

"Actually, my research wasn't quite that extensive, although I did hear a rumor that she had designs on him."

"Platitudes, beatitudes and horny as a toad. Go figure. Listen,

I gotta run. But one more thing. Did you ever suspect you had your room searched?"

"Room searched? You mean in connection with this paper?

"Yes. I couldn't prove it, but when I started getting nosy about the Home's financial situation, Van Dam got a bit uptight and was concerned that I might make some accusations about him personally. I think he had his hand in the till. But without the financials, I couldn't come close to proving it."

"Well, he stonewalled me on the financials as well, but I . . ." Jason's thoughts raced. There was something else . . . but what was it . . .

Visser interrupted his thoughts, "You caught me in the middle of a busy schedule. I gotta run. Nice to talk to a fellow Davidson Fellow. Send me your résumé when you want to get out into the world."

"Thank you for your time."

"Not at all."

So. Mr. Douglas Visser had reason to be caustic in his report. And perhaps the rumor Annie had referred to about the saintly Head Nurse wasn't a mile off after all. Platitudes, beatitudes and horny as a toad. Lord a'mercy! Who'da thunk it? But did he have his room searched? And when he remembered, his Adam's apple clanked against the knot in his tie. The mystery of the off-and-on-again computer! Holy She-it!

☦

By Thursday evening, Jason was ready to admit to himself that he was an inveterate chicken. There were two interviews he had to go through, and he was dreading both. There was the exit interview with Van Dam, and the entrance interview with Annie, which was more on his mind than the interview with Van Dam. Weak-kneed and lily-livered were adjectives that came to mind as well. That would make him an inveterate, weak-kneed, lily-livered chicken. Inveterate—wasn't that the same as invertebrate? A little more vertebrate would be desirable at this point. He decided the exit interview would go better if the entrance interview were over-and-done-with so he picked up the phone and dialed her number.

"Sure, come on over, I have a date with Jerry at nine, but you're welcome to come, too."

Jerry? Who was Jerry? "That's okay, if you're expecting comp—"

"Seinfeld! You know. Thursday night at nine o'clock? Seinfeld? Are you a stump?"

"I must be brain dead. Be right over."

The Sheltie was used to him by now and no longer made a fuss when he knocked. He took it as a good sign. The dog thought he was part of the family.

She opened the door and her arms and they embraced 'hello.' She was wearing plaid Bermuda shorts with knee sox and a white cotton turtle necked top that was pressed tightly into his chest. God, was she beautiful, he thought.

"So, Ritchie, what brings you out on a blustery night like this one?"

"The warmth of your embrace and some good comedy."

"My embrace is good comedy?" she said as she pulled away in mock questioning.

"You couldn't feel me laugh when we embraced."

"What makes you think I feel anything when we embrace?"

"I think *I* felt something, but I'm not sure. Purely from a research point of view, I think we should do that again so I can be sure." He took her into her arms again and this time he kissed her as well.

When they came up for air, she reached up and whispered in his ear, "I think I felt something that time. I think our relationship is growing."

"Do you suppose if we got married we could keep this going for a lifetime?"

"I think it would be fun trying. Purely from a research point of view, of course."

"Of course. It might even lead to a paper."

"A paper? What kind of paper?"

"Erotic non-fiction."

"That's not the kind of paper I thought you were thinking of."

"I'll bite. What kind of paper should I have been thinking about?"

"Disposable diapers."

"Maybe we could alternate the papers."

"That works for me."

*Seinfeld* was a scream. Jason noticed that when he watched alone, the program was funny but he didn't laugh out loud. When he watched with Annie, they both hooted.

After *Seinfeld*, Annie clicked off the TV and clicked on the CD player and they talked seriously about themselves and about the possibilities for their futures together. When Jason got an opening, he asked the question that had been on his mind since the first day he met her. "What I don't understand is why a beautiful, intelligent, witty girl like you remained unattached?"

"That's easy. A lot of guys wanted to do the research, but none of them wanted to do the paper. I was interested in you from the first time I met you because of the first words out of your mouth when Runner introduced us. Do you remember what you said?"

"I have *no* idea!"

You said, 'I'm doing a graduate research paper.' I thought, 'Aha, someone not only eager to do the research, but willing to do the paper. But turnabout's fair play. How come you're still unattached?"

All this time it never occurred to him that she might have the same question about him that he had about her. "I've never met anyone I really liked. I think my previous record was four dates with the same girl. You might as well know. I've never done any research, so to speak." Having said that, he wasn't sure this was the time for such stark honesty.

"Jason Richards!" She had been snuggled against him as they sat on the sofa with her legs up underneath her and her cheek on his chest. She pulled away from him to look him in the face. "You're a virgin? There's one of you left in the latter stages of the twentieth century? Be still my fluttering heart."

Damn! Was she mocking? Willard wouldn't have been so honest. Willard didn't need to be this honest. "I think I could be a good learner. I've always been a good student, especially if I had good teachers."

"Well, big guy, we'll have to be learners together. But you have to know, I don't audit these courses, I only take them for credit." Her eyes were boring in, looking for his integrity, and he was pleased it was there to be found.

"That cer-tain-ly works for me."

"Good! So tell me, when is the first day of school? I want to sign up for the lab." She leaned into him to kiss him with her mouth slightly open—at first.

The exit interview went better than Jason had expected, mostly because Van Dam was surprisingly passive and Jason wasn't as aggressive as he wanted to be. Van Dam agreed with the points that Jason felt were positive. Van Dam acknowledged the problems with a shrug or a comment about the lack of money or that obtaining good help was always a problem, or that the problem mentioned was presently being addressed by the Board of Directors of the Home. The questions that remained unasked and unanswered were, "Do you have your hand in the till?" and "Did you ever visit my apartment?" and "Are you still making it with the head nurse?"

When the meeting was over, Jason accompanied Runner back to this room where pizza was to be delivered at noon, overseen by Annie.

When they got to the room, Jason settled into the leather wingback chair and exhaled a sigh of relief. "That went easier than expected."

"Oh?"

"I expected Van Dam to be more defensive, even argumentative. But I got none of that. Then, again, I didn't ask any of the tough questions that have been raised in my mind."

Runner's eyes twinkled. "And what would those questions be?"

"Like 'Why did you stonewall me on getting the financial statements?' and 'What other kickbacks did you take, or other funds did you misappropriate besides the fifteen dollars you got from each unnecessary eye examination.' Like did you . . ." Jason hesitated. He saw no reason to bring up the mystery of the off-and-on-again computer. "Questions like that."

Runner's look was one of bemusement. "And why didn't you?"

"Two reasons, actually. One, I don't have the power to elicit the truth so I would antagonize him with nothing to gain. And two, he has the power to make your life here more intolerable than it is. He would think you put me up to it, when actually it was the previous Fellow that hinted at all the chicanery he suspected Van Dam was up to. I just can't find any evidence that he's not what

Visser suspected nor can I prove he was right."

"You also received no indications that your observations were welcome or that your report would be used as an instrument for generating change."

"Well, that's true. It's an attitude that's a little difficult to understand, unless he has something to hide. It would seem that if Van Dam cared, he would at least make an attempt. But if Visser's report didn't move him to action, I shouldn't be presumptuous and think mine will or that my un-asked questions will change anything if posed. But why not? It would seem his job would be at stake."

"Because the Home sees itself as an arm of the Church. Its mission statement is one of providing Christian care and concern to those in the last stages of life. What do modern methods have to do with Christian care and concern to those comfortably ensconced? Our Mr. Van Dam is comfortably ensconced. Boards of Directors for these types of institutions are reluctant to fire anyone, especially if the incompetent person is sincere. That goes for ministers, choir directors, church janitors, as well as nursing home directors."

"I know that to be true from experience. I remember when the principal of the Christian school I attended got the ax after years of incompetence. My father was on the Board and it was a big problem to get the guy out because, while his inaction and bungling was obvious, he was a sincere Christian, and he was an elder in one of the local churches."

"Exactly. This is the second wake-up call for Van Dam. But nothing will change. Change—new ways of thinking and new ways of doing things—are frightening and risky. This nursing home is a sample of its greater culture, and that, as you know, is something with which I have some considerable experience. It's far easier to protect the institution than to venture out into new and uncharted territories. That's as true for churches and denominations as it is for nursing homes.

"But I can't believe that denominational leaders are like Van Dam. People like Van Dam wouldn't rise to positions of leadership."

"Jason, Jason." Runner cocked his head and lowered his face the better to peer over the half-frame glasses. "Those people get to those positions *because* they are vanilla. One faction within the denomination can't afford to let leadership arise from another faction. So the leadership is typically someone who isn't dangerous to anyone or a threat to change anything. And quite frankly, with the Church's declining relevance to society, it's been unable, with few exceptions, to draw the brightest and best of its youth into the ministry. So the talent pool from which the Church must draw its leaders is sadly not what it could be. The leaders aren't the result of the survival of the fittest; what you have in leadership positions is the least controversial of the survivors.

"Most of the controversy in which I was involved would've been avoided if the Classis had leadership of substance." Runner's voice was quiet but intense as if it were urgent that Jason believe the truth of what he was saying. "There was a fumbling, halting, confused attempt to maintain the status quo, despite calls for dialogue. They didn't want to dialogue; they didn't want to wrestle with the issues I raised. I don't know if you know this, but the seminary with which I was associated sent delegations to these meetings, including its president, and they were essentially silent.

"And as further proof of a lack of leadership, I had been preaching openly in a highly visible church and writing in the publications of the denomination for years and went essentially unchallenged. If there were effective leadership, my bishopric would have stepped in and set me straight long before the issue became a controversy.

"I don't know if you are aware of the great controversy that arose in the Presbyterian Church in the 1920s. It probably signaled the beginning of the end of the influence of the Protestant movement in America. But among the leaders in the Presbyterian Church at the time were William Jennings Bryan, Harry Emerson Fosdick, and J. Gresham Machen. These were giants among men at a time when theology was considered the Queen of the Sciences, and only the best and brightest university students were accepted into seminaries and schools of theology. I don't think many would make the case that that continued to happen in the last half of the twentieth century."

"So what do you see as the hope for the survival for the institutional church?" Jason asked.

Runner was stroking his beard with his forefinger on one side of his face and his thumb on the other. "The institutional church will survive. It always has and always will. The real question is whether the Church will regain a measure of relevance to its culture. For that to happen, the Church must learn to get along with the Church. Little progress will be made until the factions within the Dutch Reformed Church can embrace each other. Then the Dutch Reformed Church will have to learn to embrace the True Dutch Reformed Church, and then the Orthodox True Dutch Reformed Church. Then those Reformers will have to embrace the Episcopalians, the Protestants embrace the Catholics, the Christians the Jews, and the Jews the Muslims."

"Do you see that ever happening?"

"It happens all the time. At Techtronics, there were a hundred and sixty-five employees representing over thirty different faiths. We were a happy family. We went to Polish, Jewish, Muslim, Eastern Orthodox, Hindu, and Baptist weddings and funerals. We celebrated and wept together. We danced and prayed together, participating in the stuff of life as brothers and sisters in the family of God.

"Where it *doesn't* happen is at most levels of the institutional Church. There's where this minister or that one won't perform your marriage ceremony because he doesn't recognize your baptism because of the depth of the water in the baptismal fount. Or you can't take communion at this wedding ceremony because your understanding of the miracle of the Eucharist is different than mine.

Or, the case of the minister at the memorial service for your nephew who didn't allow you to cry because it would be an inappropriate expression given the theologically correct understanding of the meaning of death. We could take a lesson from our Episcopal brethren who are part of the Anglican Communion. Different branches of this world-wide body are not held together by common doctrines or by theological statements, but by what they call the Bonds of Affection—they are held together by love for each other as Christ loves us.

"Is it essential that the institutional Church get its act together you might ask. Oh my, Jason, yes! Yes, for two very important reasons," Runner was becoming passionate. "First, it's a shame on all our houses that the Church is divided. But more than that, it's sacrilege that one faction denigrates the beliefs of another. Second, Hans Kung is right when he says there's no hope for world peace until the religions of the world can get along. Unless I miss my guess, future wars will be reruns of the crusades where the fault lines will be religious, as is the case presently with the Shiites and Sunni Muslims and the Muslims with the Christians.

"What we are talking about is no less than world peace, for God's sake!" Runner's voice had crescendoed to a forte.

"So how do we accomplish that?"

Runner paused for a moment as if to catch his breath. "We start by acknowledging publicly and institutionally what we all know to be true—that is none of us know *the* Truth, each of us only has our *understanding* of the Truth, human and limited, dare I say flawed, as it is. In addition, we must honor and bless those understandings that are different than our own. It's so simple; so difficult.

"The most powerful example I can think of is John 3:16 and 17. Do you know these verses, Jason?"

"Well, John 3:16 in the King James version goes, *'For God so loved the world that He gave His only begotten son, that whosoever believeth on him should not perish, but have everlasting life.'* But that's as far as I can go."

"Yes, and that's as far as our tradition goes with the texts as well. But in fairness to the Universalists, it goes on to say, *'It was not to judge the world that God sent His Son into the world, but that through him the world might be saved.'* John 3:16 is widely quoted as a proof text for limited, individual atonement while John 3:17 might lead to an understanding that the intention of the redemptive act of Christ was more universal. My question to you and my more orthodox brothers is this: Are not these verses positioned close enough in the Holy Scriptures so that I can hold on to verse sixteen with my right hand and you might hold on to verse seventeen with your left hand and, just maybe we'd be standing close enough so that we could hold hands together?"

I-94 versus I-96, thought Jason. "Why *is* that so difficult?"

"The organized Church is bigger than government and each ecclesiastical group, regardless of size, believes that God is surely on their side. And you can't go up against God just as you can't fight City Hall. Remember Hoffer's corollary to Lord Acton's axiom, 'Absolute faith corrupts as absolutely as absolute power'?

"And it's not just Christians who seemed to be handcuffed in this regard. Apostasy, which is usually defined as anyone else's understanding of the Truth different than your own, is a capital crime punishable by death in some Islamic countries. But enough of my ruminations." Runner paused as if tired of the futility of hoping for his ideals to become a reality. Then he changed the subject, "When do you expect to be finished with your report?"

"I expect to have a draft by the fifteenth of January, when I'm hoping you'll agree to review for content."

"I'd be happy to do just that. Are you going home for the holidays?"

"Leaving tomorrow. I have some shopping to finish, then I'm

off for home to celebrate the season."

"Pizza delivery!" It was Annie with the pizza. The smell of the pizza made Jason realize how hungry he had become. The sight of Annie also reminded him how hungry he had become and of his plans to do some shopping later this afternoon, at Main Street Jewelers.

☦

In the administrator's office, Van Dam was on the phone enumerating the points Jason Richards had made in their earlier meeting. "His report will make pretty much the same points the other chap made, as we might have expected. But we got the hoped-for results. Veeringa's really upset. If asked for her opinion, she'll paint a graphic picture of Runner upsetting the young man just as he has the staff and other residents. And, of course, the logical conclusion to be drawn is that the young man was unfavorably influenced by the old reprobate so as to make his report biased if not unreliable. More than I could have hoped for, Runner was the perfect foil. He peddled his religion and philosophy and distracted the kid enough so as not to be dangerous to us. So, that brings you up to date. Thanks for your time. Goodbye." Or dangerous to me, he thought as he hung up the phone.

Better one student would be discredited than the institution be destroyed. Van Dam thought he had heard that advice somewhere before. It probably came from somewhere in the Bible. He picked up his pen to add to the notes he was keeping about this whole affair. If Jason had been in the room to observe, he might have noticed Van Dam wrote with his left hand.

☦

As Jason left the Home, Our Lady of the Purple Heart was one of the ladies-in-waiting in the lobby as she had been when he arrived. He went over to stand in front of her and said, "Merry Christmas, Mrs. Kaufmann. Douglas Visser sends his greetings."

"Who?" She croaked and there was suspicious confusion in her eyes.

"Douglas Visser. He used to come to visit you. He said to say 'Hello.'"

Jason could see the old woman battle to process an appropriate answer—and then lose. "I'm a fourth-grade teacher you know." She said it proudly as if she were announcing that she had royal bloodlines.

"Yes, I know. I've heard about you." Jason's response seemed to satisfy her greatly. Jason wondered if the confusion was the result of advancing old age or the medication incident about which Visser had told him.

He paused to look around the lobby one last time. Its floors gleamed and the outdated magazines on the coffee table were arranged just perfectly, as were the plastic tulips in the imitation Delft vase. And the water damage over the doors appeared to be getting worse but it had been covered over with yet another coat of paint. Symbolic of the whole place, he thought.

It was snowing when he pushed through the doors of the Christian Arbor Nursing Home into the outside. It was a quiet, heavy snow that was covering the ground quickly, and it scrunched under his loafers as he walked toward his Honda. The world had come to appear very differently in a very short time, as had his world. He noticed there were only the remnants of Runner's grape vines to indicate the garden that had been so carefully tended just a few months before. He reflected on the short time that he had known Howard Runner. It was about one growing season.

Only one growing season, but the shape of his understanding had changed. It used to be wide. He used to know all the answers to all the questions. Everything had fit nicely into a system that had been handed to him and he had bought into it. It was wide but it was shallow and, for him, it leaked. Now he was aware that he knew few of the answers. He didn't know what all the questions were. The shape of his understanding wasn't nearly as wide, but it was much deeper. And what he knew, he owned. It was *his* structure, *his* belief, *his* conviction, *his* wager.

A growing season, but things had come into focus. He had gained perspective. He knew in tangible experience what he thought he knew before, but found he didn't know at all. And that was all that really mattered.

## THE END

Except as noted in the text, and on pages 329 and 330, all scripture quotations are taken from the New English Bible, copyright © Cambridge University Press and Oxford University Press 1961, 1970. All rights reserved.

CPSIA information can be obtained
at www.ICGtesting.com
Printed in the USA
FFOW03n2336250416
23511FF